UNDONE

THE UNTANGLED SERIES

BOOK 2

IVY LAYNE

GINGER QUILL PRESS, LLC

Undone: The Untangled Series, Book Two

Find out more about the author and upcoming books online at www.ivylayne.com

Also By Ivy Layne

THE UNTANGLED SERIES

Unraveled
Undone
Uncovered (Summer 2019)

SCANDALS OF THE BAD BOY BILLIONAIRES

The Billionaire's Secret Heart (Novella)
The Billionaire's Secret Love (Novella)
The Billionaire's Pet
The Billionaire's Promise
The Rebel Billionaire
The Billionaire's Secret Kiss (Novella)
The Billionaire's Angel
Engaging the Billionaire
Compromising the Billionaire
The Counterfeit Billionaire
Series Extras: ivylayne.com/extras

THE ALPHA BILLIONAIRE CLUB

The Wedding Rescue
The Courtship Maneuver
The Temptation Trap

Chapter One

LILY

MY EYES FLEW OPEN IN the dark. I'd been dreaming of the lake, of moonlight playing on the water, of swimming at night. Of unseen hands pulling me under, water filling my lungs.

Most of my life I'd slept like a log. In the year since Trey died, I'd gotten used to this. To waking in the dead of night, only the shadows on my walls for company.

I rolled over, fluffing the pillow under my head, trying to find a comfortable position. Sometimes I could fall back to sleep. Sometimes I lay awake until dawn.

The dream weighed me down, the dark water in moonlight. I wasn't sure if I wanted to close my eyes again or give up and read until morning.

Sleep. I needed a full night of sleep. Then maybe the nightmare wouldn't come back. I could hope.

My eyes were sliding shut when I heard it.

A thump. A shuffle. Something being dragged, or

someone walking in sock-covered feet.

I sat up, throwing off the covers, then stopped at the edge of the bed, my feet on the carpet, leaning forward, straining for a hint of sound.

Had I heard something? It wouldn't be the first time a noise woke me. The house was isolated, on the edge of the lake and surrounded by woods. Between the wildlife and the wind, nighttime sounds weren't unusual.

This was different.

Since Trey had died everything was different.

I listened, breath held, and heard nothing but the faint echo of crickets outside.

I took a deep, slow breath and reminded myself that the doors were locked. The alarm was on. The house was secure.

The last time I'd thought I heard a noise—had been absolutely sure someone was in the house—I'd called the police and ended up feeling like an idiot. Deputy Morris was nice about it.

Black Rock is a small town. Deputy Morris, Dave, had been fishing buddies with Trey. He was a friend. Sort of. Friend enough that he didn't tell me outright he thought I was making it up, but I'd known Dave for years. I could read between the lines.

If I called him right now, he'd jump in his cruiser and head over. He'd search the house from top to bottom, and when he found nothing, he'd give me a sympathetic, worried look and ask if I needed help.

I needed all kinds of help, but not from Dave Morris.

There was nothing there. It was the nightmare, that's all. Stress. Too many nights of interrupted sleep playing tricks on my mind.

I'd almost convinced myself I was imagining things. I turned, ready to slide my feet back under the covers, when it came again. A soft, shuffling thump. Not quite someone walking. Something being dragged?

I didn't know, but I'd have to find out.

I stood slowly, my palms clammy, heart racing. My robe lay at the foot of the bed where I'd tossed it hours earlier. I pulled it on, tying the belt firmly. My hair slid into my face. I twisted it into a messy knot, crushing the curls, just wanting it out of my eyes.

The house was quiet, but this time I'd heard something. I had. I wasn't making it up. I wasn't imagining things. I'd heard a noise from inside the house.

Picking up my phone, I stared at the screen. Just call Dave, a little voice whispered.

I unlocked the screen and pulled up Dave's number, then stopped. Dave's face filled my mind, the expression as he stared down at me the last time I'd called in the middle of the night. His patience would have been sweet if it hadn't been tainted by condescension.

He'd suggested maybe it was the stress of being alone. That maybe the pressure was too much. That grief could play tricks on the mind. He'd laid a hand on my shoulder, intending comfort, and said that it was okay if I was overwhelmed without Trey.

Then the suggestion, voiced so gently, that perhaps I was lonely.

Like I'd call Dave in the middle of the night because I wanted some company.

Did he think I was that pathetic? I guess he did.

I wasn't pathetic.

I was scared.

Phone in hand, I turned on my bedroom light. I'd known I was alone in the room, and still, I was relieved to see the familiar white walls, my messy bed.

In the hall I turned on the light, flicking switches on my way to Adam's room. Trey had insisted our son sleep as far from us as possible. I hadn't minded back then. My little guy was a bear to get to sleep, but once he was down, he was out. Trey joked that Adam slept like me. Like I used to. Before. Now I hated the distance between our rooms, but Adam didn't want to move.

I left Adam's light off, padding silently to his bedside. He lay face down on the mattress, the quilt shoved to his feet, his cartoon pajamas twisted around his torso.

He slept like a rock, but he moved constantly. Every now and then I'd let him fall asleep in my bed, but I always moved him to his own. I'd woken too many nights from a kick to my kidneys or a small toe in my ear. He slept hard, but he was never still for long.

Tousled blonde hair streaked white from the summer sun spread across his navy pillowcase. I ran my fingers through the silky length so like Trey's. So unlike my own dark curls. He'd need a haircut soon.

I straightened and went to the door, closing it behind me. If I'd been alone, I might have ignored the sound. Might have tried harder to convince myself I was hearing things. But I had Adam, and Adam's safety was more important than anything.

At the top of the stairs, I stopped, the darkness at the bottom a cavern hiding whatever had made that sneaky, shuffling sound. I waited, ears straining. Nothing moved in the shadows below. Nothing that I could see.

I flipped the light switch at the top of the stairs, illuminating the empty hall below. The empty hall and the alarm panel on the wall at the base of the stairs. The alarm panel with its blinking green lights. Green, not red.

Green.

My heart kicked in my chest, my breath strangling in my throat.

I'd set the alarm. There was no question. I'd set the alarm. I never forgot.

I'd grown up in the suburbs, not the country. I'd never liked the isolation of the house Trey had built for us. Even when he was alive, I set the alarm every night. I never forgot.

Those green lights glowed up at me, making me wonder. Making me doubt. I never forgot, but had I? Could I have? I descended the stairs slowly, racking my brain.

We'd had dinner early. Chicken fingers with honey mustard for Adam, along with two hated carrots. Leftover lasagna for me. After, a bath for Adam. Pajamas for both of us. Then, curled up on the couch with his favorite stuffed monkey between us, we'd watched half a movie. Curious George. Again.

Adam was crazy for Curious George, and we'd watched the movie every night for the past two weeks. Then bedtime for Adam. A story and a back rub later, Adam had fallen asleep.

I'd gone downstairs, set the alarm, and made a cup of tea before bringing a book and the tea up to bed.

I'd set the alarm while I was waiting for the water to boil. Then I'd walked through the first floor, turning off the lights, the alarm panel glowing red. Armed.

How was it green? My mind reeled at the thought. Only Trey and I had the code, and Trey was dead. The alarm had never malfunctioned. If it had, the police would have come.

Someone must have disarmed it. But who? And how? Even if someone had the code, the siren would have gone off when the door opened. The only way to disarm the panel silently was from inside the house.

That thought sent ice through my heart. No. I'd

walked the house. No one had been inside. No one. It was impossible.

Not impossible. It's a big house. So many places to hide.

I pushed the voice away. I was not going to get hysterical. There had to be a simple explanation. Maybe the power had gone out while I was sleeping.

Backup battery.

Sleepwalking? Could I have sleepwalked to the panel and turned it off myself?

At the bottom of the stairs, I stopped, turning away from the green glow of the alarm panel. The front door was closed and locked, the windows on either side dark.

Taking a breath for courage, I strode forward and flicked every switch on the panel by the door. Bright light flooded the steps outside and the path from the driveway. Beyond the path, the lake gleamed black in the moonlight, just like my dream. The lights from the dock glowed, warm and welcoming.

No one was there. No one on the lake. No one on the dock. No one on the path.

I peered into the darkness. Most of the first floor was a big open space surrounded by towering plate glass windows. Trey had designed the house with the help of a renown modernist architect. I'd hated it from the start.

This part of Maine is filled with classic New England architecture. Colonials. Saltboxes. Cape Cods. Georgians. Federals. Even a few Victorians. Painted siding. Brick. Shutters and front porches.

This place, with its flat windows and sharp corners, its metal and concrete, looked like it had been dropped from another world. Or California. Here in Maine that was the same thing.

Modern and aggressive, it jutted out on the peninsula, intruding into the lake, breaking up the shoreline.

The house Trey built demanded attention, asserting itself when it should have blended with the trees and the water.

I hated giving my address to anyone who didn't already know it. '*Oh, that house*,' they'd say. '*Why'd you go build a thing like that?*'

If I had a dollar for every time I'd heard it, I could afford to burn the place down and move away. Not that money would help. It wasn't a lack of money that kept me here.

For the first time, I was grateful for the open design of the house. One flick of a switch and I could see everything. Almost everything.

The kitchen, empty. The dining area, the sitting area, empty. The doors to the decks, all closed and locked.

I crossed the empty room and flipped more switches. The deck lights flashed on. Empty.

There was no one here. I was imagining things.

My nerves were shot, like Dave said.

I turned on the balls of my feet, phone still clutched in my hand, ready to write the whole thing off as a delusion. An overreaction.

Just two more rooms to check, and I could assure myself that I might be crazy, but at least Adam and I were alone.

I'd barely turned when a sharp crack filled the hall. Something metal clattered. Rolled.

The mudroom. It had to be. The only things down that hall were the family room, the mudroom, and beyond that, the garage.

And the back door.

When Trey died, I'd sold his guns. I didn't like them in the house with a little boy. Adam was already climbing like the monkey he loved so much, and there was nowhere I could hide the guns that he wouldn't find.

Trey had never wanted a gun safe, saying what was the point of having weapons if you have to work that hard to get to them? I wasn't a great shot. I hadn't enjoyed target practice like he did, but in that moment, I would have given anything for the weight of his Glock 9mm in my hand. For anything other than my phone.

I looked over my shoulder at the kitchen. I didn't have a gun, but I had an exceptional collection of knives. I love to cook, and my knives are my indulgence. Japanese, handmade of layered steel, they were as much works of art as tools. And each one was wickedly sharp.

Moving on the balls of my feet, I ran to the kitchen and slid open the knife drawer, pulling free my longest, sharpest blade. The handle fit my palm as if it had been made for me. I could debone a chicken like nobody's business, but I'd never thought about using the knife on a person. I didn't know if I could.

Adam slept upstairs. If Adam was at stake, I could do anything. I would do anything. But I didn't want to.

I'd raced to the kitchen. My progress toward the mudroom was a lot slower. I clutched my phone in my hand, thinking it might be worth Dave's patronizing reassurance to avoid facing whatever made that noise in the mudroom. Except...

Except the last time I'd called he'd put his hand on my shoulder, his eyes gentle and worried, and said that maybe the strain of taking care of Adam by myself was too much. Maybe I needed a break.

He hadn't said he was going to call social services. He hadn't said he planned to tell them Adam's mother was crazy and delusional. He hadn't had to.

I wasn't calling Dave unless I was sure I had no other choice.

The light in the hall should have been reassuring. It wasn't.

The family room was empty. Warm, heavy air wafted down the hall, out of place in the sterile, air-conditioned house. My fingers tightened on the handle of the knife as I reached through the door of the mudroom and pushed up the light switch with the side of my wrist.

The fluorescent bulbs in the ceiling seared my eyeballs. I blinked hard, the scene in front of me slowly coming into focus. The back door gaped open, the woods beyond the house black. Impenetrable. I couldn't see anything moving, but it was so dark beneath the trees someone could be lurking right outside the door, and I wouldn't know until he was on top of me.

The tall, metal umbrella stand by the back door was on its side, umbrellas spilling out across the tile. The crash I heard. Someone leaving?

I wanted to believe it was someone leaving.

The alternative, that someone was inside the house, was too frightening to contemplate.

My brain was stuck in a loop.

Pick up the umbrella stand.

Close the door.

Pick up the umbrella stand.

Close the door.

I did.

The flick of the lock, the bolt sliding into place, should have made me feel safe. It didn't.

The alarm was off. The door was open. Someone had been in my house.

I could have imagined the sound, the shuffle, and the thump, but I did not imagine the alarm being off. I did not imagine the door hanging open and the umbrella stand knocked over.

I stood there, staring at the locked door, trying to think. I should have taken a picture. I should have called Dave while the umbrella stand was still knocked over and the door was still open. If I called him now, with no proof, he wouldn't believe me.

But if someone had been here, I didn't want to leave the door open. I wanted it locked. I didn't know what to do. I gripped the knife and shifted my weight from one foot to the other, trapped by indecision.

Why would someone break into my house?

A thief could have made off with a fortune in artwork from the first floor alone. I hadn't noticed anything missing as I passed through the house.

At a loss for what else to do, I left the mudroom and went back through the first floor. Nothing was missing. Nothing I could see. Why would someone break in if not to steal?

I thought of Adam asleep in his bed, so small. So vulnerable. I had to protect him. I had an alarm and the best locks money could buy. Still, we weren't safe.

We should have been safe.

I'd locked the mudroom door, but I didn't know—

Had I locked someone out? Or locked them in?

I stood in the middle of the kitchen, scanning the quiet, brightly-lit house.

What do I do? What the hell was I supposed to do?

And then I remembered. Not long before he died, Trey started talking about a new security system. I'd brushed him off, hadn't really paid attention. The system we had was overkill for a small town in Maine, even considering the artwork Trey had collected.

He'd been restless and anxious those last few months. Promising me everything was fine, then talking about buying more guns and getting a better alarm. He'd been short-tempered and easily irritated. Annoyed when I asked questions, so I'd stopped.

He'd said once that if anything happened, if I needed help and he wasn't there, I should call someone. He had a card. I couldn't remember the name, but there had been a lion's head and a circle. Black on white.

Still clutching the knife in one hand and my phone in the other, I walked past the front door and down the other hall to Trey's office. I rarely went in there. Not before he died and not after. This was his space, his room.

His desk was as neat as he'd left it. Everything lined up. Everything in its place. No business cards.

I should have paid attention. I should have listened, but he'd been so erratic back then. I got used to tuning him out when he went off on a paranoid rant about guns or a new alarm. About people coming after him. If he'd been afraid for Adam, I would have taken him seriously, but it was always about him. Never us.

The top drawer slid open silently, the contents as neatly arranged as the surface of the desk. Pens lined up together, paperclips organized by size, and, in the corner, a neat stack of business cards.

Reluctantly, I peeled my sweaty fingers from the handle of the knife and set it on the desk. The blade gleamed obscenely against the warm mahogany. The first card in the pile was his stockbroker. The second for a local maid service. The third for the Black Rock newspaper.

Below that, a white card with black printing. A lion's head surrounded by a circular banner that read 'Sinclair Security'. The name underneath was Maxwell Sinclair. Two phone numbers, one toll-free and the other an area code I didn't recognize. The address beneath; Atlanta, Georgia.

Why would Trey have worked with a company all the way in Atlanta?

It was the middle of the night. No one would be in the office. Before I could think better of it, I dialed the toll-free number and waited.

The phone rang. Once. Twice. Three times. A click, as if the call were being transferred. It rang again, and a woman's voice informed me that I had reached Sinclair Security after office hours but was welcome to leave a message.

A long beep sounded in my ear and I began to babble. "This is Lily Spencer. I—my husband—my former husband—I'm a widow—uh, told me to call you if there was ever any trouble. I live—we live—I live up in Maine, and we've had some break-ins. Uh, I think. The police haven't found anything, but tonight someone got in. Turned off the alarm. I don't know what to do. I don't know if you can help, but he said if anything ever happened, I should call you, so I'm calling. Please, if you could call me back, I'd appreciate it. Again, this is Lily Spencer."

I left my number, then stabbed my finger at the screen of my phone and hung up. My cheeks were hot with embarrassment no one could see. I should have planned what I was going to say, should have thought about it, but I was rattled.

Not rattled.

I was scared.

I left the card face up on the blotter and picked up the knife. I thought about making a cup of tea. Turning on the television for company. Of walking through the house again.

I did none of it. I went to the stairs and climbed to the second level, checking every room I passed. I stopped in front of Adam's door and turned the knob, breath held, praying with everything inside me that he was as I'd left him. Safely asleep.

He'd rolled over, pushing his pillow to the floor, stuffed monkey under his head. He was still out cold, cheeks flushed with sleep, his back rising and falling in a regular rhythm.

My sweet boy. If he was okay, I was okay.

I shut the door, turning the almost useless lock on the handle, and sat on the carpet, leaning against the bed frame, the only sound in the room Adam's even breathing.

Pulling my knees into my chest, I listened for any hint of a disturbance, for any sign that we weren't alone.

Eyes glued to the door, the knife in my right hand and my phone in my left, I waited for daylight and the false promise of safety.

Chapter Two

LILY

"I DON'T WANT GRILLED CHEESE AGAIN."

"That's funny, when I asked a half an hour ago you said you had to have grilled cheese for lunch. Not peanut butter and jelly, not chicken noodle soup. Only grilled cheese."

Adam's lower lip pooched out as he scowled down at the perfectly-toasted grilled cheese sandwich. "That was before I knew you were going to use the yellow cheese."

I stifled a sigh of exasperation. *Breathe*, I told myself. *He's five. He's not being a pain in the ass on purpose.*

Except, he kind of was.

A five-year-old has three basic jobs: explore the world, give good snuggles, and drive his parents crazy. Adam was excelling at all three.

"Adam, I already told you, the grocery store was out of

the white cheese. It's yellow cheese or no cheese at all."

My stomach growled as the scent of melting cheese and toasted bread drifted across the table. I'd made Adam lunch, but I hadn't gotten to mine.

Slowly, I reached across the table saying lightly, "Well, if you don't want it, I might as well eat it for you. I haven't had lunch either and—"

"No!" Adam snatched up a triangle of sandwich and shoved half of it into his mouth, chewing furiously as he glared at me.

Bingo. The fake-out didn't always work. It was just as likely he would have crossed his arms over his chest, refusing to eat until I came up with whatever it was he wanted.

I gave an internal sigh as I watched him chomp through the sandwich. White bread and cheese toasted in butter would go straight to my rear end, but it smelled so good. I hadn't realized I'd wanted one until I'd reached across the table and my mouth had begun to water.

Pushing my chair back from the table, I set about making my own sandwich. I'd worry about the size of my rear end later.

I was spreading butter on a thick slice of bread when three heavy knocks sounded on the door. Thump, thump, thump. I jumped, muscles jerking tight, the knife clattering as it fell from my hand to hit the counter.

Adam's eyes shot up from his sandwich and fixed on me, narrowed with worry. "Mom?"

"Oops," I said, picking up the knife, stalling Adam as my mind raced.

It's just someone at the door.

It's fine.

People knock on doors. It doesn't mean anything.

I was trying to forget the night before. Trying to forget the open door, the yawning dark of the woods beyond. The dragging sound and my frantic phone call.

In the light of day, it all seemed overblown and dramatic.

Maybe I hadn't shut the door properly.

Maybe I'd forgotten to set the alarm.

Maybe I was overreacting.

The logical part of me objected to this train of thought. I knew what I saw, and I knew I didn't forget to set the alarm.

Thump. Thump. Thump. Three more heavy knocks landed on the front door. I tried not to imagine the size of the fist that made the deep, full sounds echoing through the house.

"Aren't you going to answer it?" Adam asked around a mouthful of grilled cheese sandwich.

Straightening, I wiped my hands on a dishtowel and turned to smile at Adam. "Of course. It was just so quiet the knock startled me. Finish your lunch, and if you eat it all, you can have a cookie."

"I'd rather have an apple," Adam grumbled under his breath.

What kid didn't like cookies? My kid, that's who. It was the cookies, not the kid. I was hit or miss in the kitchen. My grilled cheese sandwiches? Divine. My cookies? Not so much.

Wiping my sweaty palms on my jeans, I strode down the hall, stopping at the security panel to turn on the screen. The camera clicked on, showing a man at the door.

He was tall, the tips of his short-cropped dark hair cut off by the top of the screen. His shoulders were broad enough that only one was visible, and what I could see of his arms were corded with muscle. A black shirt with a familiar lion's head logo stretched across his chest.

It couldn't be. I'd only called the night before.

Unlocking the door, I swung it open and looked up. And up. I'm on the short side, slight except for my hips and butt. My visitor loomed over me, his face a wall, eyes flat.

My voice more hesitant than I'd like, I said, "Can I help you?"

"Knox Sinclair. Sinclair Security. You called, said you needed help."

I cleared my throat. "That was fast. I only called a few hours ago."

"Good timing. My schedule was free. So was the plane."

"I thought you'd call. I—"

I'd made the phone call but hadn't expected someone to turn up this quickly. That was weird, right? Who flies most of the way up the east coast without calling first?

Trey had left me Sinclair Security's card. What if they were mixed up in whatever Trey had been into? What if Knox Sinclair was at my door only hours after I'd called because he was already in Maine? Because he'd been at my open door last night?

Knox's dark eyes leveled on mine. I couldn't get a read on him. I needed help. I needed someone to trust. That didn't mean Knox was my answer.

"Are you going to let me in?" he asked in a deep voice.

I stepped back and waved a hand, welcoming him into the house. Pacing past me, Knox's eyes swept the entry hall and what he could see of the living room, cataloging every detail, his expression unreadable. If he was annoyed at having his day interrupted by a flight to Maine, it didn't show.

"Would you, uh, like some coffee? Lunch? I don't know how we do this." I spread my hands out in front of me palms up, at a loss.

"I'll take the coffee, no lunch. I ate on the plane. Is there somewhere we can sit down? I need to know what you're dealing with before I know how I can help you."

"Oh, of course. Yes. I'll get you some coffee and we can sit in the living room. Just let me get my son settled first. I don't want him to—" I gestured towards the kitchen.

Knox seemed to understand. He nodded, then raised an eyebrow and tilted his head in question. I stared at him, taking in his thick, dark hair, eyes so deep a brown they were almost black, sharp cheekbones, straight nose, and a full lower lip that was a lush contrast in that strong face.

His voice rumbled, "Living room?"

I dropped my eyes, a flush heating my cheeks. One second I'm not sure I can trust the guy and the next I'm staring at his lips. I needed to get it together. "Yes, sorry, I'll show you."

Knox followed as I led him deeper into the house, shutting and locking the door behind him. The living room opened in front of us and I gestured vaguely. "Anywhere you want to sit is fine. I'll be right back."

Leaving Knox Sinclair to get himself settled, I found Adam finishing the last of his sandwich. He opened his mouth to speak. I stopped him with a raised palm. "Not with your mouth full."

For a second, I was afraid he'd choke as he swallowed the giant bite of sandwich, washing it down with a generous swig of lemonade.

"Who was it?"

I busied myself making a fresh pot of coffee, thinking about what to say. I tried not to lie to Adam. He was only five, but kids have great bullshit detectors.

I wasn't going to tell him that I was afraid someone had tried to break into the house. No way. I settled for part of the truth.

"Now that it's only the two of us here, I feel like we need to upgrade the alarm system. I called the company who installed it, and they sent someone up. I need to sit down with him so he can help us figure out what we should do."

"Upgrade the alarm? You mean like laser beams so no one can walk on the floor?" Adam's eyes lit with glee. My kid was watching too many cartoons.

I shook my head. "I'm pretty sure no laser beams. This isn't a museum, baby doll, it's just a house. Even if it does have the most precious thing in the world inside."

He flashed his pure child's grin and my heart squeezed. He *was* the most precious thing in the house. In the world. I'd do anything to keep him safe.

"I have a feeling it's going to be a pretty boring grown-up meeting. How about you go into the family room and watch some cartoons?"

"TV? During the day?"

Adam didn't wait for me to say yes. He shoved back his chair and took off down the hall, not sparing Knox Sinclair a glance as he flew past the living room.

Unless Knox Sinclair had brought a lightsaber or a team of ninjas to defend the house, there was no way Adam would pry himself away from the television to investigate our grown-up meeting.

I arranged squares of freshly baked coffee cake on a plate and carried it in on a tray with two cups of coffee, a small pitcher of cream, and a bowl of sugar. Knox sat beside the coffee table, a few file folders spread before him.

He'd shifted the chair to give a view of the front door, the hallway, and the tall windows looking out over the lake. I wasn't the only one who was paranoid.

His dark eyes lifted from the paper in his hand. "These

windows are a security nightmare."

I set the tray down on the coffee table and sat on the couch beside Knox's armchair.

"Are they? I didn't know. I don't really know anything about security. Trey had the system put in when we built the house, but—"

"Trey was your husband?"

I took a sip of coffee, uneasy. I was always uneasy these days when Trey's name came up.

I shouldn't be uneasy.

I should be grief stricken. I should be mourning.

I wasn't.

I was uneasy, and I was scared.

I wasn't going to tell Knox Sinclair any of that. I settled for a nod.

"Yes, Trey was my husband. He designed the house and took care of the alarm. I know how to use it, mostly, but I don't know all the details."

"I've got them right here," Knox said, gesturing at a manila folder on the coffee table in front of him. "It looks like my father oversaw the installation personally. Shouldn't be hard to expand it if that's what we need."

Knox helped himself to a cup of coffee, ignoring the cream and sugar. He took a sip and leveled his dark eyes on me. "You called last night in a panic. Mentioned break-ins. Did someone break in last night?"

"Yes." The word was out of my mouth before I thought better of it.

Knox made a note on the paper in his hand. "What did the police say?" he asked without looking up.

"I, uh, I didn't call them."

His eyes sharpened on me. "There a reason you called us and not the police when there was an intruder in your house?"

"I, uh, I—"

Knox leaned forward. "What are you afraid of, Lily? I can't help you if you won't talk to me."

"I don't know where to start," I said, those words explaining so much and so little.

I didn't know where to start with anything. With the break-ins, with my life as a widow, with Knox Sinclair and his offer of help.

"Start at the beginning," Knox said simply.

Nothing was simple about the beginning. College, and Trey, and that first flush of heady, foolish love. That was the real beginning. But that wasn't what Knox meant.

"About a month after Trey died," I started, "I thought someone tried to get into the house. The alarm went off and the police came. They said they didn't find anything, but I heard someone out there."

"It happened again?"

"Every week or two."

"That often?" Knox asked, one dark eyebrow arched.

"It's not always someone trying to get into the house. Sometimes it's things outside that are moved. I found marks on a window like someone tried to force it open."

"Did you show the marks to the police? What did they say?"

I shook my head. "Trey's best friend Dave is a deputy with the town Police Department. He, uh, he's been keeping an eye on us since Trey died. He says it's all nothing. Probably teenagers messing around. He said the marks on the garage door were an animal trying to get at the garbage, but—"

Those dark eyes flashed up. "You have problems with animals here? Have they tried to get into the garage before?"

"No. If I leave the trash cans out, sure. We're surrounded by the woods here. Animals, yes. Raccoons and fox. Sometimes coyote. Tons of deer in the summer. But trying to get into the garage or damaging the house? Never. So if it's animals, why now?"

"Good question," Knox said in a low voice. "Have you seen anyone hanging around?"

"No. A few times I thought I heard something, but—"

"What happened last night?"

I ran through the events of the night before, trying to keep my voice steady. When I was finished, Knox set his notepad and pen on the coffee table and leaned back in his chair, propping his ankle on his knee, arms folded across his chest.

"You're sure you set the alarm. Sure you closed and locked the door."

"I'm sure," I said. "I never forget to lock up. I check the doors every night after Adam goes to sleep, and I never forget the alarm. Ever."

Straining under the pressure of Knox's steady gaze I rose to pace in front of my chair. "I know what I saw. I know what I heard. Adam was in bed. I was the only one in the house. I should have been the only one in the house. I'm not making this up."

"Sit down, Lily."

My butt plopped in my chair before I registered that he'd told me what to do in the same tone I used with Adam.

I stayed where I was. Knox wasn't friendly. He was a little scary, but he was supposed to be here to help me. I didn't want to piss him off.

He studied me, appraising, picking me apart. I fought the urge to squirm. Finally, he asked, "Has someone told you they think you're making it up?"

"Dave. Trey's friend. The Deputy. He thinks I'm exaggerating. The rest of the police agree."

"That's why you called us instead of the police last night?"

I nodded. It was enough that Knox knew I was afraid we had an intruder. He didn't have to know my other fears.

That the police would decide that I was unstable. That they would take Adam. That I wouldn't be able to stop them.

Knox flipped open the manila folder on the coffee table. "Your alarm was deactivated last night at 3:28 AM by the main code. That wasn't you?"

I shook my head, sinking my teeth into my lower lip as panic surged through me, driving me to stand, to pace, to run. I stayed put, my teeth in my lip anchoring me in place, and shook my head for a second time, afraid if I spoke, my voice would shake.

I hadn't imagined it.

Someone had deactivated the alarm while I slept using my own code.

Filling in the blanks, Knox went on, "The alarm was reactivated at 4:18 AM. Was that you?"

I nodded. Knox closed the folder. Appearing lost in thought, he picked up the slice of coffee cake I'd set in front of him and broke off a corner, popping it into his mouth. He chewed, his eyebrows drawing together in confusion as he lifted his coffee cup to his mouth, downed a swig, and washed away the coffee cake.

Had I messed it up again? How could I mess up coffee cake? How could I be so good at cooking and so awful at baking? Aren't they the same thing?

Distracted, I broke off a corner of my own coffee cake.

Dry, too salty, with aluminum notes of baking powder. Ugh. I washed my bite down with coffee as Knox had his own. Another coffee cake, down the tubes.

Holding his mug in both hands, Knox sipped again, and I wondered if he was washing the taste of the coffee cake out of his mouth. I wouldn't blame him if he were. Looking at me through the steam, he said, "Why would someone try to break into your house?

"I don't know. I don't know. I don't have anything worth stealing."

Knox's eyes drifted around the living room taking in the sculptures, the art on the walls. "Jewelry? Money in a safe? Artwork or valuables easier to move than what's in here?"

"I don't have much jewelry. A string of pearls my parents gave me when I turned twenty-one. My wedding and engagement rings. A few things here and there, but nothing valuable. Nothing worth driving all the way out here for."

"What did your husband do before he died?"

Wasn't that the million-dollar question. What *did* Trey do? It was a question I should have asked so many times throughout our marriage. I should have demanded answers. I shouldn't have accepted Trey's easy explanations.

At first, I'd been too in love to push. Later, I had too much to lose.

"Lily? Don't you know what your husband did for a living?"

"I, uh, I don't," I admitted, heat flooding my cheeks again. What wife didn't know what her husband did for a living? Knox said nothing, just raised that dark eyebrow again in query, clearly expecting more.

"We moved up here when he got a job working for a company that sold spring water. He was supposed to be in logistics and distribution. He stayed with them for about a year before he went out on his own."

"He started his own company?"

"He called it Spencer Distributors, but he never told me the names of his clients. Said it was confidential."

"Did he work normal hours? Have an office? Coworkers or employees?"

"He worked eight to six, mostly from home, in his office. He had a lot of meetings with clients and he always went to them. He traveled a lot. No employees. I always thought he should hire someone to take the load off so he didn't have to work so much, but he didn't want to. He said he liked running the whole thing himself."

"And when he died? Did you inherit the company?"

"I did, technically."

"Technically?"

"Technically the company is mine, but the attorney didn't have any information other than the LLC filing. No bank accounts, no client lists. If anyone is looking for Trey, they haven't come here."

"Bank accounts? His laptop?"

"I haven't found his banking information."

"Do you think it's possible someone who was involved in your husband's business is trying to get into the house?"

I let out a breath, deflating under the weight of his question. "It's the only thing that makes sense," I said, "but I don't know where to start trying to figure out who or how to get them to stop."

"That's my job. What about your personal finances? Any issues there?"

I wasn't sure how much information I should give to Knox Sinclair. He said he was here to help me, but I'd gotten the phone number for Sinclair Security from Trey. If the break-ins were related to Trey's business, then everything connected to him was tainted.

I had to take the chance. If Knox was here to help, I had to trust him. Just a little. A little, but not all the way.

"Everything seems fine with our personal finances. We didn't have any problems with his life insurance, no money missing from the bank accounts, everything normal with the bills."

"He left you comfortable?"

"Comfortable enough, yes," I answered, not willing to tell Knox exactly how comfortable Trey had left us.

Too comfortable. Comfortable enough that my jaw dropped as I stared at the documents from the lawyer. Where had Trey gotten all that money? It was just sitting there in the bank accounts, taxes duly paid, and I had no idea how he'd earned it.

Knox straightened his chair, then leaned forward, bracing his elbows on his knees and leveling a frank look in my direction. "This is the part that can be a little uncomfortable. What budget did you have in mind?"

"Why don't you tell me what you think I need," I said, "and I'll tell you if I can afford it."

"Fair enough," Knox said, a hint of a smile ghosting across his lips. "I think you need someone on site twenty-four/seven until we find out what's going on. I think if we want to catch whoever's trying to get in the house, we leave the system as it is."

"Set a trap?"

"Something like that."

"So how does this work? When will you send someone up?"

"Someone is here."

"You?" Nerves skittered down my spine. Could I handle Knox Sinclair twenty-four/seven? Those dark eyes, the size of him looming over me.

If he was here to keep me safe, Knox Sinclair would scare away almost any threat.

And if he wasn't?

If he wasn't here to keep me safe, I was a lot worse off than I thought.

Chapter Three

KNOX

LILY SPENCER'S BROWN EYES WERE cool with shock. She hadn't expected me to stay. Tough luck. This job was too important to trust to anyone else.

Lily was involved. I could smell it. It was all over her—her tightly wound muscles, her instinct to push me out the door.

She was involved, but how? Had she been working with her husband and my father? Did she know what Tsepov and the Russian mob were looking for?

Or was she Trey Spencer's dupe, an innocent victim he used as cover?

My gut told me Lily Spencer was innocent. Okay, no. That wasn't my gut talking. That was my cock. My cock didn't care what she was guilty of. My cock cared about her smooth, tawny skin, her cloud of soft, brown curls.

My cock wanted to know more about the curve of her hip, her high, firm breasts, her round, full ass. My cock had priorities, none of which had to do with the case.

My cock was going to have to stand down. Literally.

Don't sleep with the client. Even more important, don't sleep with the target. When the woman in question is both...the answer is simple, right?

Hands off.

No matter how much I wanted to bury myself inside her, it wasn't going to happen. Lily was off limits at best.

At worst?

At worst she could be a thief.

She could be a killer.

Even at my most suspicious, I had to admit that it was more likely Trey Spencer had been killed by Tsepov and the mob than this fairy-sized women with frightened eyes.

Likely, but anything was possible. I'd learned long ago not to underestimate women, especially the ones who looked the most vulnerable.

Pushing back my instinct to soothe the fear in her brown eyes, I said, "I'll need to stay on the property."

At the idea of me moving in, Lily flinched. Because she was wary of strangers, or because she didn't want me close enough to keep an eye on her?

"There's a guest house," she said in her low, sweet voice. "I'll show you. It's close to the house. There's an intercom between. I'll have to check for sheets and towels—"

Her voice faded as she drifted into thought, planning for an unexpected guest. She started to rise, then sank back into her seat. "We didn't talk about your fee. Onsite security is expensive, I know—"

"You have a son to protect," I said mildly, noting the flash of anger in her eyes at the implication that she would leave her son at the mercy of whoever was breaking in.

"I know that," she snapped. "That's why you're here. I can afford whatever you're charging, but I should know what that is, shouldn't I?" Her chin raised, challenge sparking in her eyes.

With a mild shrug, I handed her a folder with our contract and fee schedule. "Look that over while I let the office know the situation. If there are any problems, we'll work them out."

I rose and paced away from the sitting area, my phone at my ear. I didn't need to call in, a text would do, but I wanted an excuse to wander the first floor before Lily had a chance to prepare.

Out of the corner of my eye, I watched her flip through the contents of the folder, wincing only a little when she read the fee breakdown. I couldn't fault her for that. I would have winced, too.

She'd been right. Twenty-four-hour protection didn't come cheap. Which begged the question—why would a widow living a quiet life in the country need round-the-clock security?

Lily claimed she didn't know what was going on. I'd been doing this job too long to fall for the innocent client act.

A voice spoke in my ear. "Sinclair Security, how may I direct your call?"

"Alice, it's Knox. Let Cooper know I'm staying."

"Will do," Alice replied. "Report?"

"Nothing yet."

"But enough that you're staying?"

"You got it," I said.

"Cooper is going to want more than that, Knox. At least give me something to hold him off."

"Nothing to say. Just my gut telling me to poke around."

Alice let out a sigh, knowing from experience that pushing me would get her nowhere. She could handle Cooper.

Anyone else and he'd growl at being put off. For Alice, he'd keep his mouth shut. For a while.

Ending the call, I shoved my phone into my pocket and strolled down the hall, away from the living room where Lily Spencer waited.

The house was modern, aggressively so, and not my thing. I like wood, not metal and glass, but I couldn't deny the view of the lake was spectacular.

Trey Spencer had taste. In his home. In his wife.

The sound of a children's show drifted down the hall. The kid, banished while the adults talked business. I'd only caught a glimpse as he'd raced past the living room. Enough to see that Lily's kid was a dead ringer for her deceased husband and looked nothing like her.

Interesting.

From the corner of my eye, I watched Lily remove the contract from the folder, carefully reading line by line as she toyed with the pen on the coffee table.

She'd asked for help, but she didn't trust me. She also hadn't thrown me out. She was reading the contract, and when she was finished, she would sign.

I didn't need her fingers on the pen to tell me that. She was afraid, and she was desperate. If she was mixed up in my father's mess, I'd find out. Either way, I'd keep her safe.

Taking advantage of her distraction, I strolled down the hall to the right of the front door. Not much there. A powder room, and a closed door at the end. Well-oiled hinges moved in silence as I poked my head through.

An office. Leather and wood, with an oversized desk chair. The husband's office. I'd only known her for a few minutes, but I could see there was nothing of Lily in this room.

On my way back to the entry I checked out the kitchen. This room was Lily. Warm and welcoming, from the vanilla scented candle burning on the island to the stoneware crock of spatulas and spoons.

The country homeyness contrasted with the stark modernity of the rest of the place. If Trey Spencer consulted Lily on the house design, I doubt he'd taken many of her suggestions.

I passed the living room and headed for the other side of the house, still snooping. A quick glance told me Lily was still occupied by the contract, now several pages in.

Her shoulders tight, back straight, she twirled the pen on the coffee table. Anxious? Definitely. I just didn't know why.

A guilty conscience or good old-fashioned fear? If her story was true, she'd woken in the night to find her alarm turned off and her back door open. She thought she'd heard someone in the house. That was enough to scare the daylights out of anyone.

If her story was true.

She didn't notice me pass the living room and explore the hall to the left of the front door. Stairs to the second level rose on my right. I'd explore up there when I checked the alarm system.

Further ahead on the left was a family room complete with a huge television and black leather couches. The kid practically disappeared in the deep cushions, his attention focused on the cartoon playing on the screen. I slipped past without notice. Beyond the family room, I found the laundry room, entrance to the garage, and the back door.

Most of the square footage on the first floor was in the expansive two-story living room where I'd left Lily.

When I made my way back to Lily, the contract was

folded open to the signature page, her neat flowing script spelling out her name in blue, the date printed beside it.

Satisfaction warmed my chest. I hadn't really thought she'd turn me away, but her signature on the contract dispelled that small worry. Picking up the paperwork and the pen, I signed and tucked the contract into my briefcase saying, "I'll get you a copy of this later today. Do you want to show me where I'll be staying?"

"Of course," she said, standing and rubbing her palms over her hips. I followed her down the hall to the mudroom where she stopped and shoved a pair of hot pink flip-flops on her feet. "It's out here."

The smell of pine and summer sunshine, of lake and dirt, hit me all at once. Lily was isolated up here, miles from the small town of Black Rock. I wasn't crazy about the house, but I could see the appeal of the land.

The sun sparkled on the lake, dappled through the trees. All I needed was a hammock and a beer, and I'd be set.

Lily shoved her hands into her pockets and headed down a narrow path to the small cottage I'd seen when I'd driven in. Nothing like the main house, the rough-hewn logs and tin roof fit the woods and the lake far better than Trey Spencer's metal and glass sculpture of a house.

"Did you build this when you built the main house?" I asked.

Lily laughed, the sound light, musical. She took the steps to the porch easily, fingers trailing along the peeled logs that made up the railings.

"No. Trey wanted to tear it down, but I wouldn't let him. It's been here since the early nineteen hundreds. There used to be a Boy Scout camp on this property. It was sold off years and years ago, but some of the cabins are still around.

It's part of the town's history. You can't really see it from the house, so Trey let me keep it."

She unlocked the door and led me into the small cozy space. A brick fireplace took up almost the entire width of the far wall. The opposite wall was filled with a queen bed, the mattress stripped bare, the frame fashioned from more of those peeled and varnished pine logs. The wood glowed, lacquered until it shone. The side tables, coffee table, and small table by the galley kitchen were all made in the same style.

Watching me take in the room, Lily said, "The furniture is all local. I saw it at the craft fair the year we moved in and I loved it, but—"

"It doesn't go with your house," I finished.

"It doesn't," Lily agreed with a faintly embarrassed smile, "but it was so beautiful. I knew it would look perfect in here. As a guest cottage, it hasn't had much use, but it should have everything you need."

Pointing as she spoke, she went on, "There's a small kitchen over there. You're welcome, of course, to eat with Adam and me. I promise most of my meals are better than that coffee cake. The bathroom is over there, and there's internet, though it's not very fast."

"It looks fine. I'm going to have to check your alarm system, probably install some additional sensors and cameras. You okay with me wandering around? Letting myself into and out of the house?"

A simple question that should have had a simple answer. She'd hired me to look out for her safety. She should have trusted me, otherwise why hire me in the first place?

I knew before I asked that the idea of letting myself into and out of Lily's house would make her uncomfortable.

Too bad. This wasn't going to work if I had to ring the doorbell every time I needed to get inside. Biting her lip, Lily gave an awkward jerk to her shoulder in an approximation of a shrug.

"Of course, yes, that's okay. Adam doesn't have preschool today, so we'll be around. I'll make sure he doesn't get in your way."

"He's fine. I like kids."

"Then, uh, I'll let you get settled and go see about making the bed and getting some towels."

She was out the door a heartbeat later. I watched her hustle back to the house, her flip-flops slapping her heels in an uneven rhythm.

Lily Spencer was not what I'd expected. In the picture we had on file she'd been sleek and sophisticated, her hair straight and just brushing her shoulders. The pearls around her neck had matched the buttons on her sedate twin set. She'd been on her husband's arm, a tight smile on her face as they'd been photographed at a charity event.

Trey Spencer had looked smug. Satisfied. Lily looked trapped. I don't know why that word stuck in my head every time I saw that picture.

Trapped.

Why trapped?

A beautiful woman on the arm of a handsome man. From outward appearance, they were prosperous and secure, but something was off in her eyes, in the way she stood beside her husband but not really *with* him.

I'd expected the twin set and sleek hair. With her stiff shoulders and sophisticated armor, that woman made a convenient suspect.

This Lily did not. Her hair was a cloud of soft, dark curls. She wore no jewelry and barely any makeup. Instead of a twin set, she was in pink flip-flops, worn jeans frayed at the hem, and a T-shirt that had seen better days.

This Lily wasn't a picture clipped from the paper. This Lily was flesh and blood. She was real. This Lily might not be trapped, but she *was* terrified.

Sooner or later, I would find out why.

Chapter Four

KNOX

"MY DAD'S DEAD," A LITTLE voice piped up.

I dropped my eyes to see Lily's son standing at the base of the ladder.

I was installing new cameras under the eaves on the side of the house. Adam Spencer looked up at me through eyes the crystal blue of the Caribbean Sea, his tousled white-blonde hair tangled over his tanned forehead. His voice was matter-of-fact as he shared the news of his father's death.

I nodded gravely and said, "I know. I'm sorry."

Adam jerked his shoulder in a gesture identical to the one his mother had used only an hour before.

"It's okay," he said, "my mom and I are hanging in there."

I nodded again. Adam stood, hands hanging loosely at his sides, watching with curious eyes as I tightened the screws holding the dark gray camera to the underside of the eave where it blended in almost perfectly.

"Is that supposed to look for the bad guys? Will it stop them from getting into the house?"

"What do you know about bad guys?" I asked, keeping my voice light. My instincts sharpened at the mention of *bad guys*, but the kid was five. Odds were he didn't know anything useful. Still, it didn't hurt to ask.

Adam narrowed his blue eyes on me consideringly before he said, "I know a few times the alarm's gone off. Deputy Dave came."

"That's all?" I probed.

"Mom's been worried." He shot a quick glance over his shoulder before he went on, "She tries to pretend like everything's okay, but since Dad's been gone—" He swallowed hard.

I had to push while I had the chance. Feeling like an asshole, I said, "Since your dad's been gone, she's been worried? Or was she worried before, too?"

Adam's eyes dropped to the ground. He kicked the toe of his sneaker into the dirt, rubbing a line through cinnamon-brown pine needles, exposing the darker loam beneath.

Seeming to come to a decision, he straightened, feet beside one another in an almost military stance before he lifted his chin and said, "Before, too. My dad wasn't home a lot. Sometimes they used to yell. Then she'd be sad and worry more. Are you going to fix it?"

"I'm going to try," I said, not sure if I was telling the truth.

"How do I know you're not one of the bad guys?" Adam asked.

Smart kid. "I'm not. Promise."

I knew with absolute certainty that I was not the bad guy.

I was sure about myself, and I was sure about Adam Spencer. Everyone else was up in the air.

I couldn't promise things would go well for Lily until I knew how involved she was in her husband's business. In my father's business.

Since the day my brothers and I had uncovered the first of my father's secrets, I'd learned how deep betrayal could go. For five years we'd mourned my father's death. Right up until we found out he was still alive and on the run from the Russian mob.

He'd abandoned us once by faking his death. Now he'd made us a target for the mob's revenge. With my father out of reach, they wanted us to make good on what he stole. The problem was, we had no clue what my father took or how to get it back.

What we did know could barely fill a postcard. My father and a few compatriots had been into all sorts of dirty shit, from sketchy adoptions to trafficking for the Russian mob.

Following the money moving into and out of my father's hidden accounts led us straight to Trey Spencer. Spencer, and possibly Lily, were tangled up in all of it.

The child in front of me had nothing to do with his parents' crimes. He didn't deserve me prodding him for information, but Andrei Tsepov had threatened my mother, and the clock was ticking. If he didn't get what he wanted, he was going after my family.

I didn't have the luxury of leaving Adam in peace. I needed answers, and I needed them now.

A screen door behind the house slammed. Lily's voice drifted on the wind.

"Adam. Adam!"

Panic threaded through her words. She was trying to hide it, but she was scared. In the distance, tires crunched gravel through the trees. A car was headed down the long driveway.

Adam called out, all innocence, "I'm over here, Mom."

Lily came around the side of the house, her strides eating up the ground, lips tightly pressed together.

"What are you doing outside? You know you're not allowed to leave the house without telling me," she admonished, reaching his side and wrapping an arm around his shoulders with a squeeze of relief.

"I was just helping Mr...I was just helping—" He looked up at me and I realized we hadn't been formally introduced. I climbed down the ladder, holding out a hand to Adam, who took it and shook with a firm grip despite his small fingers.

"Knox Sinclair," I said, "from Sinclair Security."

Adam gave me a serious nod in return. "I'm Adam Spencer."

"He's not allowed outside without an adult." Lily's eyes went to the lake, glittering in the sun less than a hundred feet away. "I know you're not a babysitter, and he's a good swimmer, but that's the rule. I'd appreciate it if you could keep an eye out. Sometimes he forgets."

At that Lily gave her son another squeeze, reaching down to tickle under his arm. He squealed and turned into her side.

"Mom, I was only out here for a minute—"

The hum of an engine interrupted Adam. The three of us turned to see a police cruiser rolling down the last of the gravel drive. Lily went stiff beside me, her mouth pinched, eyes tight.

Adam broke free from his mother and bolted for the vehicle yelling, "Deputy Dave."

I shot out a hand to grab his wrist. "Not until it comes to a stop, Adam. You have to be careful around cars."

Adam relaxed into my grip. "He wasn't going to hit me."

"You don't know that," Lily said with a sigh. "We've talked about cars. You have to be careful. He might not have seen you."

Oblivious to the scolding taking place, a uniformed police officer unfolded himself from the car and strode over with a friendly smile for Lily and Adam and a flat glare for me.

"Dave," Lily said in a voice I assume she thought was friendly. Was I the only one who heard the nerves hiding under her smile? "Is everything okay?"

"Fine. Everything's fine. I headed out to get a cup of coffee and realized I hadn't talked to you in over a week. Thought I'd stop by and see how you are."

"Mr. Sinclair is here to fix the alarm," Adam said, eager to share adult news.

"Lily?" The officer asked, his eyes suspicious as they took me in. I returned his stare, not giving an inch.

He was taller than Lily, about average height, a few inches shorter than me. Dark hair, dark eyes in a face that you could see ten times and still forget. He wasn't ugly, and he wasn't good looking. Maybe to his friends, his features stood out, but on first meeting, his annoyance was the only thing about him that wasn't bland.

Adam seemed at ease with his presence. Lily wasn't but pretended to be.

Dave held out his hand to me saying, "Deputy David Morris. I was a good friend of Lily's husband, and I'm a friend of Lily and Adam's."

He tried to crush my knuckles with his handshake. I smiled easily and squeezed back long enough to be polite before pulling my hand from his grip with a quick flick of my wrist.

I'd long outgrown those kinds of childish competitions. I could take Deputy Morris to the ground in a heartbeat.

Squeezing my knuckles in a handshake didn't prove anything except that Deputy Dave thought he was top dog around here and wanted to make sure I thought it, too.

Dismissing me, he turned to Lily. "If you needed help with the alarm, I could have recommended someone."

"I appreciate that, Dave. It's fine. Knox's company put in the system in the first place. He happened to be free, so it all worked out."

"I know you've been worried about the alarm, but if you'd remember to turn it on..."

Dave trailed off, shooting me a sympathetic glance as if to say we needed to humor the little woman who couldn't remember to press all those complicated buttons.

I wasn't sure if I imagined the sound of Lily's molars grinding together before she forced herself to relax and said, "Dave, I've told you, I never forget to set the alarm."

"I know, honey, I know." He patted her shoulder. This time I wasn't imagining her clenched jaw.

I barely knew the guy and I wanted to smack him. I had to admire Lily for holding on to her composure. Deputy Dave gave her a condescending smile and said with zero subtlety, "I never did get that coffee."

Knowing her line, Lily responded, "I was about to brew a pot. Would you like to come in? Do you have time to take a break? I've got a fresh coffee cake to go with it."

"I always have time for a break with you, Lily, and I'd love some coffee cake."

Adam choked on a laugh, sneaking a glance at me. Either Dave had never tried Lily's coffee cake or he was lacking tastebuds. I hoped her cooking was better than her baking. Otherwise, I'd have to hit the grocery store in town and find an excuse not to join them for dinner.

Lily's coffee cake had been dry as dust, salty and bland

at the same time. I was almost willing to suffer through another piece if I could watch Deputy Dave do the same.

"I'm about due for a break, too," I said. "Do you have enough coffee for me?"

The scowl on Deputy Dave's face was worth every bite I'd take of Lily's coffee cake. The deputy was an old friend of the dead husband, and he was kissing up to the widow. Because he wanted her? Because they were working together?

I wouldn't blame him if he was interested in Lily Spencer. I couldn't decide if she reminded me of a woodland fairy or a skittish fawn. That delicate chin, full lower lip, curvy ass —

Yeah, I had no problem believing Dave Morris was moving in on his buddy's widow, but Lily's unease with him didn't sit right.

Dave fell in beside Lily as they walked back to the house. Adam and I trailed behind. In a low voice, I asked, "Does Deputy Dave stop by often?"

Adam jerked his shoulder in a shrug. "Sometimes. Sometimes he comes over for dinner. He used to do that when my dad was alive."

Adam's eyes cut to the lake, and I decided to drop the subject. He was a kid, and his dad hadn't been gone for that long. I didn't need to poke a raw wound.

Lily had blown out the candle in the kitchen, but the room still smelled of vanilla. She pulled the coffee cake out of the pantry and cut four slices before going to the coffee maker and setting it up for a full pot. With a hiss and spurt of steam, the fresh scent of coffee filled the air. Lily's cake was crap, but she knew how to brew a good pot of coffee.

Over her shoulder, she said to Dave, "Town's not busy today?"

"Not once we took care of the traffic after church. You know how it is on a Sunday."

"Tourist season is always a little crazy," Lily said with a rueful smile.

Deputy Dave nodded gratefully. "That it is," he agreed, taking the plate of coffee cake she handed him. "This sure looks good, Lily."

Beside his mom Adam smirked, his blue eyes twinkling in amusement. They caught on mine and I winked, sending him into a spurt of giggles. The sound of his laughter, bright and clear, brought a smile to my lips.

I took my own plate of coffee cake from Lily, setting it on the island in the middle of the kitchen. Adam looked at his mom and shook his head. He didn't have to try the coffee cake again to know it was awful.

The three of us watched deputy Dave take a hearty bite and chew, visibly quelling the urge to wince at the dry, salty, slightly metallic taste. Too much baking powder and salt, not enough sugar.

Deputy Dave was trying to get into Lily Spencer's pants. Only a man who wanted to get laid would suffer through that coffee cake. And suffer he did, forcing a smile as he chewed and swallowed, his eyes bouncing between Lily and me, suspicious and possessive.

"Knox Sinclair? Sinclair Security?"

I nodded, crossing my arms over my chest and leaning back against the counter, giving Lily a smile of thanks as she set a mug of steaming coffee beside me. Dave took his with no acknowledgement.

"You're based out of Atlanta, aren't you?"

Another nod. Dave took a step toward Lily, washing down the dry cake with a swig of coffee as he arranged himself beside her. Lily sipped from her freshened mug and eased a step away, putting space between them.

How long had Deputy Dave been trying to nail Lily Spencer? Since his best friend died? Or before?

Lily, for her part, didn't look interested. Her shoulders were so tight they were kissing her ears, and her torso leaned as far from Dave as she could without being blatantly obvious. She wanted space. Either he didn't get the hint, or he didn't care.

Dave set the plate of coffee cake on the counter. "Long way to come for an alarm upgrade. Wouldn't it have been easier to refer it to someone local? There are some good companies out of Boston."

I shrugged. "Trey Spencer was one of my father's special clients. If Mrs. Spencer needs help, we're at her disposal."

Dave inched closer to Lily, wrapping an arm around her shoulder, giving her an affectionate squeeze. A wince crept across Lily's face before she chased it away with a blank smile. The flash of panic in her eyes had me halfway to reaching out and yanking her from his side.

What the hell was I thinking? I wasn't, and it had to stop. I always thought before I acted. Always. Whatever my gut was telling me about protecting Lily, I needed to be smart.

She looked like a defenseless fawn, but looks could be deceiving. Lily Spencer was hiding things from me.

Maybe she was uncomfortable with Dave because he wanted to fuck her and she wasn't interested.

Maybe she was uncomfortable because they'd been fucking for years, had killed her husband together, and now I was in the way.

Lily had called me, poking a hole in that theory, but people panicked. She hadn't been expecting me when I knocked on the door. Maybe she regretted calling. Maybe she'd wanted nothing more than for me to leave and get out of her and Deputy Dave's way.

Dave, either oblivious to Lily's tension or not caring, gave another affectionate squeeze of her shoulder. "I keep telling you, honey, if you remember to set the alarm you don't have anything to worry about. Knox can tell you, his company put in a solid system. You don't need improvements, you just need to remember to use it. I know you've been forgetful since Trey died. You aren't yourself these days."

His eyes drifted to Adam who was poking holes through the top of my coffee cake and watching it crumble into a mess on the plate. Dave's gaze slid back to Lily as he murmured, "You have a lot on your shoulders, and it's been a hard year. No one would blame you if you can't handle things on your own."

Lily stiffened and moved from Dave's side, setting her mug in the sink. Her friend the Deputy seemed determined to convince us all that Lily was scatterbrained and irresponsible.

Lily's message had been panicked, but nothing about her struck me as scatterbrained or irresponsible.

She wasn't stupid, she was afraid. Watching Dave watch her, my gut told me that Lily Spencer had good reason to be scared. I just had to figure out what that reason was.

Chapter Five

LILY

"IT HAS TO BE HERE somewhere," I muttered. Again. I must have said that to myself a hundred times in the last hour. In the last few months.

This wasn't the first time I'd searched Trey's office. My husband had been organized. Methodical. Keys hung on the hook at the back door every time he parked the car. Shoes lined up in his closet. His pen aligned on his desk just so.

Yet somehow, he'd managed to misfile or lose almost every piece of paperwork I needed. If I wanted years of utility bills, they were here, filed by date, starting with the first month we'd moved into the house.

I had access to our bank accounts, to our homeowner's insurance. I had copies of Adam's shot records, and the will Trey left behind. None of that would help me now.

Knox Sinclair's arrival in our lives was a shock to the system. Adam and I were in a rut, existing day-to-day, not ready to figure out what came next.

The night before, as I lay in bed, I'd realized something.

Knox Sinclair was here to keep us safe. Great. Now I could sleep at night. Woo-hoo.

Except, I wasn't sleeping. The truth was that Knox could keep us safe, but he couldn't set us free. He could offer us security—security that would eventually drain my bank account dry—but then what?

What were we going to do? Stay here in his house forever? I didn't want to be here. Not in this house, not in Black Rock. The small town was beautiful, and the people were nice, but this wasn't my place. This wasn't my life.

This was the life Trey had wanted, the life he'd tried to convince me I should want. Now that he was gone, I should have been able to leave, to decide what my life was going to be.

Instead, I was trapped here by Trey's secrecy and my own ignorance. Somewhere in this house was the key to setting us free. I just had to find it. And I was running out of time.

I had to keep him safe. Adam. Nothing mattered more than my son.

My entire life all I wanted was to be a mom. Other little girls dreamed of being a doctor or a movie star. Not me. To the deep disappointment of my parents, I never had career aspirations.

I didn't want to be a lawyer, or a professor, or a ballet dancer. I didn't want to go into finance. I didn't want to win a Nobel Prize.

I wanted to be a mom and a wife. I wanted a family. I wanted to cook dinners and match socks. To drive my kids to games and practices, to pick them up from school and playdates. I wanted to rub my husband's shoulders after a long day. To read bedtime stories and play make-believe.

I'd grown up ashamed of those dreams. I was a woman in the new millennia. I could be anything. And of all those options, I wanted to be a mom.

I never understood why that was such a disappointment to my parents. In my mind, raising children is one of the most worthwhile things I could do with my life. My professor father and artist mother could only mourn my lack of ambition.

"You have so much potential," they'd said when I'd turned down an internship my father had wrangled for me in favor of babysitting. "Don't waste it with children. Do something meaningful."

It was probably a blessing that they'd kicked me out when I'd married Trey. At least I didn't have to listen to their '*I told you so's*'.

When Trey wanted to give up on getting pregnant, he'd broken my heart. He'd refused to meet with the doctor. Refused for either of us to get more tests. He kept saying everything would work itself out, but he wouldn't tell me what that meant.

Distance grew between us. He was traveling more and turning to me in the night less. I'd started to think I'd made a mistake when everything changed.

I'll never forget that night. It was the first snow of the year, and the roads were slick. I was worried about Trey driving in from the airport. The rush of relief at the rumble of the garage door took me by surprise.

I met him at the door, ready to take his bags from his hand, and found him standing there, a tiny, blanket-wrapped bundle in his arms. He pushed the bundle at me, and I'd looked down to see a red scrunched face crowned by a cloud of wispy, white-blond hair. One look and I'd fallen in love.

Adam changed everything. I was too distracted by the child I'd always wanted to wonder about Trey's constant travel and locked office door. I didn't notice when he started sleeping in the guest room. I accepted his vague excuses when I wondered why our adopted son looked so much like my husband.

He'd given me my dream, and in my joy, I let him off the hook for everything else.

I was a fool. I'd buried my head in the sand, let Adam consume me, and now we were paying the price.

I was a mother, and it was everything I'd dreamed it would be. But, in all my imaginings of hugs and bedtime stories, I'd never guessed at the fear of not being enough. Of not being able to keep him safe. Of failing him.

I had to keep looking until I found what I needed.

Where to start? I stood in the middle of Trey's office and turned in a slow circle. It looked like a layout from a decorating magazine. *The Gentleman's Office*. Tobacco brown leather sofa surrounded by dark woodwork. Persian rug. Huge desk, the surface an acre of mahogany. Trey's brown leather chair dotted with brass nubs.

No computer in sight, only the blotter and the crystal and brass pen holder. Trey's laptop was in the drawer. I pulled it out and flipped it open, entering his password. *Adam*. Not very stealthy.

The home screen popped up. I stared at it blankly. This was not the first time I'd searched Trey's computer.

You know the definition of insanity? Doing the same thing over and over and hoping for a different outcome. Buy me a ticket for the crazy train because I was going to search this thing one more time.

After half an hour of opening folders, scrolling, checking documents and doing the whole thing again, I closed the laptop.

There was nothing there. That couldn't be right. I knew it couldn't be right. Trey had used his laptop for everything. Hadn't he? There were some files that seemed to relate to the business. An accounting app. But that was it.

The laptop was strangely empty, almost as if it was supposed to look like Trey's laptop, but he hadn't actually used it. I wanted to reject that idea as soon as it entered my mind. The idea that there might be another laptop out there made my stomach twist.

If this laptop was a decoy...the implications cascaded through my brain. A second laptop meant Trey had something to hide. Something big. A second laptop was a level of deviousness, of forethought, that confirmed Trey was not the man I thought he was.

I wasn't ready to go there. I wasn't ready to accept that my husband was involved in business dealings he felt he had to hide. I wanted to think he'd just been a bad record keeper. I could have held on to that excuse if not for the meticulously organized drawers of bills I'd already found.

A man who kept every cable bill for years wasn't a sloppy record keeper. A man that careful would be good at hiding his secrets. I glared at the useless laptop on the desk as if I could demand answers it wasn't going to give.

Pushing back from the desk, I crossed the room to the closet. The walk-in closet had shelves on one side and built-in file cabinets on the other.

I'd searched here more than once. I was going to do it again. I refused to accept that what I was looking for might not be in the house. That it might have disappeared along with Trey.

It was here somewhere. I'd seen it, once upon a time. I would find it. I had to. Adam's life depended on it.

Chapter Six

KNOX

WHAT THE HELL WAS SHE looking for?

I watched Lily Spencer slam the laptop shut and cross the room to the closet. I'd planted cameras all over the house as she'd slept the night before.

I already knew that closet was office storage: shelves filled with supplies, reference books, and baskets with odds and ends. The other side had built-in file cabinets. Drawers and drawers of files, three-quarters of the way to the ceiling, with more shelves above.

Lily wasn't paying bills or balancing her checkbook. She wasn't answering email. She wasn't cleaning out the closet. There was no trash bag, no pile of things to discard.

She was looking for something.

Fortunately, I'd had the forethought to stick a camera high in the corner of the closet. From that vantage point, I had a bird's-eye view of the top of Lily's head right down into the scoop-neck of her T-shirt. For a second, I was distracted by the swell of her breasts as they rose and fell with every breath.

Okay, I got distracted for more than a second.

Get your head back on the job, Knox. If she's wrapped up in this mess with Dad, you can't afford to let your cock fuck with your head. And if she needs your help, you won't be any good to her if you're distracted by her tits.

I tried not to enjoy the view down the front of her shirt. I did. But watching her search the files was mind-numbingly boring. Whatever Lily was looking for, she wasn't finding it.

It couldn't be a copy of the will. She'd said she'd seen that document, and it was on file at their attorney's office. Access to bank accounts? Trey Spencer had left their household accounts flush with cash. Unless Lily had expensive habits, she wouldn't run out of money any time soon.

Methodically, she opened a drawer, thumbed through a file, and put it back. When she was done, she closed the drawer and moved on. As the morning passed and her search proved fruitless, her shoulders slumped lower and lower.

Two hours after she started, she'd searched every drawer. As far as I could tell, Lily hadn't found what she was looking for. Proving me right, she turned around and started on the shelves. In a few places, there were stacks of papers and file folders. Lily went through those with the same attention to detail she'd paid to the file cabinets. The rest of the shelves were filled with matching woven baskets, the dark fibers a contrast to the gleaming white shelves.

Starting from the bottom, she pulled out one basket after another, sorting through the contents before sliding it back on the shelf and starting again. One was a jumble of cables. Another old issues of magazines. None of them held what she was searching for.

The lower shelves done, she studied the rest. She'd already looked through everything she could reach, but the shelves went all the way to the ceiling. As if she followed my train of thought, she strode from the closet.

I followed her on the cameras to the mudroom where she grabbed a tall stepladder, hefted it onto her shoulder, and carried it back to the office closet. When she had the stepladder in position, she climbed up two steps and began to search the higher shelves.

Something about the way she looked told me this wasn't the first time she'd searched the office closet. She finished the shelves she could reach from the second step and climbed to the third. I winced as she leaned out over the side of the stepladder to pull a basket from the end closest to the wall.

She wasn't that high off the ground. If she fell she wouldn't really hurt herself, but with the bulky basket in her arms, her position was precarious at best. Bracing the basket against the shelf in front of her, she rifled through it, then leaned out again to replace it. I let out a breath of relief when it slid onto the shelf and she was standing on two feet once more. Her eyes went up to the next shelf.

Under my breath, I muttered, "Don't do it, Lily".

Lily couldn't hear me and probably wouldn't have listened if she had. She climbed a step higher on the ladder and went through the same routine, searching every basket on the shelf.

Again, she came up empty. She stood still for a long moment, apparently thinking as she eyeballed the top step of the ladder. The one clearly marked DO NOT STAND. She looked at the step, then the highest shelf, before lifting her foot and placing it right over the yellow and black warning sticker.

I leaned forward in my seat, gripping my knees, willing her to hold onto the shelves. Willing her not to do anything stupid. The top shelf was well above her head. She wobbled as she strained to catch the sides of the box above her with her fingertips.

I saw it happen in slow motion. Lily inched the box back, took a step to steady herself, and misjudged the width of the ladder.

I didn't hear her scream as she fell. I was already out the door.

Images of Lily, broken and bleeding, flashed through my mind as I bolted for the house. She could have hit her head. She could have broken an ankle or an arm. If she'd come down the wrong way and cracked her neck on one of those hard, wooden shelves—

Don't worry about it until you know what you're dealing with.

I burst through the door to the mudroom and raced down the hall, cursing Trey for putting his office on the opposite side of the house.

"Lily! Lily! Are you all right?" I skidded to a halt in the office to see Lily sprawled in the doorway of the closet blinking up at the ceiling, a basket upside down on top of her, papers scattered everywhere.

I went to my knees beside her, scanning for signs of injury. There was nothing. No blood, no limbs bent at an awkward angle, not even a bump coming up on her forehead.

"Lily, what happened?" I demanded, moving the basket and running my hands over her, searching for an injury I couldn't see.

"Knox?" Her dazed eyes focused on my face, and her brow knit in confusion. "Knox? What are you doing here?"

"I was outside and heard a shout," I lied. "Are you all right? What happened?"

"I was up on the ladder trying to get a box down, and I slipped."

"Are you okay? Are you hurt? Did you hit your head?"

Lily rolled her head from side to side before trying to sit up. I slid an arm under her back, lifting her. She winced at the movement.

"What?" I demanded.

"My back," she said, reaching to run her fingers under her shirt. I lifted the soft fabric to see a scrape on her right side.

"Not too bad," I said. After that fall, it could have been far worse.

Lily probed the scrape with her fingertips, biting her lip as the salt on her skin touched raw flesh. She brought her hand around to stare at her fingers. "It's not bleeding."

"Not really," I agreed, though droplets of blood welled here and there. "Mostly it's just raw. It'll sting for a day or two, but it'll heal up pretty fast."

"I guess I should count myself lucky then."

"What were you doing at the top of that ladder?" She followed my gaze to the empty space on the top shelf and back to the basket upended on the floor.

"Nothing," Lily said. Then, maybe realizing that wasn't much of an explanation went on, "Just looking for some old paperwork."

She picked up a loose piece of paper from the floor and turned it over. I plucked it from her hand and scanned.

"Auto maintenance records? For a Mercedes CL coupe? That's not your car."

"It was Trey's," Lily said, snatching the paper out of my hand, busying herself trying to organize the mess on the floor. I reached for a pile of papers, and she snapped, "I've got it."

"Next time you need something over your head, ask. Might as well take advantage of having someone around who can reach higher than you."

"Is that a short joke?"

I ignored her comment. "Don't do that again, Lily. If you need to get up to that shelf and you don't want to ask me, use the other ladder."

"It doesn't fit in the closet," she muttered under her breath as she finished shoving the last of the papers from the floor back in the box.

"Then ask for help," I said. "You want me to put this back on the shelf?" I asked.

"No, you can leave it." She dusted her hands off on her shorts, her eyes on the basket by her feet. "Do you want a cup of coffee or anything? I baked blueberry muffins."

My stomach turned over at the thought of what Lily could do to blueberry muffins if the rest of her baking was like that coffee cake. "I'm not hungry, but I'll take you up on the coffee."

I followed Lily down the hall into the kitchen inhaling the scents of coffee, blueberries, and something savory and rich. "What's for dinner?" I asked.

"Pot roast. I can't seem to get the hang of baking, but my pot roast is pretty good."

Lily was in the middle of pouring my coffee when she caught sight of the clock on the stove. "Shoot, I didn't realize it was that late. Can you take this to go? I need to get Adam from preschool."

She shoved me out the door, mug in hand, before I could object. Lily didn't want to leave me alone in her house.

As her personal security, I should have had access to the entire property, whether she was there or not. I didn't bother to object.

I already knew Lily had secrets. It was only a matter of time until I uncovered them, one by one.

Chapter Seven

KNOX

LILY DIDN'T INVITE ME TO dinner. She showed up at my door at six carrying a tray loaded with a steaming bowl of pot roast, crusty white bread, a folded cloth napkin, and a blueberry muffin.

Her eyes flitting to mine and back to the tray, she mumbled, "I brought you dinner," shoved the tray into my hands and took flight down the path back to the house, reminding me again of a skittish fawn.

Either I made her nervous, or she had a reason to keep me out of the house. Maybe both.

Lily's pot roast wasn't good. It was amazing. I'm a sucker for pot roast, it's true, but Lily's was out of this world. Tender and juicy in a rich gravy that coated chunks of potatoes and carrots. The bread was delicious. She must have bought it in town.

I watched over the cameras as Lily and Adam ate dinner at the dining room table off of the kitchen, Adam telling his mother the details of his morning in preschool.

She listened with rapt attention to stories of the Lego tower he'd built, engaging in the debate over what was more fun, construction or destruction. I remembered those days myself. The joy of seeing how tall you could build a tower. The teeter when it reached its maximum height and the gorgeous explosion of colored bricks when it toppled to the floor.

If Lily was bored by the minutia of five-year-old life, it didn't show. From what I'd seen, she gave her son attention without smothering, and he soaked it up.

It could be hard to tell with kids, but he hadn't seemed particularly broken up about his father's death. He could be shoving his emotions deep, not ready to process such a loss at a young age. Or—and this was my guess—Lily was his primary source of love, comfort, and care. Losing his father may have been difficult, but losing his mother would be devastating.

Lily would do anything to protect her boy. It was written in her eyes, in her stance when she was beside him. Whatever was going on with the dead husband's connection to my father, if Adam was wrapped up in it, then getting through to Lily would be that much harder.

I intended to have my answers. If the money was proof, Trey Spencer had been up to his neck in my father's bullshit. Lily loved her son. Would she have put him at risk for the promise of easy cash?

Watching them together, my head reminded me that people justified fucked up choices all the time, but my gut refused to accept that Lily would risk her child's life over money.

My gut remembered that my older brother Cooper had read me bedtime stories, not my mother. The housekeeper had packed my lunch and baked me cookies.

My mother had been too busy with her social life and her endless supply of martinis. My father had been a shitty husband, something I understood with new depth now that his secrets were coming to light.

Seeing Lily with Adam, I was reminded that a shitty husband didn't have to mean a checked-out mom. I was getting the picture that Trey Spencer hadn't been all that interested in his son, but Lily seemed determined that Adam have all the love and attention he needed.

Being a good mom doesn't make her a good person, I reminded myself. But didn't it?

No. It didn't. Working security and investigations had taught me that people were complicated. A career criminal might give buckets of money to charity. A pastor could beat his wife.

I'd seen it all, enough to know that a woman who loved her son could be guilty of anything. And if she'd made her choices thinking she was protecting Adam? In that case, Lily Spencer was capable of anything.

They disappeared into the bathroom and emerged half an hour later, Lily's clothes flecked with water, Adam in a pair of superhero pajamas, his blonde curls combed straight and plastered to his forehead. She tucked him into bed and read him story after story until his eyelids drooped and he fell asleep.

Just as she had described, she walked the house before settling in, checking every door and window. When all was secure, she set the alarm. I expected her to get into bed and go to sleep, but she tossed and turned for hours. It wasn't until three am that she dropped off, her body finally still beneath the covers.

Once she was out, I got to work.

It didn't take long to deactivate the alarm from my laptop and let myself in the back door. I moved in near silence through the mudroom, down the hall to the office. Closing and locking the door behind me, I reset the alarm in case Lily woke. If she checked the panel, she'd see the comforting red light and go back to bed.

Trey's laptop was exactly where she'd left it in the top drawer of his desk. I opened it and quickly determined that Lily had been trying to access a dummy account. No wonder she'd been frustrated. There was just enough here to make it look like he regularly used the computer, but it was no more than a front.

Logging out, I pulled a thumb drive from my pocket and connected it to the USB port. Lucas Jackson led our division of computer experts, and his team had come up with this little gem of an app. It should reveal all the accounts on the computer and break the encryption, letting me into everything on the hard drive.

If Trey Spencer had been a hacker on Lucas' level, the thumb drive wouldn't have done the job. In that case, I would have been on the phone dragging Lucas' ass up to Maine. But Trey Spencer wasn't a hacker, and Lucas' app looked like it did the trick.

A minute later I was in, and Trey Spencer's life was spread before me.

The banking information was the same that Lily had access to through the dummy account. Ditto for their insurance and household bills.

But the files were completely different. Where Lily found empty folders, I uncovered a treasure trove of data. Flicking through, opening, scanning, and closing documents, Trey's laptop painted a damning picture.

Everything was in Lily's name.

Everything.

The house, the cars, the investment accounts. Insurance policies for artwork and jewelry. From what I could see, it had been this way for years before Trey Spencer died.

When his car drove off that bridge, Lily became a very wealthy woman.

That sure as hell didn't make her look innocent. If Trey Spencer had been murdered, the information on his laptop provided a ton of motive.

If Lily had killed her husband, why was I here?

If she was responsible for his death, she'd gotten away with it. There was no murder investigation. The insurance paid out with only the standard delay.

Why bring me to Maine unless she absolutely had to?

Trey's involvement with my father was the wildcard.

Lily could have killed her husband and then discovered he left loose ends that threatened her and Adam. As much as I wanted to believe Lily was innocent, I didn't have a shred of proof.

Interestingly, what I didn't find was information about Adam Spencer. No birth certificate. No adoption papers. No medical bills. I didn't have to ask to know that Lily hadn't given birth to Adam.

I suspected Trey was his biological father. From the pictures I'd seen, Adam's blue eyes and white-blonde curls were a perfect match to childhood photographs of Trey Spencer. Echoes of Trey's adult face showed in Adam's childish one. They were absolutely father and son.

There wasn't a trace of Lily in him. Adam's skin was a pure ivory without a hint of her caramel tones. His hair was his father's shining white-blonde, nothing like his mother's soft cloud of spiraling, dark curls.

If Adam was the product of an agreement with a

surrogate, there should have been a contract. At the very least, there should have been a birth certificate somewhere. Trey Spencer had scanned other documents on the laptop. Why not the birth certificate?

I scrolled through the files again and checked to make sure Lucas' drive was still plugged in. The hidden account on the laptop had been packed with personal data, excepting anything about Adam Spencer, but nothing here was connected with Trey's business.

Was there a second laptop? Had it been with him when he'd died? The police report hadn't mentioned a laptop in the car, but if Trey had been forced off that bridge, his killer would have taken anything of use, including a computer.

I'd have to find a way to press Lily for more information. Trey Spencer had worked from home. It would have been hard to hide a second laptop. From our reports, he'd been driving back from dinner at his club in Bangor, a long trip in the wilds of Maine, but not one he'd make with his business computer. Had Lucas' app missed a second hidden account? Without Lucas himself, I couldn't tell.

I pulled a discrete portable hard drive from my pocket, plugged it into the laptop, and started the process of copying the files to the drive. While that was working, I installed a keystroke tracker Lily wouldn't be able to see. In the time it would take to copy the laptop, I'd check the closet.

Much like Lily, I found nothing. Bills for heating oil. Invoices for vehicle repairs. Years of utility bills. Hospital bills.

There were a handful related to Lily. I didn't need a medical degree to see that she'd been pregnant and miscarried twice. The file ended there. There weren't any bills for fertility treatments, consultations, or testing. Less than a year after Lily's second miscarriage I found a record of Adam's infant vaccinations.

Adam. Was he a key to the mystery of Lily Spencer or a distraction? It was too soon to say.

The more I discovered, the more questions I had. If Adam hadn't looked so much like his father, I might have suspected my Dad's hand in his sudden appearance. Private, possibly illegal adoptions were just one of the sordid things we'd uncovered about our father. Even Adam's resemblance to Trey didn't chase the connection from my mind.

I turned off the light in the closet and closed the door, removing my drives from the laptop and shutting it down, leaving the office exactly how I'd found it. I crept down the hall to the mudroom where I deactivated the alarm, exited the house, and reactivated it behind me.

Unlike Lily, I dropped off to sleep immediately, sliding into the darkness, my mind free to drift and dream. Untethered, my thoughts went straight for Lily.

Her soft curls. The full curve of her lower lip. The view down her T-shirt when she was in the closet. Those round, ripe breasts, the way they shifted and swayed as she'd reached for basket after basket.

In dreams I cupped them in my hands, thumbing the hard points of her nipples. I ducked my head into the curve of her neck, inhaling vanilla and spice, tasting her. I spread her out beneath me on crisp, white sheets and devoured every inch of her body until she cried my name.

I woke to find myself rolling my hips into the mattress, fucking her in my sleep, my hard cock grinding uncomfortably into the soft sheets.

I stood under a cold shower in the gray of dawn, pumping my cock with my fist, trying to think of anything but Lily, and failing miserably.

Chapter Eight

LILY

THE LIGHT FROM THE TV screen flickered, reflecting off the plate glass windows in the living room. During the day, I loved the view of the lake through those windows. At night, the dark was unfathomable. Oppressive.

I curled deeper into the corner of the sofa, pulling the soft chenille blanket over my legs and tried to focus on my movie. On-screen, Rosalind Russell and Cary Grant bantered in quick-fire explosions of words, all sharp wit and biting humor. Normally, I loved this movie. Tonight, it couldn't hold my attention.

Adam was tucked into bed after a series of arguments over everything from the temperature of his bath to the cartoon character on his pajamas. Par for the course with a five-year-old. Three books and a back-rub had him deeply asleep, his stuffed monkey clutched in his arm.

I was supposed to be unwinding in front of the TV. Instead, my ears were trained for the slightest sound. I assumed Knox was around somewhere. He'd turned down my invitation to dinner, choosing to stay in the cottage. I'd seen him only a few times during the day, stalking through the woods around the house, a dark pack on his back, tools in his hands.

I didn't ask what he was doing.

I didn't need to know as long as he was keeping us safe.

I had to trust someone sometime. Knox was as good a place to start as any.

Rosalind Russell's ill-fated fiancé came on screen, prompting a sympathetic smile. He was nice enough, but how could any man live up to Cary Grant? My mind immediately flashed to Knox.

Knox and Cary Grant weren't remotely comparable. If anything, Trey had been more like Cary than Knox.

With his easy, smooth charm, his sense of style, his ability to always say the right thing at the right time, Trey was a master of the elegant facade. It had taken me years to guess at what lay beneath.

I watched Cary talk circles around Roslyn's fiancé and had to wonder if my lifelong love of Cary Grant was responsible for my attraction to Trey.

If so, Cary had a lot to answer for.

Trey's charm and wit had been all surface and no substance. Knox was more silence than words. Action instead of empty reassurance. I couldn't help remembering Davey's visit the day before and the way Knox had studied him, then made a point of not leaving us alone. I wasn't the only one who thought something was off with Deputy Dave.

It wasn't just Knox's blunt lack of charm I found appealing. Trey had been slender. Lean and fit, but slight of build. Far bigger than me, but nothing like Knox.

Those shoulders...

Just thinking about Knox's shoulders brought a flush of heat to my cheeks. And other places.

Don't forget about his forearms, the light sprinkle of dark hair over tanned skin, muscle corded beneath. So much strength. He was tall, broad and could probably break me in two.

Why didn't that scare me? It should. Trey was dead, and with every day that passed, I was more certain his car hadn't gone over that bridge by accident.

Knox's serious, steady gaze filled my mind. He was a virtual stranger, employed by a company Trey had chosen, which should have made him instantly suspect.

Less trustworthy, not more.

So why did I want to trust him?

I needed to be sure my instincts were on target. That some deeply-buried part of me recognized Knox's innate goodness. Maybe that was it. Or maybe I was a woman alone, starved for touch, for affection, allowing her mind to be swayed by a tight ass and dark eyes.

My mind drifted to another old favorite. *Dial M for Murder*. And another. *Gaslight*. Men fooling women who wanted to believe the best of them. Just because Knox looked like an action hero didn't make him the good guy.

I focused on the movie. It worked for about two minutes. Then Cary Grant cracked a joke, and the wicked glint in his eye reminded me of the way Knox had winked at Adam as they'd watched Davey pretend to enjoy my coffee cake.

His lip had curled in a hint of a smile, but Adam had seen it and laughed along with him. Could I trust my son's instincts if I couldn't trust my own?

Adam had never warmed up to his father. When Trey was alive, their distance broke my heart. Now I could only be grateful for it. Adam was hot and cold with Davey, but Knox he took to right away.

What did Adam see when he looked at Knox Sinclair? It wasn't the ruggedly handsome face—the strong lines of his jaw that warned me off, and the lush lower lip that invited me in. It wasn't his long-fingered hands or his powerful thighs—

No, Lily. No way.

I pushed the heels of my palms into my eyes until I saw stars behind my eyelids, banishing my lustful thoughts of Knox Sinclair.

He's here to keep you safe, not to perv over. You and Adam have been doing fine without a man around. Knox can't do his job if there's anything personal between you so get your hormones under control and forget about him.

I'd get over it. I'd get used to Knox being here, and I'd stop thinking about him like this. It was only the novelty of having a man around who was even slightly trustworthy. Once I got used to him, things would change. They had to. The last thing I needed was a man to complicate my messy life.

I was so wrapped up in my head, the shrill beep of the new perimeter alarm sent me bolting off the couch with a shriek. Adrenaline spiked up my spine and down my limbs, leaving my fingers and toes prickling. My heart thundered in my chest, so loud it almost drowned out the alarm.

Fumbling for my phone, I called Knox. It rang once, twice, three times before Knox's low voice invited me to leave a message.

"Knox? It's Lily. The alarm went off, and I don't know—"

I jolted, almost dropping the phone as it vibrated in my hand with an incoming text. I ended the message to Knox's voicemail and tapped the screen of my phone. Knox.

Perimeter sensors tripped. Adam's room. Lock the door.

I took off down the hall, leaving the movie still playing in the background. I flew up the stairs, skidding to a halt outside of Adam's door, trying to get my breath under control so my wild gasps wouldn't wake him.

I eased into the dark room to see my boy sprawled across his bed, covers kicked to his feet, his too-long blonde curls splayed across the pillow. His back rose and fell with slow, deep breaths.

Adam didn't stir as I sat on the floor beside his bed, leaning my head against the mattress much as I had the night I'd called Knox.

The minutes passed like hours, dragging until a second might as well have been an eternity. The perimeter alarm cut off, leaving behind a heavy silence.

I couldn't make out anything no matter how hard I strained my ears. Not a footstep. Not the crack of a branch, the sound of a knob turning, or a door swinging open. Nothing.

When my phone vibrated again, I clamped my teeth into my lip to hold back the squeal of alarm. Another message from Knox.

Outside clear. Checking the house. Stay put.

I rested my chin on my raised knees and waited, listening. I thought I heard a door open and close. A heavy, steady tread on the hardwood floor, the sound coming into focus and fading as Knox walked past the stairs. Then the thump, thump, thump of him jogging to the second floor, the creek of the joists as he moved down the hall, methodically checking every inch of the house.

Finally, another message.

House is clear. Meet me in the living room.

I took a deep breath for the first time in a half hour and rose from the floor feeling creaky and tired. Leaving Adam still deeply asleep, I made my way downstairs to find Knox standing in the center of the living room, hands on his hips, eyes locked to the TV screen.

I'd forgotten to pause the movie. Rosalind Russell and Cary Grant were bickering. Knox watched with the same amused expression as the spectators in the film. His dark eyes turned to me as I entered the room.

"What was it? An animal?" I asked hopefully.

Knox shook his head once. "No. Human. Smaller than me, bigger than you. I'll take a closer look at the footage from the cameras later. Whoever it was had an idea that the cameras were there. The good news is they didn't get close to any of the doors or windows."

"And the bad news?"

"That they suspected there was surveillance, and they tried anyway."

I nodded, not sure what to say. I was relieved no one had gotten inside. Relieved Knox was there to search the woods in the dark instead of me. Knox was far better equipped to scare off whoever kept trying to break in than I was.

I tried a faint smile. "Your upgrades to the alarm system paid off."

The side of Knox's mouth quirked in a semblance of a grin, and he let out a rumbling noise that could have been a chuckle. "That's one way to look at it."

"I'll take what I can get," I mumbled.

Knox's eyes sharpened. "We're only getting started, Lily. I'm not going to let anything happen to you."

My throat tightened with gratitude. I couldn't force out a word, so I settled for a brisk nod.

"What's the movie?" Knox asked, inclining his head at the screen.

I swallowed hard before I said, "*His Girl Friday*. Rosalind Russell and Cary Grant. They're divorced, but they used to work together—"

Knox watched Rosalind and Carey bicker/flirt for a few seconds before saying, "They don't look very divorced to me."

"They don't, do they? But they haven't figured that out yet."

Knox stood, his thumbs tucked in his pockets, his eyes on the screen. He didn't look like he intended to go anywhere. I shifted my weight from one foot to the other, not sure what to say.

I opened my mouth and out came, "Are you hungry? I have leftover lasagna if you want something to eat. You can watch the rest of the movie..."

I trailed off, not sure where the invitation had come from. I wasn't sure it was a good idea, but it was too late to take it back.

Knox pulled his eyes from the screen and said, "Sure."

Sure? That wasn't what I expected him to say.

"Do you want me to reheat some pot roast? Popcorn?"

Knox didn't look away from the screen. "Both."

I don't know why I was suddenly so flustered. Knox worked for me. If anyone should be nervous in our relationship, it was him, right? I was the one who'd invited him to stay. It was my house. My couch. My movie.

None of that soothed the butterflies in my stomach. It wasn't a date or anything—that would be ridiculous—but every time we'd spoken, he'd been strictly business. Watching a movie over popcorn was anything but.

I paused the movie. "It won't take me long."

Knox followed me to the kitchen where I pulled out a well-used pot and turned on the gas flame, grabbing a bottle of popcorn oil from the cabinet and pouring a liberal dose inside, along with a sprinkle of rosemary and garlic powder. Knox leaned against the island, hands shoved into his pockets.

"You make popcorn from scratch?"

I swirled the pot with two hands and looked over my shoulder at him. "Of course. Don't tell me, you throw a bag in the microwave and pray it doesn't burn?"

"Pretty much."

"Then prepare yourself for the real thing. I usually add seasonings and cheese. I hope that's okay." I hadn't thought about it before adding the rosemary and garlic, but I could pour out the oil and start over.

"I'll eat pretty much anything, Lily," Knox said.

"Except my coffee cake."

Knox didn't apologize for passing on my baking. Why should he? It had been terrible. Even I knew that. "I promise my popcorn is good."

While the oil heated, I put together a bowl of pot roast from the leftovers and popped it in the microwave. "Bread?"

"Please."

I wondered what it would take to get Knox to say more than a few words at a time. I probably didn't want to know. He didn't talk much, but his eyes were alert, picking up everything, absorbing every detail of his surroundings.

His dark gaze moved around the room, soaking in the homey, country kitchen that didn't fit with the rest of the house. I'd mostly let Trey do what he wanted. I hadn't wanted to cause friction, hadn't realized how much I'd dislike the end result.

When it came to the kitchen, I'd dug in my heels. I'd

mostly gotten what I'd wanted. Instead of endless stainless steel and glass, there were touches of wood. Counters of warm, gold-flecked granite instead of concrete. Locally-crafted cabinets versus the shiny black Trey had favored. The end result wasn't quite the farmhouse look I'd pictured, but it was as close as I was going to get.

My back to Knox, I focused on the popcorn rather than trying to come up with empty conversation to fill the silence. I chattered when I was nervous. Knox made me nervous for all sorts of reasons I wasn't ready to explore, but I didn't feel the need to fill the quiet with words. Silence with Knox was comfortable. Maybe because I sensed he didn't need conversation from me.

I went about making the popcorn, adding thyme and some finely-ground black pepper, swirling the oil and kernels with every addition before putting the lid on, just in time. The first kernel popped, flinging itself across the inside of the aluminum pot with a light, crisp ping.

Leaving the pot, I grabbed an oversized wooden bowl I'd picked up at the town arts festival a few years before and set it on the counter beside the pot. The popping kernels were coming faster now, so fast I couldn't distinguish one from another. It wasn't long before they slowed, and I waited, listening, trying to find the exact moment when the last kernel had popped but the corn hadn't yet begun to burn.

Judging it was ready, I turned off the burner, pulled the pot from the stove and dumped the fragrant, steaming popcorn into the wooden bowl. Beside me, the microwave dinged. Leaving the popcorn, I got Knox's dinner from the microwave and made up a tray.

Throwing a glance over my shoulder at Knox, still leaning against the island with his hands in his pockets, I said,

"You can take this into the living room. I'll be right there with the popcorn."

Without a word, Knox picked up the tray and left the kitchen. I would have guessed that Knox's absence would ease my nerves. It did, a little, but the sense of loss took me by surprise. Without Knox, the heat and life had been sucked from the room.

I dusted the popcorn with finely ground salt and parmesan cheese, tossing it so the flavors could work their way into the nooks and crannies of every piece. I thought about getting two bowls, but there was only one couch with a good view of the television. It was easier to put the popcorn between us. We were adults. We could share a bowl of popcorn.

I entered the living room to find that Knox had made himself comfortable on the opposite end of the couch from my discarded blanket, setting the tray with his pot roast on the coffee table. I put the popcorn beside his tray and sat, busying myself with tucking the blanket around my legs and fumbling for the remote.

"I like the TV set up," Knox said, raising his chin in the direction of the screen. "Looks good in here."

"Thanks. "

He was right, it did. Trey, who hadn't been much for television, had refused to put one in the living room. We had a family room down the hall with a big flat screen so Trey could watch sports. In his world, sports and regular tv weren't the same thing. I'm not a fan of football, I don't get baseball, and soccer is boring on tv.

I wanted a place to watch my shows on the nights a game was on. We compromised with the flat screen built into one of the console tables in the living room. It wasn't much good during the day when shafts of sunlight glared on the screen, but at night, one touch of a button and the

TV rose out of the console table to face the couch. Perfect for curling up with a blanket and binge watching.

Knox used the side of his fork to cut into the pot roast, and I picked up the remote. "I'll start it over," I said. "Basically, Rosalind is on her way out of town with her fiancé, and Cary is trying to use a big story to get her to stay so he can win her back."

Knox chewed slowly and nodded, his eyes on the screen. I munched on popcorn and tried to fall into the familiar rhythm of a movie I'd seen countless times before. I'd had trouble focusing earlier, worried the intruder would come back. I wasn't worried about that anymore, but Knox's presence made it equally hard to concentrate.

He ate every bite of pot roast and set the plate back on the tray before turning to the crusty buttered bread. I hadn't baked the bread, but the garlic and basil butter on top was all me, and it was awesome. Knox must have agreed because the bread disappeared in three big bites.

He wiped his hands, finger by finger, on the napkin I'd left on the tray and settled back into the couch, his eyes still locked on the screen.

Knox Sinclair was a contradiction. Good manners. Even eating on the couch, he hadn't made a mess. His tray was as neat as it had been when he picked it up off the counter. The used napkin was folded in half, the utensils side-by-side. I remembered the way he rushed in after I fell from the ladder, his gentle hands checking me for an injury, the concern in his voice.

Knox didn't talk much, and he looked like a brawler, but he was polite and kind. I'd take kindness over pretty words any day.

I reached for a handful of popcorn, jolting as my fingertip grazed Knox's wrist. A tingle went up my hand at the brief contact, and I fought the urge to yank my fingers away. We were two adults sharing popcorn. So what if I touched him by accident?

I shoved popcorn in my mouth to distract myself. Knox did the same. A minute later he said, "This is good."

"Thanks. Better than the stuff from the microwave?"

Knox's grunt was brief but full of approval. A warm glow settled in my chest. My coffee cake had been awful, and he hadn't braved my blueberry muffins—smart move on his part—but I'd hit a home run with the roast and popcorn.

Why it mattered that Knox liked my cooking, I couldn't say. It shouldn't matter. It shouldn't matter at all.

I ignored that thought and held on to the warm glow in my chest, wondering if our fingers would brush again in the popcorn bowl and ignoring the flare of warning in the back of my head.

Touching Knox Sinclair was a bad idea.

I already knew that.

I knew and I wanted to do it anyway.

Chapter Nine

LILY

KNOX WAS WAITING BY THE Land Rover when Adam and I rushed out of the house. Adam went to preschool three days a week, had been for over a year, and every morning was still a battle.

He didn't want to get dressed. He didn't like his breakfast. He wanted different sneakers. Not all that different from our bedtime routine.

I was afraid to ask how long it would take for Adam to grow out of making every chore into a game. I loved his imagination and sense of adventure, I just wished he'd save it for times we weren't running late. Since he'd started talking, it seemed like we were always late.

We skidded to a halt at the sight of Knox in a black T-shirt and dark jeans leaning against the hood of the Land Rover, arms crossed over his chest. He said, "I'll drive."

Adam breathed, "Cool. Are you going to drive faster than Mom?"

Any thought of objecting to Knox's chauffeur services dissolved as a grin cracked across his rugged face, and he said, "I might. How fast does your mom drive?"

Adam clambered into his car seat, sitting docile as Knox arranged the straps and secured them with ease. I stood there like an idiot with my jaw hanging open. Adam never sat still to be buckled in. Neither of them noticed me.

Adam, giggling at Knox's question, considered it seriously before answering. "Mom drives like someone's grandma. My dad used to drive really fast. She yelled at him all the time. Told him to slow down, but he never listened. He had an accident in his car."

Adam delivered this information as if he were talking about a stranger and not his father. Knox's eyes flashed to me. I looked away, fumbling with the door and then my seatbelt. I didn't want to talk about Trey's driving habits or the accident that had killed him.

The police thought he'd swerved to avoid a deer in the road and skidded off the bridge. He could have. Adam was telling the truth. Trey always drove too fast. He'd loved his sleek Mercedes coupe, a car designed more for a racetrack than rural Maine roads.

The night of his accident had been clear, with a full moon. Dry roads. No traffic. If he'd lost control, it would have been the first time. And the last.

I wasn't going to think about that. Not right now.

Knox backed us out of the garage, as comfortable behind the wheel of my Land Rover as if he'd been driving it for years. I imagine Knox did everything with that same relaxed competency.

I tried not to find it so reassuring. It wasn't smart to trust a virtual stranger too much, to let his strength and capability lull me into complacency.

I'd decided to trust Knox Sinclair with our safety. I couldn't hire him for security and then go around suspecting his every move. That would be stupid. It didn't mean I should sit back and assume he was the answer to all of our problems.

"Adam's preschool is in town," I said, nerves making my voice unsteady before I swallowed and got it under control. "It's at the church on Main Street a few blocks down from Town Hall—"

"I know where it is," Knox said.

I didn't ask what that meant. He knew where the church was, or he knew where Adam went to preschool? It wasn't a stretch for someone new in town to know where the church was. Built in a classic New England style, with white siding and a tall steeple, it anchored the center of Main Street, visible from all sides.

How did Knox know where Adam went to pre-school? The answer was instantly obvious. He'd investigated us. Sinclair Security probably investigated all of their clients. Trey had been a client for years.

What did Knox Sinclair know about my dead husband that I didn't?

Adam chattered as Knox drove, telling him everything he planned to do in preschool that day. He was as comfortable with Knox as he was with adults he'd known his whole life. More comfortable than he'd been with his father.

I winced at the thought, but my discomfort didn't make it any less true. Trey'd had little patience for a toddler's babbling. More often than not, when Adam had tried to talk to him in the fragmented words of the four-year-old he'd been when Trey died, Trey had brushed him off.

He didn't want to be bothered with the ramblings of a baby, he'd told me in annoyance. '*Shut him up or put him somewhere else.*'

I'd gone out of my way to shield Adam from Trey's dismissal, but seeing the way he opened up to Knox, who laughed with him and let him talk without interruption, I realized how much Adam had been missing.

Knox was out of the car a moment after he turned off the engine, helping Adam from the car seat. Preschool was located in a squat brick box of a building, tucked behind the church. The school building wasn't pretty, but the playground more than made up for it.

The door swung open, and the sounds of screaming children assaulted our ears. Adam raced ahead of us, calling out to his friends. I put a hand on Knox's arm to stop him. We didn't need to go all the way into the classroom. Twenty kids were nineteen too many before I'd had a cup of coffee.

"One second. Let me just drop off his backpack."

I left Knox standing by the door and was back a minute later, Adam's backpack securely deposited in his cubby.

"Preschool only lasts until noon. I usually do some grocery shopping and then go to the park. If you have things to do—"

"Which grocery store?" Knox asked.

I guess that answered that question. Being trailed by a stranger as I went about my errands might raise some questions, but I couldn't deny the relief I felt having Knox by my side.

I was good at ignoring my worries during the day. Walking through the grocery store beside Knox, I realized how anxious I'd been since Trey died, always alert for anything out of the ordinary, worried, uncertain, and scared.

Did I think someone was going to come after me in the produce aisle? Of course not. We were in town, in the middle of the day, at the height of tourist season. I couldn't have been safer, with or without Knox. I still felt better with him by my side.

I decided not to analyze. I was going to enjoy feeling safe for the first time in months.

"Do you have a list?" Knox asked.

I held up my phone with the grocery list app open on the screen. "I don't need much. If there's anything you want for the cottage, just throw it in."

I meant it when I said it, but I made a face as a bag of chips hit the cart.

"Not a fan of junk food?" Knox rumbled. I swear I heard a hint of amusement in his deep voice.

"Who doesn't like chips? I usually try to keep stuff like that away from Adam. Don't be surprised if he comes begging. And if he does, try not to let him eat the whole bag."

"Deal," Knox said. "I'm assuming soda's out?"

I slid a glance at Knox. His T-shirt wasn't tight, but what I could see of his arms told me his body fat had to be in the single digits. This was not a guy who drank soda. Was he yanking my chain?

A little giddy at the thought of Knox teasing me, I let out a halting laugh. "Definitely no soda," I confirmed. We stopped in the baking aisle, and I grabbed the ingredients for chocolate chip cookies.

I refused to give up. I would learn to bake. I'd learned to cook, hadn't I?

When Trey and I got married I had no clue in the kitchen, but, between the Internet and cookbooks, I'd learned. I'd learned pretty well if I said so myself.

Baking, though, that was new. Trey hadn't wanted sweets in the house. He'd discouraged me from baking, and I'd gone along.

I'd gone along with a lot of things.

I'd gone so far, I'd almost lost myself.

A month after he died, I'd been standing in the bathroom with a hair straightener in my hand, ready to torture my curls into the smooth style Trey had loved.

All of a sudden it hit me.

Trey was dead.

Gone.

I'd dropped the straightener and sunk to the floor, tears flooding my eyes. So much effort to hold myself together, to be strong for Adam. The dam broke, and I wept until I ran out of tears.

Eyes dry, a few things had come clear.

Adam and I were on our own.

I was responsible for everything.

Including myself.

Slowly, I'd been regaining bits of my life and trying new things. I'd put the straightener away and hadn't used it since. When Trey and I met, I'd been trying the straight look. He'd hated my curls, so I'd kept up with it. But Trey was gone, and I was tired of trying to make someone else happy at my own expense.

Leaving my hair to its natural curls was the beginning. Next came my clothes as I traded twin sets and skirts for jeans and t-shirts. I still dressed up now and then, but when I was home by myself all day? Comfort ruled.

Now I was working on learning to bake. I'd always imagined being the kind of mom who made muffins and cookies, all sorts of yummy treats. I would be. As soon as I figured out how to make them taste like vanilla and sugar instead of baking soda and salt.

Practice makes perfect, right? I just had to keep trying.

At that thought, I grabbed extra chocolate chips in case

the first batch didn't work out. Who was I kidding? *When* the first batch didn't work out.

Knox gave my baking ingredients the side-eye but said nothing. We moved to the next aisle, passing shelves of packaged cookies. I waited for him to grab one in case my chocolate chip cookies turned out like the muffins and the coffee cake. He ignored the cookies and other snacks but grabbed a canister of raisins and one of oatmeal as well as a bag of apples, an extra carton of eggs, and a pint of gourmet vanilla ice cream.

I threw in a box of fruit-juice popsicles for Adam, and we headed to the checkout. I didn't know the teenager at the register. Tourist season was short but busy, and every business in town had temporary summer help.

There's an old saying: There are only two seasons in Maine. Winter and July. Like most old sayings, it was based in fact.

We got our share of visitors when the leaves blazed across the mountains in the fall, but winter came early, and tourist season hit in the heart of summer. As in, right now.

Town was packed, including the grocery store. Normally so many strange faces might have made me a little edgy, but I was glad not to have to explain Knox to anyone who knew me.

I packed our frozen food in the cooler I kept in the back of the Land Rover, adding the bag of ice I'd purchased, and arranged the rest of the groceries around it.

"Why don't you shop before you pick him up?" Knox asked.

"In the winter I do. The store isn't as crowded. This time of year, it's so busy I never know how long it'll take to get out of there."

"Do they charge extra if you're late?"

"They do, but that's not it." I nestled the eggs carefully so they wouldn't get crushed as we drove home on the curving roads, keeping my eyes from Knox. I didn't like to think about why I shopped first. Anything that hurt my baby sliced through me.

"Since Trey died, Adam gets upset if I'm late picking him up. At the end of May, I got stuck at the store, and by the time I got there, he was bawling. It took a while to calm him down, but he finally told me he thought I wasn't coming. That I'd been in an accident like his dad. Now I'm careful to be there a little early. It's a waste of gas to drive back and forth when we're so far from town, so I use the cooler."

Knox nodded in understanding. I didn't like to think about that day, Adam's desperate tears, his red face and heaving sobs. He was so young to face the loss of a parent. Grief is a difficult process for an adult. For a child? I'd do anything to make it easier for him.

"There's a coffee shop down the street," I said, changing the subject. "I usually leave the car here, get a cup of coffee, and then go to the park. That okay with you?"

Knox lifted his chin in agreement. I'd take that as a yes. We walked in silence down the hill to the heart of Main Street, passing the church where Adam was in preschool. The small coffee shop was packed, the line stretching to the door.

I got in the back of the line, resigned to wait, when I heard my name called from behind the counter. I looked up to see Dana, a junior at the high school and our occasional babysitter. She waved me over, her long, dark braids flipping over her shoulders.

"You don't have to wait behind all these tourists," she said, not even trying to lower her voice. A few of the people in line grumbled but fell silent after a look from Knox.

Dana grinned up at my companion and shot me a questioning look. Knowing there was no way I could get out of explaining, I said, "Knox, this is Dana. She babysits for Adam sometimes. Knox is up to do a few things with the house. His company worked with Trey when we built it."

Some of the excitement in Dana's eyes dimmed. House stuff was boring. Exactly why I'd explained it that way. Dana was a great kid with nice parents, but small-town gossip is a force of nature. I didn't want the widow's new lover to be the latest hot story.

Dana's natural exuberance overwhelmed her disappointment and she grinned again, ignoring the grumbles of the customers second and third in line. "What can I get you guys?"

"Iced s'mores latte for me," I said. From beside me, Knox said, "Americano. Black."

"Just a sec. You guys can wait over by the bulletin board. I'll bring your stuff there."

I was fumbling with my wallet as Knox handed Dana a bill saying, "Keep the change."

"You didn't have to do that." I led Knox to the side of the counter where creamers, sweeteners, cinnamon, and stirrers were lined up beneath a huge bulletin board packed with flyers and business cards.

Knox shrugged. We stood beside one another, comfortable in our silence, absorbing the chatter of the packed coffee shop and reading the flyers stapled and pinned in layers on the bulletin board.

Someone was trying to get rid of kittens. Not a single tab missing on that one. Guess nobody wanted kittens this summer. Someone else was trying to sell a used Honda. That one had a lot of takers. Only one tab with the phone number remained. There was an out-of-date flyer for the

4th of July concert and a new one for the Arts in the Park Festival the next week.

Dana delivered our drinks and we left, working our way through the tourists crowding the sidewalk until we got to the park. It was early enough that we were able to find a bench under a tree and we sat, Knox beside me, facing the town docks and the lake.

Black Rock was not where I imagined I'd end up. I always saw myself living in a city or near one. Trey had grown up summering in Black Rock, and he'd dreamed of living here full time. The town had charm, the people were friendly, and it was beautiful.

Still, I was lonely.

I didn't fit in, and even before Trey died, I was lonely.

We watched boats bobbing at the docks, and a young girl playing catch with a puppy, the girl doing more fetching than the dog.

I wondered, idly, how long I could sit in silence before Knox would break it. It turned out, not that long.

Chapter Ten

LILY

I LIKED THE MOVIE LAST NIGHT," he said.

"Me too. I used to watch old movies with my dad when I was a kid. That was one of our favorites."

"What are your other favorites?"

I laughed. "Oh, it's a long list. Pretty much anything with Cary Grant. And I love Hitchcock."

"I took a class on Hitchcock in college," Knox said.

"Really? Because you like Hitchcock or because you thought it would be easy?"

"Both," Knox said with a hint of a wry smile. "I majored in engineering and history. I tried to go easy with my electives."

"I could see that. I majored in education. I did most of my electives in psychology and sociology. Stuff like that."

"Did you want to be a teacher?"

A sigh slipped from my chest as I cast myself back. College felt like another life. I'd been so certain of everything.

What I wanted. What I would do. Some of it worked out. A lot of it hadn't. I stared at the sunlight playing over the water, trying to figure out how to answer his question.

"Lily?" Knox prompted.

"I love kids, used to babysit for extra money, so I thought I'd like teaching. I planned to finish my undergrad and get a Masters in Early Childhood Education. Then I met Trey, and he wanted to get married and move up here. We fell in love so fast. He wanted a family, and so did I. His parents hated me. Mine despised him. It was us against the world, and school—"

"Didn't seem that important?"

"Yeah. Do you know what that's like? When you first fall in love? Everything is so intense. The sun is brighter. Every song has a deeper meaning, like it was written just for you. When someone tells you to slow down, it feels like they don't understand."

"Did they? Understand?"

I let out another sigh and sipped at my latte. "Yes and no. Trey's parents didn't like me because I wasn't what they imagined for Trey."

"How?" Knox's eyes on me were kindly inquiring.

I looked away as I said, "Not white enough." He let out a grunt. "They denied that was it, but we knew. Little comments about my 'background' or my 'people.' My dad is an Ivy League professor of economics, and my mom's a successful artist. Nothing to complain about there, except my dad is black. Trey's parents refused to meet him but invited my mom—who's white—to come for a visit.

"They made it pretty clear what their issues were. When they couldn't scare me off or talk Trey into dumping me, they threatened to disinherit him. They weren't crazy rich, but they had money. They thought that would do the trick, but he hated when they tried to control him with money, and we were in love. Then—"

My throat closed tight, and I had to swallow. So many years gone by, but their deaths had changed everything.

"There was a fire. Trey's father forgot to change the battery in the smoke detector. They didn't wake up. They'd threatened to disinherit him, wouldn't talk to him, and a few months later, they were gone. We hadn't been married long. A part of him blamed me. He never reconciled with them because of me."

"Did you tell him not to? Forbid him from seeing his parents?"

"No, of course not. I didn't want to see them myself. They were openly rude to me, and I didn't want to deal with it. I should have encouraged him to reach out. He could have gone without me. They lived in Boston, it wasn't far. So much pride."

"Did your parents ever warm up to him?"

"I haven't seen my parents since the day before I married Trey. My father told me he wouldn't walk me down the aisle, and if I went through with it not to bother coming home. I sent them a wedding announcement, but I never heard back."

"Nothing?" I felt rather than saw Knox's head turn, the pressure of his eyes intent on my face.

I couldn't bear to see his expression, the pity I imagined was there. Years later and it still hurt to say it out loud.

"Nothing. I sent Christmas cards the first few years we were married. I know they're all right. My father is still a professor. My mother was featured in a coffee table book on oil paintings. I bought it when it came out. She's been doing beautiful work."

"Were you close before you married?"

I thought about how to answer that. How to explain the complex ties of parent and child, the expectations and the failures, the disappointment and the love.

I settled for, "We loved each other. I love them. They had plans for me. I was supposed to be someone great, to follow my father's footsteps and be a renowned academic, or inherit my mother's talent and create amazing works of art. But I wasn't either of those things. I'm just me, and the things I wanted seemed so small to them. We fought a lot when I was in college, but I never thought they'd shut me out. And then they did."

"If you'd known you wouldn't see them for all these years, would you still have married him?"

Knox was full of hard questions this morning, wasn't he? My brain needed more caffeine or my heart more courage. I didn't have to think about the answer. One thing made it very simple.

"Yes. Absolutely."

"It was a good marriage?" Knox asked. His tone didn't quite hide the thread of disbelief.

My laugh was only a tiny bit bitter. "No. No, it was terrible, honestly. We were too young to get married. We should have waited. I wonder if my dad would talk to me if I sent him a postcard that said, '*You were right.*'" I laughed again, and this time the sound was soaked in bitterness.

"So, why? Why would you marry him again?"

I turned to him, incredulous. "Adam. I would go through anything for Adam. He's the best thing that ever happened to me. I'll spend the rest of my life trying to deserve him. I'd like to think that if Trey had lived, he would have grown into a good father. A decent husband."

I stared at the lake and ignored Knox's grunt of disbelief. I didn't know what he knew about Trey, probably enough that his disbelief was justified. Given his job, I'm sure he knew more about Trey than I did.

And yeah, it was unlikely Trey would have grown into either a decent father or husband. The most realistic future, if he'd lived, was our eventual divorce and Trey sliding into the role of an absentee father. There wasn't any harm in believing there'd been hope. Especially since that hope was entirely gone.

I was done talking about myself. "What about you? Are you close to your folks?"

Knox let out a huff of breath that might have been a laugh. "It's complicated."

"Isn't it always with parents?"

"Yep. I worked with my dad until a few years ago. We're... estranged, I guess."

"You don't know?"

"That's the complicated part. I have three brothers, and we're tight. We run the company together. One of my brothers, Axel, lives in Vegas, and I don't see him as much as I'd like, but the rest of us are in Atlanta."

"Must be nice to have siblings." I'd always wanted siblings. A little brother or sister to play with. My parents hadn't been interested. One child was enough interruption in their busy lives.

"Most of the time it is," Knox agreed.

"What about your mom?" I pressed, knowing it might be rude to ask for what he hadn't offered, but I wanted to know more about the man sitting beside me. He was living in the cottage. I'd trusted him with our lives. I'd be foolish not to pry when I had the chance.

"That's complicated, too. She—" Knox trailed off. I risked a glance to see his eyes locked on the lake, unfocused as if tossed back into memory. I waited, and eventually, he started speaking again.

"I know what you mean about expectations. My mom is not a happy woman. My dad was a shit husband, and she drinks."

As always, Knox was succinct, and his words packed a punch. So much pain in such a short sentence. I whispered, "I'm sorry."

He huffed out a laugh as bitter as mine had been. "Me, too. She had plans for us. Cooper, my oldest brother, would take over the company along with Axel. My younger brother Evers and I would marry well and be her social companions.

"She always loved her social life, the parties and the lunches. She wanted us to golf and let her dress us so we could escort her around town."

I tried to imagine Knox as his mother's permanent date, playing golf and attending luncheons, but the picture wouldn't gel in my head.

I burst out laughing at the thought of this intense, quiet, capable man frittering away his life on the golf course. I slapped my hand over my mouth, embarrassed to be laughing when he was baring his soul, but when I snuck a look in his direction, a rare grin was stretched across his face.

"Crazy, right? Evers maybe could've pulled it off. Me? No fucking way. I went to college, we all did, and then, like Cooper and Axel before me, I joined the Army."

"That, I can see."

"My mother never forgave any of us. If she gets enough gin in her, she goes off on how we all abandoned her, how we don't love her, that kind of thing."

"Does she live near you?" I asked, hoping the answer was no. I didn't know Knox that well, but I hated the idea of his mother throwing her unhappiness in his face on a daily basis.

"No. She moved to Florida a few years ago. We rotate visiting. She swears now that she hates Atlanta—though she didn't when she lived there. She refuses to come back."

"Where did you serve in the Army?" I asked, letting Knox off the hook. Enough painful conversations for one day.

"I was in for a while. Started in Japan, then the Middle East. Then some places I can't talk about."

I didn't press for more. This was the most Knox had spoken since he'd shown up at my door. When I'd asked about his family, I'd figured he'd blow me off.

I never would have imagined Knox and I would have so much in common. I can't say he made me feel better about the situation with my parents, but I felt less alone. These days, not feeling alone counted for a lot.

Knox set his empty coffee cup on the bench beside him and raised his chin in the direction of the docks and the shabby hut on the end. The window beneath the striped awning was open, a line stretching into the parking lot.

The only thing new about the place was the freshly painted sign. SMILEY'S CONES.

"That ice cream any good?"

"Yeah, it is. It's great, actually."

"You finished with the coffee? Come on, I'll buy you a cone."

A warm glow spread in my chest. I slugged back the last sip of my latte and stood. "Ice cream sounds perfect."

Knox put his hand between my shoulder blades, guiding me across the park toward Smiley's Cones. He wasn't holding my hand. His arm wasn't around me. Still, the pressure of his warm palm against my spine felt like so much more than the touch of a bodyguard to a client.

The glow in my chest turned to a burn.

I didn't fight it. I loved it.

Even though I knew I shouldn't.

Chapter Eleven

KNOX

A BLACK ROCK POLICE CRUISER PULLED into the driveway for the second time in a week. I knew better than anyone that Lily and Adam were fine since I'd been watching them play Chutes and Ladders over the surveillance cameras.

I tried to ignore my twinge of guilt at spying on Lily. I was doing my job. All of them. I wasn't just here to protect Lily and Adam, I was here to find out what Trey Spencer, and possibly Lily, had been up to with my father. To do that, I had to spy, twinges of guilt or not.

I was standing by the side of the driveway when Deputy Dave pulled to a stop and got out of the cruiser. He aimed a sneer my way that I'd bet intimidated the locals.

I crossed my arms over my chest and lifted my chin. "Can I help you?"

"No. I'm here to see Lily."

I took a step closer. "She expecting you?"

"Look, guy, I don't know why you're still here, but I've

known Lily for years. Her husband was my best friend. He'd expect me to be there for her, and that's what I'm doing. If you don't like it, you're welcome to get the hell out of town."

"I'm not going anywhere until Lily asks me to," I said.

Deputy Dave's chest puffed up like a rooster. "Then start packing. I'm going in to talk to her."

I thought for a minute, weighing the inconvenience of having Deputy Dave on the scene with the benefit of more time to figure out what the hell he was up to. I already knew he wanted to fuck Lily, but something about him felt off. There was more to his hovering than a simple desire to nail his buddy's widow.

Decision made, I gave him my fakest friendly smile. "Great. I'll walk you in."

"That's not necessary—"

I ignored the deputy and strode ahead of him to the front door, rapping twice before turning the handle and calling out, "Lily? The deputy is here."

A pause, almost uncomfortably long. Deputy Dave shifted from one foot to the other, waiting for Lily to welcome him. There was a rustle of sound, and both Lily and Adam appeared.

Lily's face was arranged in a carefully friendly smile. Adam's expression wasn't friendly *or* careful.

He arranged himself beside me, crossing his arms over his chest, and glared at the deputy in irritation, muttering, "We were playing a game."

I murmured, "Were you winning?"

Adam poked the side of my thigh with his little elbow. "I was kicking her butt."

"Good job." The pleasure that flashed across his small face stabbed straight through my chest. Fuck. I kinda got why Lily said she'd do anything for the kid.

I'd heard him bitching at her at bedtime and when he didn't like his dinner. I knew he wasn't perfect. Half the time he was a royal pain in the ass. From what I've seen of kids, that's pretty much how they all are. With Adam, so far, the good far outweighed the bad.

Fuck, that grin. I couldn't wait to see what he'd do when he won the game. *If* he won. Lily was no stranger to kid's games. She might have a comeback planned.

Lily was still giving Deputy Dave her careful, polite smile that was a facsimile of friendliness. He seemed to buy it. I didn't. Lily hadn't said anything negative about the Deputy, but in my gut, I knew she didn't like him.

"Is everything okay, Dave?"

"Oh yeah, everything's fine. I was over here checking in with the Millers. The dog got out again. Went after Mabel's chickens, scared a renter."

Lily shook her head in resignation. "That dog. No matter what fence they get, he finds a way. He's sweet but full of trouble."

"Don't I know it," Dave agreed. "I thought I'd stop by, see if you're free for dinner." Lily's eyes flashed to mine, alarm, guilt, and something else I couldn't read flickering through them before she recovered her fake smile.

"Oh, that's so nice of you. I, um, I would, but I have Adam and—"

Deputy Dave shot me a look. "Sinclair here can watch him for an hour or two, can't he?"

"Oh, well, no. Knox isn't a babysitter, Dave," Lily said, confusion clouding her face.

We both stared at Deputy Dave as if he'd grown an extra head. Not that I would mind watching the kid, but as far as Dave knew I was here upgrading the specs on the security system. I was as good as a stranger.

Did he really think Lily was going to leave Adam with a man she barely knew? If he did, he didn't know Lily. I'd been here a few days, and I could've told him that wasn't going to happen.

Either Deputy Dave was an idiot—always a possibility—or he already knew Lily was going to turn him down. I was betting on the latter.

He proved me right when he let the silence stretch an uncomfortable length until Lily stepped in and said, "Would you like to stay for dinner tonight instead? I made meatloaf and mashed potatoes. I was going to put it on the table in a half an hour or so. Do you want to come in, have a beer and eat with us?"

A wide, almost smug smile spread across Deputy Dave's mouth. Yeah, he knew Lily wouldn't leave Adam. He was angling for the invite. Why? To make another run at getting into Lily's panties? Maybe.

Knowing it would drive him nuts, I said, "Meatloaf sounds great. I'll be over as soon as I wrap up my work."

Deputy Dave's eyes narrowed on me. He turned to Lily and said, "He eats dinner with you?"

Lily gave him another strained look. "Of course," she said. "Why wouldn't he?"

"I can think of a lot of reasons," Dave grumbled under his breath. Turning to give me his back, he said to Lily, "I'll take you up on that beer if you're ready."

"Sure." She held out a hand for Adam, who hung back.

"I want to stay with Mr. Knox."

I recognized that tone of voice. It was the same one he used when he didn't like his oatmeal or the sneakers Lily had put out for him.

I couldn't blame the kid. I'd rather hang with me than Deputy Dave, too. Considering I planned to spend the next fifteen minutes spying on Lily and the deputy, I couldn't have Adam in the cottage. I reached down to squeeze his shoulder.

"Another time, bud, okay? It's going to take all my attention to get this work done. I'll get to it as fast as I can and meet you in the kitchen. Deal?"

Adam's eyes narrowed on me in consideration. Just as Lily stepped forward to intercede, Adam lifted his chin at me, the gesture so adult it took me back for a moment. "K. Fifteen minutes."

I nodded. Adam raced ahead of Lily and Dave, ignoring Lily's call of, "Wash your hands and clean up the game."

I watched them walk into the kitchen, not liking the way Dave crowded Lily or the tense set of her shoulders. I didn't like the idea of leaving them alone.

I'd be watching over the cameras. If he did anything out of line, I could be there in no time.

Lily was safe and only a little uncomfortable. She could handle it. I knew all of that, and I still didn't want to leave her with him.

"Get your fucking head together," I muttered to myself as I sat at my desk and pulled up the cameras in the kitchen. Lily was the client and she was safe. I was doing my job.

She was also a potential target. I had to do that job, too.

If I had any hope of untangling the mess my father and Trey Spencer had left behind, I had to find out what the hell was going on. I couldn't turn down the chance to eavesdrop on Lily and her dead husband's best friend. Especially when I was convinced that friend had an agenda all his own.

"Fucking better keep his hands to himself," I mumbled as I zeroed in on the kitchen camera. If he put a single finger on her...

I shook my head. *Focus.* So what if he did? As long as he didn't hurt her, everything was fine. The thought of his skin touching hers made my stomach twist. I wasn't going to examine why.

I turned up the volume and waited. Lily bustled around the kitchen, pulling potatoes out of a steaming pot of water and putting them in a bowl to mash. The deputy helped himself to a beer from the fridge and leaned against the counter.

He didn't offer to help, and Lily didn't ask. They talked about town gossip, the increase in tourists for the season. I was starting to wonder if I'd been imagining things when the deputy said, "Why is Knox Sinclair still here, Lily? Shouldn't he be done with the alarm by now?"

Lily shrugged a shoulder. "He's working on a few things. He had to upgrade some wiring," she improvised.

I knew the Deputy made her nervous, but she hadn't denied he was a friend of the family. Not enough of a friend that she told him the truth. She didn't mention the intruder, the new perimeter alarm, or any of the cameras I'd added on the outside of the house.

"I don't like him hanging around."

"Why not?" Lily asked baldly, turning from the bowl of potatoes long enough to spear him with a look.

Deputy Dave shoved his hands into his pockets and shrugged. "I don't trust him."

Lily gave him a gentle smile and shook her head. "Trey must have trusted Sinclair Security. They did all the work on the house. He told me to call them if I ever needed anything. Are you saying Trey didn't know what he was doing?"

Dave cleared his throat and took a sip of his beer.

Nice job, Lily. Back him into a corner, so if he insults me, he's insulting his dead best friend.

Dave put the beer down. "I don't think you need him hanging around, that's all. Couldn't he stay in town?"

At this Lily laughed, and the sound was almost her normal, musical laugh. Almost. I wanted to hear that laugh again. The real thing. Maybe if I got rid of Deputy Dave, I would.

"Stay in town? In July? You know there's not a room to be had anywhere within a half-hour of the lake this time of year. And the cost? I don't know who would pay, him or me, but either way—" Lily shook her head again. "Why bother when the cottage is right there?"

"You shouldn't have a stranger staying this close."

"Dave, he's a security expert who's working on the alarm. The security expert recommended by Trey. If I can't trust him, who can I trust?"

Dave let it drop, changing the subject to the arts fair coming up. He never asked about Adam. Bad move. I'd only known Lily a few days and I could have told him the way to that woman's heart was through her son.

Deputy Dave would've bought himself a lot of goodwill if he'd shown the slightest interest in Adam. He wasn't that smart.

I was almost ready to shut down the laptop and join them in the kitchen when Dave tossed his empty beer into the recycling bin and excused himself.

I followed him on the cameras as he walked down the hall, expecting him to stop at the powder room. He did and came out a few minutes later drying his hands on the sides of his pants, but instead of turning and heading back to the kitchen, he ducked into Trey's office.

Now things were getting interesting. What the hell did the deputy want in Trey's office? Did he know something Lily and I didn't? He answered that quickly enough when he opened and shut the desk drawers, randomly and carelessly.

Whatever he was looking for, he didn't know where to start. But, like Lily, he was definitely looking for something.

I sat back in my chair and watched the deputy's sloppy search move to the closet. He ignored the files in favor of the woven baskets. He and Lily weren't searching for the same thing. Unless he'd already been through the files.

The gears in my mind spun. Andrei Tsepov had threatened our mother, saying our father took something that was his, and he would hurt her if he didn't get it back.

Andrei was the nephew of the former head of the Tsepov crime family. We'd dealt with his uncle more than a few times before my brother's wife shot him to save Axel. The younger Tsepov had inherited his uncle's position, and he was significantly less intelligent.

Case in point, he threatened to hurt our mother if we didn't give him back what our father stole, but he never bothered to tell us exactly what that was.

Andrei Tsepov was looking for something he claimed my father took.

My father had been working with Trey Spencer.

Both Lily and Trey's best friend were also looking for something.

Wouldn't it be interesting if that something was the same something?

It couldn't be that easy. Not that there was anything easy about this, considering I had no idea what Lily and Dave were looking for. I tucked that thought away for later, watching as Dave finished his fruitless search, attempted to straighten the blotter and pens on the desk—doing a crap job—and strode out of the office.

I'd left them alone for almost twenty minutes. Time to horn in on dinner and see what else I could learn.

Chapter Twelve

KNOX

I KNOCKED TWICE ON THE DOOR before letting myself in. I couldn't miss Lily's smile of relief when I walked into the kitchen. Deputy Dave's scowl of aggravation was almost as satisfying.

Busy pouring cream into the potatoes, Lily tipped her head in the direction of the fridge. "There's beer if you want one. Dinner is almost ready."

I looked over to the table, bare except for the placemats. "Need help setting the table?" The deputy shot me a dirty look as Lily graced me with a warm smile.

"If you don't mind, that would be great. Dishes are up there—" she nodded to a cupboard not far from the table. "Silverware is in the drawer next to the dishwasher."

I kept my smug smile on the inside as I set the table. Deputy Dave had been standing there with his thumb up his ass for half an hour while Lily worked on dinner. I would have bet he had no plans to clear the table or put the dishes in the dishwasher either.

I was guessing, from the surprise in Lily's appreciative smile, that her husband hadn't been one to help either. Dumbasses. I was eating the food too, wasn't I?

I found paper napkins in the pantry. I didn't think Lily would want me to use cloth with a five-year-old at the table. Lily pulled the meatloaf out of the oven as I finished setting the table. However bad she was with baked goods, so far, her cooking was fucking spectacular.

The meatloaf smelled so good my mouth watered. She set the bowl of mashed potatoes in the middle of the table and went back to cut the meatloaf. Deputy Dave and I both had beers, but Lily didn't have anything.

"What do you and Adam want to drink with dinner?" I asked.

Again, the look of pleased surprise. "Hmm, I'm going to get myself a beer. Adam would love some apple juice."

It was easy to tell which cups were his, lined up on the first shelf of the cabinet, all plastic and featuring brightly-colored cartoon characters. I poured Adam's apple juice, grabbed a beer for Lily, popped the top and put them on the table.

The whole time Deputy Dave stood there nursing his beer, his eyes narrowed on the two of us. I wasn't offering to help Lily with the table to piss him off, that was just a side benefit. The nights I'd eaten dinner here the table had already been set, but I'd helped her clean up.

Unlike Dave, I wasn't the kind of asshole who was going to sit around letting her wait on me hand and foot. "Want me to get Adam?"

Busy slicing the meatloaf, Lily said, "Please."

I took a few steps down the hall and called his name. He must have been hungry because he barreled down the stairs a second later in that reckless way children had. I watched his feet fly down each step, ready to catch him when they tangled. He made the descent unscathed and skidded to a stop in front of me.

"That was longer than fifteen minutes," he said with an accusing glare.

The kid didn't miss much. "I know, bud. I'm sorry. Sometimes work is like that."

Adam nodded sagely as if he knew exactly what I meant. He joined us at the table, sitting beside me. Deputy Dave took the seat beside Lily. I didn't miss the subtle way she inched her chair further from his side.

Why didn't she tell him to get lost? It was obvious she didn't like him. She didn't need him for anything, so why was he still hanging around?

Conversation was sparse as we dug in. Adam told a story about a Lego fight at preschool I couldn't quite follow. Dave wasn't getting it either, but Lily was completely clued in and nodded along, asking all the right questions.

Dave told a funny story about the neighbor's dog, the same one that had drawn him to this side of town a few hours before. Lily was starting to relax when he said, "Have you had any more trouble with teenagers? Vandalism, anything like that?"

It would have been more natural for him to address the question to me considering that I was the security expert on site. Lily, focused on her meatloaf, flicked a glance up at me. I gave an almost imperceptible shake of my head.

Picking up my cue, she lifted her eyes to Dave and said, "Nope, everything's been quiet."

"Good to hear. I was worried about you there for a while." He raised his hand to pat her shoulder, his fingers curving around to squeeze tight. My chest burned at the sight of his hand on her, at the line between her eyebrows, her tight lips.

Where did he get off touching her? Didn't he see he was making her uncomfortable?

I couldn't decide if the deputy was oblivious or enjoying the way he pushed Lily's buttons, using her innate politeness to subtly bully her.

Not for the first time, I wished I wasn't here because of my father. Wished I was only here for Lily, so I could forget all this bullshit and ask her what was wrong. Offer to help without the risk of betraying my family. I wanted to erase the worry from her eyes. To find out why she was putting up with Deputy Dave so I could get rid of him.

Lily pushed her chair back from the table, shaking off Dave's grip on her shoulder. "Dessert anyone? I made chocolate chip cookies."

Adam kicked me under the table, a smirk on his face. I kicked him back and shook my head. I was actually looking forward to trying Lily's cookies. It had become a game to figure out how she could fuck up her newest baking project.

"Sounds great," Dave said heartily. Lily returned with a stoneware plate piled high with cookies, thick and generously spotted with chocolate chips. They *looked* good, but they didn't smell like anything, not a good sign for freshly-baked chocolate chip cookies.

Adam eyed the cookies dubiously. Lily didn't look so certain herself. Dave snagged one and took a big bite, saying with a full mouth, "You seem like you're doing a lot better lately. But if you're not worried about vandalism, why did you call Sinclair to have the alarm beefed up?"

Lily shrugged a shoulder. "Oh, peace of mind, I guess."

Dave sent a pointed glance at Adam, then to Lily. "You're under too much stress. I know it's hard with Trey gone, being a single mom. No one was surprised you started imagining things. It's normal to want attention when you're lonely—"

"That's not what—" Lily's eyes flared with anger, and for once, her good manners stripped away to reveal the frustration brewing beneath. As much as I wanted the deputy gone, until I knew what he was up to, I didn't want Lily to alienate him.

I cut in, "I thought you knew Lily pretty well."

"A lot better than you do," Dave said petulantly.

Giving Lily a warning look I hoped she'd read right, I said. "This isn't the right time to have this conversation." A tilt of my head in Adam's direction. "But since we're having it anyway, Lily's perfectly capable of balancing the changes in her life with being a mom. I've spent a lot of time with her and Adam, and they're a great family."

"Look, you don't know what you're talking about. You've only been here a few days, I've known Lily for years."

"Then you should know that you're full of shit." I looked down at Adam. Oops. "Sorry, Lily."

"It's okay, Mr. Knox," Adam piped in. "I've heard the word *shit* before. Mom told me it's a grown-up word, so I'm not allowed to say it until I'm old enough to know when it's 'ppropriate. Right, Mom?"

With an exasperated sigh, Lily agreed. "Yes, that's right, Adam. But I'd prefer if you didn't say it at all, even when you're repeating what someone else said."

Adam flushed and looked at his plate guiltily. Being a five-year-old, he'd known he wasn't supposed to say it but couldn't resist the opportunity.

"This is the kind of thing I'm talking about," Dave said, trying again. "This guy is a stranger, and you're letting him practically live with you. He's not a good influence on Adam. He's got him swearing already—"

Lily grabbed a cookie off the plate and snapped with irritation, "Dave, Trey said worse in front of him, and so have you."

Seeing he was outnumbered, Dave gave in. "Lily, I'm just trying to help."

"I know, Dave, and I appreciate it. I do. I don't know what we would have done without you since Trey died. But we're okay. I appreciate the concern, but I promise, we're okay."

Dave gave an abrupt nod and took another bite of the cookie, forcing a smile as he chewed. "You made these?" Lily nodded. "They're good."

Okay, now I had to try one. The grimace hiding beneath Dave's smile told me he was a liar. I doubted 'good' described Lily's cookies.

Yep, he was a fucking liar. The cookies tasted like sawdust, and that was an insult to sawdust. They were terrible. Worse than the muffins and almost as bad as the coffee cake. Lily took a bite and chewed slowly, her face falling as the lack of flavor hit her tongue.

Adam looked up at me. "How is it, Mr. Knox?"

I set the cookie on my plate and opened my mouth to tell Adam it was fine. Instead, I said, "I'll teach you to make cookies, Lily."

Where the hell did that come from?

I could do it, that wasn't the problem. One of my best friends ran a bakery and café. She taught me to bake cookies back in high school. She'd taught me to bake a lot of stuff. I wasn't a great cook, but I knew my way around cookies and brownies. I could even make a decent cheesecake.

Deputy Dave's eyes narrowed at my offer, and Lily's brows shot up in surprise. "You know how to make cookies? Really?"

I should have made my impulsive offer into a joke. I didn't need to cozy up to the widow until I knew how deep she was in her husband's business.

She could be sweet, sexy, a great mom and still be a criminal. None of those things were mutually exclusive.

I needed to stop thinking about the *sexy* part.

Focus on 'criminal', Knox. Figure out what she and her husband were up to. You're not here to bake her fucking cookies.

I knew it, and looking at her warm brown eyes, the genuine smile on her face, I couldn't dredge up a shred of regret.

I always did the smart thing.

So what if this one time I didn't follow the rules? Who would it hurt? It was cookies. *Cookies.*

It wasn't until she smiled at me that I remembered how wound tight she was most of the time. Lily was a champ at putting on a brave face, mostly for her son, but underneath she was strained. Scared. Until I knew why, I couldn't fix that, but I could make her smile.

I wanted to see that look on her face more often, the line gone from between her brows, her eyes bright and happy. I wanted to be the one who made it happen.

That thought dragged me right down into the gutter as an image flashed in my mind of Lily naked, her smooth, tawny skin and cloud of soft curls spread before me, that same bright, happy smile curving her lips.

Fucking hell, I could make her smile like that all night if I got her in bed. I could find all new smiles, new ways to make her eyes shine...

"Can you really teach my mom to make cookies?" Adam asked from beside me. A wave of guilt washed away my lustful thoughts of naked Lily.

Christ, I was sitting next to her kid and imagining fucking her. Maybe Deputy Dave was right, and I was a bad influence. My phone rang in my pocket. I slid it out to see Cooper's name.

I'd call when I was back in the cottage. Silencing the phone, I looked down at Adam. "I absolutely can teach your mom to bake cookies."

"How did you learn? Did your mom teach you?"

"It's not just moms who know how to make cookies, bud. I have a friend, Annabelle. She bakes the most amazing desserts you've ever seen. She has one that's three kinds of cake layered together, filled with peanut butter and covered with chocolate. She taught me how to make cookies because I kept eating all of hers."

Adam nodded. "Smart of her."

"She's a smart girl," I agreed. I looked up to see the deputy smiling with satisfaction and Lily's eyes avoiding mine. I'd think about that later. I stood, picking up my plate, and looked down at Adam. "Get your plate and bring it to the sink?"

He popped up and grabbed his stuff, dutifully following me into the kitchen. Behind me, Lily muttered under her breath, "For you, he clears the table." The second his plate hit the sink, Adam took off for the stairs, eager to avoid anything else to do with the dishes.

As expected, Dave didn't do shit to help clean up from dinner. He stood, patted his stomach, thanked Lily for the meal and excused himself to the bathroom.

I would've bet a hundred bucks the bathroom wasn't his only goal. With the rest of us occupied in the kitchen, he thought he was safe for another search. I ignored him, helping Lily clear the dishes and wash up. I could check the camera feeds later.

"You don't have to help with this," Lily said.

"I can wash a few dishes, Lily. You cooked. And as bad as your cookies were, the meatloaf was great. So were the potatoes. What did you put in them?"

"Oh, shredded cheddar and roasted garlic."

"They were good," I said again. Good was an understatement. The rich garlic and sharp bite of cheddar had been way better than just *good.* I was already hoping I could cadge some leftovers for the cottage.

"You don't have to teach me how to make cookies," she said hesitantly. "I know you're here to work and—"

"I can teach you to make cookies, Lily. It's not a big deal."

"Okay. I can use all the help I can get if you really don't mind."

Deputy Dave ducked his head back in the kitchen. "I got a call, Lily. Gotta go. Thanks for dinner. Next time I'll take you out."

Not if I had anything to say about it.

Dave let himself out as I wondered where that thought had come from. First, I was going to teach her to bake cookies, now I wanted to scare off her potential dates. I needed to get my head together.

Nothing would do that better than talking to my older brother. Drying the inside of the last pot, I set it on the counter. "I've got to head out. I need to return that phone call."

"Oh, okay. Wait one sec." As I'd hoped, she'd packed a generous serving of potatoes and meatloaf in a plastic storage container. "Just in case you get hungry," she said, pushing it into my hands.

"Thanks, Lily. I'll see you tomorrow."

The cruiser was gone when I made the short walk from the main house to the cottage. A quick scan of the security footage from Trey's office confirmed that Deputy Dave had taken advantage of our distraction to search the office closet again. Again, he'd come up with nothing.

I pulled my phone from my pocket and called Cooper back. "What do you have?" he said when he answered. "What's up with the widow?"

"I don't know," I said. "She's looking for something. I have the house wired, and I've seen her searching. Whatever it is she hasn't found it yet."

I filled Cooper in on the situation with the deputy, the break-ins, and my growing certainty that Lily knew nothing of her husband's business, that, if anything, she was a victim. Cooper barked a laugh that wasn't a laugh.

"I saw the way you looked at her picture, Knox. Don't let your dick cloud your brain."

"Coop, her kid is here, okay? She's a client and her husband just died." Almost a year ago, but still too soon. Her recent widowhood was the least of the reasons I should stay away from Lily Spencer. I didn't need Cooper to tell me that.

"Whatever. I've seen how you are. You don't say a fucking thing and women fall in your lap. Don't let this woman distract you. Evers has nothing and the clock is ticking. We need to know what Trey Spencer was into. You have no idea what the widow is looking for?"

"No clue."

A long pause. I could practically hear Cooper thinking over the phone. Finally, he said, "I take it back. If you get the widow in bed, she'll trust you enough to tell you what she's looking for. Find out that way."

A wave of revulsion hit me at the thought. "You want me to be the honey trap? Fuck that. I won't do that to Lily."

"She's not 'Lily', she's the target. And since when are you too good to fuck for information?"

"Fuck off. She's not just the target, she's the client. I don't know what's up your ass, but you're being a dick. The woman lost her husband, she's alone up here with a little kid, and she's scared. I'm not going to make it worse."

"She's probably as guilty as her fucking husband. I went through the files you sent and ran them against the bank records we found. Based on the money, he was wrapped up in all of Dad's shit, running a lot of it after Dad disappeared. I don't know how they hooked up, but if he was that deep with Dad, he was in with Tsepov, and the widow was right there the whole time. Transport, arms, these fucking adoptions. This is a goddamn mess, Knox."

Adam flashed in my mind and my stomach went tight. Lily loved her son. If Trey and my Dad set up his adoption or brokered the surrogate, what would that mean to Lily? What would she have been willing to do to keep her child?

I didn't need to ask.

Anything.

Lily would do anything for Adam.

I'd been in the business long enough to know that most criminals didn't think they were the bad guys. There was always a reason, a lie they told themselves to make it okay.

Protecting the son she loved might justify almost anything to Lily. Everyone has a line. I didn't know Lily well enough to guess where she'd draw hers, especially with Adam at stake.

Annoyed with Cooper, with his insinuations and my own uncertainty, I said, "Back the fuck off, okay? I know what my job is. I'll let you know as soon as I find something."

I hung up on Cooper and took up my usual position at the desk, watching the cameras on two monitors while I searched through the files I'd taken from Trey's laptop on the other.

After Adam was in bed, Lily went straight to the closet in the master bedroom. I expected her to take off her clothes and get ready for bed. I was about to shut off the monitor when she walked past her things and stopped in the other half, still full of Trey's belongings.

She opened a drawer, rifled through and closed it, then moved on to the next. Searching again. What the hell was she looking for? I needed to know.

If she was trying to find whatever it was that Tsepov wanted, then she and Adam were in danger. Time passed, and her search grew increasingly desperate. Her jaw set and her eyes scared, she checked his pockets, looked inside his shoes, and still came up with nothing. I could feel her fear through the cameras.

Lily should have been a puzzle to solve, nothing more than a target of our investigation. At best a client and at worst a criminal. Nothing to me either way.

When the hell did it get complicated? I wanted to walk up there and demand that she let me help. Demand she tell me the truth so I could fix whatever was wrong and take the fear from her eyes.

I sat watching as she stood and walked back to her side of the closet, dragging her feet, her shoulders slumped forward. My finger hovered over the button that would turn off the camera but didn't fall. She reached for the hem of her T-shirt and pulled it over her head, her lace bound breasts bouncing as she tossed her T-shirt into the laundry bin.

The navy-blue lace bra wasn't particularly seductive. It shouldn't have been. I wanted to peel the straps down her shoulders and—

She hooked her thumbs in the sides of her jeans and pushed them down her hips, kicking them toward the hamper, leaving her standing there wearing nothing but the lace bra and a very brief matching thong. Her ass in that thong was a work of art, full and round, begging for my hands.

I stared a heartbeat longer than I should have. When her fingers went to the clasp at the back of her bra, I squeezed my eyes shut and slammed my finger down on the key to disengage the camera.

It shouldn't have been that hard.

Shouldn't have been, but it was. There was nothing I wanted more than to watch Lily peel off that bra, to see her standing there naked, just for me.

Not going to happen, I told myself. *Forget about getting your hands on Lily Spencer.*

That wasn't going to happen either.

Chapter Thirteen

LILY

WITH A FIVE-YEAR-OLD IN THE house, laundry is never-ending. I don't know how one small person can dirty so many clothes, but Adam was a pro.

Peanut butter and jelly, markers, dirt, and grass stains. You name it, he got it on his clothes. I never understood the wonder that is stain spray until I had a child. I swear I went through a gallon a month.

I concentrated on folding his little T-shirts just so, smoothing the edges into neat creases, hoping that my focus on the laundry might keep me from thinking about everything else.

It didn't.

My anxious mind couldn't decide what to stress out about and skipped from one problem to another. Like every other person on the planet, I'd had worries before Trey died. I'd wondered what I was doing with my life. If I was a good mom. I'd worried about my marriage and my husband.

Those worries were real, but none of them felt as dire as the worries that plagued me now.

Trey died and left me trapped in this house. I had access to the bank accounts, but nothing else. I'd searched his office from top to bottom. Nothing. I'd been through his closet. Ditto. I'd searched every inch of the house. I didn't know where else to look.

What if he had a safety deposit box? I hadn't found any record of one in his files. That didn't mean much now that I knew the files were missing a lot of other things as well. If he had a safety deposit box, how would I even find it?

It'd be like searching for a needle in a haystack. Different needle, different haystack, same frustration.

I should have been sleeping better with Knox nearby, but there was a ticking clock in the back of my head, counting down to disaster. I didn't know what form that disaster would take, but I knew we couldn't go on this way for long.

A quick double rap sounded on the front door. I jumped, dropping the pair of socks in my hand. I needed to chill out. Yeah, like that was going to happen.

I set the socks in Adam's laundry basket before going to the door to check the camera. Knox filled the screen, his dark, faded T-shirt stretching across his broad shoulders. My heart sped up in my chest a little. Maybe a lot. Opening the door, I looked up into his dark eyes.

"You want to make some cookies?" he asked in his low, rumbly voice.

"Sure, if you think I can manage it without ruining them."

"All you have to do is follow the directions." Knox walked behind me into the kitchen and began searching through the pantry, pulling out ingredients and lining them up on the counter.

"I've been following the directions," I protested. "You know how that's worked out." I looked at the line of ingredients on the counter. "What else do we need? A bowl and spoon?"

"The usual. Measuring cups, something with a flat top. A kitchen scale would be better if you have one."

I shook my head, baffled. Why would I need a scale to make cookies? "I don't have a kitchen scale."

His head inside a cabinet, Knox said, "If you really want to learn to bake, you need a scale. For now, measuring cups with a flat top will work. Just not the glass ones with the handle. Measuring spoons. A saucepan and a soft spatula. Cookie sheets. Two if you have them."

I started to take out what he needed, studying my glass measuring cups and wondering why they weren't good enough. Then another odd thing on his list caught my attention. "What's the saucepan for?"

"We're going to brown the butter before we mix it in."

Knox definitely knew more about baking cookies than I did because I'd never heard of browning butter for cookies. "Really? I've never seen a recipe with browned butter."

Knox waited as I pulled out the cookie sheets, standing beside the line of ingredients, looking down at his phone and tapping on the screen. Absently, he said, "It's a trick Annabelle taught me. Trust me, it's worth the trouble."

I set the cookie sheets on the counter and stepped beside him. He showed me the screen of his phone with a recipe pulled up. It was titled *Annabelle's Chocolate Chip Cookies*. Underneath in parentheses, it said *(Share this on pain of death. I'm not kidding, Knox.)*

"I don't want to get you in trouble with Annabelle," I said, only kind of meaning it.

I didn't even know this Annabelle, and already, I didn't like her. Not fair, but when he said her name, there was a warmth in his voice that bugged me. It was petty and childish, but a part of me was greedy for Knox. I wanted to keep him for myself.

"Read the recipe twice. I'm going to walk you through it, but you're going to do everything yourself."

Aside from browning the butter, the recipe was pretty basic for chocolate chip cookies. The most recent failed batch wasn't my first attempt. I set the saucepan on the stove, turned the flame to medium-low, and put the butter inside.

Knox said, "Make sure you keep an eye on that. The butter will brown faster than you think it will."

I nodded, concentrating on the next part; measuring the dry ingredients. I unsealed the bag of flour and dipped in the measuring cup, pulling it out heaped full.

"Stop."

I froze, the measuring cup still dangling in the air over the open bag.

"This is the first place you're going wrong," Knox said. "Baking isn't like cooking. Cooking you can estimate, follow your gut. Baking is chemistry. You have to follow the formula. That's way too much flour. With that mound on top, you've got at least a cup and a third. Give the side of the measuring cup a tap to settle it, then use the handle of the spatula to scrape off the rest. See the measurement beside the cups in the recipe?"

I tapped, scraped and then checked the recipe on Knox's phone. Sure enough, right beside *2 cups flour*, it said *or 250 grams.* Huh.

"Is that what the scale is for?" I asked, holding up my cup of flour for his inspection. Knox made a sound of approval and I dumped the flour into the mixing bowl.

"Cookies are pretty forgiving, but for some things, you need to use the scale. Macaroons can be a bitch."

In my experience, cookies were not at all forgiving. If baking was a science, that explained why I sucked. I'd learned to cook by following recipes, but once I got the hang of the basic principles I liked to improvise.

I was so used to it that I hadn't even noticed I was doing it with baking. I thought of all the times I'd casually measured ingredients and how often the end result tasted wrong.

I measured the second cup of flour precisely. I was carefully leveling exactly half a teaspoon of baking soda when Knox said, "Don't forget the butter."

I whirled around to find the butter bubbling away on the stove and grabbed the handle of the pan to give it a swirl. Footsteps sounded on the stairs. A moment later Adam skidded into the room.

"You didn't tell me Mr. Knox was here. What are you doing? Making cookies?"

"I'm working on it," I said, giving Adam a quick smile before asking Knox, "How do I know if the butter is ready?"

"It should be a medium-brownish color and smell kind of nutty."

I gave the butter a sniff. It *did* smell kind of nutty and was a pretty golden brown. I turned the heat off and set the skillet aside, feeling absurdly triumphant considering all I'd done was brown a little butter.

"Can I help?" Adam asked, bouncing on his toes beside me as his eyes popped from item to item lined up on the counter. "Please, please, please, can I help?"

Knox's hand settled on Adam's shoulder. Adam stopped bouncing and leaned into Knox's grip in a way that sent giddy bubbles through my chest. Knox looked down at him, crinkles in the corner of his eyes.

"Not this time, bud. If you help, your mom will never learn to do it right." Adam's face started to fall when Knox winked at him. "I think you should be on the executive team. With me."

"Executive team? What's that mean?"

"It means we're the kitchen supervisors. The Executive Chefs. Your mom is the Sous Chef, which means she has to do what we say. Also, Executive Chefs get chocolate chips. Sous Chefs don't."

Adam's eyes brightened at the idea of being my boss. I bit the inside of my lip to stop my grin. Ranging himself in front of Knox, Adam crossed his arms over his chest and gave me an imperious look. "We're the boss of you."

I nodded in agreement. "Okay, boss. What do I do now? The butter is ready, and I measured the flour and baking soda."

Adam looked at Knox, eyebrows raised in question. Knox leaned down to whisper something in his ear. Adam said to me, "Whisk together the flour and stuff."

The side of Knox's mouth quirked, and he nodded. "What he said, but first pour the browned butter into that big bowl. Then drop in the rest of the stick so it can melt."

Knox watched me carefully, snagging the bag of chocolate chips off the counter and opening it. He poured a few into his hand and dropped it down over Adam's shoulder. Adam scooped them away from Knox, shoving every single one in his mouth at the same time. I rolled my eyes but didn't say anything.

I was intent on using the soft spatula to slide every single drop of butter out of the sauté pan into the mixing bowl before I added the rest, chopped into squares so it would melt faster. I gave the dry ingredients a stir until they were thoroughly blended and turned, whisk in hand, to wait for my next order from the executive chefs.

"Measure the sugar and salt the same way you did the flour. Carefully. Then whisk them into the butter."

I took my time, overriding my natural instinct to estimate. Knox watched my deliberate movements with a hint of a smile on his lips. Adam pretended to supervise, but his little hand was creeping up to the counter, reaching for the bag of chocolate chips.

Our house was never a free-for-all when it came to candy, but I let it go. I had other priorities, namely not messing up these cookies. Once the sugar and salt were added to the butter, Knox directed me to pour in the teaspoons of vanilla and whisk again.

"Now, one egg and one egg yolk into the butter and sugar mix."

I picked up an egg and started to crack it on the side of the bowl.

"Stop."

I froze, egg in hand less than an inch from the side of the stoneware bowl. "What? What did I do?"

"Don't crack the egg right into the bowl. You're not ready for that. Break the eggs into one of those glass measuring cups, and when you know you got it right, pour the egg and the egg yolk into the butter mix."

I let out a huff of indignation but did as I was told. This wasn't my first time in the kitchen even if I was a crappy baker. I knew how to crack an egg.

I proved myself wrong when I tried to separate the yolk from the white and ended up dumping the whole egg into the measuring cup. Oops.

Adam burst out laughing. Knox was kind enough not to say he'd told me so. I got his point about putting the eggs in the measuring cup before tossing them into the butter mix. On my second try, I separated the yolk cleanly from the white. When everything was incorporated, I stopped and looked up.

Adam said, "What's next, Mr. Knox?"

"*We* eat more chocolate chips," Knox said. "Your mom keeps whisking until the lumps are all gone."

I did.

"Now we let it sit for a few minutes. Then you whisk it again for thirty seconds. Do that two times until it's thick but smooth and a little shiny."

"Oookay," I said, wondering exactly what these repeated whisks were supposed to accomplish. Everything was mixed together, wasn't that enough? Apparently not.

Adam had chocolate smeared all over his face. I snuck my hand over to snag a chocolate chip. Adam smacked my fingers.

"Sous chefs don't get chocolate chips," he said.

"Do executive chefs get chocolate all over their faces?" I asked tartly.

"This one does," Knox said. Nudging Adam's shoulder he went on, "Your mom's been doing a good job. I think she deserves a reward, don't you?"

Adam looked dubious, and before I could figure out what Knox meant, he slipped a chocolate chip between my lips. The sweet, rich chocolate melted on my tongue. My breath caught, leaving me off-balance and elated.

I rolled the chocolate chip over my tongue and went back to whisking, looking down to hide the flush in my cheeks.

"Adam, I need your help for this part." Knox nudged him closer to me. Adam straightened and lifted his chin.

"What do you need me to do, Mr. Knox?"

"Help me hold this bowl for your mom. We're going to slowly pour in the flour as she stirs."

Knox positioned Adam's hands on the bowl and helped him tilt it so the flour would slip in a little at a time. Keeping one hand on the rim in case Adam lost his grip, Knox jiggled the bowl, teasing a sprinkle of flour into my smooth and shiny mix of eggs, butter, and sugar.

Looking at me, he said, "Stir slowly. We don't want to overwork it."

I was getting good at following orders. I gently mixed in the flour, watching it disappear into the butter and eggs. Finally, it looked like cookie dough. When the bowl was empty, Knox set it aside and handed Adam the remains of the bag of chocolate chips. "Do the same thing with these. Not all at once. Your mom's going to keep stirring the same way."

The last chip slid into the dough, and Adam dropped the bag, not noticing as it bounced off the side of the counter to hit the floor. I'd get it later. He stuck his head over the side of the bowl.

"Can I lick the spoon, Mom? Can I? Can I? Can I? Please? Please?"

I thought about raw eggs and salmonella and decided some things were worth the risk. I handed Adam the handle of the spoon. He shoved it in his mouth, his cheeks bulging wide, a glop of dough sticking to his bottom lip.

Well, what did I expect? He was five, and there's no such thing as table manners where cookie dough is concerned.

"Now what?" I asked. I was pretty sure it was time to put the cookie dough on the sheet and pop it in the oven, but I wasn't taking any chances. These cookies looked too good to screw up.

"Use the scoop next to the measuring cups. One scoop per cookie, eight on a sheet. We'll bake them in stages."

Adam finished licking the spoon and started to dip it back into the bowl when Knox's hand shot out, deftly plucking it from his little fingers. "Wait until they're done, bud."

"I have to wait? How long?"

"Not that long. You can go back to whatever you were playing with and we'll call you when they're ready. They have to cook for a little bit and then cool off."

"K. But call me as soon as they're ready."

"The second you can eat them," Knox promised.

The cookies were in the oven, and Adam was upstairs. I decided to take advantage of the time alone with Knox.

Chapter Fourteen

LILY

"COFFEE?"

Knox made a sound in the back of his throat I took for agreement. I went to make a fresh pot.

While I was measuring beans I asked, trying for casual, "How well did you know Trey?"

Another sound from Knox, this one vaguely surprised. "I didn't know Trey at all. He worked with my father."

"Oh." The way Knox had said, '*He worked with my father,*' made it sound like that meant something. Trying to figure it out, I asked, "So, he only worked with your father?"

"Apparently. I looked at the files after you called, and it seems like they did a lot of business together."

That left me stumped. What kind of business? We only had the one alarm system. Trey didn't own any other property. His company dealt with logistics, not security. The more I learned the less anything made sense.

I slid the beans into the grinder and pressed the button, the noise drowning out the possibility of conversation, buying me a minute to think. I couldn't pump Knox for information if I didn't know the right questions to ask.

I racked my brain trying to see every angle. I needed help with more than security.

There was no guarantee Knox was my answer, but the temptation to open my mouth and spill everything was killing me. What would happen if I threw myself on his mercy and begged for his help?

The cliché that information is power had never been more true.

If I spilled everything, Knox would own me.

I trusted him.

I wanted to trust him.

Did I trust him that much? Could I?

A mistake wouldn't just make me a fool. A mistake would risk Adam. I couldn't take the chance, no matter how much I wanted to.

Swallowing the urge to confess everything, I dumped the coffee grounds into the filter and started the brewing process. We stood there in the kitchen, both of us leaning against the counter, Knox's arms crossed over his chest, my hands tucked into my pockets.

The scent of chocolate chip cookies filled the air, joined a minute later by the rich notes of fresh coffee. I didn't want to get too excited considering I'd made the cookies myself, but they smelled like chocolate chip cookies.

They smelled like amazing chocolate chip cookies.

Knox's explanation of why I kept screwing up at baking made sense. I went with my gut when it came to spices and seasonings. Since the beginning, I had a good feel for how much salt or pepper, how much acid or fat to use. I was definitely getting a kitchen scale the next time we went to town.

I still couldn't think of a good way to ask Knox about Trey. Trying again, I said, "You read Trey's file after I called?" Knox nodded. "How long did they work together, your dad and Trey?"

Knox's dark gaze leveled on me, serious in a face that could have been carved from granite. I felt like an ant under a microscope. What I'd asked had been wrong, though I didn't know how.

Finally, Knox's eyes shifted to the timer on the stove and he said, "That's confidential, Lily."

"He was my husband," I protested.

Knox shrugged a shoulder. "Doesn't matter."

"But I inherited his business. Doesn't that count for something?"

Another one of those long, dissecting looks. I kept my hands in my pockets but squirmed internally. Knox eventually said, "It makes you liable. Do you understand what that means?"

I gave up. The coffee was finished, and I poured two mugs. I handed Knox his and added cream to my own before I took a sip.

Did inheriting the company make me liable?

Liable for what?

The thought of being responsible for Trey's decisions was chilling. He died leaving behind more questions than answers, and I didn't even know how to ask the right ones.

In my entire life, I'd never felt more alone. The harder I treaded water, the deeper I sank. And Knox, who I thought was an ally, had looked at me with suspicion that bordered on disgust.

The buzzer on the oven went off. Cookies. The coffee was sour in my mouth. Even the smell of cookies didn't lighten my mood.

They would. My problems weren't going anywhere, but, based on the delectable scent coming from the oven, I might have baked real chocolate chip cookies. I'd take my victories where I could find them.

Chocolate-chip cookies could soothe a lot of worry.

Knox strode to the oven and opened it, peering inside. "They're done. You have a cooling rack?"

I did. I pulled it from the cabinet and set it up on the island in the kitchen. Knox took the cookies from the oven and used the spatula to carefully transfer them one by one to the rack. They looked perfect. They smelled divine.

I reached out a hand and yelped when Knox swatted it with the spatula. "They need to cool first," he said with amusement.

I snuck a look up at him and relief spilled through my chest at the quirk of a grin on his lips. Whatever damage I'd done with my fumbling questions about Trey and his father, Knox seemed to have forgiven me.

I loved that half-smile and the warmth in his eyes. I wanted more, however unwise it was.

"How long do they have to cool?" I asked, a little petulant. I wanted one of those cookies.

More amusement as Knox answered, "Not that long. Put the second tray in the oven and reset the timer. You can have a cookie when the second batch is done."

I followed orders, mouth watering. That was a long time to wait for a cookie. They looked so perfect, and they smelled so good. And *I* had baked them. *Me.*

Granted, I'd been following Knox's directions. Following Annabelle's directions to be accurate, but I didn't want to think about the mysterious Annabelle. The affection in Knox's voice when he said her name got under my skin. She'd given him her secret cookie recipe.

Knox's private life isn't your business, I reminded myself. The mysterious Annabelle wasn't the point. The point was that *I* had made the cookies, and they looked spectacular. I checked the timer on the oven. Ten minutes left. It might as well have been an eternity.

Knox was staring out the kitchen window at the lake, his back to the rack of cooling cookies. Unable to resist, I reached out a hand and broke off a piece of the cookie closest to me, popping it into my mouth.

Flavor exploded on my tongue, the cookie tasting almost like toffee, rich and buttery and sweet. Then the chocolate melting in my mouth, the crisp crunch on the outside, soft and gooey in the middle.

That chocolate chip cookie was the best thing I'd ever tasted. And *I* had made it. Triumph flooded through me, along with relief that I'd finally cracked the baking code, the rush of emotion strong enough to bring tears to my eyes.

I shoved another bite of cookie into my mouth and moaned at how good it tasted. I could eat these cookies all day. Knox's eyes came to me, his grin stretched all the way across his mouth. He shook his head.

"What are you, Adam? You couldn't wait another eight minutes?"

I swung my head from side to side in a *No*, my eyes rolled up, every taste bud alight with perfection.

So good.

It was so good, and *I* did this.

I swallowed, bouncing on the balls of my feet, not unlike my son. I felt like a five-year-old. I wasn't a failure in the kitchen. If I could bake cookies this good, I could do anything. I swallowed the bite of cookie in my mouth and immediately wanted more of the crispy, chewy, toffee, chocolatey goodness.

I reached for another cookie. Knox's hand shot out and closed around my wrist, pulling me away. I stumbled toward him, and on impulse threw my arms around his wide chest, reaching up to press my lips to his jaw in thanks.

I wasn't thinking, sugar and joy spinning in my head.

It was a thank you hug. A kiss on his jaw. That's all.

I swear, that's all.

Knox's arms closed around me like steel bars. A deep groan rumbled in his chest. He tipped his head to the side, his jaw slipping from my lips, his mouth closing over mine.

He kissed me.

Not a chaste, polite *thank you* kiss. This was something entirely different. His arms locked me to his body, one around my hips, the other across my shoulders, plastering me to all of that hard muscle.

His hold should have made me nervous. It didn't. His lips closed over mine, hungry and aggressive. Adrenaline spiked through me, and just when I might have felt a hint of nerves, his mouth softened, gentled, coaxing rather than claiming.

I melted, my lips parting of their own volition. His tongue dipped inside.

Another rumbling groan sent a thrill spiking through me. I tilted my chin, opening to him, my tongue meeting his, tasting coffee and something uniquely Knox.

My arms still wrapped around his chest, I sank my fingers into his T-shirt, gripping tight, holding myself to him as the gentleness fell from the kiss. His mouth worked over mine, his tongue stroking, lips mastering my own.

I'd dreamed of this. My dreams hadn't come close to reality.

Knox's arms tightened even more. He turned us, lifted me, and I was on the counter, Knox's lean hips between my thighs, my legs locking around his waist, the hard bar of his erection grinding into me.

Even through layers of fabric the pressure of him against my clit set sparks firing through every nerve. My head tipped back as my moan bled into our kiss. Knox's hand dropped to close around my hip, his fingers grazing my ass, tilting me into him, rocking his hips, teasing me, dragging out another moan, longer and more desperate.

I pressed my mouth up into his, kissing him harder, wishing I could blink these clothes away, could feel his skin against mine, could feel that mouth everywhere.

"What are you guys doing?"

Adam's voice cut through the haze of lust in my brain. Stiff with shock, my mind raced for a response. Knox stepped back, effortlessly disengaging from our kiss, pulling me off the counter and setting me on my feet. Air rushed into the space between us, leaving me cold.

"The cookies are done. Do you want one?" Knox asked, holding out a warm cookie. As a diversion, nothing could top cookies. The kitchen island hid any evidence of Knox's erection. Even if Adam noticed the flush in my cheeks, the glitter in my eyes, he wouldn't care when there was a cookie in front of him.

I crossed my arms over my chest to hide my peaked nipples and picked up my mug of coffee, taking a sip to hide my face. I could have saved my time. Adam wasn't even looking at me.

He snatched the cookie from Knox's hand and crammed it into his mouth the same way he had the cookie-dough spoon. His eyes rolled up in his head, bliss spreading across his face.

He chewed and swallowed before he said, cookie still filling his mouth, "Mom, I can't believe you made these. They're actually good. Really, really good."

"I know," I agreed, my voice strained. I snuck a glance at Knox. He was as cool and self-contained as ever. He didn't look at me. Didn't acknowledge me. It was as if nothing had happened.

For a second, I wondered if I'd imagined it. The tenderness of beard-burn on my cheek and my swollen lips reminded me that I hadn't imagined anything. Knox had kissed me like I'd never been kissed in my life.

I wanted more. I'd be crazy not to want more.

The timer beeped on the oven. Knox took out the second tray of cookies and added them to the cooling rack, his eyes blank as they passed through me. Clearly, he didn't feel the same.

That was for the best, wasn't it?

Kissing Knox was a bad idea.

I was his client. He was working for me. There was some connection between Trey and his father. My husband had been dead for less than a year.

So many reasons I shouldn't be kissing Knox.

I didn't care.

I wanted to kiss him again, but if his total lack of interest was any indication, I was out of luck.

Chapter Fifteen

KNOX

I WASN'T SLEEPING WELL. TO BE accurate, I wasn't sleeping at all.

In retrospect, probably a good thing. If I'd been asleep, I would have missed it. That slight, furtive sound along the back wall of the cottage. A scrape. A soft shuffle. So quiet it almost wasn't there.

No, I wasn't sleeping. I was lying in bed with my hand on my cock thinking about Lily. About that kiss. I tried to tell myself it was a mistake. I wasn't buying it. Nothing that felt that good could be a mistake.

She was small, but she fit in my arms perfectly, her curves molding to my body. I hadn't planned to kiss her.

Hell no. I'd planned to keep my hands off Lily Spencer. Way off.

Then she tasted that cookie, her eyes bright with joy and triumph, all her fear and frustration falling away in a moment of pure happiness. She'd been incandescent. So lovely.

She'd thrown herself into my arms with that wide smile.

Her lips grazed my jaw, and I was lost.

Just fucking lost.

If Adam hadn't interrupted us...

I'd like to say I would have come to my senses. I'd be lying. I hadn't been thinking of anything but Lily.

Lily in my arms. Lily pressed against me, her mouth hot and open, her tongue rubbing against mine. I'd wondered if I'd been imagining the pull between us.

Not if that kiss was any measure. Lily had been right there with me, her fingers curled into the back of my T-shirt, holding me like she'd never let go.

Fuck. I told myself to go to sleep. I could figure this shit out in the morning. Sleep wouldn't find me. I worked, pretended to doze, got up and checked the surveillance footage again.

When dawn was closer than it should be and I still hadn't managed more than snatches of rest, I finally gave up and slid my hand under the sheet, fisting my cock, squeezing hard and thinking of Lily.

Then it came. That soft, shuffling sound that wasn't a sound.

The sound that was a great, big, fucking problem.

In complete silence, I rolled from the bed and made my way to my laptop, shoving my feet into my boots as I moved. My screen came to life at a touch, divided into squares, each one showing the feed from a different camera.

I froze as I took in the scenes before me. Fucking hell.

This was not the intruder. That was a single person. Someone who wasn't a complete idiot, but sloppy and lacking in subtlety.

What I saw on the camera feeds was something different. Three—no, five figures in black, the gleam of a weapon showing on the hip of two of them. I had no question the others were armed.

The perimeter alarm would go off any minute. I had it calibrated to signal at movement close to the house, otherwise, the deer and fox would have it going off in the middle of the night.

Whoever these people were, they were serious, but it didn't look like they knew about the upgraded security. I could use that.

I grabbed my phone and called Lily. She answered after one ring. Had she been lying awake thinking about that kiss? A question for another time.

"Action outside," I said. "House is secure, but get into Adam's room. Lock the door the way I showed you. Don't open it unless I give you the signal. You remember the signal?"

"Yes. Is everything okay?"

"It will be. Just get into Adam's room."

Hoping I could keep my promise, I suited up. All black cargo pants, two Glocks at my back, a knife strapped inside my right boot, a small handgun hidden in the other. Lightweight Kevlar because I'm brave, but I'm not stupid. A balaclava to cover my face. Any edge in the dark.

One last check on my laptop. Two approaching the back door. Two headed to the front. One further back in the woods, keeping watch, maybe blocking avenues of escape.

I started on the outside and worked my way in. I was almost on the one in the woods when the perimeter alarm sounded, blaring through the trees. They weren't expecting an alarm before they'd even touched the door.

I used the first target's momentary distraction to take him from behind, wrapping my arm around his throat, cranking tight to cut off his oxygen.

He flailed wildly before his knees went out, and I had him on the ground.

"What do you want?" I demanded. "Why are you here?"

Gray eyes flared up at me in panic.

"Kto ty, chert voz'mi?" *Who the hell are you?*

"Tsepov?" I bit out

His head cut to the side in a sharp shake. *No.* The fear in his eyes betrayed his lie.

He was here for Tsepov.

Fuck.

I secured him with a set of police-grade zip-ties and pulled out a soft, narrow roll of duct tape. Tearing off a strip, I pasted it over his mouth. Another strip covered the zip ties on his wrists.

If he was any good, he'd get out of the zip ties eventually, but the duct tape would slow him down a little. My brothers made fun of me for carrying the stuff wherever I went, but it came in handy. There were very few problems duct tape couldn't solve.

I heard the two at the back door through the trees, which meant they were still outside. The clock in my head ticked faster. I couldn't see or hear the team at the front of the house. The man on the dock was in full view.

He'd be the hardest. Lily had the dock lights on a timer, and now, just before dawn, the lookout had a nice big pool of light to stand in. If I had my rifle and didn't care who heard the shot, he'd be a sitting duck.

I couldn't take the chance. A rifle shot would draw attention. Maybe I could kill them all before they got to me. And maybe there were more I hadn't seen. Lily and Adam were depending on me. If I went down, they were fucked.

The perimeter alarm sounded through the woods, but the house alarm was quiet. They hadn't breached the doors.

Not yet, but they would. Any second. With the alarm going off they were cautious, but if an alarm was enough to scare them off, they'd already be gone. Shortly after meeting Deputy Dave I'd disabled the house alarm from automatically calling the police in the event of a breech. I was here to keep Lily safe, and I didn't trust him if shit went down. I hoped I wouldn't regret that decision.

I sprinted through the woods and across the driveway, coming at the dock from the side. Just as the lookout caught the sound of my feet I dove into the pool of light, tackling him and bringing him to the ground, rolling us into the shadows.

I wanted to question him. I didn't have time. Lily and Adam were alone. I cold-cocked him on the back of the head, hoping I'd have the chance to ask questions later.

He went limp. I made quick work of restraining him before sprinting straight for the pair at the front door. With two of them, one should have been on alert while the other worked on the lock, especially with the perimeter alarm still going off, leaving them deaf to anything but its wail.

Instead, they'd both been working on getting in, one on the door and the other fucking with the keypad.

I was almost on top of them before they spotted me. Sloppy. The last time we'd had a run in with Tsepov, it had been with Andrei's uncle, Sergey. His men were tight. Well-trained and cold as ice. I would have bet the guys here were new because so far, they were a little on the stupid side.

I jumped the closest one from behind, taking him with an arm around the neck, catching him as he was raising his gun to shoot. I swung him around in the direction of his friend, using him as a shield.

Panicked at the constriction on his throat, his hand jerked, and he fired, pumping the trigger over and over. He caught the door, the side of the house, and then his partner, right in the gut.

The guy went down with a shocked groan, clapping a useless hand over the hole in his shirt, the blood gleaming black in the yellow porch light. I pulled my arm tighter around the first one's neck, flexing to cut off his air. He kicked violently, thrashing against me, getting just enough air to stay conscious.

The screeching wail of the house alarm drowned out the perimeter alarm.

I was out of time.

So were Lily and Adam.

I wrenched the gun from his hand, dropped my arm from his neck, and spun him by the shoulder. Two bullets in his chest and he went down.

I was in the house a second later, headed straight for Lily and Adam.

The last two were at the base of the stairs, jostling to see who would go first. Idiots. The one in back hooked my arm, pulling me off my feet, while the other raced up to the second floor.

Lily. I had to get to Lily.

I knew what was coming. I had no remorse. If these guys were here for a good reason, they would have shown up during the day and knocked on the door. Instead, they'd come with six men in the dark of night. Whatever they wanted, they wouldn't get it.

I swung at the guy holding my arm and missed, my fist glancing off his shoulder. Every passing second was excruciating. One more second for the guy upstairs to get to Lily. Or Adam.

I bent over, breaking the momentum of the guy holding my arm, and twisted, throwing an elbow behind me, hitting his nose with a satisfying crunch. The shock of pain stopped him for just long enough.

Shoving my shoulder into his gut, I flipped him over my back. He went down hard, at the last minute catching me behind the knee and taking me with him, tearing at my shirt and ripping the balaclava from my head.

Rolling to my back, I got my arm around his neck, ignoring the flash of heat along my arm. I braced my other hand on the side of his head and twisted. A crack of bone, and he went limp.

I surged to my feet and flew up the stairs to the sound of Adam's terrified scream.

"Mom! Mom!"

His face flashed through my mind, his eyes bright with laughter as he'd jammed the cookie dough-covered spoon between his lips.

Nothing was going to happen to him. Nothing.

I reached the top and turned the corner to see Tsepov's man with his arm around Lily's neck, a gun to her head, Adam cowering behind them. His eyes widened when he saw me, his body tensing as if to run my way.

My eyes glued to Lily's face, I shook my head. Adam stayed where he was. Smart kid.

Lily's voice shook. "Adam, go back into your room. Now."

I nodded at him. He eased to his door, staying out of reach of the man holding his mother, and disappeared into his bedroom.

Fuck, the trust in his eyes, the absolute assurance that I was going to fix this.

I wouldn't let him down. I'd die first.

Maybe Lily was tangled up in my dad's business. Maybe she wasn't.

I didn't fucking care.

A lot of things came clear at the sight of that gun pressed to her temple.

I wanted her.

I wanted Adam.

They were mine.

Trey Spencer fucked up. He put his family in danger, and then he got himself killed. His loss was my gain.

I was keeping them.

Lily's warm brown eyes now glazed with fear. Her soft cloud of curls pulled tight by the Russian's fist.

Mine.

I was keeping her with me, but first I had to keep her alive.

Chapter Sixteen

KNOX

"WHO THE FUCK ARE YOU?" Lily's captor asked in a thick Russian accent.

"I think you know who I am. And I know who you are. The question is what do you want with Lily?"

"The boss wants to talk to her. I'm bringing her in."

I shook my head. "I can't let that happen. Three of your guys are dead. The other two aren't going anywhere. You're not getting out of here with Lily. Drop the gun and let her go."

"Fuck you."

My arm hung loosely at my side, my weapon tucked behind my leg. Tsepov's guy had his arm tight around Lily's neck, the muzzle of his handgun pressed to her temple. He was too on edge. I couldn't risk bringing up my own weapon and startling him into a shot.

A seasoned professional would be deliberate about when he pulled the trigger and when he held his fire. Based on the other five guys, I doubted this one was that smart.

I wouldn't fuck around with Lily's life. Keeping my hand motionless at my side and his attention off my weapon, I said, "Why don't you tell me what Andrei wants with Lily? We'll give it to you, and you can leave."

"Orders are to bring her in."

"And Adam?"

The Russian raised his shoulder in a half shrug, the careless movement nudging the muzzle of the gun off Lily's temple. "No orders for the boy. He is—what's word? Collateral damage?"

Lily's eyes went black with rage. I saw her make the decision, saw the shift in her eyes, like a lock clicking into place. My gut twisted in icy terror as possibilities raced through my mind.

She could do anything. Launch herself at the Russian. Start struggling. Get herself fucking killed.

Eyes locked to mine, hard with determination and the same absolute trust I'd seen in Adam, she did the last thing I expected.

Lily's knees gave out beneath her. Her body dropped, limp as a rag doll. The Russian's grip around her neck fell loose at the unexpected weight, his gun hand swinging to the side.

The second the muzzle of the gun was pointed anywhere but Lily, my arm swung up, and I squeezed the trigger.

Once.

Twice.

The Russian's body jerked back into the wall, sliding to the side, smearing blood across the white paint until he crumpled face down on the carpet.

Lily landed on her ass. At the sound of the gunshot, she jammed the heel of her palm into her mouth, not quite able to muffle her whimpers.

I wanted to take her into my arms, to hold her and Adam, to promise them everything was all right.

Later. First, I had to secure the house. I grabbed the Russian's weapon from the carpet and flipped on the safety, shoving it into the waistband of my pants.

"I need to take care of this. Go into Adam's room and lock the door."

She opened her mouth to protest.

"Lock busted?"

She nodded.

"Drag Adam's dresser in front of the door. Wait there. I think I got them all, but I need to be sure."

Lily vanished into Adam's room, shutting the door. I hauled the dead Russian over my shoulder, lugging him down the stairs. I dropped him outside the front door with the other two.

At least the lock on the front door still worked. I re-secured the door and headed straight for the mudroom where the last two had entered.

Fucking hell.

They'd used an acetylene blowtorch to cut the fucking handle out of the goddamned door. The torch lay discarded on the floor in the middle of the mudroom. I shook my head.

Fewer toys, more training, and they might still be alive. My options for securing the mudroom door weren't great. I barricaded it with the hutch Lily used for hanging jackets and storing boots.

If someone was determined to get in, that hutch wouldn't stop them, but we wouldn't be here. A quick check of the garage told me the vehicles were still as I'd left them.

The laptop. If I was right and Lucas' app hadn't revealed the account Trey used for business, I couldn't leave it behind. Jogging to his office, I snagged it from the drawer and stashed it in the back of the Land Rover.

The bodies scattered all over the property were a problem. I couldn't leave them there. Lily was isolated, but not that isolated. No way in hell was I reporting them to Deputy Dave. He'd love any excuse to get rid of me.

The only option was to call Cooper and have him send in cleaners. Not ideal, but I didn't have another choice. Before I called, I jogged through the house, clearing every room.

When I was sure the house was empty of everyone but Lily, Adam, and me, I went back upstairs, rapping on Adam's door in a pattern I'd made Lily memorize.

"Knox?" she asked, the sound of dragging coming through the door.

"It's me. The house is clear. You two alright?"

The door swung open, and a small body hurtled into my legs, little arms winding around my hips, holding tight. I wrapped my fingers around the back of Adam's neck in a squeeze. He gripped me harder, his body shaking with terror or relief. Probably both.

Crouching down, I hooked my hands under his arms and lifted him, settling him into my side. His arms and legs wound around me, my free hand rubbing his back in long strokes.

"Hey, it's okay, bud. I know that was scary, but you're okay. Your mom's okay. Take a deep breath for me."

Adam buried his face into my neck, chest heaving with sobs. I expected Lily to move to take him from me, but she just stood there, eyes wide, teetering on her heels. Shit. She looked shell-shocked.

"Lily," I barked, harsher than I wanted to be. As much as I wanted to coddle her, I needed her functional. We weren't out of this yet. Her head snapped up, eyes focusing on my face, on her son in my arms.

"I need you to listen. Can you do that?" A nod. Better than nothing. "We need to get out of here. I have to make a call. Pack for you and Adam, enough for a few days. Can you do that?"

Lily processed my words in slow motion, nodding again. "Are we coming back?"

"I don't know," I said honestly. "I hope so, but plan to bring anything you can't leave behind. Two bags, easy to carry. Got it?"

"Got it."

She moved to take Adam from my arms. He clung like a spider monkey, chest still heaving with sobs. I squeezed him tighter, nudging his head up with my shoulder. His tear-swollen face raised to mine.

"I need you to help your mom, bud. Can you do that for me? I'm going to keep you safe, but I need your help."

"Are they coming back?" he asked in a thin, high voice.

"I don't think so, bud, but we don't want to find out. Your mom is going to pack some stuff. What do you need for a long sleepover?"

"George. My monkey. And my steam shovel book."

"Okay. I'm going to put you down. You go get that stuff so your mom can pack it. Can you do that?"

"I can do it, Mr. Knox."

This fucking kid. Five years old, and he had balls of steel. I squeezed his shoulder tight before nudging him in the direction of his bedroom door.

Lily took a step forward, her eyes glued to my side. "Knox. You're bleeding."

I looked to see a line of red going down my arm from a thin slice on my bicep. Now that I was aware of it, the burn flared to life. Fuck. Asshole on the floor must have had a knife.

"It's nothing. I'll take care of it as soon as I—"

The shrill of the perimeter alarm cut me off.

Fuck. What now?

I yanked my phone from my pocket and pulled up the cameras. A shiny, black, Mercedes cargo van rolled down the driveway coming to a stop in front of the house. Men spilled out into the woods.

My hand went to my weapon as my gut turned to ice. Too many. Too fucking many. Two approached the front door. I braced for attack.

They made no attempt to enter. Working quickly, they picked up the bodies, jogged back to the van and tossed them inside. One more trip and the second set of bodies was cleared.

They split up, one heading for the woods where I'd dropped the first guy, the other to the dock. Three minutes after the van had come to a stop, it was pulling away. I couldn't decide whether to be relieved or terrified.

I didn't need the cleaners. That was something. Tsepov wanted a mess less than I did. Now I knew there were more of his men out there. Were they giving up or regrouping? We couldn't stick around to find out.

Lily was looking up at me with wide, frightened eyes. "They're still here?"

"They left. For now. We need to get moving."

I cupped the side of her face in my hand, stroking my fingertip along the soft skin behind her ear and she leaned into me, the stiffness in her spine softening.

"Pack for you and Adam, okay? Be fast. Is there anything you don't want to leave in the house?"

"Trey's laptop," she said immediately.

I shook my head once. "I already have it."

Lily's eyes stayed on mine, considering. I knew she understood my comment, knew I'd been in Trey's laptop. Knew I'd been searching on my own.

I expected anger or protest. Her shoulders sagged, and she nodded. "Okay, then. If there's anything you think I need, get it. I'll get our stuff together."

"How fast can you pack?"

"Fast," she answered, turning on her heel and jogging to her room. I needed to get to the cottage, pack my own things, bandage my arm and wash off this blood. I wouldn't leave Lily and Adam alone in the house.

Adam came out of his room carrying his stuffed monkey and an arm full of books. I pointed him in the direction of his mother's bedroom. "Bring that to your mom, okay?"

He nodded and trotted down the hall. Functioning, but I didn't know for how long. I needed to get us out of here.

I thought about calling Cooper before we left and decided we didn't need the delay. My brother would want answers I didn't have. Getting us somewhere safe came first.

Lilly dropped a duffel bag in front of my feet. In her hand, she held a matching bag, only partly full. "We need to bandage your side."

"I'll get it. Don't worry about me. You need to finish packing."

Lily disappeared into Adam's bedroom, Adam following behind. A few minutes later she was out, the stuffed duffel in one hand, Adam's fingers gripped tightly in the other. "Now what?"

"Follow me." I led them to the garage and into Lily's white Land Rover. Tossing her bags into the back, I helped Adam into his car seat, buckling him in. I shut the door and opened the driver side for Lily.

"Get in." She did. I held up one of my Glocks. "Do you know how to use this?" A nod. "If anyone but me comes into the garage, shoot them and then get out of here. Do you understand?"

"I can't shoot someone."

"Yeah, you can, if you're the only thing between Adam and one of Tsepov's men."

I hit her number on my phone. She jerked in surprise as her own buzzed in her back pocket. She pulled it out with her free hand, looking from the screen to me in confusion.

"I want an open line so I know you two are okay in here. I'll be in the cottage less than five minutes. Keep that gun in your hand. Use it if you have to."

"You'll be right back?"

"I'll be right back, Lily. I wouldn't leave you here if I wasn't almost positive it was safe. Keep that gun in your hand, just in case. If you have to use it, drive out of here as fast as you can. Don't worry about me, just go. Got it?"

"Got it."

Lily didn't sound convinced, but I didn't have time to talk her into leaving me behind. I shut the driver's side door with a firm thunk and sprinted to the cottage.

My mind scanned through lists, everything I had to do in the next five minutes. The first thing to worry about was the cut on my arm. I couldn't walk around out there with a bloody shirt. I stripped off my clothes as soon as I hit the cottage, ducking into the shower, wincing at the sting.

Fucking bastard sliced me with a knife, and I didn't even feel it. The cut wasn't deep. It had already started to clot, though not enough that the water didn't hurt like a bitch. I rinsed off the blood and left my clothes on the floor of the shower where my bloody T-shirt wouldn't leave a stain.

Grabbing a clean T-shirt from my bag, I tore it into strips and bandaged the cut. As soon as that was taken care of, I pulled on fresh clothes and shoved boots on my feet.

It only took another two minutes to pack up the rest of my stuff. I was used to living out of my duffel. I zipped it closed, made sure my laptop and surveillance equipment were stored in their cases, and I was ready.

Lily's end of the line had been quiet, mostly soft murmurs from her to Adam. "Lily, you good?"

"We're okay. How much longer?"

"I'm headed to you now. Don't shoot when I come through the door."

I was only partly kidding. I needed Lily armed. I did not need her to panic and shoot me.

I squeezed through the side door, calling out, "It's me, Lily. Putting my stuff in the back. Get out and sit beside Adam in the backseat."

She did, coming to me first and handing me the weapon I'd left with her, turning it carefully so the barrel wasn't pointed at either of us. I took it and flicked on the safety. "Get into the car, Lily."

She scrambled in beside Adam and fastened her seatbelt. I was grateful for the boy's quiet, but I didn't like it. It wasn't like Adam to be silent. He sat there, clutching his stuffed monkey, his face bone white, eyes wide and pupils dilated.

Lily took his hand in hers. "Everything's okay, baby. Everything's okay."

Chapter Seventeen

KNOX

EVERYTHING WAS FAR FROM OKAY, but I wasn't going to tell either of them that.

I hit the garage remote and backed out, eyes alert for any movement in the driveway. Nothing. Just because I couldn't see them didn't mean they weren't out there somewhere, watching.

I turned the Land Rover in the direction of Bar Harbor, a city on the coast. Dawn barely kissed the horizon. We had a three-hour drive. Three hours to shake our tail if we had one. Three hours to get in touch with Cooper to find out what the fuck was going on.

I thought about doubling back towards town and taking a circuitous route around the lake to flush out anyone following us. If we were in a more densely populated area, I would have done that.

Here? Waste of time.

There were innumerable back roads around Black Rock Lake, but there was only one road to Bar Harbor. It was the only road to anywhere. If someone wanted to follow us, all they had to do was wait by the highway, and they'd pick us up eventually.

At this hour, traffic was light. Based on their performance at the house, I doubted Tsepov's men could hide if they were following us. I'd pick them up on way to Bar Harbor if they were there.

Lily was quiet as we drove, talking to Adam here and there, calming him but saying nothing to me. We needed to talk. I was done playing around, done with her hiding things from me.

First, I had to get in touch with my brothers. I called both Cooper and Evers twice, getting nothing. Finally, when the sun blazed in the sky and we were almost to Bar Harbor, Cooper answered.

"Knox. You guys okay?" Cooper was never easy going, but his voice was drawn tight. Something was wrong in Atlanta.

"In one piece. Six men attacked the house before dawn. We're fine. What's going on there?"

Cooper let out a gust of air. "It's a fucking clusterfuck. Tsepov hit Rycroft Castle. Smoky Winters let them in. He took Summer."

"Fucking hell." A quick glance in the rearview mirror. Adam was asleep. Good. "What's the plan?"

"We just traded her for Evers. It's under control. Are Lily and the kid okay? You okay?"

"I took a scratch to the arm, but we're fine. Got out of the house, headed to Bar Harbor. Summer?"

"Fine. Pissed as hell that Evers traded himself for her."

"What's the plan to get him back?"

"We're on it. Go to Bar Harbor, stay visible. Public. Alice will call you with arrangements. We need a few hours here to deal with the situation. Agent Holley is on his way. The FBI should have Tsepov by the end of the day. Just hang tight."

"Can do. I'll wait to hear from Alice."

"Don't do anything stupid with the widow," Cooper growled.

"I'm not the one trading myself to a mob boss," I said, dodging his comment.

"It was his fucking idea, the idiot," Cooper spit out.

"Of course, it was." If I'd had more time to get my head around their predicament, I would have guessed that.

Evers was head over heels in love with Summer, had been for over a year. The moron just couldn't admit it to himself. Bad enough that Tsepov got his hands on her, but to have it happen on his own job? Of course, he'd trade himself for Summer.

"Stay safe," I said.

"Yeah, you too. As soon as the situation stabilizes, I'll call."

"Got it. Later."

Lily met my eyes in the rearview mirror. "Is everything okay?"

I debated what to tell her and settled for the truth. "Tsepov hit the team in Atlanta. Grabbed my brother's girlfriend. They have it under control, but we need to stay moving until everything is resolved."

"What does that mean?" Lily asked.

"Hopefully, it means Andrei Tsepov is headed for jail. More than that, I don't know yet."

Ten minutes later my phone beeped with a text. I glanced down to see an address. *House of Blueberry: Pancakes & More*. I tapped the link and let the maps app on my phone guide us to breakfast.

A second text beeped. Alice.

Call me when you get there.

I glanced in the rearview to check the backseat. Adam was still asleep, his hand gripping his mother's, a faint line between his eyes. Lily sat stiffly, her eyes bouncing around, unable to settle.

We needed to talk. Adam was a wrench in the plans. Nothing we had to say should be spoken in front of him. It could wait. If Cooper was right, the FBI and Evers were about to buy us some time.

The pancake house wasn't far. I pulled in a few minutes after Alice's text, the gentle sway of the car parking jostling Adam from sleep. He blinked slowly.

I asked, "Who likes pancakes?"

His eyes cleared and he bounced a little in his car seat. "I do! I like pancakes. We're having pancakes?" A sudden thought occurred to him, and he slanted his mother a suspicious look. "Did you make the pancakes?"

A startled laugh burst from Lily. She leaned over and kissed her son on the cheek. "No, baby. We're at a pancake restaurant." She started to undo her seatbelt, but I stopped her.

"Hold on a second, Lily. Alice—she manages our office in Atlanta—she wants me to call before we go in. She's the one who found the pancake place. Let me check in with her and then we'll get some food."

Adam squirmed with excitement at the thought of pancakes not cooked by his mother. Lily unfastened her seatbelt but stayed where she was.

Alice answered on the first ring. "Hey, Knox. You guys okay?"

"So far, so good. How are things there? Cooper didn't tell me much."

"You know, same disaster, different day. Cooper is pretty solid on getting this settled in the next couple of hours, but he wants you to stay away from Black Rock for now. I checked out Bar Harbor. You have the little boy with you?"

"Yeah," I confirmed.

"Cool. I looked it up, and there's Acadia National Park nearby with a big sand beach. Why don't you have breakfast at that pancake place and then take them to the beach? It's public, it's in the open, and this time of year there will be park rangers all over the place."

The beach at Acadia National Park. That would be perfect. Adam could play and relax. Lily and I could talk.

"Listen," Alice cut into my thoughts, "if you need to leave the park, call first, okay?"

"No problem. We're going to need a team up here when everything is settled."

"Gotcha. Someone will call as soon as things are stable here."

"Good luck."

I hung up. I didn't like my brother with Tsepov. I liked the idea of Tsepov having Summer even less. Evers was former special forces. Tsepov trafficked women.

Between the two of them, Evers was safer in his hands than Summer. A hell of a lot safer.

If the men Tsepov had in Atlanta were as half-assed as the ones he'd sent to Maine, Evers would be fine. I'd still feel better when I heard my brother's voice. Even better when I knew Tsepov was with the FBI.

In the meantime, a big stack of blueberry pancakes would go a long way to improving the morning. I gave Lily and Adam a nod and they piled out of the Land Rover to follow me into the restaurant.

Lily picked at her single pancake and bowl of fruit.

Adam, with the resilience of a five-year-old, had no such trouble. He went for the chocolate chip stack and dug in with enthusiasm, jamming forkful after forkful of pancakes into his mouth.

He seemed to be over the trauma of seeing a man hold his mother at gunpoint. It would come back to him, but it was good to see that shocked look chased from his eyes by chocolate chips, whipped cream, and a tall glass of fresh-squeezed orange juice.

I tucked into my own stack of pancakes, liberally dotted with fresh Maine blueberries. Smaller than regular blueberries, they stained the pancakes blue, popping in my mouth with bursts of sweetness.

We were halfway through breakfast when I said to Lily, "Did you pack bathing suits?"

She nodded. "I grabbed a little bit of everything. Why?"

"Alice says Acadia National Park is close by, and it has a nice beach. Until I hear back from Cooper, she thought it would be a nice way to spend the morning."

Adam looked at me over a heaping forkful of pancake, grunting an inquiry through a full mouth.

"You want to go swimming, bud?"

He nodded, swallowing so he could say, "Can I build sand castles?"

Lily looked up from her mangled pancake. "I didn't pack your sand shovel and beach stuff. But we can play—"

"Don't worry about it," I said. "There's got to be someplace around here that sells sand toys. We'll grab some stuff and have a morning at the beach."

Lily gave me a grateful smile. "Thanks, Knox."

"Eat something, will you?" I asked, giving her plate a pointed look. "You're supposed to put the pancake into your mouth, not stab it with your fork."

Adam giggled. "Yeah, Mom. Eat your breakfast."

She made an effort, but her plate was only half clean when we left the restaurant in search of supplies for the beach.

I went a little overboard at the tourist trap where we stopped for sand toys. While Lily and Adam debated which prepackaged kit of sand molds and shovels to get, I grabbed two beach chairs, towels, a sun hat for Lily, sunscreen, a long-sleeved rash guard shirt for me, and a pair of swim trunks since I'd forgotten to pack my own. I threw in a handful of snacks and bottles of water.

July in Maine isn't as hot as Atlanta—not even close—but sitting in the sun all morning called for water, and any trip to the beach called for snacks.

A laugh bubbled from Lily's throat when she saw my pile of stuff at the register. Interrupting her debate with Adam, I grabbed the biggest pack of sand toys and tossed it on top.

"I've got it," Lily said, fumbling for her wallet.

I handed my card to the clerk, blocking her from doing the same. I should have let her pay. She was the client, after all.

Should have, but wouldn't.

I was taking Lily and Adam to the beach.

We were going to have a nice morning. I was going to watch Adam laugh and have fun and finally straighten this shit out with Lily.

She wasn't a client anymore.

She was mine, and I was paying for the fucking beach toys.

She didn't argue, still off balance. I loaded our gear into the back of the Rover and hit a drive-through coffee place because the weak shit at the pancake house was not enough.

We reached the menu to order, and I looked at Lily. "Iced s'mores Latte?"

Her eyes lit with pleased surprise. Knowing her coffee order was a friendly intimacy. In the big picture, not that important. It felt like more than a coffee order. It felt like a secret language.

She took her drink from me and sipped, staring out the window in contemplation. Adam twisted and bounced in his car seat, every mile between us and the beach stretching into eternity. Thanks to our pre-dawn departure, we were early, and the state park wasn't crowded yet. Lily and Adam changed while I got our chairs and towels set up.

I didn't like leaving them for the few minutes it took me to put on my trunks and rash guard, but stripping down on the beach seemed like a good way to get kicked out. The rash guard covered my bandaged arm well enough, and unlike a regular long sleeve shirt, wouldn't look out of place on the beach.

Adam ran to the edge of the water and stuck in his foot, then screeched and raced back, shrieking, "It's cold! It's cold! It's so cold, Mom!"

How cold could it be?

When my feet went numb a minute later, I knew exactly how cold the ocean in Maine could be.

Pretty fucking cold.

Fighting the urge to screech and run from the icy water like Adam, I forced myself to stroll out casually, praying the sun would warm me up. Every bone in my feet had turned to ice.

It wasn't anywhere close to hot enough to go swimming in that fucking water.

Hell wouldn't be hot enough to swim in that water.

Lily was biting her lip, smirking at me.

"You've never been in the ocean in Maine, have you?" she asked mischievously.

"That obvious?"

"Pretty much. I'll swim in the lake this time of year if it's hot out, but I almost never go into the ocean." Lily opened the bag of sand toys and passed them out to Adam.

The beach wasn't too crowded yet, and he'd found himself a spot closer to the water where the sand was hard-packed and wet enough to build with.

Lily sat in one of the beach chairs. I took the other. We sipped our coffee, watching Adam dig in the sand as the silence stretched between us.

Satisfied Adam was out of earshot, I asked the question that had been plaguing me since my first day in Lily's house.

Chapter Eighteen

KNOX

"LILY, WHAT HAVE YOU BEEN looking for?"

Lily stared at the clear lid of her iced latte as if it held the answers to all of life's questions.

She chewed on her lower lip. Drew in a deep breath and let it out.

Finally, just when I was about to push, she raised her head, her brown eyes strained. "I can't find Adam's birth certificate."

Her confession dropped between us like a stone.

Of all the things I'd expected her to say, that was nowhere on the list.

Adam's birth certificate.

What did Adam's birth certificate have to do with anything?

Seeing my incomprehension, she went on, "I'm sure you figured out Adam is adopted." I nodded. "When Trey brought him home, there was a birth certificate. It had my name on it. And a contract for the adoption. An agreement that named Trey and me as his legal parents. It's gone. They're both gone."

I absorbed the fear in Lily's eyes and looked from her to Adam. The summer sun gleamed on his white-blonde hair. His tan from playing outside was nothing like Lily's tawny skin.

Shit.

Her reality exploded in my brain, all of the implications of a biracial woman with a son who very much did not resemble her, and no proof that she was his legal guardian. No proof she was his mom.

Trying to clarify I asked, "Couldn't you have sent off for his birth certificate? Gotten a lawyer?"

"I was scared. At first, I didn't even think of it. I assumed the papers were where I'd last seen them. In the file cabinet with the medical bills. A few months after Trey died, I started thinking ahead to enrolling Adam in kindergarten, and when I went to look for his shot records, I realized all the paperwork relating to his adoption was gone. Including the birth certificate.

"I looked up how to send off for it, but you need to affirm who you are, your relationship to the person on the certificate. I was afraid if I said I was his mother and then I wasn't on the certificate they'd take him away. I thought about getting a lawyer, but the break-ins had already started—"

"—and with Deputy Dave implying you couldn't handle being a parent without Trey, you didn't want to say anything," I finished for her.

Fuck. She'd been backed into a corner. Black Rock is a small town. If the police were questioning her fitness as a mother and it got out that she didn't have the documentation to prove her legal right to her son...

She could lose Adam. I already knew Lily would do anything to keep her son.

"I know the adoption was legal. I saw the paperwork—"

She swallowed hard, horror dawning on her face. Her pulse pounded in her throat as her eyes met mine. "Knox? It was legal, wasn't it? I don't know what Trey—"

She dropped her head, eyes fixed on her lap. A tear rolled off her lashes to darken a spot on her shorts. Then another. And another.

I lurched to my feet, yanking my chair from the sand and moving it beside her. Sitting, I wrapped my arm around her shoulders and pulled her into me, wishing I could erase her fear.

I wanted to promise her everything would be okay. I didn't want to lie.

"Lily, we'll figure this out." I had to tell her some of what I knew about Trey, but I didn't know where to start. "From what we've uncovered so far, Trey, and my father, and some other people, including Andrei Tsepov, were working together, involved in a lot of sketchy shit. Some of it was selling kids to adoptive parents."

Lily lifted her tear stained face. "You think Trey *bought* Adam?"

How much had Lily figured out? I didn't want to break her heart, but dancing around the truth wouldn't help.

"Lily," I said as gently as I could, "I've seen pictures of Trey. Adam—"

"—looks almost exactly like him."

"Yeah."

Lily let herself lean into me for a moment longer before she pulled away. I left my arm resting on the back of her beach chair, my thumb grazing the top of her shoulder through her T-shirt.

She took a deep breath, then another, wiping her eyes with the back of her hand. "He, uh, things weren't good for a while before he brought Adam home. I was thinking maybe I'd made a mistake. We were trying to get pregnant and I, um, I couldn't. I—"

I could guess what she was struggling with. I didn't want to make her say it.

"I saw the medical bills, Lily."

I waited for her to ask how. Why. Lily was too smart for that. She'd already figured out that I was there for more than just keeping her safe.

She nodded. "So you know I couldn't stay pregnant."

I grabbed her hand. "No. I know you went through a rough time, and your husband was a shit. You never saw a fertility doctor?"

"No," she said, her voice so low it was almost inaudible. "He said there was no point. And then he brought me Adam. I don't know why, Knox."

Her eyes met mine for a second, beseeching and teary, her expression an ache in my chest. I wanted to bring Trey Spencer back from the dead so I could kill him again. So much pain, and he'd left her to handle it alone. She sniffed and looked back at her son, happily digging in the sand.

"He didn't want to be a father. He barely noticed Adam, complained about him being in the way. He didn't love me. Not by then. He didn't want me. I think he had someone else. But he brought me Adam. I didn't love Trey, but I loved Adam from that first minute."

She rubbed the heel of her palm under her eye, scrubbing a stray tear.

"I didn't want to know. My name was on the birth certificate, on that contract, and Adam was mine. I should have asked. I know that. But I had Adam, and I loved him so much."

"Lily, we'll find his birth certificate. No one will take Adam from you."

I wanted to bite back the words. Until I had more information, I couldn't know that. Not really.

"Knox, you can't promise that."

"I have resources. And I know a hell of a lot more about my father and Trey's business than you do. We'll figure this out." I rubbed my thumb over her shoulder. "I wish you'd told me."

"I wanted to. I thought about it so many times, but—"

"You were afraid to risk Adam."

She nodded. "I don't want to stay there anymore. In that house Trey built. In that town."

"Where do you want to go?"

She shrugged the shoulder under my hand and gave a helpless laugh. "I don't know. I've been afraid to plan. Afraid to do anything. As soon as I realized his birth certificate and the contract were missing, I knew we couldn't leave. I don't have anywhere to go.

"At least in Black Rock everyone knows me as Adam's mom. As long as Dave didn't start any trouble, I figured we'd be okay there, but I've been too scared to leave. Especially after what happened when he started preschool."

"What happened?"

"I tried to register him, had all the paperwork, his shot record, copy of his birth certificate, but the woman who handled registrations didn't believe I was his mom. She said she needed Trey to come in, that they'd prefer his father register him, not his guardian or step-mother."

"Bitch," I swore, hating the way Lily stared at the sand in front of her feet, her eyes dark with pain. "Couldn't she read the birth certificate?"

"Oh, yeah, she could read. And she'd known me for years, knew Trey and I were married, knew I wasn't Adam's step-anything. But she wouldn't register him until Trey came in. And that happened with someone who knew us. I started thinking about what could happen if we left and—"

"I get it," I said, gritting my teeth to force the roil of my emotions under control.

If that was the kind of bullshit Lily had to put up with, I wasn't surprised she'd been afraid to leave, afraid to tell me what she was looking for. One way or another, I was going to make this right for her. First, I had to get the whole picture of what was going on in Black Rock.

"What's up with Deputy Dave?"

"I don't know. He wasn't like this when Trey was alive. He was nice enough, always polite, but he was Trey's friend, not mine. Since Trey died, he's been... Weird."

A grin twisted my lips. "He wants to fuck you," I said bluntly.

Lily let out a shocked gasp and smacked my chest with the back of her hand. "Knox! He does not."

My grin turned into a laugh. "Lily, trust me. I'm a guy. He totally wants to fuck you. He never flirted with you when Trey was alive?"

"Not that I noticed. Eww. Gross."

"No interest in Deputy Dave?" I probed, half teasing and half serious.

"No! Oh, yuck. No. Not before, and especially not now."

"You said he was Trey's best friend. Is it possible he worked for Trey?"

Lily stared out over the water, thinking. "I guess anything is possible, but I never heard them talk about business. Then again, Trey didn't talk about business that much anyway. I guess I don't know. If I could go back and not be such an idiot—"

"Lily, don't do that. None of us can go back. If the worst thing you've done is trust your husband and focus a little too much on your kid, you should cut yourself some slack."

"I can't. Not if my being stupid put Adam in danger."

"Trey is the one who put Adam in danger. Not you," I said. "You really weren't involved in Trey's business? I'm on your side. You can trust me. I swear."

I didn't even have to think about that. I meant those words all the way to my bones. If she was involved, if she'd played even the smallest part, I'd find a way to get her out of it. I didn't need to know every detail to know Lily was innocent. Even if she was guilty in action, she was innocent in her heart.

She shook her head slowly, tears welling in her eyes again. "I almost wish I had been. Then I might have some idea what's going on. I might be able to keep Adam safe. I don't know anything. I know he worked with logistics. And he traveled a lot. He had trucks that moved stuff, though I don't know what happened to them because they didn't come to me when he died."

"What did come to you?" I probed, hoping she knew something I hadn't uncovered in the will.

"The house came to me. The house and the contents. The money in our personal accounts. The company, but it doesn't seem to have been much more than some paperwork. No employees. No equipment. No office. I didn't realize. It never occurred to me things weren't aboveboard until after he died and the attorney laid it all out. The house, the cars, all that money in the bank, and the business that wasn't a business."

"No one came looking for him? Asking about the trucks he used or unfinished jobs?"

"No. No one. It's like when he died the business evaporated. I decided not to worry about it until I went looking for Adam's birth certificate."

I believed her. Maybe that made me a fool, but I believed her.

Time to come clean, all the way. I mentally braced before I said, "Lily, I have cameras in your house."

At this revelation, she leaned forward. I was ready for her to throw a punch, slap me. Anything. Her eyes went wide, then narrowed, and I knew exactly what she was thinking.

"I didn't see anything I shouldn't. I swear. I did it partly to keep you safe and partly because I have to find out what Trey knew."

"And you thought I would know. You thought I was working with them."

"I thought it was a possibility."

She let out a huff of air and flopped back into her chair. "I should be pissed at you. I really should. I hired you to protect us, and you were spying on me instead. I had a feeling you weren't just there for me."

"I was protecting you, too." I wanted to drop my hand from the back of her chair to her shoulder. To touch her, even if it was only with a fingertip.

I kept my hands to myself. She hadn't jumped up and kicked me in the balls. That was a good sign. I tried again.

"Lily, this is about more than you and Adam. Tsepov threatened my mother."

"I should be furious right now," she said quietly, mostly to herself.

"I'm fine if you are," I said. "It was a shitty thing to do. I know that. Sometimes, in my line of work you have to make hard choices."

Lily sighed. "I guess you do. If you've been watching me, you know I'm not involved. And you searched the house? Trey's computer?"

"Not as thoroughly as I need to. But I'm not the only one who searched the house. Deputy Dave went through Trey's office twice during dinner the other night. He didn't find anything, but he's looking for something. Any idea what?"

"What? Why? If Trey owed him money or something, he could have told me." Lily tipped her head back, resting her soft curls against my arm. She stared up into the cloudless blue sky. "He was working with Trey, wasn't he?"

"I don't know for sure, but I'm starting to think he was."

Her eyes still on the sky, she said, "Who is Andrei Tsepov, and what does he have to do with anything? Why did his men break into the house and say they were taking me to him?"

"Fuck," I said, "that's a long story."

Lily tipped her head down and speared me with a no-nonsense look, the same one I'd seen her give Adam when he refused to eat his vegetables. "I'm not going anywhere. Talk."

"Okay. Andrei Tsepov is the nephew of Sergey Tsepov, who was shot and killed a few years ago by my sister-in-law. Sergey Tsepov was a bad guy. He was very good at being a bad guy. It looks like he was in business with my father, who we didn't know was such a bad guy until recently. And from what we can figure, tracking the money moving from Tsepov, to my father, to Trey, Trey has been wrapped up with them for a while."

"Wrapped up with them in what, exactly?"

"I don't want to tell you what they're into. I don't want you to know."

It was clear there'd been problems between Lily and her husband. Maybe it was wishful thinking, but it sounded like they'd fallen out of love years ago. Not being in love with her husband and knowing he was a criminal who'd put both her and his son at risk were two very different things.

I thought about some of the shit my father, Tsepov, and Trey had been into. I didn't want to bring that kind of darkness into Lily's life.

"Tell me, Knox. I'm not a child. I need to know."

"You really don't." She didn't, but that wasn't my call. Lily was right, she wasn't a child. I gave in.

"Fine. I don't know that we have the whole picture. We may never have the whole picture until we find my father, and knowing him, probably not even then. From what we've been able to find, there's been some arms dealing, a lot of transport. Tsepov moving things and using my father and Trey to do it. Drugs, though that wasn't a major part of their business. Trafficking, mostly women. And an adoption ring, highly paid surrogates, mostly."

"Trafficking?" Lily asked in a weak voice. "Arms and drugs?"

"From what we can tell, the Tsepov syndicate originated the business except for the adoptions. My father and Trey worked together on logistics. Moving product, whatever that product was, from one place to another. The only way we've been able to figure it out is that my father, when he was shorthanded, used the company as protection for some of the transport. Not often, or my brothers and I would have caught on. Often enough that we could see the pattern once we looked for it."

"But the adoptions aren't Tsepov? The adoptions were your father and Trey?"

"From what we can tell, yeah. Not all of them, maybe none of them, are illegal. Highly questionable, but not necessarily illegal."

"How is Andrei Tsepov tied up in this?" Lily asked.

"Andrei inherited the family business, and he is not following in his uncle's footsteps. He's sloppy and a little stupid. Normally that would be a good thing. For us, it's not. He's an amateur and a dumbass."

"Why would he want me? Why send those men?"

"He called us the same night you did. Said my father took something from him and he wants it back. If we don't turn it over, he'll kill our mother."

"What did your father take?"

Chapter Nineteen

KNOX

I SHOOK MY HEAD AND LAUGHED under my breath. "What did my father take? That's the question of the century. This would all be a hell of a lot easier if fucking Andrei Tsepov had bothered to tell us. I'm assuming you don't know either?"

"No. I wish I did."

"I'd bet Deputy Dave knows. Why else would he be searching Trey's office?"

"I don't have the faintest clue," Lily said. "What's going on with your brother? Is his girlfriend okay?"

"Cooper says she's fine. I'll see what Evers has to say when he gets away from Tsepov."

"Are you worried?" She answered her own question. "Of course, you are. Is he going to be all right?"

"Evers? He'll be fine. I don't like that he handed himself over to Tsepov, but he's a lot safer there than Summer was. He's sneaky. Smart. Plus, they have the FBI on the case. The phone is going to ring any minute telling us everything's good."

I mostly believed that. I was 98% positive everything would be fine. It's that other 2% that always fucks you.

Nothing was going to happen to Evers. No fucking way. He'd just gotten Summer back. He'd come back from hell if he had to, as long as Summer was there waiting for him.

"So, we sit here and wait?" Lily said, her toes digging into the sand.

"For now."

"And then what?" Lily asked, hopeful query in her warm, brown eyes.

I wasn't sure what she was asking.

What's next with the investigation? With Adam? With us?

I looked out at the water, letting her question roll around in my head. I decided to take the easy road. Business.

I was keeping Lily, but I wasn't sure she was ready to hear that yet. I could ease her into it. Evers wasn't the only Sinclair who could be sneaky.

"We'll stay in Bar Harbor for now. I'll have Cooper send a team to your house. It needs to be re-secured, for one. Even if the FBI has Tsepov, your deputy is still up to something."

"He's not my deputy," she protested.

"He'd like to be."

"I'm not so sure about that," she countered, "and anyway, I don't care. I don't want Dave Morris."

It was on the tip of my tongue to ask her who she did want. I let the opening go. For now. We'd have time. I'd make sure of it.

"After we get the house re-secured, I want to see if I can get our best computer guy up for a day or two to take another crack at Trey's laptop. I got more from it than you did, but not enough. There's something I'm missing. Unless he had another one?"

Lily shook her head. "I can't swear he didn't. What I don't know would fill an encyclopedia. But that's the only computer I ever saw."

"I want Lucas to take a crack at it. And then we tear your house apart. Adam's birth certificate and that paperwork didn't vanish. They have to be there somewhere. We'll find them."

"What if we don't?" Lily asked.

"Then we'll figure it out, Lily. I promise. You're not going to lose Adam."

I pulled my arm from the back of her chair and dropped it between us, taking her hand in mine and twining our fingers together. A shy smile spread across her face. She squeezed my hand with hers before she turned her eyes back to Adam, a flush cresting her cheeks.

The beach had filled with tourists as the sun had risen. If not for them, I would have pulled her onto my lap and done a whole lot more than hold her hand. From that hint of a blush, I hoped she was thinking the same thing.

I tried not to feel smug. So much was up in the air. Evers. Tsepov. Adam's missing birth certificate. Whatever the fuck was going on with Deputy Dave.

But Lily had come clean. She was innocent, we were alive and well, sitting on the beach watching Adam play in the sun while she held my hand.

Maybe everything else was a big pile of shit, but this was good. This was the best.

I rummaged in the bag beside me for the silly sun hat I'd bought her. Without comment, that shy smile still on her face, she put it on, shading her skin from the sun. A few minutes later she called Adam over and sprayed every inch of exposed skin with sunscreen, ignoring his strident protests. The second she released his hand he took off for his sand castle. Lily sprayed her legs and held out the can.

"Do you need some?"

I wanted to insist I didn't. I never burned. I took the can anyway and gave my legs a cursory spray. I had plans for later and they didn't involve a sunburn. They also didn't involve Lily thinking I was too stupid or bull-headed to use sunscreen.

The morning stretched on to lunch. Adam abandoned his sandcastle in search of snacks, and we all took a break to fill our stomachs with the junk food I'd picked up with the beach supplies.

Lily waded into the water up to her knees, shrieking as Adam splashed her before she bolted back out. Adam dunked himself, screamed with glee and dunked himself again before racing to his mother's lap and curling up in a dry towel, falling asleep wrapped in her arms.

She held him, leaning into my side, stroking his wet hair from his forehead. I wrapped my arm around them both, feeling like I held the whole world.

Lily's eyes were drooping with fatigue when my phone vibrated in my pocket. Cooper.

"Yeah."

"Everything's good. The FBI arrested Tsepov. Evers is with them now. He's fine. No casualties on our side."

"He's okay?"

"He's okay. Tsepov wants account numbers. Apparently, Dad took off with a ton of cash he owed the senior Tsepov, and no one looked for it after Emma shot him. Andrei figured it out and he wants it back. Seen any numbers up there?"

"No, not so far, but after last night I'm going to search the place from top to bottom. Shit. He could have told us that in the first place."

"Andrei Tsepov is an idiot," Cooper agreed. "What's going on up there?"

"Just enjoying a day at the beach," I said. "Adam played himself into a nap, and I think Lily is about to follow him."

Her head tucked against my chest, words slurring with sleep, she murmured, "I'm not sleeping."

I gave her a squeeze. Her eyes drifted shut.

Cooper heard every word. "Knox, I swear to fucking God—"

"Save it, Cooper. Don't even bother."

"Fine," he bit out. "I don't have time for that shit anyway. Now that Tsepov is out of circulation for a while I'm sending a team to Lily Spencer's house. You need cleanup?"

"No. Tsepov took care of it. But the back door has a hole in it, and all the security needs to go up a level. Or two. We're not done there. I need Lucas."

"The laptop?"

"The laptop. I'm missing something. I'd send it down, but I don't want it out of our control."

"I'll see what I can do. Alice is making arrangements. She'll text you with a place to stay, probably for the night. Shouldn't take the team long to secure the house."

"Works for me."

"Knox?"

"Yeah?"

"Be careful. We've got a little breathing room, but watch your back."

"You, too," I said, and disconnected.

Twenty minutes later my phone beeped with a text from Alice.

East Street Hotel. Check-in is at three. Have fun.

Jabbing at the letters with my thumb, I texted back

Thanks. I owe you.

Lily and Adam napped for over an hour. After waking to Tsepov's men well before dawn I could have used some sleep myself. Later.

Adam woke with his stomach growling, and we packed up, heading back into town in search of food. Lily hadn't had much breakfast, but she put away most of a sub and a bag of chips.

Adam devoured his own sub. I got a lobster roll overflowing with succulent, sweet, red and white lobster meat. When in Maine... Might as well not waste the chance to eat fresh lobster.

We found a Putt-Putt and wasted an hour. Lily was hopeless with a golf club, but Adam wasn't too bad for a five-year-old. That meant he sometimes hit the ball with the club and almost never got it in the hole without a little help. He didn't care.

Lily's eyes were too serious as she concentrated on each swing of the club, biting her lip every time she tapped the ball, usually missing whatever she was aiming for. Her mind wasn't on the game. I caught her scanning the parking lot the same way I did, looking for trouble. I couldn't blame her.

We wrapped up the game in time for check-in at the East Street Hotel. I pulled up the address Alice had texted and navigated to an elegant building downtown, across the street from the bay. Taking up most of the block, the white siding and black shutters were vintage Maine.

The uniformed young woman who checked us in gave us a blinding smile. "Oh, you lucked out. We're normally booked solid through August, but your assistant called right after a cancellation and snatched it up."

"Thanks," I said, taking the key and wondering what Alice had gotten us into. I'd imagined a small inn or one of the big chains by the highway, not this expansive, elegant hotel.

The elevator took us to the top floor where the door to our room swung open to reveal a corner suite. We walked into a living room with two balconies, dominated by views of the harbor, the blue water dotted with white sailboats.

A bouquet of roses sat on the dining table beside a silver ice bucket holding a bottle of champagne. Two champagne flutes and a box of truffles completed the picture.

Lily's eyes flicked to me and back to the roses. I flipped over the notecard reading *Enjoy your Romance Package* to see *'Have fun ;) Alice'* scrawled across the back.

"Alice," I said to Lily in explanation.

Her shy smile curved her lips, joined by a flush on her cheeks. "How did she...?"

Not, *Why did she?*

But, *How did she?* As in, *How did she know there's something going on with us?* Not that I needed more proof that Lily was as interested as I was. That kiss over cookies had been proof enough.

"Alice knows everything," I said, not telling her that Alice knew because Cooper had been bitching about me being led by my dick.

Alice was Cooper's right hand, but that didn't mean she wouldn't find it funny to piss him off by setting Lily and me up in a love nest that Cooper was paying for. I owed Alice her own bouquet of roses.

"Wow, this is nice," Adam shouted, darting across the room to bounce on one of the armchairs.

"Adam," Lily hissed, "don't jump on the furniture."

He popped up to test out the couch facing the flatscreen

TV before vaulting off and checking out the small kitchenette.

"Look, Mom, it even has a kitchen! It's like a house. Can we stay, Mr. Knox?"

"For tonight," I promised.

He gave another shout and ran for one of the bedrooms. Lily shook her head.

"I'm sorry. He's tired and wound up."

"You don't have to apologize, Lily. He's fine."

I followed Adam to see what he'd discovered. A bedroom opened off of each side of the main space, one with two queen beds and one with a king.

I dropped our bags—mine with the king and Lily's with the two queens—and did a quick walk-through. One entrance, secured by a deadbolt and a safety lock. Two balconies off the living room, and one off each bedroom, all inaccessible without a climbing rope, the safety locks un-reachable by a five-year-old.

The suite wasn't a bunker, but with Tsepov in jail, it was safe enough. Lily and Adam disappeared into their bedroom to get cleaned up from the beach.

The T-shirt I'd wrapped around the cut on my arm was glued in place by dried blood. A good soak under the shower and I peeled it off without tearing the healing cut open.

Adam and Lily didn't emerge until I was cleaned up, re-bandaged, dressed, and finished setting up extra security equipment. The sensors on the balcony doors and the main entrance to the suite were overkill, but I'd sleep better knowing they were there.

I glanced up from the laptop screen and my mouth went dry. Lily wore a cherry red sundress, the full skirt brushing the tops of her knees, a light sweater over her shoulders to ward off the coming chill. It was July, but this was still Maine. Once the sun was down, the warmth of the day would fade.

Held up by two thin straps, the dress dipped just enough to reveal the shadow between her breasts. My cock stirred, and I had to look away before I embarrassed myself. She'd been wearing less at the beach, but somehow this was different.

With her hair pulled up in a ballerina's bun on the top of her head and a light gloss on her lips she was transformed, sexy and elegant. She still reminded me of a woodland fairy, but this fairy was the Queen.

Adam fidgeted in shorts and a polo shirt, his clear blue eyes a little red from the sun, salt water, and exhaustion.

"Do you want to eat dinner at the restaurant downstairs? There's one inside that looks pretty formal, but the other one has seating outside on the second level, overlooking the bay."

Adam tugged at my pants. "Do they have kids' stuff? With crayons?"

"I don't know, bud, but I bet they do. We'll figure something out if they don't, okay?"

Adam's bottom lip jutted out and he shrugged his shoulder with a jerk. Lily said with apology, "It's been a long day."

I didn't know what that meant.

I thought I did, but I had no idea.

I was about to learn.

Chapter Twenty

KNOX

BY THE TIME WE WERE seated in a four-top overlooking the water, I had a better idea what Lily meant by *It's been a long day*.

Adam squirmed and wiggled, complaining about everything. The seat wasn't right. There weren't enough crayons. He wasn't hungry.

Lily sat beside him, trying to keep him occupied. When she finally got him interested in the maze on the back of the kids' menu she said quietly, "I'm sorry. He's tired—"

"—not tired." Adam cut in, a mulish set to his chin.

"We're all tired," I said. "Hopefully, we'll get a good night's sleep tonight. Maybe we can go to the beach again tomorrow."

I was hoping that would get a smile from Adam, but he ignored both of us, doggedly coloring his menu with the crayon. Lily turned down the offer of wine. I ordered myself a local beer.

If I'd thought we'd have a romantic dinner, I would have

been very wrong. We barely managed to get out more than one sentence at a time. Either Adam interrupted, or Lily was forced to turn her attention to him before he destroyed the restaurant around us.

Adam ordered a hotdog with applesauce. I got lobster, again. Lobster bisque and a full dinner plate. Lily skipped the bisque but joined me for the lobster dinner. Our plates arrived quickly, not a surprise since it was early and the restaurant wasn't that busy. Our lobsters had been picked from their shells for us, saving us the mess.

"I haven't had lobster in so long," Lily said.

"You live in Maine. They have fresh lobsters in the grocery store." They did, a huge tank of them swimming around right by the seafood case.

"I know, and I love them. I guess I've gotten into the habit of cooking for a five-year-old, and Adam doesn't do lobster."

The five-year-old in question shoved his plate to the middle of the table, his lower lip pooching in mutiny.

"Adam, eat your dinner," Lily said, the words so rote, so practiced, I knew they'd been repeated a thousand times, ten thousand times, over the last few years. Adam pulled his paper in front of him again, refusing to look at his mother or his plate.

"Don't like it."

"You asked for a hotdog," Lily said with hard-won patience. "Hot dogs are your favorite."

"It tastes funny, and the bread is too crunchy. It hurts my teeth."

"What do you mean it hurts your teeth?" Lily asked, exasperation gaining on her unraveling patience.

"I have a wobbly tooth, and the bread hurts. And the applesauce is chunky. I don't like chunky applesauce."

"Since when do you have a wobbly tooth? And you like apples. The chunks are apples."

"Which tooth is wobbly, bud?" I asked, not sure if Lily would appreciate me butting into their conversation. She tilted her head to the side and waited for Adam's answer.

He dropped his jaw and stuck a finger into his mouth, wiggling one of his bottom front teeth. The little sucker moved. Not a lot. It wasn't about to fall out, but it did move.

Lily's eyes flew wide, and she smacked a hand over her mouth, leaning down to touch her forehead to Adam's, her exasperation forgotten for the moment.

"It's your first loose tooth. How long has it been wiggling? Why didn't you tell me?"

"Just started," Adam said, not sharing his mother's excitement.

I checked out his plate with the partially eaten hot dog and bowl of homemade applesauce. It looked good to me. Not as good as my lobster, but still pretty good. Especially for kid food.

"Wait a second," Lily said, "you didn't have any problem eating your sub at lunch. Are you saying your tooth wasn't loose at lunch?"

"I don't know. It didn't hurt then."

Lily let out a huff of air, exasperation back in full force. "Adam, you have to eat dinner."

"Not hungry. I don't want it. Not gonna eat it."

Lily braced her elbow on the table and dropped her forehead into her palm. She hadn't been wrong earlier. It *had* been a long day. We'd started before dawn with fear and danger, but the ending had been pretty good, until now.

Dinner with a cranky five-year-old was nowhere near as bad as an invasion by six armed guys. We got through that, we could get through this.

In a low voice, I asked, "Should we have it packed up for later? Maybe he'll change his mind."

Lily nodded, her forehead still braced in her palm, and let out a long sigh. I reached across the table to bracelet her wrist with my fingers, giving a gentle tug. She sat up, her eyes tired.

Repeating her words from earlier I said, "It's been a long day, Lily. Let's eat dinner and let him color?"

"I'm sorry he's—"

"Don't worry about it. He's five. He's been a champ, all things considered. Here, you need to try this lobster bisque," I said, holding up my spoon, hoping the soup would distract her. I hadn't had lobster bisque in a while, but this stuff was beyond good.

Lily leaned across the table. I slipped the spoon between her lips. She closed her eyes and hummed as she tasted the soup.

"Oh my God, that's amazing."

It was. I took a spoonful for myself, then fed her another, still holding her hand. Adam ignored us, happy to be left to his own devices, and we managed to share the entire bowl of bisque before he slumped in his seat, let out a groan of despair, and slid under the table.

Lily's hand pulled from mine, and her head disappeared beneath the table cloth. "What are you doing under there? Get off the floor!"

From beneath the table, I heard, "Boooring. This is boring. There's no kid stuff to do."

"Draw something with your crayons."

"Don't want to. Don't want crayons. Bored. Why do we have to do grown-up stuff?"

Lily sat up, her teeth cutting into her lower lip as she struggled to get a hold of her temper. Adam wasn't always perfect, but I'd never seen him this cranky.

I'd also never seen him after being woken in the middle of the night by a man holding a gun to his mother's head, then dragged halfway across the state.

He's five, I reminded myself. *He's five, and it's been a bitch of a day.*

Lily looked like she was at the end of her rope. Despite Alice's plans, this was not the night for romance. Not that I thought there was much room for romance with a five-year-old chaperone sitting beside us.

Still, a man could hope.

It had only been a week since I'd seen Lily's picture in Trey's file. One look and I'd known. I had to be the one to help her.

She'd opened her door, and I'd started to fall. One week, and I was all the way in. I wanted Lily. Not just in bed. Not just for a night. I wanted her.

Did I want romance? Fuck yeah. Candlelight and a fancy dinner and Lily in that dress. Then Lily out of that dress. Mine.

I could wait. Adam came first. I loved that about Lily.

I love my mom. Hell, I was here partly because I wanted to protect my mom from Tsepov. But she hadn't been a mom like Lily. I couldn't remember her ever reading me a story. Giving me a bath. Tucking me into bed. Forget listening to my stories about school.

Lacey Sinclair was interested in herself. She didn't know how to love the way Lily did, with her whole heart. With her soul. Lily loved with everything she had, and I wanted some of that for me.

I couldn't love the way Lily was with Adam and then expect her to forget about him as soon as I flashed a bouquet of roses and a nice dinner.

Lily took care of everyone else. She was devoted to Adam. She cooked me dinner and stocked the cottage with snacks, just in case I got hungry. I'd bet even when Trey was cheating on her and treating her like shit, she still took care of him, cooking and doing his laundry whether he deserved it or not.

Who took care of her? From what I knew of her life, her parents, and her husband, it sounded like the answer was no one. No one took care of Lily. That was about to change.

I caught the waitress as she walked by. "Can you bring the check and three to-go boxes? We have to get this guy to bed. Long day in the sun."

The waitress smiled and promised to be right back.

"Thank you," Lily whispered in relief. "He's only going to get worse. He needs to go to bed."

"Don't need to go to bed," Adam's voice floated up from beneath his chair.

Lily ignored him, helping to pack up our unfinished meals while I paid the check. The waitress had included a twine-handled shopping bag with our boxes.

I gave it to Lily, nudged Adam's chair out of the way, and picked him up off the floor. He struggled a little, mumbling, "Wanna walk."

"Don't you want to ride on my shoulders?"

A moment of wiggling consideration. Then, "K."

I lifted him, holding onto his knees and trying not to wince when he sank his fingers into my hair. I was glad we'd stuck with the restaurant attached to the hotel. Somehow, we got Adam back to the room without incident.

I set the leftovers on the small dining table by the kitchenette, putting Adam's box into the little refrigerator. Lily led Adam into their bedroom.

She left the door open a few inches, giving me a front row seat to the nightmare that was putting a cranky five-year-old to bed.

He wanted to sleep in his clothes.

He didn't like the pajamas she'd packed.

He wasn't tired.

He wanted a different story.

Lily handled most of it with her customary calm. By the time Adam interrupted the story to complain for the fifth time, I wondered how much more it would take before Lily blew her top.

I wasn't in there with them and I was ready to beg him to please go to bed already. When he said, "I want Mr. Knox to read to me. You're not doing it right," I hauled myself to my feet.

I was used to going without sleep, but that didn't mean I wasn't tired, too. Whatever.

He's five, I reminded myself. *Five.*

Lily spotted me in the doorway, her mouth tight with fatigue and annoyance. "I'm sorry. You don't have to—"

I sat on the other side of the bed and held out my hand for the book about the steam shovel. "I can read a book, Lily. I don't mind."

I didn't. Especially if it would get Adam to shut the hell up. Momentarily satisfied, Adam leaned into me, his eyelids heavy, his stuffed monkey held tight to his chest.

"Start at the beginning," he demanded.

No problem. It's not like the book was long. I flipped to the first page and began to read. The book wasn't bad, about a steam shovel who lost his job when bigger equipment came to town and then saved the town by finishing the hole for the new library after the new equipment broke down.

By the time the hole was finished and the little steam shovel discovered he hadn't dug himself a way out, Adam's breathing was even and deep, his eyes closed.

Fucking finally. I met Lily's eyes over his sleeping body, seeing my relief mirrored in her face, lightened by a hint of wonder. She took the book from my hands and eased off the bed, pulling the covers up around Adam's shoulders.

We tiptoed out of the room, closing the door behind us. Lily stopped and turned, cracking it open a few inches. "I know he's fine, but I want to be able to hear him if—"

"Good idea," I agreed before she could apologize again.

"Dinner?" I asked, tilting my head to the table where I'd laid out our unfinished meal.

Her hand going to her stomach Lily said, "I'm starving. I'm so hungry I might eat Adam's hot dog, too. That would serve him right."

"How about champagne and chocolate?" I offered.

"I don't think I can do more than a glass of champagne," Lily said, "but I'll never turn down chocolate."

I popped the cork on the champagne, pouring us both half a glass. "You look beautiful in that dress," I said. "You always look beautiful, but I've never seen you like that."

Lily took the glass of champagne I handed her, sipping, her gaze running over my button-down shirt, open at the collar.

"Me either. I mean, I've never seen you in anything other than a T-shirt. You look... Really nice."

She swallowed another sip of champagne. I put my glass on the table and crossed the distance between us, hooking my arm around her waist and pulling her against me.

Her breath quickened, her face tilted up to mine. Nerves skittered through her eyes, but she didn't pull away.

"Are we on the same page with this, Lily?"

Lily came up on her toes, her weight shifting forward, pressing closer. I'd take that as a yes.

"I'm going to kiss you. If you don't want me to—"

Her arms were around my neck, pulling me down. That was all I needed. My mouth closed over hers, and I kissed her the way I'd been dying to kiss her since the first time.

Making chocolate chip cookies felt like a lifetime ago, though it had been barely more than a day.

Twenty-four hours ago, I'd kissed her against my better judgment.

Kissed her because I couldn't stop myself.

Not now.

Twenty-four hours, and everything had changed. This was the first kiss of many. I was going to make it count.

I wanted to peel that sweater down her arms, to slide the straps of her sundress off her shoulders, to free those round breasts, to feel their weight in my hands.

For a second, I tried to convince myself that Adam was sleeping deeply, and we could do whatever we wanted.

We could, but Lily was tired. She hadn't eaten. My body was ready to go, but it wasn't time. Not yet.

Reluctantly I lifted my head, whispering against her ear, "Dinner. I just wanted to do that first."

She stared up at me, eyes dazed, still leaning into me.

"Dinner?" she asked.

"Dinner. You need food. Lobster, champagne, chocolate. Then more kissing."

"Can we skip to the kissing?"

My cock strained against my pants, voting with Lily.

Forget food.

Kissing. Preferably naked kissing.

My cock was insistent, but it wouldn't be the first time he had to wait his turn.

"Dinner first." Cupping her chin in my hands, I met her eyes and said, deadly serious, "We have time. Dinner first. Then I'll kiss you all night if that's what you want."

Chapter Twenty-One

LILY

"I'LL KISS YOU ALL NIGHT if that's what you want."

I said the only thing that popped into my mind.

"Yes, please."

The grin that spread across Knox's face turned my knees to water and set the rest of me on fire.

He expected me to eat dinner after a kiss like that?

I couldn't *think* after a kiss like that.

I was turned upside down and inside out. The last twenty-four hours had spun me like a top. I was still spinning. When I stopped, I'd get my bearings, but right now everything was still awhirl inside me.

I couldn't forget that arm around my neck, the gun to my head. The bone-deep terror that Adam would be hurt. That the gun would go off and I'd be dead. Then Knox was there, one more person I—

One more person I *cared* about who could be hurt.

The next thing I knew we were at the beach under the

bright summer sun and Knox was declaring himself my knight in shining armor.

I wish I could say I was shocked by his revelations about Trey. I hadn't expected things to be that bad, but I'd known on some level that Trey's business hadn't been above board.

I trusted too easily.

I'd trusted Trey.

Now I was trusting Knox.

I wanted to think I'd learned my lesson, that this time I'd chosen to trust the right man. I couldn't know.

Knowing isn't trust. Trust is in the heart.

The truth is, you never really know another person. Everyone has secrets. The best you can do is go off what they show you. What they do.

By the time I understood that I was already married to Trey. Knox had shown me nothing but good. *What about the cameras?* I had to ask myself.

I couldn't blame him for suspecting me. Trey had done a good job arranging our finances so I looked guilty, and Knox had told me about the cameras, knowing I'd be mad, wanting to be honest anyway. That had to count for something.

Maybe it was the way he'd promised we'd find Adam's birth certificate, promised I wouldn't lose my son.

I'm not a child, and I'm not stupid. I knew Knox couldn't promise me those things. He didn't control the universe. Without those papers, the deck was stacked against me no matter how powerful the Sinclairs might be.

Yesterday he'd looked at me like I was a criminal. He'd told me I might be liable for Trey's crimes. Today he swore he was on my side.

I believed him. Maybe I shouldn't, but I did. Something about Knox... I couldn't not believe.

He didn't bullshit. Didn't charm. He didn't talk fast to get what he wanted. Knox laid it all out. He was who he was. He didn't talk unless he had something to say.

How could I not trust this man? A man who kept his cool through dinner with a cranky five-year-old, and still had the patience to read that five-year-old a book until he fell asleep?

It's one thing when it's *your* five-year-old. I love Adam more than life, and by the time Knox came in, I was ready to smother him with a pillow.

Anyone who thinks that sounds bad has never had a five-year-old.

Now we were alone. Finally alone. And everything had changed.

He took my hand, leading me to the table. I followed, wobbling a little, my knees still weak from that kiss, my head still spinning from everything else.

I sat in front of my takeout container of lobster. It was cold, but it still looked good. Knox set my refilled glass of champagne in front of me and sat on the opposite side of the small table.

I took a bite and let my eyes wander our suite, suddenly too shy to look at Knox. That kiss had my brain all muddled.

I'd heard of the East Street Hotel. On a weekend in July, a two-bedroom suite didn't come cheap. I'm not wealthy, but Trey left me taken care of. I wouldn't take advantage of Knox.

"This room must have been expensive," I said, sneaking a quick glance at Knox. "I'll pay for it when we check out."

The look Knox gave me almost made me laugh. Amusement and impatience warred on his face. "No. You're not a client. Not anymore. Anyway, Alice partly did it to piss off Cooper. I'm not going to ruin her fun."

"Why would Alice want to piss off Cooper? Doesn't she work for him?" I asked, wanting a glimpse into Knox's life.

"I'm not sure if Alice works for us or we work for her. The place would fall apart without her. Alice is with Coop more than anyone. Evers and I like getting out of the office, but Cooper runs everything. Alice is his right hand."

"Is it like a love/hate thing?" I asked, trying to get a picture in my head.

Knox took a sip of his champagne, thinking before he said slowly, "No it's a love/dumbass thing."

"What does that mean? Which one of them is the dumbass?"

"They're both dumbasses. But mostly Cooper. Alice was married until recently, but her husband was a loser and he was never around. Cheated on her. Told her he didn't want kids and then got his girlfriend pregnant. A total asshole. She's way too good for him. Once they split, we all figured one of them would make a move, but so far, nothing."

"Are they going to stop being dumbasses?"

Knox rolled his eyes to the ceiling and the side of his mouth quirked up. "No one knows. We thought about starting an office pool, but if Alice finds out, she'll kill us all. I don't mind pissing Cooper off, but Alice likes me. I want to keep it that way."

"If this hotel suite shows how much she likes you, I don't blame you," I said.

"Yeah, this is partly that Alice likes me, and partly wanting to annoy Cooper."

"Because of how much it costs?" I asked, not sure I understood.

Sinclair Security had a private jet, and I'd seen the cases of surveillance equipment Knox brought with him. It's not like they were running the company on a shoestring.

Knox shifted in his seat, suddenly uncomfortable.

"What? Why would the suite make Cooper angry?" I forked another bite of lobster in my mouth and watched emotions flicker across his face.

"Cooper doesn't think I should be involved with you."

Of course, he didn't. "Knox, I get it. You're trying to figure out what's going on with your dad, and I was married to his partner in crime. I understand why your brother would want you to stay away from me."

"Cooper doesn't get to call the shots. He doesn't know you."

"And you do?" I asked, meaning the question as a friendly tease. It came out dead serious. I'd only known Knox for a week. He didn't really know me either. His next words showed me how wrong I was.

"I know you, Lily. I know you're in a shit situation and doing the best you can. I know you're a great mom, and when something is important to you, you work for it and you won't give up. I know you're kind, sometimes when you shouldn't be. You're patient. Honest. I know you're as beautiful on the inside as you are on the outside. And I know keeping my hands off you for the last week was one of the hardest things I've ever done."

My cheeks got hot, and I found myself staring at my half-empty plate in embarrassment, not sure what to say. That was a lot of compliments.

I thought I was going to say thank you. Instead, I admitted, "I've had a hard time keeping my hands off you, too."

Knox's dark eyes flared with heat. I glanced to the cracked door of Adam's bedroom. He was asleep. I could only cross my fingers and pray he'd stay that way.

Knox in a worn T-shirt and cargo pants was one thing. Drool-worthy for sure.

Knox in a button-down with the collar open? He was so hot he was nuclear. I was a little dizzy at the thought of opening those buttons, getting my hands on all that tanned skin.

His eyes on mine, he said, "Eat your dinner, Lily."

Unlike my son, I didn't argue. I ate my dinner, wondering what was going to happen when my plate was clean.

We finished quickly, pushing our take-out containers aside at the same time. Knox left our champagne on the table but picked up the box of chocolates and walked to my side, taking my hand and pulling me from my chair.

I followed him to the couch, struggling to decide where I should sit—was it too desperate to sit next to him? Should I pick the other side of the couch or get over my nerves and sit right on his lap?

I decided on something in between. I could have saved myself some time. Knox hooked an arm under my knees and turned me, pulling my legs over his lap. I sank back into the arm of the sofa, looking up at him.

I'm not tiny, only a little on the small side, but Knox loomed over me. Taller, broader. Bigger all over. Was he big *all* over? Was I going to find out?

I couldn't tell the difference between nerves and anticipation, butterflies at war in my stomach, my lungs tight, heart racing.

I hadn't been touched by anyone other than myself in years. After the few times I tried to initiate sex with Trey and he wasn't interested, I'd given up. Anything physical between us had dried up a long time ago. Knox was my first kiss since Adam was born.

I lay there, staring up at Knox, not sure what to do next. That was okay. Knox had a plan.

Without saying anything, he pulled a truffle from the

box of chocolates and held it up to my lips. I took a bite, not expecting the gooey fudge center that spilled out. Knox watched my mouth, his pupils dilating as my tongue flicked out to lick my lips.

Hooking a finger in the strap of my sundress, he tugged it down my shoulder. It was the kind with a shelf bra built-in, and with another tug it slid all the way down, baring my breast.

Knox was completely silent, the look on his face so focused, so hungry, I thought I would melt. Holding the half-eaten chocolate between his fingers, he smeared gooey fudge across my nipple.

Holy shit.

He'd barely touched me, and I was ready to explode. Slowly, so slowly, he leaned down, the anticipation stoking the fire between my legs and drawing my nipple tight. He smashed the chocolate between his fingers and pressed it into my hard nipple, covering me with chocolate.

Sparks shot through me, an overload of sensation. The heat of his hand against my breast, the cool chocolate, the wash of his warm breath. His mouth dropping ever closer. So close.

I arched my back, my breast reaching for his mouth, my legs moving on his lap. Restless. Needy.

His face dropped out of my line of sight for an endless moment before his mouth closed around my nipple, sucking hard, licking at chocolate and skin, feasting on me. His hand closed around my breast, lifting it, serving me to him.

His fingers trailed along the inside of one knee, sliding up to touch me where I needed it the most.

I tried to be quiet. I tried so hard, but his name slipped out in a plea, a benediction.

"Knox. Oh, please, Knox."

He lifted his head, his lids heavy with desire for me. His hand on my thigh moved higher. I parted my legs, rolling my hips, inviting him closer, deeper.

"Shhh, Lily."

I sank my teeth into my lip, trying to keep my mouth shut. Anything so that Knox and I weren't interrupted. Anything for more of this. More of Knox.

"I love the way you taste," he said against my skin. "I want more."

"I think that's the chocolate," I gasped, my breath hitching in my chest.

His lips moved against my nipple, sending shivers down my spine, a bolt of need straight between my legs. "It's not the chocolate. It's you."

Knox pulled my other strap from my shoulder. My dress slid to my waist. Lifting my legs, he moved from the couch to the floor, stripping my dress over my hips, leaving me in nothing more than a white lace thong.

His voice rough, he said, "Lily, fuck. I'm glad I didn't know you were wearing this at dinner. I was half-hard just seeing you in this dress."

I laughed, giddy at the idea of Knox getting hard seeing me in a sundress. I didn't know about that, but the sight of him in that white button-down definitely left my lace thong wet. He peeled the thong down my legs, a rush of heat hitting me at being naked while he was still fully dressed.

With anyone else, it would have been too vulnerable. Not with Knox. Never with Knox. All of a sudden, his hand was in front of my face. I blinked to see another chocolate. I'd forgotten about the chocolate. He ran the corner over my lower lip. "Open."

I did and sank my teeth into the truffle. Buttery, sweet caramel melted across my tongue. I let the flavors dissolve, watching as he broke the candy in half and spread it across my other breast.

I thought I was ready when his mouth touched my skin. I wasn't. His lips closed over my nipple, feeding on flesh and chocolate and caramel, his tongue working hard to taste every scrap of sugar and me.

My head tipped back, I stared at the ceiling, every nerve winding tight, wanting to scream it felt so fucking good. So good. Better than my own hands, so much better than Trey even back when he used to try. No one had ever made me feel like this.

Knox's mouth on my breast was so distracting I almost missed his fingers between my legs. Searching, they found me slick and ready. His fingertips stroked over my opening, grazed my clit before painting me with the melting chocolate and caramel, coating my pussy in sweetness.

What was he...? He couldn't.

He wouldn't, would he?

His fingertip slid across my lower lip and I opened for him automatically, sucking hard, an explosion of sweetness and a trace of my own salt. I licked every bit from his fingers, my body trembling beneath him, my nerves, my senses wound so tight I thought I'd explode.

Licked clean, Knox pulled his fingers from my mouth, drawing a line down my body, over my collarbone, between my breasts, across my stomach to dip inside me, filling the tight, slick channel.

I sucked in a gasp at the sudden fullness, almost missing Knox sliding down my body to spread my legs with his shoulders.

Oh, oh, God, he was going to do it.

His mouth closed over my clit, feasting like he had at my breast, but this time, oh my God, this time, I smacked my hand over my mouth, biting into my palm to shut myself up.

The orgasm hit hard and fast, drowning me in bliss. Waves and waves of bliss. Knox didn't stop. He sucked at my clit, licked me, pulling with his lips and tongue until every bit of chocolate and caramel was gone.

Struggling for breath, boneless, I let my legs fall open further, unable to bring myself to move. I thought he was done. Just a second and I'd sit up, finally undo the buttons on that white shirt.

Knox was far from done. Pushing my thighs wider, he closed his mouth over me, his tongue diving deep, licking into me, the stubble on his upper lip teasing my clit.

That mouth. I came again, my body surging up, the orgasm taking me by surprise. His hands closed over my hips, holding me still as I tried to rock into him, away from him. I didn't even know.

My body was out of my control, short-circuited from so much pleasure. I'd never come twice in a day, much less twice in ten minutes.

I didn't think it was possible. I wasn't sure it was. Maybe I'd died after the first time I came. I'd heard of death by chocolate. Maybe this was death by orgasm.

My mind and body disconnected, I looked down between my breasts at Knox's dark head moving between my legs and thought that if I'd died, I must have done something right because this had to be heaven.

Chapter Twenty-Two

LILY

KNOX RESTED HIS CHEEK ON my thigh, his dark eyes seeking mine, satisfied. Smug. Exactly the way I felt.

I didn't have to look hard to see the tension hiding beneath his satisfaction. I'd come. Twice. I'd lay there and let Knox have his delicious way with me.

Now it was my turn. Or his turn, depending on how I looked at it. Either way, I wanted to get my hands on him. My hands, my mouth, everything.

At the thought of pushing his shirt off all that warm skin, of finally touching him, I found the energy to sit up, nudging him back so I could put my busy fingers to work.

One button.

Two buttons.

I was glad he hadn't bothered with a tie. I slid the backs of my fingers under starched cotton, the heat of his skin branding mine, smooth as silk stretched over hard muscles.

His heart thumped against my hand. He was so still, so patient. Restrained. That thundering heartbeat gave him away. Knox was no more relaxed than I was.

Finally done with the buttons, I pushed the shirt off his shoulders and stopped to take in all the beauty that was Knox Sinclair. Oh my God, his shoulders. I'd seen them in a T-shirt, but it wasn't the same.

So much muscle. A little dizzy from the sight of him, I planted my mouth on the hollow of his throat where his pulse beat. Salty and sweet, he tasted so good. Smelled so good. Like soap and Knox.

I found myself sliding off the edge of the sofa, coming to my knees in front of him, my shyness nowhere to be found.

His mouth had been between my legs. What was there to be shy about?

I wanted to touch and taste. I wanted to absorb every inch of him, to feel him shudder with pleasure that *I* gave him. I wanted to take all the joy he brought me and give it back tenfold.

I wanted Knox to have everything. That thought in mind, my hands skimmed over his body to find his belt.

I had it open and his pants unbuttoned with a flick of my fingers. Then he was in my hand, long, and thick, and so hard.

Big. Too big, maybe. After five years, his fingers had been more than enough, and his fingers were nowhere close to the size of his cock.

I wasn't going to worry about it. Knox wouldn't hurt me. Knox would never hurt me.

I wrapped my fingers around his length and squeezed, loving the way he groaned deep in his throat.

Leaning back, I said one word. "Up."

Knox didn't need further explanation. He rose to sit on the edge of the sofa. I hooked my fingers in his pants and boxer briefs, pulling them down as he moved, kneeling between his legs, that long, thick cock right in front of me.

It had been a long time since I'd been face to face with a man's equipment. I'd never been face to face with anything that looked like this. I should have been sated after two orgasms, but my pussy clenched on empty air at the sight of Knox Sinclair's erect cock.

I still wasn't sure it was going to fit, but I absolutely wanted to find out.

Knox's hands closed over my upper arms, not pulling me closer or pushing me away, just hanging on. His lids heavy, eyes dazed, he said, "Lily, fuck, Lily."

I knew what he wanted. It was what I wanted. I flicked out my tongue and licked a long stroke, ending with a swirl around the head. Again. Salty and musky. So good.

His head tilted back, eyes closed, he hummed deep in his throat. I licked again, wondering if he would fit into my mouth.

Only one way to find out.

Parting my lips, I slid them over the head of his cock, sucking hard, taking as much of his length as I could.

My oral skills were not impressive. Lack of practice. From the rumble in his chest, the squeeze of his hands on my arms, I didn't think Knox minded.

I closed one hand around him, squeezing and twisting in time to the movements of my mouth, touching as much of him as I could. I licked and sucked, tasting him, already addicted to the way he moved against me, the hungry sounds in his throat, and his complete restraint. He held on tight, but he didn't push. He didn't demand.

"Lily, Lily, I'm going to—Lily, I—"

I was pretty sure I knew what he was trying to say. I wanted it. I wanted Knox Sinclair to come in my mouth. I wanted him to be mine just as much as I was his.

So many thoughts swirling in my head, so much want and need. So many things I'd never expected to feel.

My head was so crowded, it's no surprise I missed it at first.

A cry. A whimper.

Not from Knox. Not from me.

The second time there was no missing anything.

A tortured shriek cut the heavy air, coming from behind Adam's door.

My blood ran cold, lust wiped away in an instant.

Gently but firmly pushing me away, Knox bolted to his feet, yanking up his pants and boxer briefs as I rocked back on my heels, wrestling the straps of my dress over my shoulders.

Knox beat me to Adam's room, throwing the door wide, light spilling inside to illuminate the bed.

Adam was alone. No man with a gun. No threat. Just my baby boy twisting in his sheets, tears wet on his cheeks, eyes open but unseeing, small arm reaching out, fingers grasping and closing on empty air.

Words fell from his lips, garbled and tangled. I sat on the edge of the bed, taking his hand in mine. "Adam, Adam, baby, it's Mom. I'm right here. It's Mom."

"Mom, Mom, Mom—," he cried in despair, his fingers gripping mine, eyes not seeing me.

Oh, fuck. I hated this.

Night terrors. He'd had them a few times after Trey died. His doctor had told me it wasn't uncommon in children his age and could sometimes be precipitated by stress. What was more stressful than losing a parent?

It had only happened a handful of times, and never since then. I should have guessed that the attack might have sparked them once more.

I pulled him from beneath the covers and gathered him into my lap, wrapping my arms around him, whispering in his ear, "I'm right here, baby. I'm right here."

The bed sank beside me as Knox sat, wrapping his arm around my shoulder, pulling us closer. He studied Adam's face with concern.

"Is he awake? His eyes are open, but—"

"Not really. It's a night terror, like a nightmare, but he can't wake up. It happened a few times after Trey died. Scared the heck out of me."

Almost inaudible, Adam continued to whimper, "Mom, Mom, Mom."

"He doesn't see you?"

"I don't think so. The first time it happened it broke my heart. He was calling for me, and I was right there, but he didn't see me. Couldn't hear me."

"What do we do?" Knox reached out to brush Adam's sweat-damp hair off his forehead, cupping my son's cheek in his big hand, worry spread across his features.

"This," I said, rocking Adam against me. "Just this. Hold him and reassure him until it passes."

"Is this from yesterday?"

"Probably."

Knox let out a heavy sigh. "Lily, I'm sorry. I should've known. I should've stopped it from happening."

"Knox, don't. Don't do that. You told me we can't go back. We could hash out *what if's* forever and it wouldn't do us any good. *If I'd known Trey was involved with the mob. If you'd realized they'd come after us.* Even if you had, who would have expected six of them to attack in the middle of the night?"

"I should have kept you safe," Knox said.

"Stubborn," I said. "Knox, this is one thing I've learned since having Adam. I can't keep him safe from everything. I can try. I do my best. That's all you can do. Try your hardest and hope it's enough. Last night, it was enough. We're here. We're safe."

"Adam—"

"—will be okay. I promise, Knox. He'll be okay." I thought wistfully of where we'd been a few minutes before, half-naked on the sofa, Knox filling my mouth. "I'm sorry about—"

I couldn't bring myself to say what I was thinking. *I'm sorry we were interrupted. I really wanted you to come in my mouth.*

I'm an adult. Talking about sex shouldn't be that big a deal. In the heat of the moment, it wasn't. Now, with my terrified five-year-old cradled in my arms, I couldn't bring myself to say the words.

I didn't need to. Knox's arm tightened around me before his lips pressed gently into my hair. "Lily, don't ever apologize for taking care of your son. Ever. I can wait. Adam can't."

His arm dropped, and he stood, ordering, "Stay right here."

Like I was going anywhere. Knox strode from the room, returning a few minutes later missing his pants, his button-down traded for a well-worn T-shirt.

I didn't look. I swear I didn't look. Okay, just a peek.

Sadly, his erection had subsided. Not really sad, considering we wouldn't be able to do anything about it, but as impressive as his erection had been, I couldn't help but miss it.

I owed him one. Two if I wanted to get technical.

Knox sat beside me again and reached for Adam. "Let

me take him for a minute. You can change into something else. I think we all need some sleep."

Not sure what would happen, I leaned forward, passing Adam into Knox's strong arms. Adam continued to mumble my name under his breath but turned into Knox's heat, pressing his cheek to Knox's chest.

I imagined the thump of Knox's strong heart under his ear, the rhythmic sound reassuring on an instinctive level. Adam's tightly wound muscles relaxed a fraction. Knox dropped his head, his chin resting on the top of Adam's head, crooning softly, "Shhh, Adam. Everything's okay. Everything's okay."

Tears hit my eyes at the sweetness. Adam had a father for the first four years of his life, but he'd never had this. Never had a man read him a story. Never had a man offer him a shoulder ride. Never had a man hold him in his arms and promise him he'd be okay.

I tore my eyes from Knox holding my son and went through my bag in search of the nightgown I'd packed. A stretchy version of the sundress I'd worn to dinner, it had narrow straps, a V-neck, and swirled around my knees. Patterned with white clouds wearing sleeping caps, it was cute and a little silly.

I took the nightgown into the bathroom, getting ready for bed quickly in case Adam needed me. Knox didn't seem to mind cute or silly, his eyes flaring when I walked out of the bathroom.

He stood, carrying Adam. "Is there anything you need from in here?" I shook my head, confused, following Knox as he crossed the suite to the other bedroom, explaining, "My bed is bigger. We'll sleep in there."

My heart melted. Not only did Knox understand that I intended to sleep with Adam, he was going to stay with us.

He held my baby like he was precious, carrying him to bed and laying him between us, taking the spot closest to the door. Protecting us every way he could.

I slid beneath the covers, looking over Adam's head to Knox, his eyes heavy with exhaustion, his arm thrown over Adam, fingers wrapped around mine.

“Sleep, Lily,” he said, his voice rough.

I did.

Chapter Twenty-Three

LILY

ADAM SEEMED FINE WHEN WE woke in the morning. So did Knox, a glint shining in his dark eyes when he pressed a good-morning kiss to my lips.

In the light of day, memories of the night before left me flustered, a little shy, and a lot turned on.

We headed out to breakfast, then back to the beach, pretending we were a normal family on a normal holiday. I didn't realize how on edge I was until Knox's cell phone rang. The conversation was short, mostly consisting of '*uh-huh*'s' on Knox's side before he hung up.

"There's a team at your house fixing the back door and tightening security. Alice got us a late checkout at the hotel. We can go back to the hotel in a few hours, have lunch, and head home. Okay?"

"Sounds good," I agreed, mentally quailing at the thought of going back to my house.

Knox wouldn't bring us there if he didn't think it was

safe. I knew that. The idea of walking through the door still made me feel a little sick.

It didn't matter. We had to go back.

Knox was going to help me search the house. Given his job, I was sure his search would be a lot different than mine, especially since he didn't have to hide it from me anymore.

We were going to find Adam's birth certificate and the adoption contract. Maybe we'd even find the account numbers Andrei Tsepov wanted. Then we'd be free. All of us. Knox, me, and Adam.

What then? I wondered for the first time in months.

Since the moment I'd realized Adam's birth certificate was missing, I'd stopped planning for the future. Without Adam, there was no future.

If I had Adam's papers, and Knox had his account numbers, would that be it? Nice knowing you, thanks for the good time?

I'd only known Knox for a week. It was probably a little too soon to think about where things were going, but I've never been a fling kind of girl.

Watching Knox with Adam, I knew I didn't want this to be a fling. I wanted Knox. I wanted him for me. I wanted him for my son.

I didn't think about finding someone else after Trey died. He'd been gone for less than a year, and I'd had worries about Adam to occupy my time. On top of that, Black Rock is a small town with a very limited pool of available men.

Even more limited when I considered that Trey and I had been the only mixed-race couple in Black Rock. Maine isn't exactly overflowing with diversity. I'd bet there were more than a few single men in town who wouldn't mind a date but wouldn't want to bring me home to their mom's for Sunday dinner.

It was hard enough to imagine finding a man I could love for me. It wasn't just about me anymore. Everything I did affected Adam. Any man I chose had to love him, too.

Too soon, Lily, way too soon. One dinner out, one bedtime, and you're sizing Knox up to be your new baby daddy. First, you have to get past all this other crap. Then you can think about forever.

I was trying to keep my head straight. Really.

I tried not to let Knox dig deeper into my heart every time he picked Adam up and tossed him into the freezing water, every time Adam screamed with delight and begged, "Do it again, Mr. Knox! Do it again."

I closed my eyes as a secret part of me imagined whispering the exact same thing. *Do it again, Mr. Knox.*

I watched my little boy play in the ocean and tried not to think about that box of chocolates and everything Knox had done with them.

Inappropriate, Lily, I reminded myself.

Inappropriate maybe, but I couldn't forget a second of it. Couldn't help but wonder when we could do it again. Not soon enough.

We had enough time after the beach to rinse off and throw our stuff in our duffel bags before we had to check out of the hotel. We made a quick stop for sandwiches, Knox getting another lobster roll, and Adam mysteriously not complaining about his wiggly tooth as he devoured a meatball sub.

One more stop for drive-through coffee, and we were headed back to Black Rock. Adam fell asleep on the drive. Knox dropped his hand to tangle his fingers with mine, and we rode in peaceful quiet all the way home.

When we pulled in the driveway, everything looked exactly as it should. No bodies in the front yard. No blood stains on the dock or the front porch. No visible signs of increased security.

The only thing that didn't fit was the large, shiny, black SUV parked in front of the house. Knox took a long look at the SUV and swore under his breath, "Fuck me," too quiet for Adam to hear, loud enough that I knew he was not happy.

"What? What is it?"

With a reassuring smile, he squeezed my fingers once before he let go. "Nothing's wrong, Lily. Just company I wasn't expecting. Brace yourself."

Instead of opening the garage, he pulled the Land Rover up behind the SUV and jumped out, taking a minute to free Adam from his car seat. Not wanting to miss whatever was going on, I hopped out and joined them as the visitors in the SUV got out.

There were three of them. A man with dark hair and apple-green eyes, so tall and broad he made Knox look normal sized.

I swallowed hard. There was something about him—he looked like he'd been carved from granite. This was not a guy I'd like to piss off.

From the back seat on the driver's side emerged another man, as tall as Knox but not quite as broad, with sandy, close-cropped hair, and a roguish grin on his lips as he said, "Hey, y'all."

Knox shot him a dirty look. "Don't 'Hey, y'all' me. What the f—" A quick catch of the profanity. "What are you doing here, Griffen? I asked for Jackson. Not you."

From the other side of the car came a female voice brimming with laughter. "You didn't ask for me either, Knox, but you got all three of us."

Knox's dark eyes rolled to the sky in irritation. A woman came around the side of the SUV, a little taller than me, with ocean-blue eyes and tousled, chin-length auburn curls. She took the arm of the behemoth Knox had called Jackson. This must be Lucas Jackson, the computer expert.

I didn't have to be a genius to figure out that the woman, whoever she was, was with him. I'd heard him mention Griffen, so it wasn't a tough guess that Griffen worked with them.

"You must be Lily," the woman with Lucas Jackson said. "And you have to be Adam." She held out her hand to Adam. Pleased to be treated like an adult, he took her hand and gave it a firm shake.

"I'm Adam Spencer. What's your name?" Adam asked.

"My name is Charlie Jackson. I'm married to this big guy here." She tipped her head at the giant beside her before turning to me. "Sorry for the invasion. Lucas has been gone for a week, then he came home and walked right into Evers' thing. I wasn't letting him take off for Maine without me. Griffen tagged along to be nosy."

"Excuse me, *Griffen* tagged along to be nosy?" Griffen asked with a roll of his eyes. She laughed again, not the least bit offended.

"Okay, *Griffen and I* tagged along to be nosy. Cooper wanted to come, but he couldn't leave the office."

"I'll bet," Knox said, looking less than happy at the arrangements.

With another wide smile, Charlie went on, "Really, sorry for the invasion. We won't be any trouble, I promise."

"That's a laugh," Knox said from beside me. "All you know how to be is trouble, Charlie."

"That's not true!"

With a laugh that sounded like rocks grinding together, Lucas Jackson squeezed his wife against his side. "It is true,

Princess. But I like you that way." Her cheeks flushed, and she leaned into his embrace.

"The honeymoon is over, guys. Enough of the PDA," Griffen grumbled.

Lucas shot him a derisive look. "That's why you're still single. The honeymoon is never going to be over." Charlie beamed at her husband.

Adam piped up, "Are they gonna kiss now?"

"I hope not, little man," Griffen said. "Let's get this stuff unloaded, just in case."

Knox emptied the Land Rover of everything but the beach toys, dropping our bags on the front porch. "I'll bring the stuff upstairs in a minute. Don't touch it while I park the car"

"Yes, sir," I said with only a little sarcasm. If he wanted to bring the bags up, I wasn't going to argue. I had two beds to make.

Following my train of thought, Knox said, too quietly to be overheard, "I'm staying with you. Why don't you give Lucas and Charlie the cottage?"

I stared at him blankly for a second. He was staying with me? Like, in my bed?

Well, what else would that mean, Lily? Duh.

The real question was, did I mind?

It took a millisecond for my brain to answer with a resounding, *No! Of course not, you idiot. Why would you mind having that man in your bed?*

My internal debate flashed through my mind, leaving me speechless. All I managed was, "Okay. I'll go make the beds."

Knox dropped a quick kiss on the corner of my mouth before turning back to the Land Rover. Adam started to follow him, but I grabbed his hand, leaning down to whisper, "Do you need the bathroom after that long ride?"

His eyes flashed wide as if he'd only just realized he needed to go. Turning on his heel, he bolted for the front door. I raced ahead to unlock it, letting him in before disaster struck.

I was well acquainted with the vagaries of the five-year-old bladder. If Adam was running for the bathroom, I'd better make sure he had a clear path.

It wasn't long before the guys were sequestered in Trey's office, talking business. I probably should have insisted on being there. This was my house. I was technically a client. My dead husband was their father's partner. So many reasons I should have been a part of whatever plan they were cooking up.

I didn't want to. I wanted to let Knox handle it.

This is how you got into trouble with Trey. You let him take the lead. You didn't ask the tough questions.

Knox wasn't Trey. He wasn't.

I know my judgement about men isn't the best. If it were, I never would have married Trey in the first place. I couldn't stop wondering if I was being a fool again. Was I putting my trust in another man who would only use me and leave me worse off than before?

No. I wouldn't believe that about Knox, no matter what my lingering doubts whispered in my ear. Knox was here to help. They all were. What would I have to offer in whatever conversation they were having in Trey's office? I wasn't a security expert. I knew nothing about Trey's business. I'd only be in the way.

I couldn't quite convince myself that letting Knox take over was the right thing to do. But, with Adam curled up on the couch in front of a cartoon, tired from spending most of the day at the beach, and guest rooms to prepare for my visitors, I had other things to worry about.

I could press Knox for details later.

I needed to get organized. I'd have to run into town to pick up something to make for dinner, but first I wanted to deal with the guest rooms.

Charlie tagged along with me.

Chapter Twenty-Four

LILY

"I CAN HELP," CHARLIE SAID, "IT'S the least I can do for showing up uninvited and unannounced."

"I don't mind, you're more than welcome," I said automatically, before realizing that it was true. I was curious. It was clear that Griffen and Lucas were more than co-workers, Charlie more than a co-worker's wife. They were friends. Good friends. I wouldn't pass up the opportunity to learn more about Knox by getting to know the people he cared about.

Charlie trailed behind me down the path to the cottage, her arms filled with folded towels. When the cottage came into sight, she exclaimed, "It's adorable! Is it original to the property, or did you build it?" Under her breath, she mumbled to herself, "Looks original. That roof is gorgeous."

"It was here when we bought the land, and I talked my husband into renovating it. It's perfect, isn't it?"

Charlie followed me inside, taking in every detail from the fireplace to the rustic furniture. She dumped the towels on the bed and circled the room. "Lucas and I flip houses," she said, explaining her interest.

"I thought Lucas was a computer expert at Sinclair Security."

"He is. He's been very part-time these days with the renovations. Things have been busy at Sinclair. I have my contractor's license, so I manage most of our work. I bet this was fun. I'd love to get my hands on something like this. You did a great job bringing it back to life."

"Thanks." A warm glow spread through me at her praise. I loved the little cottage. "Knox thought since you and Lucas hadn't seen each other in over a week, you might want some privacy."

"Much appreciated," Charlie agreed, moving her stack of towels to the bathroom and coming over to help me remake the bed with fresh sheets.

"Lucas doesn't travel often. Not like he used to before we were together, but every once in a while, he goes out of town on a longer trip. This one felt like it lasted forever. Then, just when he got back, Evers' thing happened. He never even made it home. Ran into Cooper in the parking garage. They worked around-the-clock on that, and by the time he got home last night he fell right into bed."

She paused and thought for a second before she corrected, "Well, not *right* into bed but, you know. Close enough."

I thought about the way Lucas Jackson had hugged his wife. I imagined he'd found the energy to make up for their time apart before he'd passed out the night before.

"How many houses do you usually work on at the same time?" I asked. I'd never met anyone who flipped houses for a living, and after my small experience with the cottage,

I was interested to know what it was like to do the same thing on a much larger scale.

I also hadn't missed Knox calling Charlie *nosy*. She seemed nice, someone I'd love to be friends with under different circumstances. The fact was, I didn't know how much of my situation was confidential and how much wasn't. Of the parts that were my story alone, I couldn't think of any I was willing to share.

The uncertainty with Adam's birth certificate.

My bad marriage and the death of my husband.

My estrangement from my parents.

Whatever the heck was going on with Deputy Dave.

It had taken me over a week to talk about any of that with Knox. However nice Charlie seemed, I wasn't spilling my guts after five minutes of pleasant conversation.

Charlie took the bait, and it wasn't hard to keep her talking, especially since so much of her life was intertwined with the Sinclairs. I never would have guessed Charlie Jackson was born Charlie Winters, the youngest daughter in the notorious, scandalous Winters family.

The Winters were American royalty, and the family company, Winters, Inc., seemed to own half the world. I couldn't imagine Charlie Winters needed to work. I was shocked when she admitted she'd been an executive at Winters, Inc. until her brother, Aiden Winters, CEO of Winters, Inc., had called her into his office and fired her.

I couldn't imagine getting fired by my own family. I thought of my father and changed my mind. I could totally imagine my father firing me. He'd cut me off for marrying Trey, hadn't he? Still, Charlie's older brother sounded like he was devoted to her.

"He said I wasn't happy. Controlling jerk," she laughed with clear affection. "I moved out of the family house into this rundown heap I'd bought in the Highlands—even though I had no clue what I was going to do with it—and discovered Lucas Jackson living right next door. Aiden never fails to remind me that I never would have met Lucas if he hadn't fired me."

"You and your brother are okay now? You're not still mad?"

Charlie looked surprised at the concept of holding a grudge against her brother. "Mad at Aiden? Not anymore. That was two years ago. He apologized, and I got him back. Aiden practically raised me. I can't stay mad at him for long."

"How did you get him back?"

Charlie hesitated before saying, "Um, it was a little... immature, but, well, Aiden likes whiskey. Really, really expensive whiskey. He won this bottle of Macallan Select Reserve Single Malt in an auction. After he fired me, when I moved out, I stole the whiskey."

"How expensive was it?" I asked, wondering why she looked embarrassed. How expensive could a bottle of whiskey be?

Another of those hums in the back of her throat. "Between the whiskey and the special edition decanter... Let's just say I could have sold them and bought a pretty nice car."

"Wow." That was all I could say. There was whiskey that was worth more than a car? Between growing up in a town filled with Ivy League college kids and marrying Trey, I thought I knew about life with the upper crust. Clearly, I'd missed some things.

"Did you drink it all?"

Charlie grinned. "I shared it with Lucas. Then I jumped him on my back porch. Totally worth it."

Ending up with a man who loved you like Lucas seemed to love Charlie would definitely be worth it.

Finished with the cottage, we walked back to the main house. Charlie took in all the details of Trey's dream house as we headed up to the rarely used guest room.

"This is the complete opposite of the cottage," she commented.

"I know. Trey, my husband, designed it. He loved it."

"But not you?" she asked.

I refolded a towel, not wanting to think about Trey and how much I hated this house. "The cottage is more my style."

"Then you're going to love Knox's place."

I wanted to ask for more details, my heart taking off in my chest at her assurance that I'd ever see Knox's house. I was afraid to assume too much. *Too soon, Lily,* I reminded myself.

Since Charlie didn't mind talking, I asked, "How long have you known Knox?"

Charlie shot me a shrewd glance over the sheet we stretched across the guest bed. She knew when she was being pumped for information.

"Since I was born. His dad and my dad were best friends. We all grew up together. Knox is like another big brother. We always got along well when I was little. Evers and Axel liked to tease, and Cooper was so serious, but Knox was patient with us little kids."

"I've noticed that. His patience. How much older is he?"

"Ten years. He's Aiden's age. They're tight, Aiden, my other brother Jacob, and my cousins Gage, Vance, and Annalise. They're all around the same age as Cooper, Evers, Knox, and Axel."

Knox poked his head into the room. "You telling Lily all my secrets?"

Charlie laughed, the sound comfortable. Confident. This was a woman who knew she was loved. Knew she had a place in the world. I'd only known her an hour, but I liked her a lot. I envied her even more.

Charlie shot Knox a wink. "Not yet. I'm saving your secrets for later."

"How about you tell her the good stories and keep the bad ones to yourself?"

With exaggerated sincerity, she said, "I can't do that, Knox. I only have good stories about you."

I sniggered. Charlie helped me spread the quilt across the bed and fold it down before she said, "Maybe I should tell her about that time with the spiders when you and Evers and Gage—"

"Not another word." Knox shoved his hands into his pockets, looking a little sheepish. "First of all, I was thirteen. Second of all, the spider thing wasn't even you. It was Annalise, and she was ten. Ten and determined to keep up with the boys."

"Yeah, you guys showed her," Charlie said, skepticism heavy in her voice. Turning to angle Knox out of the conversation she said to me, "They put dead spiders inside her shoes. I was only three, but I swear I remember the screams. She was so mad. It took her a while, but she got them back."

"What did she do?" I gave the pillows on the bed a final fluff.

Knox shuddered. "She hid a snake in my bed."

"She did not," Charlie countered. "She found a snakeskin in the woods and hid it under your pillow. Obviously, I couldn't hear those screams, but Cooper says they were impressive."

"I did not scream. Much. Evers screamed louder."

"That's because she snuck a dead mouse under his sheets. According to Ev, it was pretty gory."

I looked between them, still jealous, but loving that Knox had this sprawling extended family, filled with pranks and teasing and affection. I'd spent so much of my life alone. Isolated. Not fitting in.

Wanting to hear more, I asked Charlie, "What else did he do?"

"Nothing," Knox said with a glare for Charlie. "I was an angel. The perfect child. Ask anyone who isn't Charlie."

"Actually, you're better off asking me. I was only kind of kidding before. Most of my stories about Knox are good ones. Now, if you wanted to know about my older brothers and cousins, I've got plenty of bad stories about that crew."

"You have no idea, Charlie. You're the baby. We all went easy on you. Tate and Holden—Charlie's brother and cousin—are the youngest boys of all of us. They caught hell until they got big enough to fight back."

"And the rest of you got old enough to stop being jackasses," Charlie finished.

"When did we grow out of being jackasses?" Knox asked with a straight face. Charlie laughed so hard she snorted.

"Apparently not yet," she said through her giggles.

Knox rolled his eyes to the ceiling once before saying to me, "Do you have enough food in the house for everyone? I can't remember what there was before we left."

I mentally inventoried my pantry and freezer. There wasn't a lot left in the fridge. Enough for Knox, me, and Adam, but not when I added three more.

"Thanks for thinking of it, I do need to run to town. It won't take me long."

"I'm driving. Normally, I'd say these guys are good to watch Adam, but after last night—"

"What happened last night?" Charlie asked.

"He had a night terror," I said slowly, not sure I wanted to talk about it, and unwilling to be rude to Charlie when she'd been so nice. "He seems fine today, but—"

"You don't want to leave him alone. I get that. Knox is right, we wouldn't mind watching him, but I understand wanting to keep him close. Tate had night terrors for a while after his parents died."

"I remember," Knox said solemnly.

I wanted to ask what they were talking about, but I didn't have Charlie's confidence. Asking felt too much like butting in.

Keeping my questions to myself, I checked my watch and realized we'd have to move fast to get to the store and be back in time to make dinner.

"I'll get Adam and meet you at the car," I said.

Knox nodded, and I started the all too lengthy process of prying Adam from his cartoon, ushering him to the bathroom and into his shoes.

Knox was ready to go when we got to the garage. Adam grabbed one of the coloring books I kept by his car seat and started to draw.

Seeing he wasn't paying us any attention, I asked in a low voice, "Why did Tate have nightmares?"

Chapter Twenty-Five

LILY

I WAITED, WONDERING IF KNOX WOULD answer. It wasn't my business, but I wanted to know anyway. He took a deep breath and let it out slowly, his eyes on the road ahead. Reaching across the center console, he took my hand in his before he answered.

"You know who Charlie is, right?"

"That she's a Winters? Yeah."

"So, you know her aunt and uncle, her cousin Tate's parents, died when she was a baby. Tate would have been about three and a half. Then Charlie's parents died when she was ten."

"They were—" A quick glance into the rearview at Adam, blissfully distracted by his crayons. My voice too quiet for him to overhear, I continued, "I always heard it was a murder/suicide, but there was that movie about it being a cover-up."

"That movie was total bullshit. The police called it murder/suicide. Both of them. But yeah, they were murdered. Tate was too young to understand that part, but his whole life changed overnight."

"Losing a parent is tough at any age, but both? When he was so young? I can't imagine."

"They were all close, which made it worse. I don't even remember spending time with my parents before I was Adam's age. Babysitters. A nanny. My brothers, but not my parents. The Winters weren't like that."

I doubted Knox realized how lonely he sounded when he talked about his childhood. He was close to his brothers, but it wasn't the same as love from a parent.

My parents had walked away from me when I was an adult, but at least I had memories of a childhood filled with love. Especially from my mom.

"You were close to them, too," I said, realizing that he wouldn't have been much older than Tate when the first set of Winters parents had died.

"Yeah. Aiden, Gage and I were pretty much inseparable. I spent more time at Winters House than I did at home. Losing them was..."

I squeezed his hand. "I'm sorry I asked, Knox. I wasn't thinking." I didn't like that I was the reason for that somber look on Knox's face.

"Lily, you can ask me anything." His dark eyes, sad and serious, fell on me for a moment before moving back to the road. I could feel the sincerity in them, the truth. It humbled me.

I rubbed my thumb across the top of his hand, words jumbling in my mouth, nothing coming out.

So much feeling swirled inside me for this quiet man. I was falling way too hard, way too fast, for a man I barely knew. As much as I tried to stop, I couldn't seem to catch myself.

Unaware of the struggle inside me, Knox said, "Anyway, it took Tate a few months to start sleeping well again. The kids—Tate, Vance, Annalise, and Gage, moved into Winters House. It wasn't that big a move. Anna and James' house was part of the estate, and they'd grown up treating Winters House like it was their own. Olivia and Hugh were like another set of parents, but they'd still lost their own. And Tate was so little. I remember hearing Olivia talk about it, but I forgot until Charlie brought it up. I should have thought about it last night, but—"

He fell silent for a moment, his eyes on the trees lining the road as if searching for something in the dense woods. Finally, he said, "None of us likes to think about that time."

"I'm sorry I brought it up," I said, wishing again that I hadn't asked.

"I meant what I said. You can ask me anything, Lily. There's stuff I can't tell you—things about the Winters that are their business, and some of my time in the military is confidential—but I'm an open book for you."

We stopped at a red light, the late July traffic in town slowing us to a crawl. I tugged at Knox's hand until he turned to meet my eyes.

"Me too," I said, wishing I could offer more than just the truth. Wishing I could offer him everything. "I know there are a lot of reasons not to trust me. Trey and your dad. You've only known me a week. But I'll never lie to you. I promise."

Knox pressed his mouth to mine for only a second before the light changed and the car behind us honked. Tourists. No townie would honk.

A quick glance at me, his dark eyes still serious but sweet, he said, "I trust you, Lily."

I wanted to believe him. Part of me did.

Knox drove past the grocery store and pulled into the parking lot of the only pizza place in Black Rock, distracting me from my worries about honesty and how fast was too fast to fall for a man I'd just met.

"What are we doing here? We don't need pizza."

"You don't have to cook for all of us, Lily. It's too much."

"It's not too much." I turned in my seat to face Knox. "I want to cook dinner. The pizza here is awful. Really. Your friends flew all the way up here to help—"

"*Lucas* flew all the way up here to help. The other two are just here to butt in."

"You know what I mean. I never get to cook for people. Trey and I... We didn't have those kinds of friends. Friends you invite over for dinner. And he was gone so much. I love to cook, you know that, but I never get to cook for people. I can throw together something in time for dinner that would be so much better than takeout pizza."

Knox closed the distance between us with a soft kiss on my lips. "You don't have to convince me, Lily. I love your cooking. I just didn't want to dump a bunch of work into your lap."

From the back of the car, Adam interrupted. "Did you kiss my mom, Mr. Knox?"

Crap. What was I supposed to say to that? I don't think Adam had ever seen me kiss any man, even his father. By the time Adam was old enough to pay attention, kisses were long gone between Trey and me.

True to form, Knox knew exactly what to say. With an easy-going smile, he turned to face Adam. "I did kiss your mom. Is that okay with you?"

Adam thought about it, his eyes ping-ponging between me and Knox. Just when I thought I was going to die of embarrassment at being caught kissing by my five-year-old, he said, "I guess it's okay. It's kinda weird, but whatever. Girls have cooties."

"I'm glad I have your blessing," Knox said wryly.

Adam hadn't appeared too concerned, but I knew my kid. If he didn't like it, he would have said so. Anytime Dave got close enough to put a hand on me, even a friendly one, Adam noticed and did his best to separate us.

To Knox, I'm sure he'd sounded like a distracted five-year-old, but I knew we had Adam's approval. I just had to make sure he didn't get his hopes up and start looking to Knox for something more.

Whatever Knox said, I was still a client and we were still a case. We had Andrei Tsepov and those account numbers between us. All the damage Trey had done working with Knox's father. The threat to Knox's mother.

It was all tied to me through Trey. Through my own willful ignorance. Maybe through Adam's adoption.

I wanted to believe that nothing would change once we solved our problems. I couldn't afford to be that naïve. Not anymore.

The three of us made quick work of the grocery store. I grabbed everything I needed for seafood linguine and bruschetta.

We loaded up on sandwich makings and chips, Adam chortling with glee to see bag after bag of junk food dropped into the cart. Knox stopped us in the baking aisle, pulling up another recipe on his phone and tossing ingredients into the cart. Unsweetened chocolate. Sweetened condensed milk. Cocoa.

"What are you making?" I asked, all that chocolate making me think of what Knox could do with chocolate. I'd never be able to look at my favorite sweet again without thinking of Knox and his talented fingers. His mouth.

I missed what he said in my lust fog. "Huh?"

"I'm not making anything. You're going to make salted caramel brownies."

"We still have the chocolate chip cookies."

Knox shot me a sideways look. "Griffen found them while you and Charlie were in the cottage. He has a sweet tooth. Between him and Lucas, we're almost out of cookies."

"Okay. If you think I can handle salted caramel brownies."

Knox dropped a quick kiss on my cheekbone, sending a warm flush through my body. "You can handle it," he said with quiet confidence. I wished I felt as sure.

As I'd promised, dinner didn't take long to throw together. We had enough cookies left to crumble over vanilla ice cream with hot fudge and cherries for an easy dessert.

We gathered around the table of the kitchen, every seat filled for the first time in memory. My linguine was a hit. As usual, Adam picked around the seafood, eating the shrimp but ignoring the scallops and lobster. Lucas made up for it, devouring his first plate while the rest of us were only halfway done. He got up, returning with a second serving, piled high.

Charlie poked him in his very muscled arm. "It's a good thing you're so gigantic. Otherwise, with the way you eat you'd be as big as a house. And not in a good way."

Lucas swallowed before he spoke. "I eat this much to stay this big, smart ass. And you'll have to forgive me, it's the first time I've seen a home-cooked meal in... how long, Princess?"

Charlie laughed. "I don't know, when was the last time we ate at Winters House? Does that count? This Princess doesn't cook."

"No complaints here," Lucas said with an affectionate smile for his wife. "Takeout works fine. Anyway, Mrs. W and Abel would miss us if we didn't show up to cadge dinner a few nights a week."

"That's true." In explanation, Charlie said, "I grew up with a cook, so I never learned how. Then I moved into our place in the Highlands—so much good takeout nearby. Plus, I was trying to renovate the house. I didn't even have a kitchen for the first two months."

"And by the time she did," Lucas filled in, "we'd started flipping houses together. She didn't have time to learn how to cook. Most days she's out the door before the sun is up, and she comes home exhausted. I could learn to cook, but I'd rather spend my free time doing other things."

I did not ask what *other things* he meant, considering the pretty blush on Charlie's cheeks and the sparkle in her blue eyes.

Doing *other things* with Lucas Jackson was probably a lot more interesting than learning to cook.

Maybe I should be grateful Trey hadn't been interested in sex after the first few years. On second thought, nope. I'd rather have spent the last seven years madly in love, getting all the sex I wanted, rather than teaching myself how to make a good pasta sauce from scratch.

"Aaanyway," Charlie said, dragging out the word to cover her blush, "I thought of a good Knox story to make up for telling Lily about the spiders."

"That's okay Charlie, we don't need any more stories," Knox said. "Really."

"You mean a story about Mr. Knox from when he was a kid?" Adam asked, leaning forward in interest. Charlie leaned across the table, almost meeting him halfway.

"Exactly."

"You knew Mr. Knox when he was little, like me?" Adam was enthralled at the idea that his new hero had once been a kid.

"Not exactly. Mr. Knox is older than me. Really, really old. By the time I was born, he was already ten."

Adam's eyes widened as he looked at Knox. "That *is* really old."

Everyone around the table laughed as Knox said under his breath, "I'm only thirty-five." Adam's eyes went even wider. "Really, really old," he whispered in awe.

I bit my lip to hold back the laugh, squeezing Knox's knee under the table. Leaning over, I said against his ear, "Should I buy you a walker?"

"Watch it, Lily," he breathed back. "A little less mouth or I'll have to spank you later."

"Promises, promises," I singsonged quietly, raising my eyes to see Griffen studying us, his eyes serious, but his lips curled in a half smile.

For a second, I'd forgotten we weren't alone. My eyes went back to my son, embarrassed to be caught flirting. Adam was oblivious, bouncing a little in his seat, saying to Charlie, "Tell me, tell me."

"Okay. So, I grew up the youngest in a big family. Knox and his brothers were kind of like my brothers. I was the littlest. I was always trying to keep up with the big kids, and I never could."

Adam nodded sagely. "Sometimes I try to play with the bigger kids at school and they won't let me because I'm too little. I'm not even in kindergarten yet."

"So you know what I'm talking about," Charlie said with an understanding nod. "I guess I bugged them a lot, though I don't know how because I was a *very* good little girl."

A snort of laughter from Knox, who caught Adam's eye and shook his head in a negative. He stage-whispered behind his hand, "She got in trouble all the time. *All the time*."

Charlie let out a huff and looked at the ceiling as if praying for patience. "I'm telling the story, Knox. Not you. And I was a very good little girl."

"Nobody's buying that, Princess," Lucas cut in. She ignored him and continued her story, talking only to Adam and pretending the rest of us weren't there.

"Knox's house was in the same neighborhood as ours. If you wanted to drive from one to the other it took a little bit, but a long time ago our dads figured out that if we cut through some other people's yards, they could get from one house to the other in a few minutes. The neighbors didn't mind, so the bigger kids were allowed to walk from Winters House to the Sinclair's house."

"Were you allowed?" Adam asked.

Charlie shook her head. "I was not. One day, the big kids decided that they were going to leave Winters House, where they were playing video games, and go to the Sinclair's house. I don't remember why."

"Because the game we wanted to play was in my room," Knox supplied, "and you guys didn't have it at your place."

"I should have guessed. An excellent reason to tromp through the woods. To get a different video game."

Charlie rolled her eyes, but Adam looked at Knox and nodded in agreement. He didn't even have a gaming console, but he was looking forward to getting one after hearing all about it from other kids in preschool.

"I wasn't playing with the big kids because they wouldn't let me—" a scowl at Knox, "but I didn't want them to leave because then there wouldn't be any kids around. I can't remember what my mom was doing, but she was busy with Mrs. W and she didn't notice when I followed the boys out of the house."

"Did you get lost?" Adam asked, a little breathless.

"No," Knox cut in. "She got stuck."

"Stuck? How did you get stuck?"

"I haven't heard this one," Lucas said. "What did you get stuck in, Princess?"

"Not in, on," Knox clarified.

Charlie thrust out her chin. "Are you telling the story?"

"You are, Charlotte," Knox said. "Carry on."

Charlie's eyes narrowed at being called *Charlotte*, but she looked back to Adam with a smile.

"The house I grew up in is surrounded by a big stone wall. There are a few gates in the wall, and they all have big locks. I was only six, so I didn't have a key. And since I was six, I never considered what I would do when the boys went through the gate ahead of me and locked it behind them."

"What you should have done was turn around and walk home," Knox said, interrupting again.

Charlie ignored him. "But there was a big tree next to the wall."

"Not close enough to climb over, because my dad was in charge of your security, and he never would have let that happen," Knox added.

Charlie continued to ignore him. "I thought if I could climb the tree, I could get over the wall. I was a good tree climber, even when I was six."

Adam looked at Knox for confirmation. "She was an excellent tree climber," he confirmed. "Too good."

"That might be true," Charlie admitted. "I climbed the tree. I climbed way, way up the tree. So high I could see over the wall, but Knox is right. The branches were trimmed, and there was no way I could get to the other side. I wasn't close enough. And then I looked down."

"What happened when you looked down?"

"I realized how high up I was," Charlie said with a dramatic screech, her eyes wide with surprise. "Then I was too scared to climb down. I was stuck."

"What did you do? Did you have to spend the night in the tree? Didn't you get hungry?"

"I started to scream. I screamed really, really loud. I screamed for a really long time."

"She screamed for like five minutes," Knox corrected. "You cannot believe the sounds little six-year-old Charlie could make."

"They all heard me. My cousins, Vance and Gage. Knox's brother Evers. They all heard me. But only Knox came back to see what was wrong."

"Someone had to see what you were screeching about before we all got in trouble."

"You were the only one who came back," Charlie said again, gracing him with an affectionate smile.

Focusing back on Adam, she said, "Knox climbed up that tree. As far as he could. The branches where I was sitting were very thin, and he couldn't get close. But he talked to me, calming me down until I managed to inch my way back to the trunk. He grabbed me, put me on his shoulders, and climbed all the way back to the ground. Then he walked me home."

"Did you get in big trouble?" Adam asked, sneaking a look at me. I tried to give him my best 'Mom Face' so he didn't get any ideas. The last thing I needed was Adam climbing to the top of a tree and getting stuck.

"I didn't get in trouble because Knox didn't tell. He

made me promise never ever to leave the house by myself, but he didn't tell."

Adam stared up at Knox with reverence. "You rescued her. You saved her from falling out of the tree and then you didn't even tell."

Knox leaned across me to Adam and said, seriously, "She could have gotten badly hurt. I was scared. I would have gotten a grown up if I thought I had time, but I was afraid she'd fall out of the tree. We were both very lucky."

Ignoring the caution in Knox's words, Adam said again, "You saved her. You climbed all the way up and saved the Princess. Like in a book."

"Not like a hero, bud. I never told anyone this, but I was so scared that after I walked Charlie home, I ran for the woods and threw up."

"But you did it anyway," Adam protested. "Even though you were scared. That's what Mom says being brave is. Doing hard stuff even though it's scary. From the book with the frog and the fox."

"Kid's got a point," Charlie said.

Knox shook his head. My heart tumbled at his feet. He hadn't tried to play the hero to Adam, when another man might have soaked up that worship, embellished his role in the story. No, Knox had exposed his own fear without hesitation.

What kind of man was he? Strong enough to take out six armed men on his own. Even stronger to admit when he was afraid.

How could I not fall for him?

I was setting myself up for pain when this was all over.

I couldn't find it in me to care.

I had Knox for now. That would have to be enough.

Chapter Twenty-Six

LILY

CHARLIE AND LUCAS EXCUSED THEMSELVES after helping with the dishes. I used their departure to sell Adam on the idea that it was bedtime. It was a little early, but he needed the sleep.

I tucked him into bed in his own room, hoping he'd stay there. It had been a few years since I used it, but I pulled out his baby monitor and plugged it in. After the last few days, I wanted an ear on him.

He chattered as I tucked him in, mostly about our guests and Knox saving Charlie from the tree. Once he was done talking and I started reading, he fell asleep like he normally did—right in the middle of the story.

I came back down to find Knox and Griffen talking quietly over a beer. Trying to think of what we could do with the rest of the evening, I said, "Do you want to watch a movie?"

"No, he doesn't," Knox said, just as Griffen agreed, "A movie sounds great, thanks, Lily."

The smile he sent in Knox's direction was smug and amused. The side of Knox's jaw flexed as if he were grinding his teeth together.

"I'll make popcorn," I said, "you guys can pick the movie."

I felt Knox's eyes on me as I escaped to the kitchen. It's not that I wanted to watch a movie with Griffen. He seemed like a nice guy, and I was glad he was here, but the only person I wanted to watch a movie with was Knox.

Alone.

Naked.

Forget about the movie, all I wanted was Knox.

That wasn't going to happen. Not yet.

I wanted Knox all to myself, but not enough to be openly rude to a houseguest, even one who'd shown up uninvited.

When I came back with two bowls of popcorn, Knox was stretched out on the couch, Griffen in the armchair. They'd settled on an 80's action movie I'd seen a million times. I handed Griffen his bowl of popcorn and looked at Knox, suddenly unsure how to sit.

I didn't want to be too obvious in front of Griffen. Knox had been affectionate with me in front of his friends, but that wasn't the same as me sitting in his lap.

Knox took the bowl of popcorn from my hand and pulled me onto the couch, settling me against him. He tugged the coffee table closer and put up his feet. I did the same, snuggling happily into his side.

Problem solved.

The movie started, but I don't remember a minute of it. All I could think about was Knox. The heat of him beside me. The hard length of his thigh under my hand. His strong arm wrapped around my back.

A few minutes into the movie, his lips brushed my ear. "Adam go to sleep okay?"

I let out a little sigh as I fell harder. "He did, but I brought the monitor down just in case."

"Good thinking," Knox agreed.

We fell silent, watching for a little longer. Knox's arm dropped, nudging me forward so his fingers could wrap around my hip, his thumb tracing circles, branding me through my shorts.

It was an innocent touch. He had his hand on my hip, not between my legs, but the firm swirl of his thumb echoed all over my body, leaving me flushed and restless.

I was beginning to regret being polite to Griffen. I should have pointed him to the television and dragged Knox upstairs.

Knox's lips brushed my ear lobe. I waited for him to say something. His teeth closed over the soft flesh, his nose nuzzling my cheek. I pressed my knees together, trying to stem the growing heat between my legs.

If Griffen weren't here, Knox could stretch out with me on top of him. I could slide my hands under his shirt, put my mouth all over his chest. Taste those hard muscles. Lick his warm skin. Feel the rasp of his chest hair on my cheek. Unbuckle his belt and push his jeans down—

Knox bit into my earlobe again and sucked, soothing the sting from his teeth and sending a bolt of need straight to my clit.

If he kept this up, I wouldn't make it through the movie.

"Everything okay over there?" Griffen asked. The smirk in his voice came through loud and clear.

"Fine," I croaked.

"Why don't you go to bed, Griffen," Knox suggested.

"I'm not tired yet. I'd rather watch the show," Griffen said evenly. I realized he hadn't said *movie.*

He said *show.*

Meaning us.

The heat of embarrassment joined lust until I was boiling over. Any more of this and I might combust and evaporate.

"I'm your boss," Knox shot out, "and I say *go to bed.*"

Griffen didn't try to hide his amusement. "Technically, Cooper's my boss, and he told me to keep an eye on you, so I guess I'm just doing my job. Why, am I bothering you?"

Knox came to his feet, scooping me up as he moved, snagging the monitor off of the coffee table with one hand and dropping it on my chest.

"Enjoy the movie," he announced flatly.

My cheeks caught fire at Griffen's laugh. I tucked my face into Knox's chest, sure I'd die of embarrassment if I met Griffen's eyes.

"Put me down," I said as soon as I thought we were out of earshot.

"No way. Griffen's going to regret messing with me."

"He was messing with you?"

"Oh, hell yeah. He didn't want to watch that movie. I mean, who doesn't want to watch John McClane? But he'd be just as happy going to bed early for once or reading a book. No, he knew I wanted to be alone with you, and he thought it'd be fun to fuck with me. I'll get him back later."

"Wait, he thinks we came up here to, uh—"

The words stuck in my throat.

What was wrong with me?

You are a grown woman, I lectured myself. *You were married. Why can't you talk about sex with Knox?*

Because it wasn't just *sex* with Knox.

It was so much more than two bodies coming together. My heart was tangled with all that lust. It felt so big. Important. More. So much more than just sex.

My lack of experience and innate shyness only left me more self-conscious.

Knox didn't seem to mind any of it. My lack of experience, or my shyness. He dropped me in the middle of my bed, propped his hands on his hips and looked down at me like a conquering warlord.

"I don't care what he thinks we came up here to do," he said. "I only care about you and me."

"Okay," I whispered, my throat dry with nerves and desire. Knox crossed the room to shut and lock the door. He placed the monitor on my dresser, turning the volume all the way up, filling the room with static and the faint strains of the lullaby playing in Adam's room.

Coming back to the end of the bed, he grabbed my ankle, dragging me close enough to reach the waistband of my shorts.

"The house is secure," he said matter-of-factly, unsnapping my shorts and pulling them down my legs, taking my panties with them.

"Griffen is downstairs, and Lucas will hear the perimeter alarm if it goes off. Which it won't."

Taking my hand, he pulled me to a sitting position. As soon as I was up, he whipped my shirt over my head, my arms flying into the air automatically.

"Adam's asleep. We'll hear him if he needs us."

This time, I didn't need a prompt. Reaching behind me, I unsnapped my bra and tossed it to the floor.

Knox's eyes went black, narrowing on my tight nipples. Rising to my knees, I crooked a finger, beckoning him closer. I couldn't seem to talk about sex without fumbling like a teenager, but I could do this.

I'd been imagining doing this all day.

The second he was in arm's reach my hands went to his belt. "Take off your shirt," I ordered, busy getting his pants off.

"I like you bossy," he said in a growl, complying immediately. He kicked off his pants as he threw his shirt over his head.

Knox stood before me completely naked.

That body. Oh my God.

He was perfect. Every part of him was perfect. Strong and big, with tanned skin and hard muscles, a sprinkle of dark hair on his chest.

I knelt on the edge of the bed and reached for him, my hands on his hips, sliding back to close over his tight, perfect ass.

Squeezing, pulling him closer, I ducked my head and finally did what I'd been thinking about all day. I parted my lips and took the head of his cock in my mouth.

I heard a groan from above me. "Oh, fuck, Lily. Lily, baby."

I'd never wanted to do this before, had never imagined how it would be to make a man like Knox feel so much, to know it was me—my mouth, my lips, my tongue—doing this to him.

I could have stayed there all day, but he brought his fingertips to the sides of my face and nudged me backwards. His cock popped from my lips and sprung back. I gripped him, his hard length pulsing beneath my fingers.

Before I could ask why, Knox said, "I need you, Lily. I needed you before I even met you."

I knew what he was asking. I slid back on the bed, leaning against the pillows, and spread my legs in welcome.

Chapter Twenty-Seven

LILY

KNOX WAS ON ME IN a heartbeat. I was caught in a cyclone of sensation, his mouth sucking at my nipples, moving from one to the other, his fingers plucking and pinching, sending sparks ricocheting through my body.

His mouth was so wet, so hot, so hungry. Demanding. Softening me with his need, leaving me languid and on edge at the same time, the contradiction muddling my brain.

I was a spring wound too tight, ready to snap.

Low moans rolled from my throat. All I could say was his name.

"Knox. Oh, Knox."

Something hot and hard traced the seam of my pussy, teasing out moisture. Not his cock. A callused fingertip circled my clit, and I shivered.

One finger dipped inside. Then two. I was wet. So wet. Ready.

I reached for him. I wasn't above begging. I wanted to feel him inside me. Knox made me wait. He parted my legs, dropped his head between them and licked. God did he lick. And suck. And taste. I couldn't stay still.

I wanted more. I wanted everything. He pinned me to the mattress with hard hands, holding me captive under his mouth, drawing me closer and closer to the edge.

"I need to fuck you, Lily. Do you want that? Do you want me inside you?"

Was he serious?

Just the words sent white-hot bolts of lust arcing through me. I couldn't make the hungry sounds in my throat turn into words.

In answer, I bent my knee and let my leg fall open. That was all Knox needed. He kissed the inside of my thigh, then moved up to bite my hip. I heard the crinkle of foil or plastic.

I hadn't even been thinking of protection. Idiot. I didn't have time to be glad Knox was prepared. He was over me a second later, his weight pinning me to the mattress, the head of his cock pushing inside me, stretching me almost painfully.

I needed him so badly the pain only gave the pleasure an edge. He rocked into me slowly, gently, feeling how tight I was after so many years untouched.

Emotion welled in my heart. I knew what he needed, and still, he was gentle.

It wasn't just emotion. It was love. I wasn't going to lie to myself anymore. It was stupid as hell to fall so fast, but I loved Knox.

I wouldn't tell him. I couldn't. I did the only thing I could think of. The only thing that felt right. I raised my knees, locked my feet behind his back, and surged up, taking him to the root.

His eyes closed, the ecstasy spreading across his face the most beautiful thing I'd ever seen. Those hard cheekbones and dark eyes suffused with a joy only I could give him.

I wrapped my arms around his shoulders, hanging on tight as he groaned in my ear. "Lily I need—Lily I need to—"

I held him with everything I had and whispered, "Fuck me, Knox. Please. Fuck me."

His chest rumbled and his hips snapped forward. I thought I had all of him, but as he fell into a hard, fast rhythm, I realized there was more.

The grind of his pubic bone against my clit, the stretch of his cock inside me, the rasp of his chest hair over my nipples all drove me out of my mind. Out of my body.

The orgasm was a thunderclap, leaving me deaf and blind, boneless and tingling, holding onto Knox, those last few thrusts throwing me higher. Further.

I couldn't breathe, wasn't sure I knew my own name, but I knew the man inside me. When he finally let it take him under, I kissed him.

Everything I couldn't say in words, I said with my mouth, giving him my heart. My fear. My love. My want for him—to keep him with me, to make him happy, to give him anything he needed.

In that moment I didn't care if loving Knox was stupid or reckless.

I didn't care if my heart would end up broken.

I didn't want to protect myself.

I wanted to love Knox.

Knox collapsed to his side as if every muscle in his body gave out at once. He rolled, taking me with him so he didn't crush me. I sprawled on top of him, feeling the loss as his cock slipped from my body.

I knew with a condom it wasn't smart to keep him inside. I wasn't worried about getting pregnant, but until we talked about it—and we hadn't— it was better to be smart about condoms.

Maybe thinking the same thing, Knox eased out from under me, pressing a kiss to my forehead. "Be right back."

He was, slipping under the covers a few minutes later, pulling me back into my half-sprawled position on top of him. He nuzzled his mouth into my hair.

"I love your hair. So soft. When you opened the door that first day, I thought it couldn't possibly feel as soft as it looked, but it's even softer. Smells like the beach."

"Coconut," I murmured. "I use coconut oil."

He was so warm, the thud of his heart under my ear lulling me into a dream of Knox and me. Together.

His hand stroked down my back, tracing a circle over my tailbone and sweeping back up again. When I thought I could form words into a sentence, I asked, "How many of those condoms do you have?"

His laugh rumbled under my ear. A wave of embarrassed heat took me and dissolved when he said, sounding a little embarrassed himself, "A box. I bought it in Bar Harbor. Not that I thought—I wasn't assuming, but—"

I pressed a kiss to his chest. "I'm glad you did. How many do you think we can use in one night?"

Knox hooked his hands under my arms, hauling me up his body and settling me over him, my legs straddling his abs. His half sleepy, sated smile had an edge. Dark eyes glinted up at me as his hand covered my breast, squeezing a nipple between his thumb and forefinger.

I squirmed against him. I'd kind of been joking when I'd asked how many condoms we could use, but with his hands teasing me, his hard body between my legs, and that look in his eye, I was definitely ready for another round.

His cock stirred. Knox wasn't ready yet, but he would be. I pressed my mouth to his, kissing, rubbing his tongue with mine, our breath mingling, hands stroking.

My forehead pressed to his, I lifted my hips and shifted, trapping his hardening cock between his stomach and my pussy.

Oh yeah, I was totally ready for another round.

The scream sliced through the room, severing me from my dreamy arousal. Knox went stiff, his hands tightening on my hips reflexively before he rolled, taking me with him. He was off the bed, yanking on his clothes while I was still trying to get my legs to work.

Another scream and my brain kicked online.

Adam. *Adam.*

No alarm. There was no alarm. It's a nightmare.

Ignoring my clothes, I lunged for the robe hanging on the back of the bathroom door, sliding my arm through the sleeves as I groped for the bedroom door. I had to get to Adam.

Knox's hand closed over my shoulder, pulling me back. Driven by instinct, I tried to dive past him, but he put his body between me and the door. "Lily, wait. Let me go first."

The absolute command in his tone broke through my panic. I held back long enough for Knox to clear the hall before me. He kept a hand on my arm, holding me behind him as he made sure there wasn't any danger standing between me and my son.

Adam was alone in his room, sitting bolt upright, eyes wide, panicked. Like the night before he whimpered, "Mom, Mom, Mom."

Unlike the night before, this time he saw me. I fell to my knees on the carpet, pulling him into my arms. He buried his head in my neck, wetting my skin with his tears, murmuring my name over and over. Knox took the floor beside us, his back to Adam's bed, pulling us into his arms, his forehead pressed to my temple, his hand rubbing Adam's back.

"It's okay, buddy. It's okay. Your mom's right here. Everything's okay. Everything's okay."

I don't know how long we sat there. Griffen appeared in the doorway, probably having heard Adam's screams and the pound of Knox's feet as he ran down the hall. Without saying a word, Knox looked up and nodded. Griffen nodded back and disappeared.

After a while, Knox tightened his arm around me, urging me to my feet, taking Adam so I could get up. Adam curled his arms around Knox's neck, pressing his cheek to Knox's wide chest and letting out a sigh.

I didn't realize I was crying until Knox lifted his hand and wiped a tear from beneath my eye.

"He'll be okay, Lily."

That wasn't why I was crying.

My heart was too full. I was a lost cause. Seeing Knox hold Adam like that got me deep inside. I had no defense against a man like this, one who would hold my child with such tenderness, even after that child had interrupted him in the middle of sex, not once, but twice.

Knox didn't seem to mind. Knox didn't blame Adam. He didn't blame me. He shifted gears and did what needed to be done. In this case, comforting a scared five-year-old boy who'd seen a man hold a gun to his mother's head not forty-eight hours before.

Maybe if Trey hadn't died, Adam would have been more resilient. I wasn't just his mother, I was his only parent.

Knox tucked Adam in on the side furthest from the door, waiting by the side of the bed while I changed into a nightgown.

"You get the middle," he said, holding up the blanket.

I climbed in, wrapping my arm around Adam. He snuggled into me out of habit, his little hand closing over mine as he fell back to sleep. The bed dipped, and Knox got in, his heavy arm coming over me and Adam.

I wanted to say so many things. To tell him I loved him. To say thank you. Thank you for everything; his kindness and the orgasms. For keeping us safe. For being Knox.

I couldn't figure out how to put the words together, afraid it was too much. I wouldn't be able to live with it if I scared Knox away.

I didn't know how long this thing between us would last. I wanted to keep Knox as long as I could. If that meant I kept my feelings to myself, I could live with it, as long as I still had Knox.

Chapter Twenty-Eight

LILY

"DID YOU TAP THE SIDE of that measuring cup?" Knox asked.

Oops. I'd leveled it off with a knife, but I forgot the tap. Obediently, I struck the side of the knife against the measuring cup and watched as the flour fell into the air pockets, leaving me less than the half-cup I needed.

Eventually, I was going to get this right. I scooped flour from the bag again, tapped a few times and then leveled it off. Knox leaned into me, aware of Adam and Charlie's watchful eyes, and settled for dropping a kiss on the top of my head.

"Good job."

I checked the recipe on Knox's phone. One cup of sugar. One cup of sugar? Twice as much sugar as flour? I was working on another one of Annabelle's recipes. If these brownies were as good as the chocolate chip cookies, I wasn't going to question her, but that's a lot of sugar.

Adam giggled quietly. I looked over to catch him shoving a handful of chocolate chips in his mouth, joined by Charlie, who had a smear of melted chocolate on her bottom lip.

"Hey, I need those for the brownies."

"Here." Charlie topped off the measuring cup with chips and handed it to me, keeping the open bag for her and Adam. I dumped the chips into a bowl set over a pot of simmering water. From the other room, we heard Lucas swearing to himself. Adam giggled again.

Charlie rolled her eyes to the ceiling before looking at me in apology. "Sorry, he's not used to little ears."

"It's okay," I said. "Adam knows better than to repeat words he's not allowed to say, right?"

"Right," Adam agreed, the word garbled through a mouthful of chocolate chips.

I kept my eyes on the melting chocolate as I beat eggs together with sugar and vanilla, the recipe taking all my concentration. I knew Knox would make sure I didn't screw up, but I wanted to do this right. So far, my only mistake had been forgetting to tap the side of the measuring cup with the flour. Otherwise, I'd learned my lesson.

Measure carefully and follow the directions.

Lucas appeared, filling the doorway of the kitchen. His size was startling, even more so given that he moved in complete silence. A man that big should lumber like an elephant. Instead, he was a ghost.

Charlie poured him a cup of coffee, sliding it into his hand while tucking herself into his side. He sipped gratefully.

"How good was your husband with computers?" Lucas asked me.

I turned from the stove. "He was okay, but he wasn't a hacker or programmer or anything."

"You sure?"

I looked at Adam, who appeared completely disinterested in any talk of his father. I couldn't tell if he truly didn't care or was pretending not to care in the hopes that we'd say something interesting in front of him. I wasn't sure it mattered.

I wouldn't talk badly about Trey in front of Adam, but the fact was Trey had left us in trouble. Things were complicated enough without me bending over backwards to try to pretend he'd been father of the year. Adam was five. He wasn't stupid.

"Honestly? I'm realizing there's a lot I don't know. I guess it's possible he was a secret hacker, but as far as I could tell, he was good enough to handle online banking, to use a spreadsheet and a word processor, but I never saw him do anything more advanced than that. He couldn't get the TV remote to work half the time."

Lucas nodded and sipped his coffee in contemplation. Finally, he said, "Davis had access to tech he got from Tsepov."

I had no clue what he was talking about, but Knox said, "Yeah. I remember. You think he fixed up Trey's laptop?"

"Somebody did. I doubt it was Trey Spencer."

"Can you get in?"

"I will. I'm almost there. Where's Griffen?"

"Searching the house," Knox answered with a quick glance at Adam.

Lucas followed his eyes to my son, looked at me and nodded. He gave Charlie a squeeze. "Thanks for the coffee, Princess." Then he was gone as silently as he'd come in.

"He'll get it," Charlie said with all the confidence in the world. "No one can keep Lucas out if he wants to get in."

"That's true," Knox agreed. "Once we get things wrapped up with Tsepov, I want to find out who he has working for him. If his hacker is good enough to slow Lucas down, I want to know who it is."

I tuned out Knox and Charlie's conversation, checking the recipe again before taking the now-melted chocolate off the simmering water to cool. I didn't want it hot enough to cook the eggs when I dumped it into my mixing bowl. In another bowl I sifted together the dry ingredients except for the sugar, sneaking a square of caramel for myself.

Just before my chocolate timer went off, Lucas let out a shout of triumph that echoed down the hall from Trey's office. I took that to mean he'd broken into the laptop. Charlie slipped out of the room and came back almost immediately with a wide grin on her face.

"He's in," she confirmed. Now I just had to hope all that effort was worth something.

The buzzer went off and I mixed the chocolate with the eggs, then the wet ingredients with the dry, and poured the whole tempting mess into the pan I'd already buttered and floured.

I slid the pan into the oven and set the timer for half an hour. I still had to make the caramel sauce, but I wouldn't tackle that until the brownies came out of the oven. Adam lost interest in my cooking project as soon as I plucked the bag of chips from his hand and put them away.

"Can I go play Legos?"

He'd clung to my side more than usual over the last few days. While part of me knew how he felt, I nodded, relieved at the return to normalcy. "Go ahead. I'll call you when the brownies are done."

"Don't forget," Adam yelled as he raced down the hall and up the stairs to his room.

Griffen came in, shaking his head at the question on my face. "I didn't find anything. There's a spot under the stairs where the paneling looks a little off." Catching Knox's eyes, he said, "I'd check there, and take apart Trey's desk. My guess is whatever he hid, it's in one of those two places. I looked everywhere else."

"Lucas got into the laptop," Knox said

"He find anything?"

"Don't know yet."

Apparently not worried about interrupting Lucas, Griffen grabbed a cup of coffee and headed down the hall to the office. The rest of us followed. Lucas stared into the laptop screen, a smug smile on his face. "I found the books for the business. The real books."

I noticed a thumb drive stuck in the side of the laptop.

"Anything else?" Knox asked, leaning over Lucas' shoulder to check out whatever was on the laptop screen.

"A file with a list of account numbers."

"The account numbers we're looking for?"

"Too soon to tell," Lucas said. "I can leave the laptop here, I don't need it anymore, but I'll bring everything back to Atlanta and let you know. I need to do a little more digging."

My knees went a little wobbly at the idea that Lucas might have found what they were looking for. If they had the account numbers, Knox didn't need me anymore.

No. I wanted Knox to find the account numbers. I wanted his mom to be safe, his family to be safe.

If Tsepov had his money, he'd forget about me and Adam. I wanted Tsepov to go away, right? Of course, I did.

Then why did I feel so deflated at the knowledge that Lucas might have solved Knox's problem and not mine?

Griffen hadn't found Trey's hiding place. I still didn't have the adoption contract or Adam's birth certificate.

Griffen looked at his watch. "We need to head to the airport soon."

They were leaving for Atlanta after lunch. Charlie had to meet her subs at their latest flip house first thing Monday morning, and there wasn't much more Lucas and Griffen could do up here.

I'd be sorry to see them go. Much less sorry to be alone with Knox, especially since I wasn't sure how much longer he'd be around.

A beep erupted from my phone and Knox's simultaneously. The driveway alert. Not quite an alarm, it let us know a car had turned off the main road and down the long, narrow driveway.

I wasn't surprised to see the Black Rock cruiser pull up in front of the house. Who else would be here but Dave? Knox's hand closed around my elbow when I moved to answer the door. "Let Lucas get it."

I didn't have to ask why. Lucas grinned. "Why? Who's this?"

"The deputy I told you about."

"Oh. Yeah, let me answer the door."

I didn't laugh at the expression on Dave's face when Lucas opened the door, but I wanted to. His jaw dropped a fraction as his eyes scaled up, and up, to where Lucas' head brushed the doorframe.

Dave took an involuntary half-step back before he straightened his shoulders. "I'm Deputy Dave Morris of the Black Rock police. Who are you, and what are you doing in Lily Spencer's house?"

"Lucas Jackson with Sinclair Security. Is there something wrong, officer? Something I can help you with?"

"I, uh, I came by to take Lily to lunch." Dave leaned around Lucas, eyes searching for me.

Lucas didn't move out of the doorway. "Lily has plans for lunch. I'll tell her you stopped by."

"I'm not leaving until I see Lily," Dave said mulishly.

Lucas didn't move. I was a little curious to see how long the standoff could go on, but I didn't know if I'd be in Black Rock on my own after Knox eventually left. It wouldn't pay to make Dave angry.

I pulled free of Knox's hand and moved into the doorway, nudging Lucas to the side.

"Hey, Dave. You working on a Sunday?"

"I'm on call. Wanted to see if you could leave Adam with Sinclair and go to lunch with me."

From behind me, I heard a choked laugh. Charlie. I wanted to laugh, too.

Why did Dave keep asking me out?

What was the point?

Knox claimed he was attracted to me, but I didn't see it. Unless he was trying to get me into bed, so he'd have better access to the house. Knox had said he was searching for something. Either way, it wasn't going to happen.

"Dave, I'm so sorry, but you can see I have company—"

"They work for you. They're not company."

I closed my eyes in a long blink, hoping it hid my annoyance. "Dave, I'm sorry, but I'm not free for lunch, and I told you, Knox isn't here to babysit."

"What is he here for, exactly?" Dave challenged. "This is Black Rock. We don't have any crime. A couple of teenagers messing around isn't anything to worry about, Lily."

He stepped closer, lowering his voice as if he could keep

his words confidential. Ridiculous, considering that Lucas stood right next to me, Knox, Griffen, and Charlie only a few steps away.

Dave could whisper and they'd still hear every word.

"I'm just worried they're taking advantage of you. Convincing you you need protection and running up their bill. You're fine. You don't need them."

Lucas put his arm around me in a show of friendly affection. Dave's eyes narrowed. He started to speak. Lucas got there first.

"Didn't Lily tell you? Sinclair isn't billing her. She's not a client. Trey was tight with the old man. His sons consider Lily's security a family issue, so you don't need to worry about us soaking her for equipment and monitoring she doesn't need. We're here to look out for her. Got it?"

Dave's shocked eyes turned to me. "Lily? Is that true?"

I didn't know what to say. It was the first I'd heard of it. Lucas stepped back and Knox took his place, sliding his arm around my waist and pulling me into his side. I tried not to think about how well I fit there as he said in a low voice, his eyes on mine, "I told you you weren't just a client, Lily."

He'd said that, but I hadn't believed it. I wasn't sure I did even now, but I didn't mind them using that story to get Dave off my back.

Temporarily out of protests—and reasons to hang around—Dave stepped back off the porch, his eyes hard on Knox's arm around me.

"Okay, Lily. You know you can always call if you need something."

"I know. Thanks, Dave."

He threw up a hand in a halfhearted salute before getting into his car, gravel spitting out from beneath his wheels as he executed a jerky three-point-turn and shot down the driveway.

My eyes on the dust clouds he left behind, I couldn't stop my laugh when Charlie said, "What's up with the deputy? Was that weird, or is it just me?"

"No, Princess, that was weird. What *is* up with the deputy?"

Slowly, I said, "He was best friends with Trey. He feels an obligation to look after Adam and me since Trey died."

Knox choked back a laugh. "Deputy Dave has his eye on Lily. And, when he invited himself over for dinner, I caught him on camera searching Trey's office."

Griffen and Lucas' attention sharpened. Griffen asked, "You think he was working with Trey?"

"It's a possibility. If he wasn't, he wants something he thinks is in this house."

The timer for the brownies went off. I ducked out from under Knox's arm and went to pull them from the oven. The others followed me into the kitchen as I set the brownie pan out to cool and started working on the caramel sauce.

From behind me, I heard Griffen say to Knox, "Tsepov may not be in custody for long, you know that, right?"

Knox grunted in response. I'd take that as a *yes*. I hadn't really thought about it, but someone like Andrei Tsepov probably had good lawyers and plenty of money for bail.

Griffen continued, "If he gets out, I think the three of you need to come home. It's not safe for Lily and Adam to be on their own."

"We'll see," was all Knox would say. I understood Griffen's logic, but I didn't like the idea of leaving Black Rock.

If I had Adam's birth certificate and the adoption contract—legal proof I was his mother—I'd be out of here like a shot.

Without that, I wasn't going anywhere.

Chapter Twenty-Nine

LILY

"HEY, DO YOU CARE WHAT happens to Trey's desk?"

Knox asked the question with innocent expectation, but there was a spark in his eye that hinted at destruction.

Did I care what happened to Trey's desk?

Not the tiniest bit.

"Do what you have to do," I said.

Knox nodded and disappeared. He'd spent the day before pulling apart the crawlspace under the stairs where Griffen thought Trey might have had a hiding spot. It had been nothing more than conduit and pipes. Now it was a great big mess.

I didn't care about the mess. I cared about not finding what we were looking for. I cared about being trapped in this house. In this town. I cared about Adam's safety.

Knox could tear this place to the ground, and if he found that birth certificate in the process, I'd rejoice.

After a long debate, we'd taken Adam to preschool the day before. He'd had enough upheaval. He needed normalcy, but neither of us felt comfortable dropping him off and driving away.

Instead, I grabbed us coffees and joined Knox in the car to stake out the church. On a Monday morning, the church was not the center of excitement. No excitement was good but boring. Very, very boring.

We picked up Adam, hit the grocery store for more supplies, and headed home, Knox to tear apart the crawlspace and me to start packing.

Packing for what? I wasn't exactly sure.

One way or another, Knox had promised we'd solve the problem of Adam's birth certificate. I'd chosen to believe him, to push away the doubt gnawing in my gut and believe in Knox.

Once I had the legal paperwork proving that I was Adam's mom, we were not staying here. I didn't know where we were going. It didn't matter yet. We were going somewhere, so I might as well prepare.

I packed in two stages. First, I set aside enough to hold us for a few weeks if we had to leave quickly.

I was still reeling from the sudden attack of Tsepov's men, from finding out what Trey had been into and how much danger he'd landed on our doorstep. Andrei Tsepov was in FBI custody, but no one seemed convinced he'd stay there.

If he got out, we wouldn't be safe in Black Rock. I wanted to be ready for anything. Just in case.

It was past lunchtime when my stomach growled, and I looked at the clock. I'd left Adam in his bedroom, occupied with the agonizing decision of which five toys he wanted to take with us.

If we had to leave in a rush, I wanted Adam to be prepared. I stuck my head into his room to find him frowning down at three stuffed animals, a garbage truck that made sounds when it rolled, and his favorite book.

"The book doesn't count as part of the five, baby doll. Set aside the books you want, and if it's too many, we'll figure it out later. Are you hungry for lunch?"

As if his stomach woke at the sound of the word *lunch*, Adam popped to his feet, wrapping his arms around his waist and doubling over. "I'm so hungry, Mom."

I raised an eyebrow. Leaning down, I pressed my ear to his stomach, pretending to listen. "Uh-huh. Maybe... Okay, absolutely."

"What did it say?" Adam asked, mostly sure his stomach hadn't said anything, but not entirely convinced.

Deadly serious, I responded, "It said that you want broccoli with hot sauce. That's fine, I bought broccoli at the store yesterday, and we have plenty of hot sauce."

"No way! I only eat broccoli if you put cheese on it, and I don't like spicy. Tell my stomach I want something else."

"What *do* you want?" I asked, taking his hand and walking down the stairs.

"I don't know, what do we have?"

"Broccoli and hot sauce," I answered.

"Moooom." Adam pulled his hand from mine and ran down the hall to Trey's office. "Mr. Knox! Mom's trying to make me eat broccoli and hot sauce for lunch. Make her let me have something else!"

He skidded to a halt in the doorway and stopped, bracing his hand on the frame. "What did you do?" he asked in awe.

I hurried my steps to catch up, clearing the doorframe to find Knox sitting in front of Trey's desk, surrounded by scraps of wood. It looked like he'd taken a hammer to the inside of the thing.

Walking around to the other side I crouched and looked underneath. The frame of the desk remained, but the internal structure had been pulled apart.

On the floor beside Knox sat a strongbox, about a foot and a half long, maybe twelve inches wide, and at least 4 inches tall. Trey could have hidden a lot in a box that size. I couldn't imagine how he'd stashed it in the desk.

My heart sped up, my chest tightening, leaving me breathless. Knox caught my gaze and gave an almost imperceptible shake of his head. His eyes landed on Adam, then back on the box, and I understood.

"Lunch?" I asked, doing my best to sound normal. Knox got to his feet with a fluid grace.

"I'm not that crazy about broccoli with hot sauce," he said, "I thought we got deli meat yesterday. I was thinking a turkey sandwich with cheddar and some chips."

I hummed in the back of my throat, pretending to think it over. "You sure? A turkey sandwich is better than broccoli with hot sauce?"

Knox's laugh rumbled behind me. His arm shot out to wrap around my waist, pulling me into him. Lips dropping to my ear, he murmured, "I'll eat anything you make me, Lily. Even broccoli with hot sauce."

Adam raced ahead of us, seating himself at the table and starting a serious discussion with Knox about which books to bring on our trip.

I leaned into the refrigerator to pull out lunch meat and cheese, avoiding Knox's curious glance at the mention of a trip.

I wasn't ready to admit I was okay with leaving. One step at a time.

Knox helping, I assembled sandwiches by rote, shaking a pile of chips on each plate and finishing the meal with sliced strawberries, the entire time my mind fixed on that black strongbox in Trey's office.

I don't remember what we talked about over lunch. I barely tasted my sandwich. All I could think about was the box.

Finally, plates cleaned, Adam took off, his mind made up on three of the books he planned to pack. The second he was out of earshot, I said, "When did you find that box?"

"About two minutes before Adam walked into the room. I need a little time with the lock. I don't want to force it until I know what's inside. Any chance you have a key?"

I pushed back from the table and went to the junk drawer in the kitchen, the central repository for all sorts of stuff we had no idea what else to do with. Including keys. There were extra keys to the house, keys to the cottage, both new and the original keys that no longer worked. Keys to the outlet covers down on the dock. Nothing the right size for a strongbox.

Knox sifted through the bin of keys himself before agreeing that the key to that strongbox wasn't in my junk drawer. I followed him back to Trey's office and watched, fascinated, as he pulled out a small, black, zippered case and opened it to reveal a set of shiny silver sticks. What was he going to do with those?

Clearly, I watched too many old movies and not enough detective shows. It was apparent as soon as Knox pulled two of the silver sticks from the case and slid them into the lock of the strongbox. Concentrating, making tiny shifts in the position of the lock picks, he said under his breath, "Slide the light closer, Lil."

I did, watching as his fingers flexed and turned. He traded out one of the silver sticks for another and went back to probing and turning. The lock popped open.

I'd expected to feel a surge of triumph. Excitement. Instead, my stomach sank, heavy with dread. What if it wasn't there? What if we didn't find it?

Knox lifted the lid, and despair was shoved out by a surge of hope. Legal size envelopes. Documents. Knox shuffled through them, holding up a hand when I reached out.

"I know you want to see what's here, but give me a sec."

I let my hand fall to my side with a low grunt of frustration, ignoring the quirk of Knox's lip at the sound. He wouldn't think it was so funny if our positions were switched and I was hogging all the newly discovered...whatever it was.

Trey had hidden a strongbox in his desk, hidden it so thoroughly Knox needed to tear the thing apart to get to it. What had he put in there? And why?

Knox held up an unsealed, white, rectangular envelope and shook out the contents. A piece of paper with handwritten notes and two documents, 8.5 x 11, identical in almost every way, from the watermarked red and white paper to the state seal on the bottom corner.

Issued by the state of Alabama, both of them showed Adam Michael Spencer, Adam's birthdate and Trey Carlisle Spencer as the father. One birth certificate had the mother's name scratched out, the ink completely scraped off the heavy paper. The other certificate listed me.

I stared at the two documents, completely nonplussed. Two? My voice sounded thin and weak to my own ears as I asked, "Is one of those a fake? They can't both be legal."

Knox held them up to the desk lamp, studying the weight of the paper and the impressions left by the seal.

After a few minutes, he lay them on top of the desk, side-by-side.

"My lawyer in Atlanta has some experience with family law. What he doesn't know he can refer out. I'll ask him to look into this. These both look legitimate. I think when you adopt a second certificate is issued. The good news is that you have a birth certificate—"

"—the bad news is, it might not be the one on file with the state," I finished.

Knox slipped both birth certificates back into the envelope and examined the other piece of paper, the hand-written notes in a kind of shorthand that didn't make any sense to me. L.G. Who was L.G., and what did they have to do with Adam's birth mother?

Knox ran his finger down the neat lines of notes, stopping on one to murmur, "LeAnne Gates. Son of a bitch."

He moved his finger back to the top and started again, clearly seeing something in the numbers and notes that I didn't. When he was done, he said, "Payments. L.G. LeAnne Gates. The dates on these—he was still paying her when he died."

I had no idea what to make of that. My head spun, new information swirling in a whirlwind. I tried to reach out and grab bits and pieces, to assemble them into some kind of pattern that made sense.

If even one of those birth certificates was accurate then Trey was, in fact, Adam's biological father. Ongoing payments to LeAnne Gates filed with the birth certificate meant they went together. The birth certificate was missing the mother, but the payments... LeAnne Gates had to be Adam's mother. Why else was he paying her?

What if she hadn't wanted to give him up? The idea that Trey might have taken Adam from her was a stab to my heart. I felt it as a physical pain, stealing my breath. I leaned over, clutching my fist to my chest, struggling for air.

I couldn't give up my son. But what if he wasn't mine? What if she missed him? Mourned for him?

"Hey, hey, Lily, talk to me. Talk to me, baby."

Knox pulled me into his lap, wiping tears from my wet cheeks with the side of his thumb.

"Lil, Adam's upstairs. You don't want him to see you crying. What's wrong? Are you upset about this stuff? The birth certificates and the payments? We have a certificate with your name on it and a place to start looking for the rest. Now I know what we're dealing with. This is good news. This is progress."

"What if—" My throat locked on a sob of anguish. "But what if—" I swallowed hard. "What if she didn't want to give him up? What if she wants him back? She's his biological mom and if she wants him back—"

"No, no, baby. First of all, LeAnne Gates isn't Adam's mother. She's over sixty. But she should be able to tell us what happened. And even if her name is the one scratched out, I guarantee you, there is no way LeAnne fucking Gates wants Adam."

I barely registered his arm squeezing me to his chest as his words penetrated the panic in my heart.

Knox knew her.

He'd recognized her name. That's what he meant when he said, *'Now I know what we're dealing with.'*

Afraid to hope, afraid to let go of fear, I whispered, "How do you know? Maybe she loved Trey. I know he was having affairs. Maybe she thought he was going to leave me, that Adam would bring them together. Maybe—"

"No, Lil. I promise you. I know who LeAnne Gates is. She doesn't want Adam. Likely she sold him to Trey."

Sold him? My jaw dropped and I stared at Knox, speechless. *Sold him?*

Knox sat back, wiping my cheeks again. "You know my father and Trey were involved in adoptions involving large amounts of money, right?" I nodded. I wasn't exactly sure what that meant, but he'd mentioned it.

Knox continued, "We haven't untangled the whole thing yet, but we know there were women they paid to act as surrogates. We've dealt with LeAnne before, and that woman doesn't have a maternal bone in her body. Believe me, the only thing she sees in any child is a paycheck."

"I can't—"

Knox lifted a hand to cup my cheek, pulling me in for a soft kiss. Against my lips, he murmured, "No, you can't, Lily. You will never understand a woman like LeAnne Gates. You don't have it in you."

He leaned back, sliding his hand across my shoulder, down my arm, to thread his fingers with mine.

"This is good news, Lily. I doubt LeAnne Gates has any rights to Adam, but she can tell us who might. She will. All we have to do is wave enough money in front of her and she'll give you anything you want."

I let out a long breath. Only one good thing had come from my disastrous marriage to Trey.

Adam.

Once I'd learned what Trey had been up to, I'd seen the money he'd left me as a curse. I'd need some of it to get started in a new life. I wasn't sure I wanted the rest. But for this? To secure Adam's safety?

I'd spend every penny if I had to.

I'd never imagined my problem could be solved with

something as simple as money. But then, money is only a simple answer when you have it.

"So, we go see this LeAnne Gates?" I asked.

"I'd like to talk to our lawyer first. But then, yeah, I think we go see LeAnne Gates."

I nodded, my eyes falling on the still mostly full strong box. "So, if we have the birth certificate, and we have evidence of payments to LeAnne, what's the rest of this stuff?"

"I don't know, let's find out."

Chapter Thirty

LILY

KNOX PULLED OUT ANOTHER LARGE, white envelope and checked the contents. More notations like those he'd said indicated payments to LeAnne Gates, but if the notes listed the recipient, neither of us recognized who it was.

Knox set it aside and picked up another envelope, this one manila, sealed shut with two folded-down aluminum prongs. Nothing was written on the front or back to indicate what might be inside.

Knox pulled out three sheets of paper. The first was a receipt that appeared to come from an auction house in New Jersey. Trenkley Auctions. I'd never heard of it, but I recognized the item in the photograph.

A small, dark blue box with gold detailing, a frame of sparkling faceted stones running along each edge of the lid, a larger stone on each corner.

In the center of the lid more sparkling stones surrounded a miniature oil portrait of a bearded man from another age. I didn't know enough about art or history to place the box, but his dress wasn't modern. Nothing about the small box was modern.

Until this moment, I'd completely forgotten about it.

It used to be right here in Trey's office, on the table beneath the window by the armchair. When had it disappeared? When Trey was alive, I didn't come in here much. Seeing the box in the grainy photograph on the receipt, I realized I hadn't seen it in over a year, maybe more.

Knox ran his finger around the frame of the image. "Holy shit. I wondered what happened to this."

"What do you mean? That was Trey's. He used to keep it in here and—"

Knox's eyes sharpened on my face. "And? Do you remember when he got it? When it disappeared? Are you sure it's not here anymore?"

Flustered, I tried to think. "When he got it…um, Adam was still a baby. He put it on that table."

Knox and I both looked at the table across the room. An antique, the three-legged side table had a circular top of polished wood. It held a lamp aimed at a small oil painting on a stand. Nothing else. The spot where the box had been was empty.

"Three years ago sound right?" Knox asked, his finger on the date at the top of the receipt.

"Yes, that's around when I first saw it. I don't know when it disappeared. It would have to be before he died because I didn't do anything with it. I forgot about it until I saw that picture. How do you know what it is?"

"It used to be my father's. And this—" He pointed to the amount at the bottom of the receipt.

$39,872.56 Almost forty thousand dollars. Wow. Maybe the sparkly stones on the top had been real.

"This—" Knox tapped that number again, "is way fucking off."

"Too much?" I asked.

Knox's laugh had a tinge of bitterness. "No. Way too fucking little. Do you know what this is?"

"An ugly box?" I asked, trying to cut the mood with a joke. Knox's eyes crinkled at the corners when he shook his head.

"It's not the prettiest thing I've ever seen, I'll give you that. It's also Faberge. And not just Faberge. It's Imperial Faberge. See this guy?"

He tapped his finger on the photograph of the miniature portrait on the top of the box. A man stared back at us, with a neatly trimmed beard, an impressive mustache, and hard eyes. A row of medals decorated his formal red jacket.

"This guy was the Emperor in his military uniform. Faberge designed it specifically for his birthday."

Faberge? Imperial Faberge? As in, that ugly little box had belonged to an Emperor of Russia? And Trey just put it out on the table in his office with a toddler walking around? I looked back at the receipt. $39,872.56. *That* was underpriced?

"How much is it worth?"

"In today's market? I don't know exactly, but when my dad had it, he told me the last Imperial Faberge snuff box that sold at auction was in the UK. It went for well over two million pounds and that was more than a decade ago. This one? Hard to say. The art market changes all the time. A fuck ton more than forty thousand dollars. At least a few million US."

Knox set the receipt aside, scanning the two pages that had been in the envelope beneath it.

"Motherfucker." His fingers stabbed the lines of numbers. "Recognize these?"

"No. Should I?"

"Those are the account numbers Lucas found on Sunday. He's still trying to track them down."

"What does this mean? This is your dad's box? How did Trey end up with it?"

"No fucking clue. My guess?"

"Yeah?" I was glad Knox had a guess because I was all out.

He traced his fingers down the lines of numbers, then looked back at the receipt. "My guess would be that my dad was supposed to give Trey part of what's in those accounts. Instead of giving Trey his share of the cash, he gave him this, selling it through the auction house."

"The auction house was in on it? Like money laundering?" I asked, trying to wrap my head around what Knox proposed.

"Exactly like money laundering. But Trey didn't get the provenance because they didn't represent it properly in the auction. And if he didn't get it from my dad, it's probably because my dad never had it in the first place. I'll have to check with my brothers, but I'd bet this box originally belonged to Sergey Tsepov."

"If we knew where it was you could offer it to Tsepov to get him to leave you alone. There's no clue in there as to what Trey did with it?"

"Nope."

"Crap." So far, Trey's strongbox was filled with more questions than answers.

Knox returned the auction receipt to the envelope, resealed it with the little silver prongs, and placed it on top of the envelope holding Adam's birth certificates.

Beneath that were more loose papers, documents, a wad of cash wrapped in a paper band as if it had come from the bank. Knox flipped through and murmured under his breath, "About twenty grand."

What the hell, Trey?

Why was twenty grand sitting in a box in his desk? Knox tucked the money into the side of the box and lifted out another manila envelope, again sealed with two silver prongs, this one bulging in the center. Knox opened it and out slid a stack of letters.

All of them had been opened, the tops of the envelopes jagged and torn. Knox turned over the first. My heart stopped when I saw the address in the upper left corner.

Rose Adams.

Hanover, New Hampshire.

My mother. The letter was addressed to me. I snatched it up, checking the date. A month after my wedding. My mom had written me a letter?

Knox flipped through the rest of the envelopes. He reached the end and handed them to me in a stack. "All addressed to you. Based on the postmarks, they stopped coming a year ago."

My hands shaking, I pulled the letter out of the first envelope.

> *Lily,*
>
> *Your father and I received your wedding announcement. I wish that I could tell you I was happy for you. I can't. I can't help but feel this is a terrible mistake.*
>
> *I know what your father said, but if you want to come home, if you ever need to come home, I'm here.*
>
> *I hope things with Trey work out.*
>
> *Love,*
>
> *Mom.*

It wasn't an apology for kicking me out, but it was far more than I'd expected. Hands shaking, eyes blurred with tears, I slid the letter back into the envelope and turned it facedown on the desk. Knox watched over my shoulder as I opened the second envelope, postmarked a few months later.

> *Lily,*
>
> *I hope you're well. I haven't heard from you. I know we parted on unpleasant terms, and I know I was vocal about my unhappiness over your marriage.*
>
> *What's done is done. I miss you. I understand if you don't want to visit, but please write or call. I've never gone this long without seeing my little girl.*
>
> *Love,*
>
> *Mom*

"You didn't know she wrote?" Knox asked quietly.

My throat tight with the tears streaming down my cheeks, I shook my head.

My father had told me not to come home if I married Trey. I thought he'd meant it. Maybe he did. Clearly, my mom felt differently.

At the thought of her beating back her fierce pride and reaching out, then getting no response, I choked on a sob.

My mother was bold, strong, and, much like my dad, she hated to admit when she was wrong. She must have missed me terribly to write these neutral, vaguely apologetic letters. I placed the second one on top of the first and opened the next letter, dated almost three years after my marriage.

Dear Lily,

You haven't written me back. You must think I deserve that after the way your father and I behaved when you got married. Maybe I do.

Your life is yours to live. Someday, if you have a child yourself, you'll understand the overwhelming need to protect and how it can be so misguided. My own parents never spoke to me again after I married your father. I missed them every day.

I'm ashamed that we did the same thing to you.

I was wrong to let your father throw you out.

I was wrong not to come after you.

I won't intrude on your life by showing up where I'm not wanted, but please know, Lily, your father and I miss you so much. Please forgive us.

Love,

Mom

I slid the letter back into its envelope and spread the first two letters out on the desk in front of me. Both the same address, the place we'd lived when we first married. The third letter came to our address in Black Rock.

How would she have known? Every letter had been opened and read by my dead husband. He'd known how deeply I'd grieved the loss of my family and yet he'd hidden these letters. Why would he do that to me?

I worked my way through the rest of the letters, tears streaming from my eyes as my mother grew more and more desperate in her pleas. The final letter began,

My dearest Lily,

I would give anything to hear your voice again. I received your letter. It's not like the woman I know

to be so unforgiving. We were wrong. We want to make amends. Please reconsider and accept our apology.

As you've asked, this will be the last time I write. I love you. Your father loves you. We want nothing more than to see you again. We were wrong in so many ways. Don't make us pay for the rest of our lives.

All my love, always,
Mom

"I never—" I couldn't finish the words. I'd never written to my mother. Trey must have—

I closed my fingers around the letter and gave into the sobs clawing at my throat. All these years, I'd hated myself for not being good enough, hated them for not loving me anyway.

I'd stayed with Trey in part because leaving would be admitting I'd sacrificed my family for nothing. I'd stayed because I thought I had nowhere to go. No one who wanted me.

As soon as that thought crossed my mind, I knew why Trey kept the letters from me. As long as I only had him, I'd stay. Trey had given me Adam when he had no interest in being a father because a child would tie me to him.

Why? I would have sworn he didn't love me anymore. Why not let me go?

I didn't have the answer for that. I probably never would. Trey never did like for anyone else to play with his toys. Maybe it was as simple as that. He didn't want me, but he didn't want anyone else to have me either.

I clutched the last letter in my hand, turning my face into Knox's broad chest, and bawled like a child. I cried for the lost years, for my mother's broken heart and my own. For all the time I'd wasted married to a man who'd given me my son but broken my heart over and over.

Knox held me on his lap, rubbing my back, surrounding me with strength. When my tears tapered off, he said, "Do you want to go see them?"

I nodded into his shirt. When I thought I could speak, I whispered, "Soon. Not yet, but soon."

"Then we'll go. As soon as you're ready, we'll go," Knox promised.

As soon as I was ready.

My mother's final letter crumpled in my fisted hand, I thought *Now* and *Never*. All these letters from my mother, and nothing from my father. It didn't matter.

I couldn't get my bearings. Too much was changing. Everything I thought I knew was wrong.

Eventually, I got off Knox's lap and pretended to function like a normal person. I went through the rest of the day in a haze, packing without thinking, my mind on those letters.

On Trey.

On Knox and LeAnne Gates.

On the Faberge snuff box worth millions that Trey had left sitting on a table like it was just another knick-knack.

I was looking into a fun house mirror reflection of my life, and I recognized nothing. Knox, seeing my distraction, put Adam to bed while I was still shoving things into boxes in my closet.

He joined me in my room, closing and locking the door, setting the monitor on the dresser with the volume turned up, the sounds of a lullaby drifting through the room in crackly, ghostly notes.

I didn't want to talk. I didn't want to think. I just wanted Knox. Knox, who hadn't lied to me. Not really.

Knox, who hadn't hurt me. Knox, who'd done nothing but protect me, body and heart.

I didn't know how to say how grateful I was. I knew how to show it. I pushed him back on the bed and climbed on top, straddling his hips, my hands desperate, yanking at his shirt, trying to pull it over his head.

He stopped me, his fingers braceleting my wrists, and met my eyes, searching for something. He must have found it because he released my hands and cupped my face in his.

"Lily, everything's going to be okay. I promise."

I gave a jerky nod, words piling up and tangling behind my tongue. I didn't know what to say, how to say it. I tugged on his T-shirt again. Knox did a half-curl off the mattress, reaching behind his neck to tug his T-shirt over his head. He tossed it to the floor and cupped my face in his hands one more time.

"Do what you have to do, Lily. I'm yours."

That was all I needed to hear. I unleashed all of my confusion, my hurt, my love, my pain, my need, and gave it all to Knox.

Tasting him, licking and sucking, kneading his muscles with my fingertips, guiding him inside me and riding until he arced beneath me. Taking my own pleasure and giving him his.

When we were done, Knox rolled out of bed to take care of the condom, coming back with a warm, wet washcloth. I tried to take it from him, but he evaded my grasping hands with a firm, "Lay still. Let me do this."

Drained from my orgasm and the frenzy of emotion, I lay there, body soft, the upheaval in my heart finally quiet. When he was finished, Knox slid under the sheets to curl his body around mine. His arm wrapped around my chest, and I held on with everything I had, Knox the only anchor I trusted in a world turned upside-down.

Chapter Thirty-One

KNOX

I WAS ON THE PHONE WITH my lawyer when the driveway alarm beeped. Opening my laptop, I flipped to the camera that covered the drive.

A fucking Black Rock cruiser. When would this guy give up?

"Got a visitor, I'm going to have to call you back."

"Don't worry about it, Knox. I'll call you when I've got something together."

I disconnected and stood, beating Lily and Adam to the door. It was early, almost time to leave to take Adam into preschool. I knew normalcy was important, but I didn't like the idea of taking him to preschool.

My instincts told me to hold Adam and Lily close, to guard them against any threat.

So many balls in the air, most of them a threat to Lily and Adam in one way or another. I couldn't let my feelings cloud my logic. That would only put them in more danger.

I was still tempted to bar the door and keep everyone out, including Deputy Dave. Unfortunately, Lily was more civilized than me.

"It's Dave," she said unnecessarily, reaching for the handle. I shut down my need to stop her, instead standing behind her with my hand on her shoulder, marking my territory. If I couldn't do it in a more primitive way, I'd settle for this.

Lily swung open the door to reveal Dave holding a bag from the town's doughnut shop, the white paper stained with splotches of grease, the scent of fresh donuts drifting in the door. Out of nowhere, Adam raced to join us, skidding to a stop and yelping with delight at the sight of the doughnut bag.

"Are those for us?" Before Deputy Dave could answer, Adam screeched again and snatched the bag from his hands, darting for the kitchen.

Lily exclaimed in a familiar, exasperated tone, "Adam! I'm so sorry, Dave. Do you want to come in, have some coffee?"

I almost felt sorry for the guy, watching the way his face fell as whatever plan he'd concocted was torn to shreds by Adam's donut theft and my proprietary hand on Lily's shoulder.

My pity dissolved as Dave's forlorn expression melted into something darker. Eyes hard, he stared at my fingers where they touched Lily. I pulled her into the shelter of my body, resisting the urge to shove her behind me.

She wouldn't appreciate that level of protection, and Dave wasn't enough of a danger to justify it. That didn't mean I wasn't ready to act if I needed to.

Lily stepped back a little, holding the door open. "Dave? Did you want to come in for coffee?"

"I don't think so," he spat out, trying to glare at me and ending up looking squinty. "Didn't take you long, did it? Do you know how many months I've been working on her? Close to a fucking year. She's got her legs crossed so tight nobody gets in there. I'm not surprised they had to adopt Adam. She's so fucking frigid she's ice cold."

I was in motion before the last of his words registered. Swinging Lily behind me, I lunged, my fingers sinking into the collar of Deputy Dave's uniform shirt as I tossed him out the door, catching him with a roundhouse punch on his way. He landed in a heap, blood dripping from the corner of his mouth.

So much for not letting feelings cloud my logic.

"Get the fuck out," I said. "Unless you have a legal reason to be here you aren't welcome on Lily's property. Got me?"

Dave's eyes overflowed with bitter venom. He said nothing, wobbling to his feet, backing up before he turned and headed for his cruiser. Behind me, Lily breathed, "Knox, what have you done?"

Without turning around, my eyes on the cruiser backing out of the drive, I said, "Nobody talks about you like that. Ever."

"But he's a deputy. You could get in trouble—"

"I'd like to see him try."

She wasn't wrong, and I knew it.

I'd hit a cop without justifiable provocation. Any man—hell, any woman—would understand why I'd thrown a punch and tossed him out of the house. That didn't mean I wouldn't have a problem if he pressed charges.

Deputy Dave was exactly the kind of douche who would press charges over a punch he knew he fucking had coming.

I ushered Lily back into the house, closing and locking the door behind me. We had Adam's birth certificate. My lawyer was working on getting a copy of the certificate on file with the state, as well as putting together whatever legal papers we'd need to get the surrogate to relinquish any claim to Adam, once we paid LeAnne Gates to tell us who she was.

It was time to get out of Black Rock. I dug my phone out of my pocket to call Cooper. He answered with a rushed, "Good timing. I was about to call."

"What happened?"

"Tsepov walked. Twenty minutes ago. His lawyer convinced the judge he isn't a flight risk, got the judge to grant bail, and he's out. We had men on him, but he lost them. You three need to move."

"Perfect timing because I just punched out the local cop."

"Fuck, Knox. What did he do, talk shit about your girlfriend? Griffen said he wanted a piece of her."

"No comment."

I expected a scathing retort, but Cooper laughed. "I'll send the plane."

Thinking quickly, I said, "Find a strip near Hanover, New Hampshire. Worst case we can go out of Logan in Boston, but if you can find someplace near Hanover, that would be better."

"Hanover? Got it."

"Tomorrow. We'll want to spend the night."

Hanover was the best option for so many reasons. We couldn't leave New England without seeing Lily's parents now that we'd found those letters, and Lily's parents' house was the last place Deputy Dave would look for us. As far as he knew, Lily hadn't spoken to them in years.

"Keep me posted," Cooper said and hung up.

Lily's eyes were wide with panic. "Hanover?" she asked, her voice wobbling, thin and uncertain.

"Hanover," I said. "Hanover, and then Atlanta. You want to see them before we leave, don't you?"

If she didn't, I'd call Cooper back, and we'd change our plans. Lily had been through enough. If she wasn't ready, we'd wait.

She sagged against me. "I do. I do, so much. I'm just—I'm scared. What if—"

I slid my arms around her. The hits kept coming. Everything she'd learned about Trey, her fears for Adam, the letters from her mother, Deputy Dave's harsh words after she'd considered him a friend. So much I couldn't shield her from.

"The longer you put it off, the harder it will be. If it doesn't go well, we're out of there, okay? I promise."

She nodded, her forehead brushing my chest. "Tsepov got out of jail?"

"We knew that might happen."

"I know. We're mostly packed. Any idea how long we'll be gone?"

How to answer that question? I could take the easy way out—shrug and say a week or two. Or, I could lay it out, tell her how I felt and let the chips fall.

I put my hands on her shoulders. "Do you want to come back?"

Lily's mouth opened to answer, but nothing came out. I pushed my advantage.

"I want you and Adam to come to Atlanta. I want you and Adam with me, in my house, but if that's too much, I can find you a place. Between Jacob's building and Charlie, I'll find you a place."

"You want us with you?" Her question was barely more than a whisper.

"If it's up to me I'd say bring everything you can pack, hire someone to do the rest, put the house on the market, and don't come back."

Light bloomed in Lily's eyes. "How can you be so sure?"

I brushed her cloud of curls back from her face, cupping her chin in my hand and dropping a soft kiss on her mouth. "I just am. I've waited my entire life to feel the way I feel about you, Lily. If you want to slow things down, I can wait. We need to get out of town for now, but if you're not ready to leave Black Rock yet—"

"I am. I am. I just—I didn't want to assume—I didn't know if you—"

"I do. More than anything." Straightening, I focused on what had to get done. "We can leave the Land Rover here. I'll have someone drive it down to Atlanta later. I have to return my rental anyway, so pack as much as you think will fit in the back. We'll take that with us, load it on the plane, and whatever's left we'll have packed up and moved down later when the rest of this is settled."

Lily stepped back and nodded. "I can do that. How fast do we have to move? I already put some things aside, organized what we might want now versus later, but if we have the whole SUV..."

I knew what she meant. The SUV I'd rented was massive. We could fit a soccer team in that thing. Lily had set aside bags suitable for a commercial flight, but she could take a lot more than that between the SUV and our plane.

"It's about five hours to Hanover. I think we should try to leave by lunch. Does that work?"

"That works. I'm on it."

"Lily," I called out. She stopped and turned, already distracted with everything she had to do in the next few hours. "I don't think Dave is going to press charges. If he comes back, tell him you don't know where I went."

"Where are you going?"

"Nowhere without you, but he won't know that."

Shadows moved through Lily's eyes. I waited for her to object, to ask for an explanation. Anything. Instead, she said, "Okay."

She turned on her heel, then stopped abruptly and threw herself into my arms, planting a kiss on my mouth. As soon as the warmth of her lips left mine, she was gone, flying up the stairs.

I didn't know what I'd done to earn such trust, but I'd do everything I could to deserve it.

I was moving too fast. Cooper would go ape shit if I moved Lily into my house. I didn't fucking care. I'd told her the truth. I'd waited my entire life to feel this way. Maybe things would change, maybe they wouldn't, but I wasn't going into this assuming it would fall apart.

I wanted Lily.

I wanted Adam.

I'd give her space if that's what she needed. As long as she was mine.

Chapter Thirty-Two

KNOX

IT DIDN'T TAKE ME LONG to get the rest of my things together. So far, we hadn't been interrupted by an invasion of Black Rock cruisers with their lights flashing. I wasn't sure if that was a good sign or a bad one.

I met Lily on the stairs, taking a massive duffel from her hands before it pulled her off balance and she tumbled to the bottom.

"What the hell are you doing?"

"Bringing the bags down."

"I'll get the bags. Is everything together upstairs?"

"In a big pile in the middle of my bedroom. My stuff, Adam's stuff, a few boxes of things I don't need right away, but I don't want to leave in the house. I need to pack a bag from the mudroom—shoes, jackets, stuff like that, but otherwise, we're ready to load up."

"Got it." I found everything neatly organized in Lily's bedroom. A few trips, and I had the back of the SUV loaded. Adam dogged my heels, asking question after question, most of which I couldn't answer. Fortunately, he was easy to divert with little tasks, happy to help me carry odds and ends.

Lily left another over-stuffed duffel by the back door, this one filled with whatever she wanted from the mudroom. I found her in the kitchen cobbling together lunch from leftovers and food that would spoil before the end of the week. Adam complained about the odd mix of food on his plate until Lily gave him what I thought of as 'Mom Eye', and he shut up.

The shrill of the perimeter alarm cut through the house as Lily was clearing the table. She jumped, a plate sliding from her fingers to shatter on the floor. I circled the table to lift her clear of the sharp slivers of ceramic surrounding her bare feet.

A shadow passed by the window at the front door. Behind me, Adam raced for the front door, calling out, "Deputy Dave."

"Adam, don't!" I yelled.

The driveway alert hadn't sounded. If he was here on official business, he would have come in his cruiser. I set Lily on her feet, away from the remains of the broken plate, and sprinted for the front door.

Adam was already swinging it open.

He froze for a split second, stumbling back as he saw Dave's normally affable face contorted with rage and desperation. The deputy lunged for Adam, his fingers closing over the shoulder of Adam's t-shirt.

His gut overriding his brain, Adam was already scuttling back, away from the door. Dave's desperate grasp came up short. Adam bolted for Lily, barreling into her arms. She stopped only a few feet away, her eyes wide and fixed on the man she'd thought was her friend.

Dave held a Taser in my direction, waving it threateningly. I would have laughed if I hadn't known that would push him over the edge. A Taser? He'd have to fill out paperwork if he discharged his service weapon, but seriously. A Taser?

Then again, his weapon was on his hip. He was an asshole, but he wasn't completely incompetent. As long as he had that gun on his hip, he was a danger.

Ignoring me when he saw I wasn't going to approach, he focused on Lily, all pretense at friendship wiped away. "Give me the box, Lily. I'm tired of this bullshit. Trey owes me. He said it was mine. Give it to me, and I'll go."

"Were you working with Trey?" Lily took a step out from behind me, confusion and betrayal nudging her guard down. I shot out an arm to block her approach.

Dave sneered. "Yeah, I was working with Trey. You're such a fucking idiot. So much shit he did right under your nose, and you never thought to ask about any of it, did you? Just make your pot roast, read books to your dumbass kid and never wonder where all that money was coming from. Did you ever ask Trey what he was doing on those business trips? Who he was fucking when he stopped fucking you?"

Dave's wild eyes flicked to Adam and back to Lily. "I know you don't have proof that he's yours. Give me the box or I'll call social services and you'll lose the only thing you care about."

Adam was oblivious to the threat, but Lily turned to stone, her eyes blank with panic. I was going to fucking kill this guy. I stepped in front of her, blocking him from her view. "What box, Morris?"

"The fucking Russian box, you asshole. I know it's worth millions. Trey said it was mine. Hand it over and I'll walk away."

"It's not here," I said. "I've torn this house apart. I found the receipt but no box. You're out of luck."

"It can't be gone," Dave cried, desperation drawing his voice into a whine. "It was in his office. What the fuck did you do with it, you bitch? I've been looking for months."

I didn't give Lily a chance to respond. "She didn't do anything with it. It's gone."

"Then give me cash. I know he left you flush. He owes me."

"Lily doesn't have any cash in the house." Technically I wasn't lying. The strongbox with the twenty grand was safely packed in the SUV. I wouldn't risk Lily and Adam over twenty grand, but that wasn't the kind of money Dave Morris was looking for.

"Then let's go the to the bank," Dave shot back, his greed short-circuiting his brain.

"How do you expect to pull that off?" I asked conversationally. "You going to hold the gun on her in front of the teller?"

"She can write me a check." He was grasping at straws. Whatever he'd done for Trey, he hadn't been using his brains.

"That's going to leave a hell of a paper trail. You're out of options, Morris. Turn around and leave."

Dave lurched forward, lunging at me but not getting close enough to strike. His control was disintegrating, falling to dust as his frustration grew.

This was his endgame. He wasn't going to walk away without getting what he wanted.

I could feel Adam behind me, squirming against Lily. I turned to close my hand around his upper arm, holding him still. Lily pushed him further behind me, edging to the side, out of my protection. I couldn't shield them from Dave if they wouldn't stay fucking still.

"Dave," she said, "I don't know what Trey did with the

box, but there's stuff in the house. Artwork. I have a little jewelry. It's not worth what the box was, but you can have it. I don't care. Whatever Trey owed you, it doesn't have anything to do with me."

"It has everything to do with you, you fucking bitch. He was supposed to leave it all to me. I've been his friend his entire life. You're just some cunt he picked up at college to piss off his parents."

A wounded sound from Lily at the harsh epithet. Adam pulled from my grip, going for his mother. I shoved him further behind me, moving both of us a step too far from Dave and Lily.

In slow motion, I watched as Dave shot out an arm to grab her. She was still too far away, his fingers skating over her shoulder, closing around a chunk of her hair. He yanked, dragging Lily off her feet.

Everything went red at her scream of pain.

Diving to the side, I pulled her out of his reach, shoving both her and Adam behind me. "Garage. Now."

I heard more than saw Lily grab Adam and take off down the hall. I was on Dave before he could get his bearings, throwing punch after punch.

I was done with this fucker.

Done with his crude comments about Lily.

Done with his entitlement.

Done with this little man thinking he could threaten my woman. My boy.

Just. Fucking. Done.

Deputy Dave Morris wanted to be a player, but he was about to leave the stage.

I pulled back to take a good look at the blood streaming from his nose and mouth. His dazed eyes met mine in disbelief, lips closing and opening, sounds choppy.

"—oo 'an't. 'oo 'an't."

"I can, and I did, motherfucker." I snagged the cuffs from his belt and secured his hands behind his back before tossing him over my shoulder. Deputy Dave might press charges this time, but we wouldn't be here.

I jogged through the woods, dumping Dave in the dirt beneath the pine trees and refastened the cuffs behind his back.

"One last thing," I said, "Lily's house is wired, inside and out. I guarantee you that you won't spot all of the cameras. If I catch you breaking in again, I won't call the state police, I'll call Andrei Tsepov. He doesn't like loose ends, and right now, he can't afford a fuckwad local cop drawing attention to his business. Got me?"

I saw the exact moment he understood, the impotent rage in his eyes dissolving into abject terror. Yeah, he got me.

I left him there, handcuffed to the tree. Dave was no genius, but he wasn't a complete idiot. He'd figure out a way to get free. It didn't matter. He wouldn't be found on Lily's property, and we'd be long gone.

Jogging back to the house, I cleaned up his blood from the floor, packing away the paper towels to dispose of on the road.

A quick shower, change of clothes, and I tossed the last of my gear into the SUV. Lily was waiting in the passenger seat, a wet towel pressed to her temple. Adam babbled non-stop, filled with worried questions she couldn't answer.

At the sight of me, he fell silent. I slid into the driver's seat and reached over to nudge Lily's hand from her temple. My gut turned at the raw patch of skin, bleeding sluggishly. It was tiny, not bigger than a dime, but that didn't matter.

It was Lily, my Lily, and she got hurt under my watch. I leaned in closer, pressing my forehead to hers. "I'm so sorry, baby. That shouldn't have happened."

"It's not your fault, Knox. I should have stayed behind you. I wasn't thinking."

"You okay?"

"It stings, that's all. Where's Dave?"

I sat back, fastened my seatbelt and hit the garage door remote. As we pulled out, I sent Lily a wink.

"Handcuffed to a tree in the woods two houses over. I don't think he'll be bothering you anymore." Tossing her my phone, I said, "Set the alarm, Lil. We're hitting the road."

Chapter Thirty-Three

LILY

FIVE HOURS IS A LONG time to be stuck in a car with a five-year-old. A lot of people think New England is a bunch of little states all squished together, but Maine is pretty big. The drive to central New Hampshire was beautiful and endless.

It didn't help that I was twisted with nerves, imagining what might happen once we reached our destination. I carried my mother's letters in the front seat with me, reading them again and again, reassuring myself that I was wanted.

She'd missed me. I thought I'd never see her again. Years of grief and loss had been bottled up, and the letters popped the cork, letting it all out in a fountain of heartbreak and need.

Need for my mom. For my dad, as strict and distant as he'd been. Stingy with hugs, quick to disapprove, but he'd loved me.

Some parents hurt with neglect. My dad was the opposite. My dad hurt because he loved too much, and with that love came expectations and ultimatums.

I watched Adam in the rear-view mirror, happily kicking his feet while playing a game on my phone. Screen time restrictions were lifted when we were stuck in a car for hours. In between stops for the bathroom—far too many of them—I'd give anything to keep him quiet.

What would they think of Adam? Would they care that he was adopted? That he was mine yet not mine? I couldn't bear the thought that we might reunite, and I'd have to leave because they couldn't accept my son.

I couldn't bear the thought, but I had to acknowledge it was a possibility. They hadn't accepted Trey. What made me think they'd accept a child who was clearly Trey's and just as clearly had not come from my body?

I'd protect Adam from anything, including my own parents. I prayed I wouldn't have to.

For most of the drive, it felt like we'd never get there. Then, familiar landmarks came into view. My stomach knotted, and I wished the drive would never end.

I didn't want to do this. I wanted to be past this part, past the awkward introductions and the uncertainty. I reached out to touch Knox's arm. He turned his wrist and closed his fingers around mine.

"It's going to be okay, Lily," he said, too low for Adam to hear. "And if it's not, we're out of there."

I nodded, my throat too tight to talk. If it wasn't okay, we'd leave. Simple as that.

And from here to Atlanta, and Knox's family, and a whole new set of worries. His brother didn't approve of our relationship. Lucas, Charlie, and Griffen had been great, but Knox's brothers—

Can it, Lily. Obsess over one thing at a time. If you try to worry about all of it at once, your brain is going to explode.

My brain might explode anyway.

By the time the SUV pulled into my parents' driveway I was so nauseous with nerves I thought I was going to throw up. Knox's hand pressed to my back, urging me to lean forward and put my head between my knees. His fingers stroked up my spine, easing my tight muscles.

"You want me to go first? Clear the way?"

For a second, I wanted to say yes. Yes, please go fix this for me so I don't have to see the rejection in my dad's eyes. The disappointment in my mother's face.

No freaking way, Lily, I lectured myself. *Grow a spine. You have a son. You can forgive yourself for the past, but not if you keep making bad decisions. Woman up and go knock on the door.*

Sucking in a breath through my nose, I held it, letting it out slowly before I sat up and unsnapped my seatbelt. "I can do this. I'm ready," I lied.

"You want us to wait in the car?" Knox asked. He did not like that option. I loved that he offered it anyway. I could pretend to be brave, but I couldn't do this alone.

"No. I think you two should come with me."

I got out of the car, my hands shaking only a little as I unfastened my seatbelt. I met Knox at the hood, taking Adam's little hand in mine.

"Where are we, Mom?"

"This is the house where I grew up. We're going to see if your grandparents are home."

"Really? You lived here when you were little?"

"I did. And it looks exactly the same."

The flowerbeds in the front of the house were different, of course. My mother had inherited her mother's love of gardening, hence her name, Rose, and mine. She changed the design of the beds almost every year, but, flowers aside, everything was the same.

The same pristine white siding and forest-green shutters.

The same wraparound porch with white swing. Walking distance to campus with a sunlit studio tucked in the backyard, it was the perfect house for a professor and his artist wife.

I didn't know my father's class schedule anymore, had no idea if they'd be home, but I hadn't had the nerve to call ahead.

Looking down at Adam, I forced a bright smile. “Should we ring the bell?”

He darted ahead, dragging me along with him. Knox followed behind. I rang the bell, listening to it echo through the house, the familiar tones bringing on a wave of nostalgia so sharp tears stung my eyes.

Silence inside, but that didn't mean anything. If my father was in his office, or my mother in her studio, it might take them a while to investigate the ring of the bell. I gave it thirty seconds and rang again, blinking away the moisture in my eyes.

Finally, the steady cadence of feet in the hall. Too heavy to be my mother. My breath grew tight.

Between the two of them, I'd rather see my mother first, but I'd take what I could get.

The door opened.

My father stood there, looking exactly the same and alarmingly different. Older. His walnut skin was wrinkled at the forehead. There were threads of gray in his close-cropped dark hair. Reading glasses tangled around his neck, but those weren't new.

His slouchy khakis and worn argyle cardigan with leather patches on the elbows were exactly the same. My dad dressed like the stereotypical stuffy professor he was. No amount of teasing from my more flamboyant mother could prompt him to try anything else.

His eyes flared with surprise when he saw me. The hint of emotion kindled hope in my heart. Then surprise was sucked away, and his face went blank.

"Lily. You're here."

"Yes. I—"

Why hadn't I thought about what to say? Five hours in the car, reading my mother's letters over and over, and I never planned what to say.

From beside me, a little voice broke into the silence. "Are you my grandpa?"

I squeezed Adam's hand, sending a prayer to the heavens that my dad would say the right thing. My father looked at me in question.

"Dad, I'd like you to meet my son, Adam."

Another flare in my father's eyes, an emotion I couldn't read. I'd never been able to read him well.

To my relief, he bent a little at the waist and held out a hand to Adam. In his measured, professor voice, he said, "Yes, if you're Lily's son, I would be your grandfather. It's nice to meet you."

He hadn't exactly held his arms open in welcome, but it was better than nothing. Shifting awkwardly on the doorstep I said, "I, uh, I—"

Realizing I was making a mess of this, I stepped back to nudge Knox up to my side.

"Dad, this is Knox Sinclair. He's—"

Knox stuck out his hand and gripped my father's, giving it a firm shake. "I'm with Lily. May we come in?"

My father stepped back, his eyes darting from Knox to me to Adam and back to me. "I'll get your mother."

He left us standing in the hall and strode in the direction of the back door. She must be working in her studio.

I'd grown up in this house, but I didn't feel comfortable exploring. Not yet. Not until I knew we were welcome. From what I could see, everything looked the same. Same dining room furniture, the living room sofa in the same navy velvet with the same tapestry blanket draped over the back.

The screen door at the back of the house slammed shut. My mother strode down the hall, back straight, chin high, long blond hair streaming behind her.

Her loose, poppy-red shirt flowed over skinny jeans to feet covered in paint-splattered Converse sneakers. Truly, most of her was paint splattered. Nothing new there.

Closer to Knox's height than mine, she towered over me, arms crossed over her chest, gaze appraising. I felt the weight of it as she absorbed me. My poofy, natural curls, gone wild in the humidity of summer. My freckles, darker from playing in the lake with Adam. My casual sundress and sandals.

She let out a breath I hadn't realized she was holding, her arms coming around me with wiry strength, drawing me close. Mouth at my ear, she breathed, "Lily. My baby. My baby girl. Oh, Lily."

I wrapped my arms around her slender body, burying my face against her shoulder. She smelled the same, like flowers and earth and turpentine. My chest hitched with a sob, and I held her tighter, able to say only, "Mom. Mom."

Adam tugged at my dress. His brows knit together, eyes shadowed with worry, he pulled harder. "Mommy?"

I pulled away from my mother and closed Adam's hand in mine. "Mom? This is Adam. My son."

My mother's eyes fastened on Adam's face, fixed on his features. I knew what she saw. Trey. Not me. I braced, ready to scoop up my boy and take off if she gave even the slightest hint he wasn't welcome.

Abruptly, her grey eyes filled with tears. She dashed them away with the back of her hand and dropped to her knees, opening her arms in a hug. Adam went to her, his voice muffled by her paint-stained shirt. "You're my grandma? Why is everyone crying?"

In the crisp voice that had delivered so many parental lectures, she answered, "Because we haven't seen each other in a very long time, and we're happy to be together now."

"Why would you cry when you're happy?"

"Because my heart is so full it hurts, just a little. A good hurt. I never imagined I had a grandson."

"I didn't know I had a grandma."

I was a huge jerk. It was Trey's fault our estrangement had lasted so long, not mine. I still felt like a jerk for not telling Adam he had grandparents he'd never met.

If Adam thought it was weird adults cried when they were happy, he'd be shocked as hell to grow up and discover we felt all sorts of things that made no sense. Grief at what wasn't lost. Guilt where there was no fault. The human heart knows no logic, no matter how we might wish it would.

My mother stood, keeping an arm around Adam's shoulder. Her assessing stare landed square on Knox. Not waiting for me to jump in, he dealt with her the same way he had my father.

"Knox Sinclair. I'm with Lily." As if that were explanation enough. For now, it would have to be.

Holding her counsel, my mother gave a brisk nod. "I see." Dismissing us, she reached for Adam's hand. "Was it a long drive? Do you need the bathroom and a snack?"

As always, mention of the bathroom reminded Adam of his bladder. Dancing from foot to foot, he nodded. "It was so long. We were in the car forever. After Mr. Knox hit Deputy Dave, we had to leave and—"

"Why don't I show you the bathroom and get you something to eat?" she interrupted with an arch look at Knox and me.

"K. Is this where my Mom lived?"

Knox slipped his arm around my waist as we followed them down the hall to the kitchen. "He threw us right under the bus, didn't he?" Knox said, amused.

"Little booger." I couldn't even be mad. He was five. Seeing Knox hit Dave had been the height of excitement in his short life. His hero, taking out the bad guy. Of course, he'd told my Mom. He probably would have told the gas station attendant if there'd been one.

Adam was already in the powder room when we reached the kitchen. My mother's cool eyes didn't miss Knox's arm around my waist.

"Tea? I have a new blend. Does Adam like apples and peanut butter? We can take it outside so he can run around in the yard."

"No tea for me, Mrs. Adams," Knox said.

"I'll take some. Adam loves apples and peanut butter. And the yard would be great."

My Mom's tea blends were hit and miss. Some were heavy with fruit and flowers, ambrosia whether hot or iced. Some tasted like the rich garden soil she loved so much. I was hoping for fruit and flowers instead of dirt, but I'd drink it either way.

With a glance down the hall at the closed bathroom door, my mother asked quickly, "What happened to Trey?"

Knowing we didn't have much time, I said, "He died. Almost a year ago."

"And the deputy?" This question she aimed at Knox.

"Trey left Lily some trouble. I work in security. I came up to help."

"And stayed?" she asked archly. Knox gave a single nod of his head, holding her eyes with his. Whatever she saw there must have satisfied her. "Are they safe? My daughter and my grandson?"

"For now," Knox said. "We can only stay the night, and then I'm going to move them somewhere secure until my brothers and I can clean up Trey's mess."

For the first time, raw emotion broke through my mother's controlled expression. "Only one night? You just got here."

"We'll come back," I cut in, "as soon as it's safe to stay longer. This is the last place anyone would look, but—"

"What the hell did that bastard do?" she asked, aiming the question at Knox.

"You don't want to know, and I can't tell you. Lily and Adam are almost clear of him. It won't be much longer before this is over."

I hoped Knox was telling the truth. With Tsepov missing and Dave to deal with, I wasn't sure it would be that easy.

Down the hall, the rush of a toilet flushing interrupted. A second later I caught the sound of water running into the sink. Grownup time was over. Knox met my eyes and cocked a brow. I knew what he was asking, and I nodded.

"I need to check the house, secure the property while we're here, just in case. That okay with you, Mrs. Adams?"

"Of course. Do what you have to do. My husband should be in his office upstairs. He can show you around."

Knox disappeared as Adam came back into the room. My mother loaded glasses of iced tea and Adam's snack on a tray. We followed her out the back door to the seating area on the porch overlooking the yard.

Adam went straight for the sliced apples and peanut butter, gobbling them down as if he hadn't eaten in days. I took a glass of iced tea from the tray, the scent of melon and strawberries drifting to my nose. My mother sat beside me on the wicker loveseat.

Quietly, so Adam couldn't hear, she murmured, "You named him after us. Adam."

So much to say that I couldn't. Not with my son sitting right there. I settled for, "I never got your letters. Not until yesterday. He hid them."

My mother drew in a shocked breath. "You never got my letters? Any of them?"

"No."

"And that letter. You didn't write it."

"I didn't know. I didn't think you wanted me to write. Whatever that letter said, it wasn't from me."

Her face fell, grey eyes clouded. "Oh, Lily. We should have come up there. We should have known."

"I don't know how you could. I didn't know how bad it would be."

Adam shoved the last apple slice into his mouth and stared down at the yard with longing. "Mom, can I?"

"Sure. Stay inside the fence."

"There's a swing on one of the trees, Adam," my mother cut in.

"You still have that old swing by your studio?"

"Your father has some colleagues with young children. He keeps it up so they have something to play with."

Adam ran to the swing I'd loved as a child, and my heart squeezed, torn between joy that he'd share one of my favorite memories and pain at how much I'd lost. My parents had a whole life I knew nothing about. Friends, their children, so much day to day that I'd missed.

“How bad was it?” my mother asked as soon as Adam was out of earshot.

Chapter Thirty-Four

LILY

NOT THAT BAD," I SAID quickly, not wanting her vibrant imagination to scare her. "He just...didn't love me. And I was too stubborn to admit I was wrong. Then he brought home Adam, and I couldn't leave him."

"He's a beautiful boy. Sweet."

"He's the best. I'm sorry I—"

She straightened and said sharply, "No, Lily. Don't be sorry. There's enough sorry on both sides. We can't go back. Let's not waste any more time on things we can't change."

"That's what Knox says."

"He sounds like a smart man."

"He is. I—" My voice hitched in my throat. Why is it so hard to admit when I'm wrong? Sucking in a quick breath, I spit it out. "I made a terrible mistake with Trey."

"Lily—"

"No, let me say it. You and Dad were right. I should never have married him. He—I think he married me out of rebellion, and maybe I did the same thing. Once we were together— His parents hated me. He blamed me for keeping them apart, and then they died, and nothing was ever the same again."

"Those bigoted assholes."

My laugh was watery with tears.

My mom never shied away from criticizing me. I wasn't outgoing enough. Confident enough. I had no ambition.

She could be my harshest critic, but she was always first in line to defend me. She was allowed to criticize her daughter, but God save anyone else who tried. She knew it had been hard growing up in this mostly-white town as one of the very few children of an interracial marriage.

I think she'd always felt a little guilty they hadn't chosen to raise me somewhere with a more diverse population. A place where I might have looked around the classroom and seen anyone else who looked like me.

There were times when I wondered who I would have grown into if I'd lived in a place like that. Somewhere I fit in. Somewhere I wasn't always *other*. My father said everyone has challenges, and this was mine. He wasn't wrong, but that didn't mean I hadn't struggled.

My mother smoothed my hair back from my forehead. "And Knox? How long have you been together?"

Crap. Another awkward conversation. The truth wasn't pretty, but I wouldn't lie about Knox. Not about Trey either. The time for covering Trey's ass was long gone.

"Like Knox said, Trey's business had...issues."

"Are you in trouble?"

"I didn't do anything wrong. I didn't know about it. But Trey's business partner was Knox's father, and he *is* in trouble. Because of Trey, some of that trouble is after me and Adam. Knox came to help, and we, well, you know."

My mother winked. "You saw that fine young man and decided you owed yourself a little fun?"

My face went hot. That was my mother. Never one to shy away from anything, including teasing her only daughter about sex.

I couldn't even talk about sex with Knox. I wasn't going to talk about it with my mother.

Feeling like a kid, I took a quick sip of my iced tea, watching Adam on the swing. "Something like that, yeah."

She raised her hand, her fingertips brushing the raw spot where Dave had ripped out my hair. "What happened here?"

In the worry over seeing my parents again, I'd almost forgotten the injury. "Oh, that."

"Did Knox do this?" she asked, leaning forward as if ready to find Knox and drive him from the house.

"No, Mom. No. No. This was the deputy. And it's my fault." I tried to think of an explanation that would satisfy my mother and not take the next year to get through.

"Trey's best friend is a town deputy. Turns out he's dirty, part of the problem Knox is helping with. He came by this morning, and I got too close. Dave grabbed me, got my hair."

"Why didn't Knox keep him away from you? Isn't that his job?"

"He had his eye on Adam. Honestly, it was my fault. I promise. Knox has been great. Really great. Adam loves him, which is nice because his father never bothered with him."

Out of the corner of my eye, I spotted Knox and my father in the side yard. Knox leaned over and attached something to the fence. A motion sensor? My father stood behind him, hands on his hips, glowering.

My mother followed my gaze to the two of them. "We missed you so much, Lily."

"Dad barely said hello." I couldn't hide the bitterness.

My mother sighed. "He missed you. You know how stubborn he is. It's an Adams trait, that stubbornness." She raised an eyebrow at me, and I squirmed.

Her eyes moved to him again. "I don't know that he'll admit he was wrong. Or tell you how much he regrets everything he said the last time you were home. But he does, Lily. I know he does."

I didn't know what to say to that. Did it matter? If he couldn't tell me he loved me, couldn't tell me he'd missed me, did it matter? It was the emotional equivalent of the old, 'If a tree falls in the forest and no one sees it...'

If he never says he loves me, never shows it...

I looked away from my father, still glowering at Knox as he moved down the fence. Whatever. I wasn't going to bang my head against the wall over my father's emotional unavailability.

Expecting him to start handing out hugs and vows of love was setting myself up for pain. I'd had enough of that. So had he.

That's how we got into this mess—expecting the other person to be who we wanted them to be instead of who they were. Maybe I could decide to believe my mom and take his love on faith. Isn't that what love is? Faith?

If I could trust Knox, love Knox, after such a short time because I believed in him, couldn't I do the same for my dad?

"It's okay if we stay tonight?" I asked, tired of dwelling on my dad. "I don't even know if you had plans."

"We didn't, and it wouldn't matter if we did. Of course, you can stay."

"I wasn't sure—" I mumbled.

"I deserve that. We deserve that. We should have come up there. You're always welcome in your home, Lily. Always." Her voice hitching a little, she said, "I don't know how I'm going to say goodbye to you tomorrow."

"It won't be goodbye, Mom. I promise. Just *see you later*. The situation with Knox's dad is complicated. It's going to take time for us to resolve. But once we do, we'll come back. I promise."

Adam spotted Knox and my father and abandoned the swing, running over to follow Knox as he checked the property line, placing more sensors here and there.

With a quick look at her watch, my mom noticed the time and went in to finish making dinner. I followed. We moved in an easy routine in the kitchen, my mother cooking and me setting the table.

I entertained her with stories about my failed attempts at baking. She pretended to gasp in horror at the idea that I used real sugar in my cookies, offering her recipe for carob-hemp bars.

I wrote it down, but I was a lot more interested in taking another crack at those salted caramel brownies. The first batch had been good, but they were long gone. I needed another taste test. And more chocolate.

Dinner was awkward despite my mom's attempts to keep the conversation moving. My father sat stiffly, entering the conversation only to jab at Knox with questions.

"What exactly do you do for a living?"

"Where are you from?"

"How long have you been seeing my daughter?"

Knox absorbed his questions calmly, answering them all. He didn't let my dad ruffle him, didn't get impatient or annoyed. Knox did a much better job under the inquisition than Trey had.

Trey met my parents at school a few times, but the night I brought him home to announce our engagement, my father had peppered him with pointed questions until Trey lost his temper and stormed out in a huff. I'd followed, furious with my father for picking on my fiancé.

I watched Knox's lips curl at my dad's latest surly inquiry and thought about all the ways I could thank him for putting up with my dad.

We lingered at the table over a bottle of wine, my father finally deciding he'd grilled Knox sufficiently. Instead, he regaled us with the details of his latest paper on globalization and its impact on entrepreneurship in developing countries.

I'm sure his graduate students found it fascinating. Economics was not my thing. I'm not going to say that hearing about his research was as good as a sleeping pill, but I started trying to hide my yawns a few minutes in.

My mother smiled as I pressed a hand to my mouth for cover and glanced at her grandson, taking in Adam's drooping eyes and exhausted slump.

"We can pick this up over breakfast, can't we Louis? I don't know about Knox, but Lily and Adam look like they're about to drop."

"It's been a stressful few days, Mrs. Adams," Knox said.

"I told you, call me Rose. Let me show you to your rooms."

Knox waited until we were upstairs before saying to my mother, "I'm staying with Lily and Adam."

It was rare that I saw my mother completely flummoxed. She stared at Knox, her mouth gaping open before she snapped it shut. "Knox, I understand that you and Lily have an adult relationship, and I'm not a prude, but Adam is young and impressionable, and this is—"

"This is our house. In our house you follow our rules," came my father's unyielding dictate.

Out of habit, my spine went stiff. I hated that tone, the assumption that his word was law and everyone around him would fall into line.

When I was a teenager, I always lost my temper when he talked to me like that. Knox, much like he had been at dinner, was completely unruffled.

He leveled an equally unyielding look at my father. "I appreciate that, Mr. Adams. If our arrangements don't suit your needs, we'll find somewhere else to stay. Until this situation is resolved, Lily and Adam aren't out of my sight. Understand?"

"This house is safe," my father sputtered. "I watched you augment the security. No one is getting in here."

"Probably not," Knox agreed. "Nothing is more important to me than Lily and Adam's safety. I'm not taking any chances. If you can't accommodate us, we'll leave and come back for breakfast."

My father opened his mouth. I could tell by his expression he was going to lay down the law again, as stubborn as ever. His mouth snapped closed as my mother smacked him in the gut, knocking the wind from him just enough to shut him up.

"Louis. Let it go." Putting her hand on my shoulder, she said to Knox, "I understand your concern. Lily's bedroom still has a double bed, a little small, but there's room on the floor for the air mattress we have in the closet. The guest room has a queen, but there's no room for Adam."

"Lily's room and the air mattress will be good. Thank you, Rose." Knox said, looking to me for directions.

My father grunted, pushing past us down the hall. I figured that was the last we'd see of him until breakfast, but he returned a few moments later carrying a bag I recognized from my days of sleepovers. The air mattress.

Taking it, I said, "Thanks, Dad."

"See you in the morning," he muttered and disappeared again.

My mother watched him go and let out a sigh of exasperation. "Do you need help making up the bed, Lily? The linens are in the hall closet where they always were."

"No, we've got it, Mom. Thanks."

"All right then, sleep well."

After a tight hug for me and a kiss to the top of Adam's head, she followed my father down the hall to their bedroom. I turned to Knox, raising my eyebrows. "That was awkward."

"Lily—" Knox started to say.

I cut him off. "Don't apologize, Knox. It's been a long time since anyone cared what happened to Adam and me. I'm not going to ask you to stop because it makes anyone uncomfortable."

"Good. Because I'm not going to stop, even if you ask."

I didn't try to hide my smile. "Let's get this bed made so we can go to sleep."

Knox followed my lead, getting sheets and a pillow, helping to usher Adam to the bathroom down the hall and then into his pajamas. It was only a little weird to slide into my childhood bed beside Knox.

First of all, Knox was way too much man for a double bed. And second, the last time I'd slept in this bed I'd been newly graduated from college. A lifetime ago.

I was exhausted, but it was hard to settle surrounded by remnants of my childhood. We lay there, Knox spooning me, his arm around my waist, listening to Adam babble about the swing and his grandparents until he sank into a mumbling recitation of the alphabet, something he did now and then to sing himself to sleep.

In the half-light of the moon, I watched Adam's eyes droop closed, his little voice still murmuring through the A-B-C's. In my ear, Knox whispered, "Your father is a tough nut, yeah?"

I choked on the laugh. "That's one way to put it."

"After I left you with your mom, I found him in his office. He was standing over his desk, crying. When he saw me, he pretended it didn't happen."

"Of course." What, my father acknowledge that he had an emotion other than stubborn pride? Hell would freeze over first.

"He wiped his eyes and led me around the house, barely said a word, but Lily, when I found him, his shoulders were shaking, tears streaming down his face. I don't know if he can tell you. Maybe he never will, but he was standing there weeping because you were home. I thought you should know."

"Thanks, Knox," I said, my voice hoarse.

The steel band around my heart loosened a little. The only time I'd ever seen my father cry was at his mother's funeral. That he would cry over me said more than any words. Maybe he did love me, even if he couldn't tell me.

Tucked against Knox, my son within arm's reach, I slept like a baby once my eyes finally slid shut. The smell of coffee and bacon woke me in the morning. I sat up, blinking against the sunlight streaming into the room. Knox was already awake, quietly tapping away at the screen of his phone. At my movement, he glanced my way.

"Morning," he said in a low voice full of promise.

I was overjoyed that my son was safe and happy and still asleep. Not so overjoyed that he was in the same room as Knox and me.

Not that we were going to do anything in my parent's house, but still. Sleeping with Knox in front of Adam was one thing. Adam waking to find us making out on the bed? Not going to happen.

I glanced at Knox's phone as it vibrated in his hand. "Everything okay?"

"Yes and no. LeAnne Gates is missing."

"Missing? What does that mean?"

"It looks like she took off. We don't know for how long, why, or who with. No signs of forced entry, or a struggle, and it looks like she packed for at least a week or two. Maybe more."

"Okay, so what do we do?"

"Cooper has someone looking for her. He also has people looking for Tsepov, but so far, the guy is vapor. Not in Atlanta, not in Vegas. Nowhere. Axel told Cooper there are some rumblings in Vegas. His organization is unhappy with the way he's handled the situation with Trey and my father. He's getting pushback. It's not safe for us in Atlanta."

"What are we going to do?" I asked

"Do you trust me?"

I didn't have to think about the answer. "Of course, I trust you."

"Then let me figure it out. I'm going to keep you and Adam safe. We'll find LeAnne Gates and deal with Tsepov and my father. I promise. Right now, we're going downstairs to have breakfast with your parents."

A thousand questions flooded my mind. Where would we go? How long would we stay? Where was LeAnne Gates?

I shoved it all aside.

I trusted Knox.

I'd worry about the rest later.

"Okay. Let's go get some breakfast."

Chapter Thirty-Five

KNOX

THE FLIGHT FROM HANOVER WAS uneventful if you ignored Adam's enjoyment at his first plane ride. Lily shook her head in wry amusement, murmuring, "He's going to be spoiled, thinking this is what flying is usually like."

Lily had boarded the plane without asking our destination, taking in the luxurious interior with wide eyes as she settled Adam with a coloring book and crayons into one of the leather seats.

Our company plane was a luxury we could have done without. As a line item expense, it was hefty, but our clients paid for the extra layer of security it provided. In cases like this, it was ideal.

We took off from the small, private airstrip in Hanover after filing a flight plan for Atlanta. An hour into the flight we diverted, with no one to answer to but the tiny airfield where we landed.

The flight to Tennessee wasn't long. Adam only had to use the bathroom twice, less interested in emptying his bladder than an excuse to unsnap his seatbelt and explore the plane, testing out the sink, the seats, the lock on the door and everything else he could get his hands on.

Griffen met us at the airport with a Sinclair Security SUV and a house key. He'd even remembered a booster seat for Adam. We exchanged few words as he took our place in the plane and we took his in the SUV. A few minutes after we'd landed, we were on the road to our destination.

Lily waved to Griffen but didn't say anything until we were belted in.

"Okay, where are we? I know this isn't Atlanta."

"The middle of nowhere in Tennessee. Close enough to get to Atlanta quickly if we have to, far enough away that no one will think to look for us here."

"Okay."

And that was it. *Okay.* Her trust meant more than she could know.

I followed our GPS to the small cabin I'd borrowed from a friend.

I wanted this business with Tsepov resolved. I wanted answers about Adam from LeAnne Gates. I wanted a normal life with Lily and Adam by my side.

Normal life would have to wait. The next best thing was having Lily and Adam all to myself. No Deputy Dave, none of Tsepov's goons, no nosy friends to interrupt. Just the three of us, safe and secluded.

The cabin was rustic, but it sat in the center of a hundred and fifty acres on the side of a mountain. A stream bisected the property, carrying water that was biting cold and crystal clear.

A stone's throw from the cabin, the stream ran into a pond big enough for swimming and fishing. It was a far cry from the modern monstrosity Trey had built on Black Rock Lake. I wondered if Lily would mind. The cabin was better than sleeping in a tent, but not by much.

Lily and Adam piled out of the SUV. Adam started for the water. I caught him with a hand on the shoulder and redirected him toward the cabin. "Let's get settled in, bud. Then we can check out the lake."

Lily stood in front of the porch, taking in the small, A-frame cabin. Built of pine stained dark brown, with a covered porch that looked like it had been tacked on as an afterthought, the cabin was unimpressive at best. I braced for Lily to climb back into the SUV and ask me to take her anywhere else.

I shoved my hands into my back pockets. "It's basic, I know, but it has everything we'll need. It's completely off the grid. Solar panels, no Internet."

I climbed the steps to the porch and opened the door, wincing at the wave of stale heat. The cabin had been closed up for weeks, the air inside musty. Lily followed me in, taking in the main room.

Old, patched couches surrounded a cast iron wood stove we wouldn't need this time of year. I flipped a switch by the door. The ceiling fan hanging from the peak of the roof spun lazily to life. It didn't do much to clear the stuffy air.

I made my way around the room, opening the windows and inserting the screens left leaning against the walls. This high in the mountains a good cross breeze would make it bearable inside, even in the first week of August.

Lily found the narrow hallway off the kitchen that led to the small bedrooms. One had a set of bunk beds. The other bedroom was almost completely filled by a queen-size bed.

Lily turned to look at me. "We're going to stay here?"

"It's nothing fancy, but—"

"How long can we stay? Will it just be the three of us?"

I realized Lily wasn't complaining about the accommodations. "We'll stay until Cooper gives us the okay to come back. At least a week, maybe more."

Lily leaned into me, her arms wrapping around my waist. "We're safe here?"

"I'm going to set up the perimeter alarm we had at your parent's house and add some more security to the windows and doors. I don't want you and Adam going into town for groceries. But, yeah, we're safe here."

"Sounds good to me."

Adam ran down the hall shouting, "Can we go swimming?"

"Not yet, bud."

It took the rest of the afternoon to get moved in. After we got the rest of the windows open and our things unloaded, Lily splashed with Adam on the rocky shore by the little dock. There was a canoe in the shed I promised I'd clean of spiderwebs and dead bugs. First things first.

Once I had the security bolstered by my equipment, I left Lily and Adam to run to town and stock up on groceries. I was only gone an hour and a half, but every minute was an eternity.

They were secure at the cabin, as safe as I could make them short of locking them up at Sinclair Security. I wouldn't be comfortable with them out of my sight until Andrei Tsepov was neutralized.

I returned to find them working on a puzzle laid out on the coffee table. Lily jumped up when I entered, taking the first set of grocery bags from my hands.

"There's a ton of things to do here. Piles and piles of paperbacks, puzzles, board games, cards."

"So you won't get bored?"

"Between the pond, and the woods, and all those books and puzzles? Nope. Neither will Adam. What about you?"

"This place belongs to a friend. I've never made it up here, but he swears the fishing is great. There's trout in the river and the pond. I've got you and Adam and a fishing pole. Sounds like heaven to me."

Lily beamed up at me. After we put the groceries away, I grabbed a beer and joined her on the couch to tackle the puzzle.

If I'd known how good those weeks at the cabin would be, I would have kidnapped Lily that first day.

You learn a lot about a person after three weeks of isolation. Without distractions, it doesn't take long to figure out how compatible you are.

I already knew Lily and I were a perfect fit in bed. Not much could top getting Lily naked. Day to day life with her was a close second.

Cooking. Washing dishes. Putting Adam to bed.

Take away the distractions of TV, cell phones, work, and there were no barriers. I'm not what you'd call a chatty guy. I could go days, and have, without talking to anyone.

I liked talking to Lily. Liked talking to Adam. What I liked more was knowing that we didn't have to talk at all. We could sit for hours, working on a puzzle saying barely anything, then pull out a board game and find ourselves talking half the night.

Between hiking, learning to fish, and swimming, Adam went to bed early every night, sleeping deeply, his nightmares a distant memory.

Once he was out, I had Lily all to myself. It was a good thing Adam slept like a rock, because our bedrooms weren't that far apart.

Lily and I made ample use of ours, and the rest of the cabin besides. I fucked her everywhere I could get my hands on her after Adam was asleep.

In the lake under the glittering moonlight.

On the dock.

In the hammock we'd found in the shed and hung between two pine trees.

Once in the canoe, though that ended with us both drenched and me dragging the canoe out the next morning, grateful we'd swamped it near shore.

Adam had almost grown out of naps, but the few times he fell asleep in the middle of the day we took advantage.

It was hot. August in Tennessee usually is. Lily and Adam never complained. We didn't spend much time indoors during the day, anyway. When it got too stuffy inside, we moved to the covered porch, taking our puzzle or board game with us.

On the few days when the heat grew too oppressive for the mountain breezes to chase off, we floated in the pond on cheap blow-up floats I'd grabbed in town. The pond was small, but the mountain stream running through it kept the water fresh and crisply cold, even on the hottest days.

I could have stayed at the cabin for another three weeks. I could have stayed forever.

After only a week in Maine, I knew I wanted Lily and Adam for my own. Hell, I'd seen Lily's picture in a file and known. Her face had tugged on something deep inside me, the answer to a question I hadn't known I'd asked.

The day she opened the door to the house she'd shared with Trey, I started to fall. By the time we arrived at the little cabin, I'd accepted all of that.

Those lazy weeks together still changed everything. I wasn't falling for her, I was long gone, in so deep I'd never be able to let them go. Life without Lily and Adam was unthinkable.

I wanted this, all of it. Lily. Adam.

Adam already felt like he was mine. It didn't matter that I wasn't his father. I was the one who taught him to bait a hook, steadied his hands while he reeled in his first fish. I was the one who helped him beat his mom at cards, smiling every time he cried out, "Go Fish!" with unabashed glee.

I could have stayed forever.

The end came far too soon.

I went to town every few days to check for messages on a burner phone. Every time, Cooper had nothing. We learned only two things in the weeks we were gone.

One, that the accounts Lucas tracked down were empty. Every cent was gone. Tsepov was looking for millions of dollars that had vanished into thin air. Or my father's pockets.

And two, the birth certificate on file with the state of Alabama was the one bearing Lily's name as his mother. The original birth certificate, the one with his biological mother on it, was sealed, following Alabama's procedure for handling adoptions. As far as the law was concerned, Lily Spencer was Adam's mother.

Bad news and good news, none of it enough to bring us home. Not until the morning I checked my phone after grabbing fresh donuts and saw Cooper's name on the screen.

If I'd known where his brief message would lead, I would have barricaded us in the cabin for the rest of eternity.

Even in my ignorance, I thought about it. I wouldn't abandon my brothers. Couldn't turn my back on my family.

Sitting in the parking lot of the grocery store in town—the only place I got cell reception—I read Cooper's message. Everything inside me wanted to erase it, to turn off my phone and drive back to the cabin, pretend I never read his text.

Gates and Tsepov surfaced. Time to come home.

I couldn't run from this. Lily couldn't run. Neither of us would be free until we talked to LeAnne Gates and dealt with Andrei Tsepov.

Wishing I could do anything else, I tapped out a message into the burner phone.

On our way. First thing tomorrow.

Then I went to tell Lily and Adam our vacation was over.

We weren't ready to face the real world, but the world was ready for us.

Chapter Thirty-Six

LILY

I WAS ALMOST AS NERVOUS AS I had been on the way to see my parents. At least I was used to my parent's disapproval.

Knox's family was a whole new set of people who I desperately wanted to like me and who had good reason not to.

I already knew his brother Cooper wanted me nowhere near Knox. Griffen, Lucas, and Charlie had been great, but they weren't his family.

I had a temporary stay of execution. Knox wanted to take us home, to his house, before we braved the Sinclair Security offices and figured out what to do about LeAnne Gates.

The transition from the highway to the congestion of Atlanta was abrupt. We descended from the mountains into miles and miles of rolling green hills, exits only popping up here and there, and then Knox got off the highway and we came to an abrupt stop in dense traffic.

He lived *here*? I couldn't see Knox surrounded by all this concrete and exhaust. He'd been so at home in the woods of Maine, content with the isolation of the cabin.

I knew he lived in Atlanta, but I'd never been to the city before, hadn't spent a lot of time in cities in general, and I had no clue what to expect.

A few miles after we left the highway, Knox turned off of the main road, took a right, then a left, and we found ourselves on a two-lane byway shaded by tall, old-growth trees.

"How far is it to your house?" I asked. I'd completely lost my bearings. First, we were in the country, then the city, now it felt like we were in the country again.

"This is Buckhead. I live close by, a few miles from the house I grew up in and Winters House. The Sinclair offices aren't far, so it made sense to stay in the area."

Knox was nervous, too. Because he was worried what his brothers would say? That they wouldn't like me? He already knew Cooper wanted me gone.

I couldn't think of any other reason for Knox to be nervous about bringing me home.

We turned onto an even narrower road with mailboxes set every few hundred feet. Knox slowed in front of one and turned down a smoothly-paved driveway, the dark strip of asphalt curving to disappear into the trees.

"The, uh, lot is a good size, but the house is small. I didn't need much. And anything in Buckhead is expensive so—"

Knox trailed off. We turned the corner of the drive and a house came into view. Nothing like what I'd expected.

"This is it?" I asked, too surprised to be more gracious.

Knox cleared his throat. "I, uh, yeah. This is it."

Knox lived in a fairy-tale cottage. Steeply peaked eves slanted down, framing diamond-paned mullioned windows trimmed in dark wood. Rough siding was stained a dark green—forest-green—with lushly overflowing planters hanging off the rail of the covered front porch. Stacked stone detailed the foundation and corners of the house, an earthy contrast to the copper gutters glinting in the sun.

This wasn't at all what I'd expected, and it was utterly charming. Better than a fairy-tale cottage. It was real, and it was so completely Knox, I was already in love with it.

"Did you do the planters on the porch?"

I had to ask. Not once had I seen him show any interest in gardening. Rubbing the back of his neck, a ruddy flush on his cheeks, he said, "I have a service. It's—do you like it?"

"You have to ask? Knox, it's beautiful. It's just not what I expected. It's so pretty."

"Did you think I lived in a dump?"

"No." I slapped his arm on a laugh and turned to unfasten my seatbelt so I could get out and explore in person. "This is just, honestly, not the kind of place I'd guess a single guy would live in. Like I said, it's pretty. It's gorgeous."

Knox didn't say anything, the red staining his cheeks speaking for him. He let Adam out of the SUV and preceded us to the door. "I'll unload the car. You can take a look around."

Good, because I was planning to.

Knox swung the door open, saying, "I reset the thermostats and checked everything before we left the cabin, so it should be good. Just, uh, make yourself at home."

I wasn't sure I liked the way the Sinclair's technology meant they could see and hear everything everywhere. The number of cameras Knox had at my house was a little creepy. On the other hand, it was awfully nice to walk out of the Atlanta heat into a cool, air-conditioned house.

I stepped through the front door, admiring the way it was curved at the top instead of square, how it appeared to be made from roughly cut wood held together by black iron straps. It looked like something from a movie about hobbits or witches and wizards.

A small wood and iron peek-through door was cut in at eye level, so if someone knocked, you could open it to see who was there without opening the whole door. I was sure there was more sophisticated surveillance I couldn't see—this was Knox, after all—but the peek-through door was too cute.

Inside, the walls were roughly-finished plaster painted a dark cream, the style bringing to mind a house centuries-old. The cozy front entry had stairs on one side leading to the second level and opened into a two-story great room that looked out into the woods behind the house.

A wide stone fireplace dominated one wall of the room. The other side flowed into the kitchen and eating area with more stone, granite, and gorgeous chestnut cabinets.

The inside was as much fairy-tale cottage as the exterior. Not in a feminine way. There wasn't an overstuffed throw pillow or scented candle in sight. Furnished in shades of brown and green with blue accents, the cottage was Knox through and through.

I was still standing in the middle of the great room when he came back carrying two duffel bags. "The bedrooms are this way."

I followed him up the stairs by the front door. At the top, we turned right, and I found myself in a short hall, a bedroom on each side.

One of them was decorated in shades of blue, with a double bed tucked under the eaves. "Adam, this look okay for you?" Knox asked.

Adam took in the cozy, slanted roof, the armchair with foot rest in the corner and the double bed, bigger than the one he'd left at home. "Cool, Mr. Knox. Can I put my stuff in here?"

Knox sent me a questioning look.

Was I going to pretend we'd stay anywhere else? No, I wasn't. I didn't think I could bring myself to leave Knox. It would have been hard enough after we left Maine, but now?

Three weeks of being at his side and the idea of sleeping without him, living without him, was unthinkable. Not going to happen.

Still, I had to give him an out. "You're sure you're okay with this?"

"Lily, don't even ask. I want you here. Both of you."

"Okay, then. By now you know what you're getting into." Unzipping the duffel bag where Adam had shoved his stuffed animals, I said, "Here you go, kiddo. I'll do your clothes, but you can unpack your toys. We'll get the rest in a little bit."

Adam was instantly distracted. I followed Knox back to the top of the stairs and across a walkway overlooking the great room, bordered by the slant of the roof on one side and a black iron rail on the other.

I'd been so distracted downstairs I hadn't noticed the walkway above. At the other end, Knox opened a door into the master bedroom.

A big wooden bed dominated the wall opposite the door. Tall windows with more of those diamond-shaped panes looked out into the woods. The open door to the bathroom gave me a peek of a huge soaking tub and oversized walk-in shower.

"Did you decorate this?" I could not see Knox picking out furniture.

His laugh answered my question. "No. No way. I bought it from the family who built it, and they had good taste. It's a lot newer than it looks, so I didn't have to update anything. Jacob—Jacob Winters—has a good decorator. I told her what I liked, and she did all the work. Anything that doesn't fit probably came from my old place."

"It's perfect. Everything is beautiful."

"Yeah?" Knox dropped the duffel bag and turned to face me, uncertainty in his dark eyes. "You like it? Enough to stay?"

I wrapped my arms around him, determined to chase the question from his beautiful eyes.

"I'm happy anywhere you are, Knox. I was happy in that little cabin. I would have been happy in a tent. And whatever your house looked like would have been fine as long as you're there with me. But this place is beautiful. I love it. I—"

The words almost stuck in my throat. I couldn't believe I hadn't said them yet. Those weeks in the cabin had been perfect. A dream. This, standing in Knox's bedroom, in his house, in his city—this was real. This was life. It was time to take a chance.

Knox asked all those weeks ago if I trusted him. The answer was yes. It was yes then, and it was yes now. The answer would always be yes, as long as Knox was asking.

Going up on my toes, I pressed my lips to his. "I love your house, and I love you. I've loved you for a while, and—"

I didn't get out another word. Knox's hands cupped my face, holding me as his mouth devoured mine, saying everything with his lips he didn't have to say with his voice.

He lifted me, my legs wrapping around his waist as soon as my feet left the ground. Three long steps and my back hit the wall, Knox's mouth hungry and demanding.

Who knows what would have happened if Adam's voice hadn't floated down the hall? "Mom, where's my box of toys?"

Knox pulled back, resting his forehead against mine, panting lightly. "First time I've wished we were alone," he said with a rueful laugh.

I shifted so he could set me on my feet. His arms tightened, keeping me still. Voice hoarse, he called out, "One second, bud. I'll get it out of the car."

Forehead on mine, voice a rumble, he said, "I love you, too. I think I've loved you since I saw your picture in that file, since you opened your door and looked like you wanted to slam it in my face."

Even then he'd been able to read me like a book. I wouldn't pretend I hadn't wanted to slam the door in his face, but letting Knox Sinclair in had been the best decision of my life.

"I love you," he said, "and I love Adam."

A beep sounded somewhere in the house. Knox straightened. Pulling his phone from his pocket he looked at the screen and swore.

"Fuck. Seriously?" Shoving his phone back into his jeans, he dropped a quick kiss on my temple and muttered, "Prepare for the invasion."

Chapter Thirty-Seven

LILY

KNOX OPENED THE DOOR TO reveal a cluster of people on his front porch. Strangers. A cold pit of nerves opened in my stomach. Wiping my suddenly sweaty palms on my hips, I stepped aside to let the invaders in.

A tall man with icy blue eyes and the same thick, dark hair as Knox spoke first. "What the hell are you doing here? I thought you were coming straight to the office."

"We were getting there," Knox said easily. "Did something happen? You can't wait an hour?"

Taking in his scowl, I guessed this was Cooper. He didn't answer Knox's question, just glared at us, his face and build so like Knox's own it set me back for a minute.

From behind him stepped a petite woman, shorter than me and tiny. Not just slender, but built on a small scale, her bones delicate, almost birdlike.

Curious eyes of sky blue were framed by lush, dark lashes. Her mouth was a cupid's bow of red, her hair black as night and chopped bluntly at her chin. She wore a full-skirted dress embellished with cherries and could have stepped straight out of a poster for a nineteen fifties sock-hop.

With a sweetly mischievous smile, she held out a hand to me. I shook it gently, surprised by the strength in those slender fingers.

"These lunks have no manners. I apologize on their behalf. I'm Alice. You must be Lily. It's so nice to finally meet you."

I'd pictured Alice as taller and tough as nails. Looks must be deceiving. No way a pushover could handle the Sinclair brothers and the rest of the guys who worked for them. This cheerful, quirky, sprite of a woman was the last thing I'd imagined, but beneath the warm welcome in her eyes, I saw a hint of steel.

"If there's anything you need, let me know. If Knox isn't around, I can help."

"Thank you," I said sincerely.

The man behind her held out a hand, studying me with friendly eyes the same ice blue as Cooper's. "I'm Evers, one of Knox's brothers. The other one is Cooper, not that he bothered to introduce himself. It's nice to meet you, Lily."

"Nice to meet you too, Evers," I murmured, flicking a quick glance at Knox, his arms crossed over his chest as he glared at Cooper.

Alice followed my gaze, and her mouth twisted into a scowl. She poked Cooper sharply in the side, interrupting his glare-off with Knox. Cooper looked down, the irritation in his eyes a mirror of hers. He raised an eyebrow in haughty query. She cleared her throat and sent an exaggerated look at me.

Cooper's eyes rolled to the ceiling before he nodded at

me. "Lily, I presume?"

As if he didn't already know. I nodded back.

"Cooper," he confirmed. No handshake. That was okay. I wasn't sure I wanted to get close enough to Cooper Sinclair to shake his hand.

He looked down at Alice and raised that dark eyebrow again. I could practically hear the words, *Good enough?*

Alice harrumphed and mumbled something under her breath that sounded like *stubborn ass*. The two of them didn't seem to get along, but, according to Knox, Alice had been running their office for years.

I couldn't see Cooper Sinclair putting up with someone he didn't like, especially in such a key position. Then again, hadn't Knox said they had a love/hate kind of thing? Something like that. There was no time to jog my memory.

Cooper took charge. "Now that the introductions are over, we need to get to work. We had eyes on Tsepov in Vegas an hour ago. Everything is quiet here. This is the best time for you two to make a run at LeAnne Gates."

"We just got here, Cooper," Knox protested. "As you know since you practically chased us through the door."

"He's been driving all day," I protested, crossing my own arms over my chest and staring down Cooper. "He needs a break and lunch before anything else."

Cooper raised that eyebrow again. So much snottiness in one dark arch. "My brother doesn't need a mother hen. And he doesn't need some woman telling him what to do."

Oh. My. God. That autocratic know-it-all tone dug right under my skin. It was the same tone I'd heard from my father for way too many years. I'd hated it then, and I hated it now.

I wasn't always good at sticking up for myself, but this wasn't about me. This was about Knox. Lifting my chin, that stubbornness my mother bemoaned leading me into trouble again, I said, "I'm not a mother hen, I'm looking out for him. That's what you do with people you care about. Or maybe you didn't get that memo."

Cooper's eyes narrowed on me for a long moment during which I deeply regretted every word I'd said. Knox was silent, but wrapped his arm around my waist, molding me to his side. He didn't need words to say whose side he was on.

Cooper's eyes softened, and he shook his head in resignation. "We brought lunch. Let's sit down, get some food, and we can talk about what to do. Is that acceptable?"

This last part was aimed at me. My voice stuck in my throat, I gave a jerky nod. The men dispersed to the kitchen, clearly comfortable in Knox's house.

Alice hung behind. "I'll run out to the car and bring in the food. Lily, do you want to help?"

I joined Alice, following her to another of the ubiquitous black Sinclair Security SUVs.

"Don't mind Cooper," she said in a low voice. "He feels responsible for everything going on with his father. He's worried about his mother, and what happened with Evers and Summer, and then Knox takes off and comes back with a ready-made family—" She shrugged a shoulder. "He loves his brother. If Knox is happy, he'll be happy. He just needs a little time to get used to it."

I didn't know what to say to that except, "Thanks."

"I got lunch for Adam," Alice said, her head buried in the backseat of the car. She passed me a brown paper bag filled with wrapped sandwiches and bags of chips. "I wasn't sure what he'd want so I got grilled cheese and peanut butter and jelly. But, if it's okay with you and he can wait, maybe it would be better to feed him lunch after the rest of us eat. You might not want him in on the conversation."

I realized what she meant and knew she was right. Again, I said, "Thanks, Alice. And thanks for that hotel suite. And for thinking of the beach. It could have been an awful few days, but you helped make it fun."

Alice straightened from the back of the car, her arms loaded with bottles of iced tea and cans of soda. She winked at me, her cherry red lips curved into a grin that proved the mischief I'd seen before had not been a phantom.

"You're very welcome. Lucky they had a cancellation—there wasn't much else available in Bar Harbor. Not on a summer weekend. I need to get up there myself someday. It looked fantastic."

"It was beautiful," I agreed, "and the lobster was out of this world."

"Bet Knox liked that," she said. At my surprise, she went on, "There's not much I don't know about these guys. I've been running the office for ages."

Slanting me a confidential look, she said in a low voice, "Long enough to know the number of women who've crossed the threshold of this house... Single digits. I might even be able to count them on one hand and have some fingers left over."

I didn't know what to say, not ready for the cool relief spreading through my chest. Knox hadn't talked much about past relationships, and I hadn't asked. A man like him must have had a ton of women. I didn't want to know.

"It's been fast, but—"

"Knox knows his own mind. He always has. And he's not one to be stupid over a pretty face. I've never known him to get personal with a client. Ever. And believe me, he's had the opportunity. Knox is strictly business. Always.

Cooper will get over it. Try not to hold it against him while he's being an ass. I know it's tempting, but he's a good guy underneath."

"I'll take your word for it," I said, still working through the idea that Knox didn't usually bring women into his house. That he never got involved with clients.

I'd known what we had was different. Special. Hearing it from Alice made it real.

Knox said he loved me. I knew I loved him. I'd put up with a lot for that. An annoying older brother didn't even factor. Besides, Alice's friendly assurance went a long way to helping me let it go.

I followed Alice back into the house with the bag of food and met the others at the beautifully beaten-up farmhouse table on the far side of Knox's kitchen. He didn't appear to have a dining room, but the table was big enough to seat everyone with room to spare.

I set the bag of sandwiches on the table and turned to Knox. "Adam can stay upstairs while we talk. Is the car locked? I want to go get his Legos and bring them up to keep him busy."

With a smile, Knox kissed my cheek. "I'll get them. I had a few more bags to grab anyway. Be right back." He disappeared. A second later, the front door opened and shut behind him.

I expected Cooper to jump on the chance to warn me off, or something equally irritating and archaic. He didn't. Surprising the heck out of me, he changed the subject completely.

"Let Knox do the talking when you're at Gates'. When she realizes who you are— Let Knox take the lead. The woman is poison. Way over your pay grade."

"You know her?" I asked carefully.

"I do. I dealt with her on similar business a few months ago. Let Knox handle her," Cooper repeated.

I opened my mouth to protest that I could speak for myself.

Cooper held up a hand to stop me. "I'm not implying that you can't handle yourself. I'm saying Knox is going to want to protect you. That will be a lot easier if you don't engage."

"He's right," Evers put in. "It would be better if you stayed here—"

"I'm not staying here," I said before he could finish.

"That's why I didn't bother," Cooper said, annoyance creeping into his voice again.

Wryly, Alice chimed in, "You can't expect her to stay home. We're talking about her son."

It was nice to have an ally. "I'll keep my mouth shut, okay? I need to know what happened, what that woman has to do with Adam. He's my child. But that doesn't mean I'm going to barrel in and screw everything up. It's too important, and I trust Knox."

I squirmed inside under the weight of two identical sets of ice-blue eyes. I wasn't sure I could keep my mouth shut, but I was going to try.

Knox and I wanted the same thing. If the best way I could help was to sit there with my mouth shut, that's what I would do.

If I'd had any idea what I was getting into, I would have made a different promise.

I would have promised to kick LeAnne Gates' ass.

Straight to hell.

Chapter Thirty-Eight

LILY

KEEP MY MOUTH SHUT.

I had no clue how hard that would be.

Cooper had called her poison.

Poison was an understatement.

The flight to Huntsville was only an hour. I hadn't wanted to leave Adam behind. It sounds crazy, but in five years we'd never been separated by more than a handful of miles.

I'd never traveled without him. Why would I? It's not like Trey and I went on romantic weekend getaways or I went home to visit my family. It was always Adam and me.

Getting on that plane without him, even with Knox by my side, felt like tearing off a limb. I had to leave him. There was no way I was bringing him anywhere near LeAnne Gates. Not until we knew what part she'd played in his birth and adoption. Not when Cooper called her poison.

Knox seemed confident that he could handle whatever we'd find when we finally saw LeAnne Gates. I wasn't so sure. If she was over sixty, I doubted she'd been involved with my husband.

She definitely wasn't Adam's mother, which meant there was another woman involved. Someone who might have a claim to my son. Someone who might want him back, no matter what Knox said.

Alice volunteered to stay with Adam at Knox's house, keeping him company until we got back. He watched me go with uncertain eyes, his hand tightly clasped in Alice's, her smile warm and reassuring.

I was uneasy leaving him with her, no matter how much I liked her. Knox said he'd trust her with his life. That would have to be enough.

Thanks to Alice, a car was waiting for us when we landed. The drive to LeAnne Gates' gated neighborhood took less than twenty minutes. At the entrance, security refused to let us through. Knox got out of the car, exchanged tense words with the guard, and held out his hand for the phone.

I don't know what he said, but two minutes later he slid behind the driver's seat, putting the car into gear as the gate swung smoothly open. We found the house after only a few turns down nearly identical streets packed with carbon copy McMansions.

It looked like no one lived here. No cars parked in the street. No bicycles abandoned in the driveways. Knox slowed in front of 57 Arcadia Drive and stopped the car.

I swiped on lip balm and tugged at my skirt. I'd changed into a sundress and pulled my hair up into a bun before we left Knox's house. It felt wrong to meet the woman who held my fate in her hands wearing shorts, my face surrounded by frizzy curls.

No amount of makeup or pretty dresses could ease the twist in my stomach or dry the sweat from my palms. Knox waited for me in front of the SUV, taking my hand as we approached the house. The door opened before we got there.

For a second, I was sure we had the wrong house. The woman in the doorway was taller than me, her platinum blonde hair streaked with threads of gold. Her oddly-beautiful lavender eyes were eclipsed by heavy black liner and thick mascara.

We must have interrupted her work-out. She'd pulled her hair into a high ponytail, secured by a hot pink scrunchie and sweatband that matched her cropped exercise top and the tiniest pair of bike shorts I'd ever seen.

Cleavage was everywhere. So much cleavage, the skin was wrinkling between her breasts from the force shoving them together. I was pretty sure I could see the bottom curve of her ass hanging out of the bike shorts.

This couldn't be LeAnne Gates. Knox had said she was in her sixties. I would have put this woman in her late forties, at worst.

She said nothing, studying Knox with her lavender eyes before they came to me. When her eyes met mine, understanding bloomed. This woman knew exactly who I was.

Her mouth twisted into a scowling smirk. Wrinkles bloomed around her hot pink lips, and I could almost believe her age. Either this woman was a model for healthy living, or she had an ample budget for the best that cosmetic surgery had to offer.

Propping a hand on her hip she opened her mouth. "Well, well, well, if it isn't one of Maxwell's boys and the grieving widow. I haven't talked to your father, so I don't know what you want with me."

"Let us in, and we'll tell you. You don't want to do this on your front stoop," Knox said.

Her hand twitched, and I thought she'd slam the door in our faces. Maybe thinking better of it, she stepped back and let us in. We followed her into the formal living room by the front door. Knox stopped in the entrance, and I bumped into him, so distracted by her decor I wasn't paying attention.

Pink and green. She might have called it rose and avocado, but by any name the color palette was hideous. Her velvet couch was a rusty shade of gold that brought to mind the days of disco.

Every single thing in the room you could sit on was covered in clear plastic slipcovers. Afternoon sunlight angled through the window, glaring off all that plastic, giving the room a glow that left me wanting to close my eyes for relief.

"You boys haven't found Maxwell yet?" LeAnne asked, snagging a crystal glass from the bar cart in the corner and filling it with a generous slosh of vodka. She didn't offer either of us a drink, not that I wanted one.

I hadn't missed the mockery in her voice and pressed myself to Knox's side in comfort. The situation with his father was bad enough. She didn't have to laugh at him over it.

I remembered what Cooper said. *Poison*. I was beginning to see what he meant.

Pulling a pack of cigarettes from somewhere—there was no way those bicycle shorts had pockets—she brought it to her mouth and flicked the lighter that appeared in her hand.

I squinted at her outfit, trying to imagine where in the cleavage-baring crop top and tiny bicycle shorts she'd managed to stash a cigarette lighter. I didn't think I wanted to know.

I watched her light up and exhale a puff of smoke in our direction. So, her youthful appearance didn't owe itself to healthy living. She sat in one of the chairs, the plastic crinkling, probably sticking to her bare legs.

Knox ignored her taunt. "We're not here about my father. Exactly."

"I should have known. You have the widow so you must be here about Trey. He was a good fuck. Kinky. We had fun, but there wasn't much between us. You know, since he was married and all."

LeAnne Gates made no effort to hide her venom. My mouth opened before I thought better of it. "You and Trey? Aren't you a little... Old for him?"

Knox's hand tightened on mine in warning.

I know, I know I said I'd keep my mouth shut, but really? She was going to start by bragging about sleeping with my husband?

Oddly, I felt no sting at the confirmation he'd been cheating on me. He'd thrown my heart away so early in our marriage—what he'd done with his body hardly seemed important.

"Oh, you know Trey," she said, crossing her legs in a way that might have been suggestive if I wasn't so grossed out. "All those issues with his parents. He had a real mommy complex. We weren't working together long before things got... personal. You know what I mean."

I knew exactly what she meant, but this time I kept my mouth shut as promised. I had to or I would have thrown up all over her.

As it was, bile rose in my throat, the acid burning deep. I saw it as soon as the words left her mouth. She was like a trashy version of Trey's mom. Mrs. Spencer had blue eyes instead of lavender, and a haughty New England accent versus LeAnne's Southern, but otherwise...oh, gross. Just ick. The platinum hair, their height, even the curvy build. All the same.

I swallowed hard, fighting back the need to vomit at the thought that Trey had been fucking this woman because she reminded him of his mother. My heart squeezed, feeling sorry for him for a split second before it swerved back to...ugh, gross.

LeAnne soaked up every drop of emotion in my face, mistaking my disgust for the pain of betrayal, savoring her defeat of me with a smile. She bounced her crossed leg, her hot pink toenails flashing in the light.

"If Maxwell had had a piece like Trey working with him when we started, the job would've been a lot more fun. He sure as hell livened up the last few years. Especially when he came back wanting a kid of his own."

No, I was wrong. This did hurt.

I couldn't stop the flinch as those words hit my brain. *Came back wanting a kid of his own.* As if I didn't even factor in the equation.

Knox studied LeAnne for a long moment before coming to a decision. His hand on my lower back, he urged me to the couch, and we sat as if this were a friendly meeting. Nothing more than a chat over drinks. Except LeAnne was the only one with a drink. She tossed back a slug of vodka and waited.

"You brokered the deal for Trey's son?" Knox prompted.

"You don't know?" Her eyes landed on me, speculative. "Isn't that interesting." Then her face went hard. "You know how this works. Since you're Maxwell's boy I might be willing to talk, but I don't do shit for free."

"I know how it works," Knox agreed. "How much?"

"Depends on what you want," she said, exhaling a stream of smoke aimed straight at my face. I resisted the urge to fan it away, keeping my eyes on her and my mouth closed.

Even if I wanted to talk, I wasn't sure what I'd say. At this point, I was better off letting Knox lead.

"Everything," Knox said. "Specifically, the circumstances of the child's birth, and copies of any paperwork pertaining to the exchange. For a start."

"Paperwork?" Her eyes narrowed on me. "Trey brought all that home with him. He didn't leave it for you? Puts you in a sticky situation."

"Don't get cocky," Knox warned. "Were you aware the FBI is involved with my father's business as it pertains to Andrei Tsepov?"

LeAnne took another swig of her drink, her eyes cutting to the side. I guessed she did know, and she wasn't happy about it.

Knox went on, "We have some excellent hackers on staff. Between Trey's laptop, his files, and everything my father left behind, we've got plenty that implicates one LeAnne Gates of Huntsville, Alabama. Jerk me around and the next knock at your door will be from the FBI. Do we understand each other?"

LeAnne Gates lifted her chin in defiance and exhaled another noxious stream of smoke, but when her lungs were empty, she gave a jerky nod. "I still want the money."

Damn, this woman had balls.

"We'll pay what's fair," Knox said. "Tell me what happened with Trey and the baby."

I was glad Knox didn't use Adam's name. I didn't want to hear it spoken in this room, with this woman. I didn't care that she'd had her hands on my husband, but I didn't want to know that she had anything to do with my beautiful little boy.

Adam was innocence. This woman was anything but.

Chapter Thirty-Nine

LILY

"WHERE DO YOU WANT ME to start?" she drawled, her eyes heavy on me, something inside them hungry and vicious. "That one couldn't stay pregnant. Lost a couple, and Trey was getting frustrated. We'd been fucking for a while, and obviously, he knew what my businesses was since he took point for Maxwell after he came on board."

Turning her face to angle me out of the conversation, she looked at Knox and said in a low voice, "He was having second thoughts. He didn't want to divorce her. She was convenient."

I bit my bottom lip to keep my mouth shut. It's not like I couldn't hear her. I was sitting right next to Knox.

"I realized that when I went through his files," Knox said.

It took everything I had to stay silent. What did that mean? Why was I convenient? Because I was cheaper than a housekeeper? Knox's next words were a slap to my face.

"He had everything in her name. If Trey ever ran into trouble, the authorities would have looked at Lily as the ring leader, not Trey."

"Bingo." LeAnne stabbed her cigarette in the air at Knox, a smirk on her pink lips. "That, and like most men, he didn't know how to admit he'd made a mistake. But he didn't want his boy—"

A meaningful glance in my direction before she shifted her eyes back to Knox, "Tainted. You know what I mean. He wanted his kids to look like him. He didn't want a mutt."

Tainted? That bitch. A wave of vicious fury hit me, leaving my heart racing and my gut twisted. *Tainted?*

I beat back the roil of emotions as Knox jerked forward, his body vibrating with rage. My hand tightened on his, holding him in place, his anger somehow dulling my own.

Trey had been an asshole. This woman was worse. But Knox would regret losing his temper. We needed LeAnne Gates if I wanted to find out what had happened with Adam.

I leaned into Knox's side and whispered, "Don't. It's okay, don't."

He sat back, his anger leashed but not weakened. His tone deadly, eyes black with fury, he said to LeAnne, "Watch. Your. Mouth."

LeAnne gave a negligent shrug of her shoulder and ground out her cigarette, lighting another. "You wanted to know. You want to be mad at somebody, be mad at her dead husband. His words. Anyway, they had some incompatibility or something. I don't remember."

My head spun. "Rh incompatibility," I murmured.

LeAnne snapped her fingers. "That's it."

"Rh incompatibility is treatable," I protested. "My doctor should have checked. They could have fixed it."

LeAnne shrugged, unbothered by the idea that she'd just turned my life upside down. "Trey decided not to tell you, make it seem like you just couldn't stay pregnant. But then he had the idea to get a baby the old-fashioned way." She cackled, the sound grating every nerve. "You know, *our* old-fashioned way."

Knox let go of my hand and wrapped his arm around me, the heat of his body anchoring me.

"I know you're not the mother," he said to LeAnne, "so where'd you get the girl? Where is she?"

LeAnne's odd lavender eyes went dark. "You won't find the girl. I can promise you that."

"If you were sleeping with Trey," I croaked, "what did you—how did you—"

LeAnne's laugh dripped with pity. "I can see why he went looking elsewhere. When I was done working for Maxwell in a direct capacity, I started organizing things for him. Finding girls, matching them with the right guy, all that. I had a girl, not that reliable, but she made pretty babies. Blonde and blue-eyed like Trey. She was adventurous, didn't care what I asked her to do as long as there was money or a fix at the end of it."

"She was a junkie?" Knox asked sharply.

"I kept her clean when she was pregnant. When Trey was in town, I'd have her here, and the three of us would fuck. It didn't take long for her to get knocked up. I usually kept an eye on her when she was working for me, but as a favor to Trey, I had her here. The whole time. Fuck, that girl was a pain in my ass. But Trey cut me in on extra, on top of my usual, and she gave him a healthy baby boy. He got his blonde-haired, blue-eyed kid, and a way to keep her from asking for a divorce."

Her words sank in slowly, working their way through

layers of shock. Trey and LeAnne. His lies about my fertility. The distracting thought of LeAnne, Trey, and an unknown girl in a threesome. Yuck.

Finally, it registered. "Trey wanted a baby to keep me from leaving?"

"Mostly, yeah. All men want a son, I guess. If our business is any clue, all men want a son." She rolled her eyes. "But he knew you were going to walk. He didn't give a shit, except he couldn't have lawyers poking around in his finances."

Trey had known I was thinking about a divorce. He'd had Adam to stop me from leaving, knowing the only thing that would keep me at his side was a child, the child I thought I couldn't have myself.

All those months grieving the child I'd never carry, and it was a lie. How had I been so naïve? I guess I should count myself lucky he kept me with him by giving me Adam. He could have gone to the Russian mob and asked Tsepov to take care of his problem.

A faithful wife at home made for good cover, I guess, especially if you put everything in her name. I'd been so wrapped up in Adam I never paid attention to the rest. I was an idiot.

Knox asked the only question left. The only one I cared about. "And the girl? The girl Trey got pregnant?"

LeAnne Gates took a long drag on her cigarette and ground out what was left in the crystal ashtray in front of her. Huffing out the smoke she said flatly, "Dead. Almost two years ago. Got another payday out of her, but she couldn't stay clean after that. OD'd."

My chest hurt at the disinterest in her voice. She'd worked with this girl, had sex with her, delivered her to my husband to impregnate, taken her child for money, yet she spoke of her death as if it was little more than an inconvenience.

Cooper was wrong. Poison was too gentle a word for LeAnne Gates.

"Where's the contract?" Knox asked.

"What do you need the contract for? Everything is legal. The birth certificate on file has her name on it with Trey as the father."

"Just in case," Knox answered in a deceptively easy tone. "Just in case the girl isn't dead. Just in case you're full of shit and she comes knocking on our door. Just in case, and none of your fucking business. How much do you want for it?"

Knox leaned forward, ready to play hardball. My stomach clenched, my head spun, too much stress and all that cigarette smoke pushing me to the edge of nausea again. I jerked to my feet, legs shaky. I needed sugar and bubbles. And to get the hell out of this house.

"Do you have a ginger ale or a soda or something?"

An annoyed look from those lavender eyes. LeAnne gestured behind me at the bar cart in the corner. I lurched in that direction, giving LeAnne and Knox my back. Looking again, I saw a mini-fridge built into the bottom of the cart. I opened it and pulled out an ice-cold ginger ale.

She and Knox were negotiating in low voices, Knox in a glacial tone I'd never heard from him before. She demanded a million dollars. I caught Knox's disbelieving laugh.

If we got a copy of that contract, if I could leave this house knowing that Adam was really and truly mine, I'd pay every last penny I had. Anything. I took a long sip of the ginger ale, lingering on the far end of the room where the smoke was less concentrated. Where I didn't have to see LeAnne's sneering smile.

My eyes trailed around the room, taking in a bookshelf, a plastic plant on a fake marble stand, and a curio cabinet with a mirrored back, its frame made of glaringly shiny brass. I wandered closer, curious to see what kind of things a woman like LeAnne Gates collected.

My eyes caught on a familiar sight and I froze.

It couldn't be, could it? How—?

I didn't have to ask.

Trey.

My goddamned lying bastard of a husband.

Sitting on the top shelf of the curio cabinet, beneath a bright accent light, was a small blue snuff box, diamonds glittering on the lid.

Holy crap.

I turned to get Knox's attention, then thought better of it and started across the room to take my seat beside him. There was a reason Cooper had told me to keep my mouth shut. Intrigue is not my specialty.

Throw me a five-year-old and I'm a pro. Negotiating with a procuress for an illegal contract for a child that was a result of the threesome she'd had with my husband and a drug addict? I could leave that in Knox's lap.

I was crossing the room when Knox's phone rang. He glanced at it and silenced the call. Two seconds later, it rang again. Giving it a long, measuring look, he stood and left the room to answer. A second later his body locked tight.

That couldn't be good.

Chapter Forty

KNOX

THE VOICE IN MY EAR was terrifyingly familiar. I'd missed the second call, but he left a message that sent my world tilting sideways, tipping me out of reality and into a nightmare.

Knox Sinclair. I know you have the numbers. I have your house surrounded. Charges are planted. Send your men in and I'll blow it up. Fail to give me my money and I'll blow it up. Try to get the woman and the boy out and...you get the picture. I look forward to hearing from you.

For far too long, I stood there, unable to move, unable to breathe, the thud of my heart deafening in my ears. Adam. Alice. How?

As if he could read my mind, a text came through. A picture of my house, exactly as I'd left it, except for the small, white block beside the front door, black wires protruding in a tangle. A second picture, another white block, this one at the corner of the house. Another by the garage.

I called Alice. Voicemail. We already knew Tsepov had access to tech. He probably had the signals blocked at the house. I'd have to think of a way to warn Alice.

First, the accounts. They were empty. I couldn't let Tsepov learn the money was gone while he still had Adam and Alice.

"Knox?" Lily hovered on the edge of the living room, worry heavy in her eyes. Fuck. I held up a finger. She stayed silent, but she didn't leave. Fuck.

Normally my first call would be to Cooper. I thought of Alice, trapped in my house, surrounded by bombs. Not Cooper. Not yet.

I needed to talk to Tsepov, and I absolutely couldn't call him. Not with Lily standing right there. I thought about telling her to get into the car. She trusted me, but she also knew me. She knew something was wrong. Chances of getting her out of here? Zero.

I texted in response to the message.

> Get rid of the explosives and I'll give you the numbers.

An answer shot back in seconds.

> I see what's in the accounts, then I let them go.

Fuck. That was exactly what I couldn't let happen. I had to buy time.

> I'm not in Atlanta. I need time.
>
> Get me the money or I'll blow the house.
>
> You blow the house, you'll get nothing.
>
> You have two hours.

I had to hope that would hold him. The clock was ticking. Way too many things could go wrong, with two lives in the balance. Cooper might call Alice, Alice might notice the wireless and mobile signals were down. Adam might want to play outside. Anything could happen.

We were done here.

A tug on my sleeve. I looked down to see Lily at my side. So quiet her voice was almost inaudible, she asked, "What's wrong? What happened?"

I thought about lying, almost managed to convince myself it was the right thing to do. I didn't need Lily to lose it. Not now. I thought about it, and I knew I couldn't do it.

Aware LeAnne was listening, I matched Lily's almost silent tone. "I need you to be strong for me, Lily—"

I didn't have to finish. Her skin turned to ash beneath her normal tawny glow. "Adam," she breathed.

"Tsepov has the house surrounded. Adam and Alice don't know. They're fine. But we need to get him the account numbers." I didn't mention the bombs. Lily didn't need that much truth. Not yet.

She swayed against me, pupils so wide her eyes were almost black. Sucking in a breath, she pressed her forehead to my chest, body trembling, the struggle to control her panic taking every ounce of her attention.

"Lily—"

"I'm okay."

"We need to go," I urged.

"Wait. Just give me a minute."

We didn't have a minute. I gave her another few seconds anyway. Her breathing evened out. She straightened and pressed the heels of her palms to her eyes, then wiped beneath with her fingertips, erasing any signs of tears.

Voice tight and barely a whisper she said, "You can't give him the numbers, right? Because there's no money in the accounts. And not enough time to put it there."

"Right," I confirmed.

"What if we could give him something else?"

"We can try," I started, "ask him how much he wants. I'll give him everything I have if it will get Adam back."

Between the money Trey left with Lily and my own savings, we had assets. None of them were worth shit if we lost Adam.

Lily shook her head. Reaching out, she took my hand and tugged me back across the hall, ignoring LeAnne's curious gaze. I wanted to tell her we didn't have time to waste, that we had to deal with LeAnne and get moving, but I couldn't bear to shut her down after delivering such devastating news.

Lily pulled me past LeAnne to the far end of the living room, coming to a stop in front of a garish brass curio cabinet.

"What if we give him that?"

Holy fucking shit. The snuff box. Why would Trey have given it to LeAnne Gates?

"Get it," I said.

Lily opened the curio cabinet. LeAnne twisted in her seat. When she saw what Lily was doing, she surged to her feet, vodka sloshing from the crystal glass in her hand.

"What the hell do you think you're doing? Get your hands off my stuff."

"I believe this is mine," Lily said, her voice coated in ice.

This was a Lily I'd never seen before. She wasn't shy or tentative. This was a woman who would do anything to save her son. LeAnne Gates no longer scared her. Nothing scared her but Adam coming to harm.

"That's not yours," Leanne insisted, striding across the room, vodka spilling over her fingers. She reached to snatch the snuff box from Lily's hands. I closed my fingers around her wrist and yanked her back.

"Interesting," I said, holding her away from Lily,

"because we have a bill of sale that says it belonged to Trey. And Trey left it to Lily. Do *you* have a bill of sale?"

Lavender fire burned in Leanne's eyes. "I don't have a fucking bill of sale. Trey gave it to me. It's mine."

Lily held onto the snuff box with both hands, her spine poker straight. Her usually warm eyes were frigid as she stared down LeAnne.

"I'm taking the box. I'll give you a hundred thousand dollars for the contract. Or, we walk out of here and you get nothing. Decide."

Leanne looked from me to Lily, her lower lip quivering. Was she about to cry? I didn't give a fuck.

Dropping the pathetic act the moment she saw no one cared, LeAnne ground her teeth together and said, "Two hundred thousand."

Lily took my arm, the box tucked against her chest. "Let's go."

We turned for the door.

"Wait!"

We stopped, Lily looking over her shoulder. "We don't have time for this," she said.

"One hundred thousand. I'll take it. I'll get the contract."

Lily released my arm. Leaving her by the door, I said, "Stay here."

"I'm coming with you," I said to LeAnne, dogging her heels as she led me to a home office on the second floor. It looked unused except for the file cabinet built into the desk, stuffed full of papers.

Rifling through, she muttered, "I know you don't have the cash on you. Don't even think about stiffing me, or—"

"I'm the least of your worries right now," I told her, honestly. "Andrei Tsepov is on a rampage. What do you think he'd do to you if he found you with that box?"

Her face went white.

"You'll get the money. I'll be in touch. Unless you can't find the contract."

She tore a folder from the drawer and shoved it at me. I scanned the few pages, seeing all I needed. Trey and a woman's name I didn't recognize listed as the parties to the contract. In the section assigning parental rights: Trey Spencer and Lily Spencer.

"Why did Trey give you the box?"

"He owed me," she shot back, her chin raised in defiance.

Lie. I'd bet anything he asked her to hold it for him, spreading out his assets, just in case.

She turned her head to the side with a jerk and lit another cigarette. I closed the folder with the contract and walked away, leaving LeAnne behind.

"Wait, what about my money?" she called down the stairs.

"We'll be in touch," I said over my shoulder.

She might get her money. She might not. At that moment I could not possibly have cared less.

I had to get my boy back.

Chapter Forty-One

KNOX

"CAN YOU DRIVE?"

I expected Lily to balk, but she took the keys from my hand and switched directions, moving to the driver's side of our rental.

"Would you set the GPS in the car?"

I punched in the address to the private airfield where the plane was waiting and let her take over. I had calls to make before we were in the air.

A minute into the drive and I knew Lily had this under control. She drove smoothly, as fast as she could but not fast enough to get us pulled over. We didn't have time to waste on a ticket.

Before anything else, I called the pilot. I wanted the plane ready to take off when we got there.

The next call was a lot harder.

Cooper.

It was too dangerous to leave him out of the loop. Too much could go wrong before we got to Atlanta. If it were anyone else but Alice I wouldn't think twice.

All of us had experience in crisis situations, first in the military and then years of working with clients in touchy situations. Cooper wasn't in charge because he was the oldest. He was in charge because he never faltered, never lost focus, never let emotion rule.

Cooper was a fucking machine. Except this was Alice. And where Alice was concerned, all bets were off.

I didn't have a choice. I glanced at Lily, her eyes on the road, knuckles tight on the steering wheel. I loved the Lily I knew. Her shyness, her occasional uncertainty, was a part of her, and I loved that part as much as everything else.

This woman sitting beside me—this woman who would do anything to save her son—she wasn't the woman I wanted every day, but I loved Lily more knowing she had this resolve inside herself for Adam. For someone who was hers.

She was making good time, the traffic lights changing in our favor, one after the other. I could practically hear the clock ticking in my head. Less than two hours.

I tried Alice again. Straight to voicemail. Fuck.

Braced for the explosion to come, my finger hovered over Cooper's name on the screen of my phone. I made a split-second decision and hit the name below his.

"Hey, man, on your way home? Things go well?"

"Evers, we have a problem. You in the office?"

"Yeah."

"You alone?"

"Yeah," he said more slowly. "What happened? Are you okay?"

"Lily and I are fine. Alice and Adam are not. Tsepov has the house surrounded. I'm on my way and I'll need backup."

A long silence. His voice precise, calculating, Evers said, "Cooper's going to flip his shit. I'm assuming Tsepov said to come alone?"

There was only a hint of irony in his words. I heard the thump as he pushed back from his desk, the sound of voices as he moved down the hall.

"Yeah. Don't send anybody or he'll shoot, yada, yada."

"He wants the account numbers," Evers said.

"Yeah."

"Fucking hell. We're fucked—"

"No," I cut him off, "we're not. I don't have time to explain, but I have something to trade. We'll hit the airport in a minute. I need to talk to Cooper, but not until you're in his office so he doesn't do anything—"

"Stupid, got it. Get on it. I'm here."

Evers disconnected. Before I called Cooper, I texted to Evers,

> Charges planted around the house. Didn't want L to hear.

Then, I called Cooper.

"What the fuck?" my brother answered. "You guys okay?"

"We're fine." I didn't have time to ease him into it. "Tsepov has Alice and Adam." I heard Evers in the background, quietly filling him in on the explosives and Tsepov's demands.

Complete and utter silence from Cooper.

I braced, waiting for him to swear, to yell, to throw the phone. Anything. There was fucking nothing.

I pulled the phone away from my ear to check the screen in case I'd disconnected. The time counter on the call ticked-up, second by second.

00:21

00:22

00:23

00:24

Nothing from Cooper.

Just when I was about to hang up and call Evers, a harsh breath sliced through the speaker like a blade. Cooper's voice was guttural, the sounds barely words.

"I'm going to slit his fucking throat."

I tried to decide if coldly enraged Cooper was better than a Cooper who was swearing and throwing things.

Better for Alice.

Better for Adam.

Not so good for Tsepov.

That was fine. As long as Adam and Alice were okay, I didn't give a shit what happened to Tsepov. Agent Holley might since he was trying to build a case, but we'd deal with the FBI later.

"When I get my fucking hands on him—"

"Coop," I barked into the phone. "We have an hour and forty-five minutes before I have to be there. Before we need to make the trade. I don't have time for you to get your shit together. I need you now. Alice needs you now."

Another grating breath, the hiss of Cooper sucking in air. Once. And again. I could practically see him closing his eyes, using his steady breathing to calm his nerves the way he'd learned years ago.

Good. This was good. I waited, the clock in my head ticking down as I followed the map on the screen of the rental. I had another few minutes before we were on the plane. Once we took off and rose above the cell towers, I'd lose the connection. I couldn't afford to lose contact until we had a plan.

"How much cash can you get your hands on?" I asked. "I got something from Gates we can use instead of the money in the accounts but adding cash to the deal won't hurt. Just in case he doesn't recognize it."

"What? What did you get from Gates?" Cooper ground out.

"The Imperial Faberge snuff box," I said.

A beat of silence and then, "What the fuck? How did she have it?"

"Long story. Not important. I have the box. It's probably enough on its own, but—"

"I'll get the cash. We need to end this shit."

"We're almost at the airport," I said. "I tried calling Alice. Twice. I can't get through. I'm almost positive he's got the signals blocked. We need to let her know. There's a safe room in the basement—"

Lily shot a hopeful glance in my direction before her eyes went back to the road and she swung the car into the airport.

"Alice knows where it is," I went on. "She knows the code, knows how to get into the safe with my weapons. If we can tell her what's going on—"

"What do you have in the house? If there's no cell signal, and he cut the cable so there's no Internet, no phone, what else do you have?"

I'd been racking my brain for the answer to that question since I realized Tsepov had blocked the cellular signals.

"Not much," I admitted. "There's the wireless network inside the house. It's probably live even if he's cut the Internet."

"Your alarm has a separate cellular signal, doesn't it? Wired in away from the house?"

All the alarms we installed had an independent cellular line, so they could alert emergency services if the power or phone lines were down. Even if someone was using a device to block a cellular signal. The alarm was hard-wired to a mini cell tower hidden in the woods. Tsepov's men wouldn't know to look for it, and it was far enough away from the house that whatever he was using to block the signal wouldn't affect it.

"It's our standard system," I said, "so, yeah, it has a cellular line, but it's not connected to the wireless network in the house."

"But that gives us a live signal going into the house," Cooper said. "We can't trigger the alarm without risking Tsepov's men panicking and blowing the house. You don't have a speaker system on the alarm, do you?"

"Fucking no. It was just me and I—"

I never thought I'd need one. Never imagined this scenario. For clients? Sure. But for me?

We always tell people the most important thing your system protects is the people inside the house. I'd always been on my own, and I could protect myself just fine. My system, what I had of it, was the best. I'd left off most of the bells and whistles, never thinking I'd need them.

Lilly brought the car to a halt as close to the plane as she could. We were out the second it rolled to a stop, racing for the open door of the plane.

"Boarding now. I'll lose you once we're up. Stay with me."

"Gotcha. Evers is working on the cash. He's getting Lucas so we can figure out if there's a way to patch the signal going to the alarm into the network in the house."

I buckled in, Lily beside me, and took her hand in my free one. Closing my eyes, I tilted my head back, trying to picture every square inch of my house, to put the pieces together in a shape we could use.

So much shit connected to the Internet. Fucking everything, from the smart speakers to the refrigerator. The goddamn coffee maker had an app so I could start a pot from my fucking phone, and the printer—

I sat up with a jerk. The fucking printer.

I didn't have a home office per se. I lived five minutes from work. If I needed a desk, I went to the office. Every once in a while, I worked from home, spreading out any paperwork on the big farmhouse table in the kitchen.

We tried to stick with electronic files versus hardcopy for anything sensitive, but some of the admin shit we printed out old school.

While I hadn't succumbed to the trend for a home office, I did have a printer in the utility room by the kitchen. A multifunction copy/scan/fax/printer device, its connection to the phone line would be useless, but it *was* on the wireless network.

"The printer," I said. "In the utility room. It's not that loud, but it's fucking stocked with paper. Alice will hear it. If Lucas can get can patch the alarm to the network, maybe—"

In the background, I heard Lucas grumble, "It's fucking designed so it *doesn't* connect with the fucking network."

The plane lurched forward as its wheels left the ground. Cooper pulled his phone from his face, his voice distant as if from the other end of a long hallway. "I don't give a fuck. Make it connect."

Doing the same with my own phone I called to the cockpit, "How long till we land?"

"Forty-five minutes," came the answer.

"We'll be there in forty-five minutes."

The plane gained altitude, cutting through the blue sky into the clouds. Any second, we'd leave the reach of cell towers and the phone would cut off. No Wi-Fi on the Sinclair Security plane, which meant no cellular calls. I'd always liked that before.

The private plane was a hefty expense, one we'd decided was worthwhile. Adding Wi-Fi? That ran a cool quarter-million, and for a number of reasons, we'd decided to skip it.

Cursing myself as a cheap bastard, I told Coop, "Anything happens, call the sat phone. I'm about to lose you. I'll call the second we land."

Cooper disconnected before the call dropped. From beside me, Lily said, "You have a safe room?"

"In the basement. It's basic, but it's bombproof and bulletproof."

"Do you think Lucas can hack into the network? Will Alice hear the printer?"

More than anything I wished I knew the answers to those questions. "I hope so. I fucking hope so."

Lily fell silent. I'd always loved that we didn't need to talk, but never like I did then. Every nerve in my body was strung tight. I didn't think I could have handled words, handled having to reassure and calm. I could barely keep myself together.

My grip on Lily's hand was too tight. Her fingers dug into mine. She was my lifeline, and I was hers. We held on with everything we had as each excruciatingly slow second ticked by.

Lucas was the best. He would figure it out. Evers would get the money. Cooper would somehow keep himself from burning the world to the ground to get to Alice. The plane would land, we'd give Tsepov his fucking box and his money. We'd end this once and for all. With everyone safe.

I had to believe that. I had to believe I was going to hear Adam's infectious giggle again. I had to believe he would be all right because there was no alternative.

Not for Lily and not for me. I wanted my family—Lily and Adam and me. Together.

Without Adam, it would all fall apart. Lily would fall apart. And I would go right with her.

This was not my fault. I knew that. This train wreck had been set in motion by my father, by Lily's husband, long before we'd met.

It was not my fault.

And yet Adam was trapped in my house under my watch, his fate balanced in the hands of a man who so far had proven to be a fucking moron. A dangerous fucking moron.

All it would take was a careless finger on the wrong switch and the house would be obliterated, Alice and Adam along with it.

Thinking of Cooper, I forced myself to breathe, drawing air in slowly, filling my lungs and emptying them. Creating calm. Focus. Pushing back the fear, the utter mind-numbing terror, that this whole thing would slip out of my hands, and Adam with it.

Chapter Forty-Two

KNOX

I ALMOST WEPT WITH RELIEF AT the jolt of the tires hitting the runway. We'd barely come to a stop when Lily and I were up, unbuckling our seatbelts and bolting for the door. She muttered under her breath, "Open it, open it," the copilot slanting her an annoyed look.

I ignored him and called Cooper.

"You on the ground?"

"Yeah," I said, following Lily down the steps to the tarmac. "Headed for the car. Did you get it?"

"Lucas bitched the whole time, but he managed to patch the cell signal on the alarm to your network. We sent a file to the printer from our end. It looks like it's been printing for twenty minutes. You've got to be out of paper by now. No fucking clue if she saw it because you don't have any goddamn cameras in your house."

Racing through the tiny terminal to the parking lot I barked, "Why the fuck would I have cameras in my own house?"

I knew for a fucking fact Cooper didn't have them in his.

He didn't answer my question. I could only hope Alice had heard the printer, that she and Adam were tucked away in the safe room.

I had to think that because the other option—that they were wandering through the house unaware of the danger they were in, that they might try to go outside or realize there was something wrong with the phones—.

No. I couldn't do anything about that. Except give Tsepov what he wanted and convince him to call off his goons.

I slid behind the wheel of the SUV I'd left in the lot.

"Evers have the money?"

"He scraped together a million," Cooper said. "What do you think?"

"I need to text Tsepov and let him know I'm on my way."

"And the money? The box? What do you want to offer?"

"Cooper, if you're about to fucking suggest that we low-ball him—"

"Shut the fuck up, you asshole. I'm not going to fucking lowball Tsepov when Alice's life is on the line."

"So we give him all of it," I confirmed. "I'm good for it—"

"I don't give a fuck about the money, Knox. We'll figure it out later. Are you headed here?"

"I can't bring Lily."

I felt Lily go stiff beside me, but she didn't say a word. No fucking way I was bringing Lily anywhere near Tsepov. Bad enough he had Adam and Alice. I'd need everything I had to get this done. Lily would be a distraction.

"Text Tsepov," Cooper cut in, "Tell him you'll meet him at your house, in the driveway just past the curve. You'll be hidden from the road, not close enough to the house to make him nervous."

"That works," I agreed.

"Evers has a team together. They'll take position in the woods, far enough out that Tsepov's men won't spot them."

Tsepov had said to come alone. Standard bad guy orders.

Evers knew what he was doing. If he'd put the team together, they'd be invisible, and we already knew Tsepov's men weren't the top of the barrel.

They'd never see Evers coming.

I knew that, and still, I didn't like it.

Cooper went on, "Drive here. Pull into the garage. I'll have someone bring Lily up. I'm coming with you."

Cooper disconnected. I pulled up the number Tsepov had been using and handed my phone to Lily.

"I need you to text for me."

She took the phone and waited.

"Tell him—In Atlanta. Meet you in the middle of my driveway in twenty minutes."

Lily's fingers tapped the screen. When she was done, she looked up. "Is that it? Should I send it?"

"That's it."

Less than a minute later my phone chimed. Lily read, "Twenty minutes. Come alone."

"Tell him—Bringing Cooper. He has what you want."

Another minute and a second chime from my phone. Lily read, "Fine. Only Cooper. Eighteen minutes."

Lily handed my phone back. "What an asshole," she said, her voice shaky.

"You got that right," I agreed. She reached out, wrapping her hand around mine. I held on as we made our way through the streets of Atlanta to Sinclair Security. The four-story building was sleek, the exterior mirrored, flashing graphite in the summer sun.

I pulled into the parking garage and came to a stop

by the elevators. Lily was unbuckling her seatbelt when I leaned across and cupped her chin in my hand bringing her face to mine for a quick kiss.

"The next time I see you I'll have Adam," I promised.

Lily's eyes met mine, her pupils too wide, her face still a little gray, but she gave me a resolute nod. "I'll see you soon," she said and slid from the car.

Cooper took her place, a small black gym bag on his lap. I threw the SUV into gear and headed out.

"You couldn't find a briefcase?" I asked, preferring sarcasm if it would hold back everything else.

We were so close. So close, and with every turn of the wheels, I grew more aware of all the ways this could go wrong.

Cooper ignored my taunt about the briefcase.

"Is Evers in position?" I asked, trying to focus on the job at hand.

"He's there," Cooper confirmed. "Where's the box?"

I jerked my head at the backseat. Cooper turned and reached to retrieve the snuff box, wrapped in the cardigan Lily had brought to ward off the air-conditioned chill of the plane.

"Think he'll go for it?" I asked Cooper.

"If he doesn't, there's always Plan B," he said ominously. I came to a stop at a red light and chanced a look at my brother. I couldn't remember the last time I'd seen him like this.

His ice blue eyes, so like my father's and Evers', were locked down. Impenetrable. A knot in his jaw flexed. I didn't say anything else. No point. We'd done what we could do. Now, all we had was hope.

A few minutes later I turned down my driveway as I had so many times before. For the first thirty feet, everything looked normal. It could have been any other day.

We came around the curve and the illusion fell apart. There were men in black gear holding rifles interspersed through the woods. A shiny, black sedan blocked the driveway.

I pulled the SUV to a stop. Cooper reached for the door handle. My hand shot out and grabbed his arm. "I'm talking."

It was a measure of how tightly strung Cooper's nerves were that he grunted in acknowledgment but didn't argue. Holding the gym bag and the box, still wrapped in Lily's cardigan, Cooper got out of the car.

I held on to hope. Hope that Adam and Alice were okay. Hope that Cooper would keep his shit together long enough to get them back. Hope that none of Evers' guys tipped off Tsepov's men. Hope that somehow, we'd all get out of this alive.

Andrei Tsepov emerged from the sedan. Tall, slender, elegant in a dark suit, he sauntered toward us with the arrogance of a king.

A hard stare fell on Cooper's full hands. "That doesn't look like account numbers."

There was no point in bullshitting him. "We found the numbers. The accounts are empty. We have something else."

Tsepov's dark eyes flared with rage. "I want what's mine, you fucking greedy—"

His right arm lifted as if to signal. Cooper moved, drawing Tsepov's eye. He said nothing, but peeled back the edge of Lily's sweater, tilting the snuff box so the diamonds caught the light.

Tsepov's head jerked around, his attention zeroing in on the flash of all those stones. His arm dropped to his side. He took a step forward, mesmerized.

"You know what it is?" Cooper asked, his voice flat, deadly.

Andrei Tsepov nodded, eyes locked on the snuff box, his hand reaching forward as if to snatch it from Cooper's grasp.

I took a step to the side, blocking Cooper and the box from Tsepov's gaze. "It was Sergey's," I said. "He gave it to my father."

"It should be mine." Tsepov's voice was breathy with awe. Then, firmer, "It's mine."

"I'll give you the box and a million dollars cash. Get the charges off my house and it's all yours."

Tsepov eyed me for a long moment, thinking before he said, with an easy shrug of one shoulder, "What's to stop me from taking it? These woods are filled with my men. They're armed and you're not. I could take the bag, the box, and blow the house anyway."

Beside me, Cooper growled low in his throat. Of all the fucking times for my rock-solid brother to lose it, it had to be now.

I said, "You could, but your men aren't the only men in these woods, and if you blow the house, you'll die. If you pull a weapon on either of us, you'll die. Or, you could take the box, the money, and agree that whatever problem you have with my father, we're out. My brothers and I, our women, our mother, our families—we're all out of it. We give you that box and the cash, and your issues with my father stay between you and my father. Agreed?"

Tsepov's teeth ground together, his chin jutting forward as he processed my demand. Maybe I should have bargained for my father's protection, too. Tried to end this whole thing once and for all.

Fuck that. Andrei Tsepov wanted revenge on my dad. Fine then, he could have it. Adam's life wouldn't be in danger if it weren't for my dad.

I was done protecting him. He was on his own. My concern was for the innocent. For my family. My father no longer qualified.

"If I agree," Tsepov said slowly, "your father is still fair game."

"My father is on his own," I confirmed.

Tsepov leaned to the side, trying to see around me, needing Cooper's assent. I stepped out of the way.

"And you? You agree?" Tsepov demanded of Cooper.

In a voice so tight I thought it would snap, Cooper said, "I agree. We're out. The women, the child, our mother—our family is out. Whatever you need to do to my father, have at it."

It tore at me. Buried under all that anger, under the betrayal, the rage, the futile wish that he was the man I'd always hoped he could be, it tore at me to throw my father to the wolves.

He should have been so much more than this.

I'd grown up wanting him to be the hero, never realizing how much he was the villain. A part of me wanted to save him. Wanted to believe he could be redeemed.

The time for that had passed. I had people to protect. My father was no longer on that list.

"We have a deal," Tsepov said, taking a step forward, his hands reaching for the bounty he thought he'd earned.

I moved to block him from Cooper.

"I want the charges off the house. You can keep your men in place, but get the fucking charges off my house or you get nothing."

Irritation flashed across his face before Tsepov raised his phone and spoke a single word. I didn't catch what it was, but two men emerged from the woods and headed for the house.

One of them went to the front corner, crouching to remove a white rectangle of C4. The other did the same at the front door.

Cooper put the sweater-wrapped box in the bag with the money and moved to hand it to Tsepov.

Chapter Forty-Three

KNOX

IN THE QUIET OF THE summer afternoon, all hell broke loose.

A shot rang out from inside the house. Then another. Before we registered the live fire, the house shook, a plume of smoke rising from the side of the garage.

One of the charges had blown. At the sound of the shots and the explosion, Tsepov's men scattered like rats, melting into the woods.

Cooper shoved the bag at Tsepov and took off in a sprint. I was on his heels, Andrei forgotten. Cooper threw himself at the door, stumbling as it gave easily, unlocked. He bellowed Alice's name.

No answer.

I opened my mouth to scream for Adam, then stopped. I didn't want to scare him. Cooper's shouts were bad enough.

The house was silent except for the crackle of fire faintly coming from the direction of the garage. The acrid scent of smoke drifted down the hall.

Cooper bolted toward the basement, skidding to a stop at the open door of the utility room. The tile floor in front of the printer was piled with paper, all of it bearing the same message.

HOUSE SURROUNDED. GET TO SAFE ROOM.

HOUSE SURROUNDED. GET TO SAFE ROOM.

HOUSE SURROUNDED. GET TO SAFE ROOM.

HOUSE SURROUNDED. GET TO SAFE ROOM.

It was hard to tell if the pile had been disturbed, but from the single sheet crumpled by the door, I thought Alice had gotten our message.

Cooper must have thought the same because he was at the basement door a second later, his feet pounding down the stairs.

He shouted Alice's name. At the anguish in his tone, my heart stopped. Alice lay crumpled at the base of the stairs, my Walther PPQ inches from her open hand.

Ten feet away, deeper in the basement, lay a second body, this one dressed in black like the rest of Tsepov's men.

Cooper knelt at Alice's side, his fingers at her throat, feeling for a pulse. The pool of blood beneath Tsepov's man told me I didn't need to do the same for him.

"Alice?"

"Alive. Heartbeat stable." His hands slid gently beneath her head. "Hell of a bump here," he said, his fingers lingering behind her ear.

Alive. It was all I needed to hear. I was at the safe room door, punching in the code. I tore the door open the second the lock disengaged.

Adam sat cross-legged on the floor, his lip caught between his teeth as he studied a puzzle laid out on the carpet, a juice box and a bowl of goldfish by his side.

He looked up to see me and grinned.

"Mr. Knox. Where'd Alice go? We're playing a game, but she didn't come back. She's getting cookies."

"We'll get you cookies in a minute," I said, relief giving my words buoyancy. "Are you—" The house shook above us, the steel-lined concrete of the safe room stable as everything around us shifted.

Cooper moved like lightning, scooping Alice into his arms and bolting up the stairs. I did the same with Adam, holding him close to my body to shield him. I had no fucking clue how much C4 was left on the house or what set it off.

Had the explosion been an accident or were they going to take the house down around us?

Another charge went off, this time at the back of the garage. This close it was deafening. The house shook again, the floor rolling under our feet. Cooper stumbled, almost going to his knees with Alice before he caught himself and lunged for the door.

Feet pounding, conscious only of Cooper ahead of me and Adam's hot breath in my ear, I ran for the SUV. It was still where we'd left it, but the sedan was gone, gouges in the grass beside the driveway evidence of Tsepov's escape.

I wrenched open the back door. Cooper lay Alice down along the seat, her eyes still closed. Evers emerged from the woods, Griffen beside him.

Griffen took one look at the situation and jumped behind the wheel, throwing the vehicle into gear before Cooper had his door shut. I stepped back, giving them room as he reversed down the drive and out of sight.

Evers scanned Adam and then me.

"He okay?"

"He's okay," I confirmed. Evers touched the mic at his ear. "Call it in. Cooper has Alice. They're headed to the hospital. Adam is unharmed. He's with Knox. Have someone take Lily to my house." To me, he said, "Alice?"

"Unconscious, with a bump on her head. No other visible injuries."

He nodded, eyes worried. Alice had been with us for years. She was family. If anything happened to her—

Evers shook off his worry and smiled, moving into Adam's line of sight. Adam burrowed into me, his eyes wide and a little wild after our crazed flight from the house.

"Hey, Adam, I'm Evers, Knox's brother. I didn't get to meet you before. You like swimming?"

Did he like swimming? What the fuck was Evers talking about?

My heart pounding at our narrow escape, relief had slowed my processing power. I got it when Evers said, "I live right around the corner. Unlike Knox, *I* have a pool. You want to go swimming?"

"I left my bathing suit inside," Adam said, his face falling as he looked back at the house and caught sight of the garage engulfed in flames. "Are the firemen coming?"

"They're on the way, kid," Evers reassured. "It's my pool. I don't care if you want to swim in your underwear."

Adam brightened and looked up at me. "Can I swim in my underwear, Mr. Knox?"

"It's good with me, bud." I shot Evers a grateful look.

"One of the guys is bringing my car around. Lily will be there soon. This'll be easier with you guys out of my way. I have to deal with the fire department and call Agent Holley. What are we looking at inside? Anything?"

"Alice got one. Basement. Weapon looked like mine. Any clue what happened?"

"Nope. My guess? The one in the house was looking for leverage in case the hand-off went bad." Evers sent a meaningful look at Adam. "I was on the wrong side of the house to see, but the explosion feels like an accident."

We wouldn't know until Agent Holley had time to examine the scene, but Evers' analysis made sense. There was no denying that the sight of Adam with a gun to his head would have tilted negotiations in Tsepov's favor.

"Makes sense. Good thing Alice remembered her training."

Evers gave a nod. One of our black SUVs nosed down the drive. I slapped his shoulder once and took off at a jog, Adam in my arms, belting him in the back as soon as it stopped.

We didn't have a booster seat, but this one time I didn't think Lily would mind. I owed Evers big time for handling all the bullshit that was about to rain down on his head.

I backed down the drive, turning away from my burning house without the slightest twinge of regret.

It was a house.

Adam was safe. Alice was a little banged up, but Cooper said her heartbeat was steady. Until I heard differently, I was going to assume she was fine. Two for two. If I counted getting Tsepov off our backs for good, it was a complete victory.

In light of that, I wasn't worried about my garage. At the wail of sirens, I relaxed even more. The fire department would stop the flames before they spread much further.

Evers' house, as he'd told Adam, was around the corner. We beat Lily there. Using the key on the ring from the SUV, I let us in, directing Adam to the bathroom as soon as we cleared the threshold.

After almost five weeks with the kid, I knew any transition required a bathroom break if we wanted to avoid disaster. The tiny bit of normalcy steadied me like nothing else could.

Adam was safe. I waited by the door for Lily, taking a minute to send Tsepov one last text.

You have the money and the box. This is done.

I'm coming for your father. Stay out of my way.

I ignored the stab of regret as I answered.

He's all yours.

Then Lily was there, bolting out of the SUV in the drive and flying up the stairs to me, her eyes wild. Adam was just leaving the bathroom, wiping his wet hands on the front of his shirt as she flew through the door, her eyes landing on him immediately.

"Adam!" she cried, darting forward and scooping him into her arms, holding him close, her face buried in his neck, tears streaming down her face.

"Mom, there's a fire, and Mr. Knox and his brother said we could go swimming."

Oh, to be a five-year-old, where a house fire and swimming ranked the same level of excitement. I wrapped them both in my arms, pressing my cheek to the top of Lily's head, her soft hair tickling my nose.

"Everyone's okay, Lily. Everyone's okay."

Well before she was ready, Adam started to squirm, not understanding his mother's desperate need to hold on to him.

"Mom, put me down. I wanna go swimming. Mr. Knox said I can swim in my underwear. Can I? Can I?"

With a Herculean effort, Lily loosened her grip and set Adam on his feet. Her voice wobbly and her eyes wet, she said, "It's okay this time, baby."

"I'll show you where the pool is." I led them out to Evers' deck and down the stairs to the pool. Adam tore off his clothes as he ran, screeching with delight before he cannonballed into the shallow end.

Taking Lily's hand, I led her to the steps, and we sat, getting rid of our shoes and dropping our feet in the cool water.

"Alice?" she asked. "They said Cooper took her to the hospital."

"No word yet. She'll be fine," I said, hoping I was telling her the truth. I filled her in on everything else, forgetting I hadn't told her about the bombs before I left her at Sinclair Security.

She smacked my shoulder twice before she shoved with both hands, trying to dump me in the water. Despite her effort, she barely moved me an inch.

I had it coming. Leaving out the bombs was a pretty big omission, not that I regretted it. With a sigh, Lily let it go, shifting from anger to remorse.

"Your house," she said, "oh, Knox, your beautiful house."

I leaned over and plucked her from the edge of the pool, settling her into my lap. "It was only the garage, Lil. The fire department is already there. They'll catch it before it spreads. Anyway, I was thinking we need a bonus room."

Too stunned to follow, she asked, confused, "A bonus room? What are you talking about?"

"A bonus room. Like a playroom kind of thing. We only have the three bedrooms. Ours, Adam's, and the other one can be a guest room, or maybe another kid's room if that's how it works out. Either way, we need a playroom. Kids need space. And maybe, while we're at it, I'll put in a pool. Adam needs a pool."

"A pool?" Lily asked faintly. I stroked the side of my thumb down her arm.

"Don't you want a pool?"

"I—" Her voice failed her as she looked at Adam, splashing at a bug, then back at me.

"You—" I prompted. Lily leaned back to look up at me, her mouth gaping open and closed like a fish.

I caught her full lower lip in my teeth for a second before resting my mouth on hers. Her lips moving against mine she whispered, "Kids?"

"If you want more," I said.

"Do you?"

I pressed my mouth to hers again before I said, "I have you, and I have Adam. That's all I'll ever need. But if you want more, I wouldn't mind another."

"What if I can't?"

"Then we'll adopt. Or we'll foster. Or we'll be happy with Adam. Seriously, Lily, I don't give a fuck. As long as I have you two, I'm good."

Lily scowled at the profanity. That's when I knew the shock was fading and I had her back.

"I wouldn't mind trying for more," she confessed, shifting in my lap so she had a better view of Adam, happily doggy paddling from one side of the shallow end to the other, splashing as much as a five-year-old could in a limited space.

He saw her watching and stopped, treading water long enough to shout, "Look, I can do a handstand underwater," before disappearing beneath the surface, his little feet popping up and wiggling a moment later. Lily clapped in appreciation when he surfaced.

"I'm all about trying for more," I said. "I think we should start right away."

Lily's eyes flared. "Right away?"

"Maybe not right away. We should probably let things settle for a while."

We watched Adam splash in the water. He'd had enough upheaval in the past year. In the past few weeks. A new baby might be too much. And we had time.

"I think we should practice," Lily murmured. "Make sure we know what we're doing."

"I like that plan." I nuzzled her neck, sucking a little at her warm skin. She squirmed on my lap.

"Not right now," she protested, breathless.

"Not right now," I agreed. "Tonight. After our little chaperone is asleep"

"Tonight." Her eyes warmed, and she relaxed, settling into me, resting her head on my shoulder.

"I'm not too heavy?" she asked.

I wouldn't have moved her even if she were. I told her the truth. "No, Lil. You're perfect. And I like you right where you are."

In my arms, exactly where she belonged.

Epilogue One

LILY

THE DAMAGE TO KNOX'S GORGEOUS fairy-tale cottage was not as bad as it could have been. The fire department got the flames under control before they spread from the garage, leaving the rest of the house mostly undamaged, aside from the lingering smell of smoke.

When he heard what had happened, Aiden Winters invited us to stay in Winters House until the repairs were complete. We packed up our things—again—and took up residence in the grand estate.

I was a little overwhelmed, to be honest. I wasn't used to having a cook and housekeeper. I don't know what I expected the Winters to be like. I'd met Charlie, so I should have had an idea, but I still thought they'd be, I don't know, cold. Pompous and self-important, like Trey's parents, but more so. That much money. That much power. How could they be anything but?

Aiden Winters was a little formal, but really, they were like any other family, just with a bigger house. A much bigger house. Winters House is massive. I've stayed in smaller hotels.

Adam and I were fish out of water twice over—living in a new city, with a family we didn't even know. The Winters provided more than enough entertainment to ease us through that awkward first week in Atlanta.

Aiden's great aunt Amelia was in her eighties, but she was a hoot. His sister-in-law Sophie, also Amelia's nurse, did her best to keep Amelia in line. That first night, Amelia snuck a cookie under Adam's broccoli and a fake cockroach under mine. It didn't take me long to figure out that not much kept Amelia Winters in line, even Sophie.

Everyone loved having a child in the house again. They spoiled Adam rotten, the older family members—mainly Aunt Amelia and the housekeeper, Mrs. W—aiming raised eyebrows at the younger Winters women.

Aiden's girlfriend, Violet, was about to start graduate school. Kids were not in her plans yet. Used to dealing with Amelia and Mrs. W, she just aimed a raised eyebrow back and ignored them.

Sophie, on the other hand, flushed and looked away. I had the feeling Gage and Sophie Winters were working on a new addition to the Winters clan.

Knox didn't waste our week at Winters House. The first day he tracked down Charlie and sweet-talked her into taking on his garage renovation.

Charlie had given Knox an arch look. "I'm sitting on a flip that's already running behind, racking up expenses every day I don't have it back on the market. I'm not giving you the family discount."

Knox had only shrugged. "I wasn't going to ask for it. You work hard enough as it is without doing it on the cheap. Can you fit me in or not?"

Charlie's lips quirked up. "You know I'll fit you in. What do you want to do? I'm thinking three cars and a bonus room."

"That's why I came to you, Charlie."

Charlie and Lucas figured out a way to turn the two-car garage into three, adding a bonus room above, as well as a guest room on the first floor that Charlie cleverly tucked away behind the kitchen.

Knox hadn't been kidding about turning his current guest room into another kid's room. I don't know how they did it, but, based on the sketches, the house wouldn't look any different from the front. The side with the most changes faced the woods, and none of the additions would disturb the whimsical look of the place.

Knox wrote Charlie a check. I peeked at the zeros and handed him a check of my own. I was no freeloader. Knox tore it in half. "I let you pay off Leanne Gates."

I opened my mouth to protest, and he held up a hand. I glared at that hand but let him talk.

"You wanted to use the money from Trey to pay off Gates, and I didn't argue."

He hadn't. It seemed fair, using Trey's ill-gotten gains to settle the threat they'd caused.

Knox went on, "Put the rest of that money away for the kids' college fund. I take care of my family."

I rolled my eyes. "Sexist much?"

Knox shoved his hands in his pockets and looked down at me, thinking. I wasn't sure I was going to like what he'd say when he was done.

"Lily," he said finally, "I don't want you to feel trapped. You want to stay home with Adam, and we want to have more kids, right?" I nodded in agreement. I did want those things. "Keep your money. Put it away or spend it however you want. Keep it as a nest egg and we'll use it for the kids' college, or we won't use it at all. Okay?"

I nodded, words stuck in my throat. I couldn't imagine ever feeling trapped with Knox, but I loved that he was determined to make sure I never would.

"Did you call your mom?" he asked, changing the subject.

"She said anytime is good."

"Then let's go to Hanover. We have time while Alice gets kindergarten straightened out for Adam and Charlie's working on the house."

"Can you leave again so soon?" He'd been away from the office for three weeks while we were at the cabin, unable to work remotely because of the isolation.

"I'll bring my laptop. The semester's started, so your dad can't come here, and Adam can miss the first week of kindergarten. We need time with your parents. Anyway, Axel is bringing Emma and my mom to Atlanta. They'll have him to pick up my slack, and—."

"—you'd just as soon not be here when your mom shows up," I finished for him.

Tsepov was still missing. He had his money and he had his Faberge box. So far, he hadn't made any moves against the Sinclairs. Just that morning, Axel had called to tell us there was an attempted coup of Andrei's operation.

Apparently, his people weren't impressed by his obsession with revenge, or his disorganized leadership. The coup had failed, but barely. Axel didn't like the instability in his hometown, so close to his wife and mother.

The Sinclairs were circling the wagons, and while I knew they felt better having their mother under multiple layers of security, they were dreading her return to Atlanta.

We stayed in Atlanta for a few more days, Knox organizing his responsibilities so he could leave again, me getting Adam set up with a pediatrician and delivering all his paperwork to Alice, who was taking care of getting him into kindergarten.

She was back at work, seemingly managing the entire universe from her desk, though Cooper—according to Alice—was hovering like a mother hen.

Knox and I made final decisions on fixtures and colors with Charlie and helped the pool guy stake out the location for the small lagoon-shaped pool Knox insisted we have in the backyard.

I signed a contract with a realtor in Black Rock to put Trey's house on the market and hired a company out of Bangor to pack up everything we'd left and ship it to Atlanta.

We hadn't heard a thing from Deputy Dave. Knox's threat to send Tespov after him must have done the trick. The day the moving company showed up to start packing I braced for a call from Dave or the Black Rock police, but there was nothing. Soon enough, the house would be sold. Then Dave, and Black Rock, Maine, would be behind me.

We spent two weeks in Hanover with my parents. To my shock, my mother put Knox and me in the guest room and Adam in my old bedroom with only a slight harrumph from my father. We horrified my mother by showing off my newly acquired sugar-laden baking skills.

It sounds silly, but I think my chocolate chip cookies went a long way to winning over my father. It was a little late to be overprotective considering he'd thrown me out years before, but I finally realized his glares and pointed questions were his way of telling Knox he hadn't made the cut.

One taste of those chewy, decadent cookies, packed with real sugar, and he started to melt. That's what happens after decades of sugar-free carob hemp bars. My mother only complained a little. Having her daughter home and a grandchild to spoil were more important than her anti-junk food edict.

Eventually, it was time to go back to Atlanta. Cooper called threatening to fly up and drag us back. Alice had Adam enrolled in kindergarten and he was eager to settle into his new life. Knox's house—our house, as he kept insisting—was still under construction, but the work was isolated to the garage and the back of the house. As long as we parked in the driveway, we could move in.

My Land Rover and all of our belongings from Winters House were waiting when we got back. Adam went to his first day of kindergarten with only the usual nerves at starting a new school. I'd worried that a new school would be one stress too many, but he rolled with it, eager to make friends.

Knox went back to work, and I did my best to get settled in. It helped that Knox's family and friends reached out to make sure I felt included. I saw Charlie almost every day when she stopped by to check on the garage addition.

At Sophie and Amelia's request, I brought Adam by Winters House to swim a few days a week. Knox had somehow managed to get a pool contractor working while we were gone, but pools don't spring up overnight. Amelia claimed that she needed the excitement of a five-year-old to keep her young, and Sophie seem to love having a kid around.

One afternoon I headed out to run errands, restocking Adam with school clothes since he seemed to have grown two inches overnight. Knox had offered to pick Adam up from kindergarten and I jumped on the opportunity to shop without a complaining five-year-old latched onto me like a barnacle.

Adam and Knox had hit it off from the first day, but lately, they'd grown even closer, whispering, then stopping abruptly when I walked into the room, going off every few days to do something together, just the two of them. I didn't pry, especially not after seeing the way Adam bloomed under Knox's attention.

I arrived home not much before five to find the driveway mysteriously empty of construction vehicles, only Knox's SUV parked in front of the house.

Reaching for the handle of the front door, I was surprised to find it already turning under my fingers. The door swung open to reveal Adam wearing a pair of long pants, a button-down shirt, and a bow tie I'd never seen before.

He said nothing, handing me a hand-drawn invitation, the artwork clearly Adam's, the printing Knox's.

You are cordially invited to join Adam Spencer and Knox Sinclair for dinner.

The picture below was something I think might have been food on a plate. I didn't ask.

"You made me dinner?"

"Well, we didn't exactly make it, but—just come in."

Adam grabbed my hand and pulled me to the kitchen where Knox waited, standing beside a dozen roses in a crystal vase and a box of chocolates. Knox wasn't wearing a bow tie, but he was in a gray suit with a crisp white button-down, undone at the neck.

In all the time we'd been together I'd never seen him dressed so formally. My knees went weak as I took in the breadth of his shoulders under the dark gray wool jacket.

He should wear suits more often, if only so I'd have an excuse to take them off.

I dragged my eyes away from Knox to look back at my son and the expectant expression on his face, then to the flowers and the chocolate.

"What—what is this?"

"Adam and I decided to make you dinner."

Adam opened his mouth to explain further but clapped it shut at Knox's head shake. The table had been set with more flowers, placemats, and cloth napkins. Wow. They went all out.

Adam grabbed my hand again and led me to the table, stopping to pull my seat out for me. "What a gentleman," I commented.

From across the kitchen, Knox said, "You can sit, Adam. I'll bring dinner to the table."

"K, Mr. Knox," Adam called back, excitement sparkling in his eyes. Knox slid a bone china plate in front of me piled with lobster and a twice baked potato—an almost exact replica of the meal we'd eaten in Bar Harbor all those weeks ago, right down to Adam's hot dog.

This time he ate it, finally accustomed to the loose tooth that continued to wiggle but had not yet fallen out. Unlike that meal in Bar Harbor, he was not the world's most horrible crank-monster. He chattered happily about school, the kids he liked, comparing their Legos to those at his preschool, all the while sneaking expectant looks at Knox.

Knox seemed to be communicating something back, but I had no idea what. I wasn't worried about it. My two men were blindingly handsome all dressed up, though, admittedly, in completely different ways. I was a little thrown to see Adam in his bowtie, without a fidget or a request to change into something more comfortable.

When Adam exhausted his store of information about kindergarten, Knox updated me on the status of construction. His early departure from work gave him a chance to catch Charlie on the site and she'd promised the garage would be done in a matter of weeks.

The second he took his last bite of hot dog. Adam whispered to Knox, "Now? Now?"

Knox answered with another brief shake of his head. What were they up to? As the last bite of lobster slid between my lips, Adam asked again, insistently, "Now?"

A smile cracked Knox's face. "Now. But I'll do it. You stay put."

Adam did as he was told but squirmed in his seat with impatience or anticipation. Maybe both.

"Close your eyes," Adam ordered me, bouncing up and down so much I thought he'd fly right off the cushion onto the floor. I raised an eyebrow and Knox confirmed, "Close your eyes, Lily."

I did. A few seconds later Adam cried out, "Open them! Open them!"

A squeeze of my shoulder and Knox's low rumble, "You can open your eyes."

Sitting in front of me was one of Annabelle's chocolate tarts, my favorite, the dense chocolate drizzled with caramel and sprinkled with sparkling crystals of salt and sugar.

The sparkle of the salt and sugar didn't come close to the brilliant fire of the ring nestled in the center, propped up by two plump raspberries.

A ring?

A ring was the last thing I expected.

I thought of us as a family already, Knox and Adam and me. Somehow my mind hadn't gone from that to a ring. Not yet.

We talked about it like it would happen eventually, but we never got down to specifics. How and when was still up in the air, and we absolutely hadn't talked about a ring.

A ring. I hadn't thought about it, but if I had, the ring before me was exactly what I would have chosen for myself. An emerald cut stone on a slender platinum band, it was elegant, almost understated, but not quite. The stone was a carat or two too big to qualify as understated.

I looked from the ring to Knox, standing beside me, silent and oddly tense.

Adam, who didn't have a speck of Knox's patience, burst out with, "Mr. Knox wants to marry us. And then he'd be my dad. When are you going to say yes? Say yes already, Mom."

Say yes.

As always when I had too much in my heart and no idea how to let it out, my throat locked up. Not a word made its way past my lips.

Instead, I looked up at Knox and nodded, a tear of pure joy spilling over my lashes to run down my cheek.

This man. It would have been a *Yes* anyway, but Knox making Adam a part of his proposal, telling Adam he wanted to marry *us* and not just *me*...

I knew what I wanted.

Knox.

For me. For us. For the children we'd add to our family.

Knox, and only Knox.

Knox plucked the ring from the raspberries and slid it on my finger. It fit perfectly, the stone sparking cool fire against my skin. Still unable to get a word through my tight throat, I threw myself into Knox's arms, pressing my lips to his.

He kissed me once, taking his time, before he said, "So, that's a yes?"

In answer, I kissed him again.

Adam let out a whoop of triumph, diving around the table to join us. Knox bent down and picked him up, bringing his head level with ours.

My son threw his arms around both of us, pulling us into a messy jumble of a hug that only brought more tears to my eyes.

"I can call you Dad now, right? Do I have to wait until after you guys get married?"

Oh, hell, I was never going to be able to get a word out if they kept this up. I nodded again, but Knox answered for both of us.

"You can call me Dad now if you want, Adam," he said, his voice thick with emotion. Adam let out another whoop, all but deafening me before squirming to be put down, shouting, "Time for ice cream!"

Knox set him on his feet, and Adam ran straight for the freezer. Knox leaned back, wiping the tears from my cheeks with the sides of his thumbs. "You like the ring?" he asked.

Managing to force words through my tight throat, I said, "I love the ring. I love you."

Knox cupped my chin in his fingers, pressing a gentle kiss to my lips before dropping his hand to take mine, lifting my fingers to the light. His dark eyes were hot with possession as he studied the glitter of the diamond on my finger.

In a murmur only I could hear he said, "I want to see you wearing that ring and nothing else. You have no idea how long I've been waiting to see it on your finger."

"How long have you two been planning this?"

"We went ring shopping as soon as we got back from New Hampshire."

"You and Adam went together?" I thought of the times they'd snuck off to do guy stuff. In a million years I never would have guessed that *guy stuff* was picking out my engagement ring.

"I wanted to make sure he knew that we're a team. That this isn't about me and you. It's about the three of us."

Overwhelmed, all I could manage was, "You guys are so sneaky."

Knox dropped a kiss on the corner of my mouth. "Get used to it."

Adam returned to the table with the ice cream and a scoop. With a grin, Knox dropped my hand and strode across the kitchen to shut the freezer door Adam had left hanging open.

He paused at the island, nudging the box of chocolates beside the roses and meeting my eyes. Without a sound, he mouthed, "For later."

I shuddered from a wave of pure, liquid heat.

I knew what he could do with those chocolates.

Knox still hadn't seen the can of whipped cream and the chocolate sauce I'd picked up at the store the day before. I'd learned that baking required precision, but I planned to follow my instincts with the whipped cream and chocolate sauce. I had a feeling Knox would appreciate my instincts when it came to whipped cream and chocolate sauce.

I sat at the table with my two guys, listening with half an ear as Adam chattered away, planning the wedding of his dreams, complete with a spaceship built out of Legos and a honeymoon riding roller coasters. I love my little guy, but I was not getting married in a spaceship built out of Legos. I'd break that sad news to him later.

For now, I took a bite of Annabelle's chocolate tart and basked in the joy of the moment.

My family.

My future.

Knox had been right. That first day, I'd opened the door and my gut urged me to slam it in his face. He was a stranger. A threat. An unknown. I'd been afraid to hope, afraid to trust.

A whisper deep in my heart had urged me to let him in.

Following my heart led me into trouble more than once, but it also gave me the greatest gifts I'd ever know. My son.

And Knox.

My love. Soon to be my husband.

I shouldn't have been surprised by his fairy-tale cottage of a home. It was a perfect fit since Knox was my dream come true.

Epilogue Two

COOPER

I WASN'T READY FOR THE SOUND when it came.

Bang.

Bang.

A fist pounding on my door.

I looked at the woman in bed beside me, her nearly-black hair a sharp contrast to the white of the pillow. Even in the dim light of the room her lips were red, her lashes dark fans on her cheeks.

If whoever was banging on the door woke her up, I was going to kill them. If she woke up, she might remember where she was. She might leave. I wouldn't let that happen.

I liked her right where she was. Asleep in my bed. I preferred her in my arms, where she'd been a moment before the asshole at the door interrupted.

Pulling on a pair of pants, I grabbed my weapon from the bedside table and strode through my apartment. With a stab of my finger at the panel, I woke up the screen to see the face of the man I was about to kill for disturbing my sleep.

I had to blink at the image that flicked into view.

Are you fucking kidding me?

It couldn't be.

I had to be hallucinating.

As a teenager, betrayal sparked a flicker of rage in my heart. Nearly a year ago that spark ignited, the flames growing hotter day by day. At the sight of the man on the screen, those flames erupted into a raging inferno.

In an instant, my control evaporated. All I could see was red.

I was going to fucking kill him.

I wrenched open the door and stared into the ice blue eyes of Maxwell Sinclair. My father.

My father, who faked his death five years before, leaving us to grieve with no answers.

My father, who'd stolen money from the mob, making his family and the people we loved into targets.

My father, who had broken so many laws I couldn't keep count.

My father, who moved through life thinking only of himself, leaving destruction in his wake.

My father, who stood at my door, wearing the cocky grin I'd learned to hate.

I did the only thing I could, the thing I'd dreamed of doing for far too long.

Lunging at him, I swung, my fist connecting with his jaw in a solid thunk, sending a shockwave ricocheting up my arm.

My father flew back to sprawl on the carpet in the hallway, his head lolling to the side, blood trickling from his mouth.

My chest heaved, lungs tight with adrenaline and rage.

A slender yet strong arm slid around my waist. Sky-blue eyes looked up at me, concern and amusement battling in their depths.

"I think you knocked him out," was all she said.

We both froze at the rustle of feet on the carpet. A small figure came into view.

Her too-big sundress sliding off her shoulder, a bedraggled bear tucked under her arm, she looked up at me with a familiar pair of ice blue eyes.

"You hit my dad."

From beside me, Alice muttered, "Oh, shit."

Exactly.

Never Miss a New Release:

Join Ivy's Reader's Group

@ ivylayne.com/readers

&

Get two books for free!

Don't miss the series that started it all.

The Alpha Billionaire Club Trilogy.

Also By Ivy Layne

THE UNTANGLED SERIES

Unraveled
Undone
Uncovered (Summer 2019)

SCANDALS OF THE BAD BOY BILLIONAIRES

The Billionaire's Secret Heart (Novella)
The Billionaire's Secret Love (Novella)
The Billionaire's Pet
The Billionaire's Promise
The Rebel Billionaire
The Billionaire's Secret Kiss (Novella)
The Billionaire's Angel
Engaging the Billionaire
Compromising the Billionaire
The Counterfeit Billionaire
Series Extras: ivylayne.com/extras

THE ALPHA BILLIONAIRE CLUB

The Wedding Rescue
The Courtship Maneuver
The Temptation Trap

About Ivy Layne

Ivy Layne has had her nose stuck in a book since she first learned to decipher the English language. Sometime in her early teens, she stumbled across her first Romance, and the die was cast. Though she pretended to pay attention to her creative writing professors, she dreamed of writing steamy romance instead of literary fiction. These days, she's neck deep in alpha heroes and the smart, sexy women who love them.

Married to her very own alpha hero (who rubs her back after a long day of typing, but also leaves his socks on the floor). Ivy lives in the mountains of North Carolina where she and her other half are having a blast raising two energetic little boys. Aside from her family, Ivy's greatest loves are coffee and chocolate, preferably together.

Visit Ivy

Facebook.com/AuthorIvyLayne
Instagram.com/authorivylayne/
www.ivylayne.com
books@ivylayne.com

Made in the USA
San Bernardino, CA
05 June 2019